THE DEVIL'S PLAYGROUND

THE DEVIL'S PLAYGROUND

A Novel

CRAIG RUSSELL

Doubleday · New York

Copyright © 2023 by Craig Russell

All rights reserved. Published in the United States by Doubleday, a division of Penguin Random House LLC, New York, and distributed in Canada by Penguin Random House Canada Limited, Toronto.

www.doubleday.com

DOUBLEDAY and the portrayal of an anchor with a dolphin are registered trademarks of Penguin Random House LLC.

Front-of-jacket photographs: (film strips) © MarsBars / E+ / Getty Images; (snake) © Graphic Compressor / Shutterstock
Jacket design by Michael J. Windsor

Library of Congress Cataloging-in-Publication Data
Names: Russell, Craig, [date] author.
Title: The devil's playground : a novel / Craig Russell.
Description: First Edition. | New York : Doubleday, [2023]
Identifiers: LCCN 2022039193 | ISBN 9780385549011
(hardcover) | ISBN 9780385549028 (ebook)
Subjects: LCGFT: Novels.
Classification: LCC PR6118.U85 D49 2023 | DDC 823/.92—dc23/eng/20220831
LC record available at https://lccn.loc.gov/2022039193

MANUFACTURED IN THE UNITED STATES OF AMERICA

1 3 5 7 9 10 8 6 4 2

1st Printing

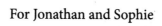

For Jonathan and Sophie

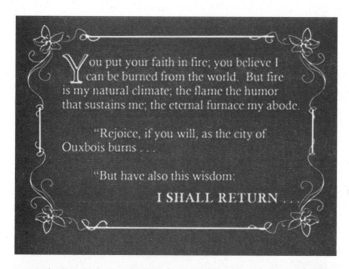

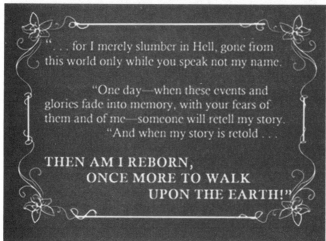

Surviving intertitle cards from *The Devil's Playground,* 1927, Carbine International Pictures Inc.

The Devil's Playground, once regarded as "the greatest horror film of all time," is now considered lost.

PART ONE

1

1967
Sudden Lake

It takes hours to find, as he knew it would.

Smooth highway asphalt yields to blacktop cracked into snake-skin scales by a caustic sun, which in turn yields to powder-dry dirt track. Paul Conway's Rambler makes its dust-cloud-waked way across an ocean of scorched earth navigated by no other cars, unbroken by any truck stop, gas station, or island of habitation where he can pause to ask directions. The only other vehicle he encounters is the rusting wreck of a truck on the side of the road, forsaken, flaked, and faded, slowly being comminuted into the desert by twenty years of excoriating abandonment.

Other than that, all there is, is the vast, pale, hot-as-hell desert stretching gray and white, yellow and rust, all the way to where the mountains rumble dark on the horizon.

Conway remembers someone once saying there was a special beauty to the desert. But he can't recall who said it, or even if it had been a real person or just a character in a movie. It wouldn't be the first time he's gotten the two universes confused. Maybe they hadn't even been talking about a real desert, but a set: a cinematographer's *idea* of a desert. Whoever said it, Conway doesn't see any unique beauty. For him, the desert is empty of beauty. Empty of anything. Dead space.

Then again, Conway knows he doesn't see or experience the world the way others do. He never has, and it led him to the profession he now pursues, now excels in. Part of that innate otherness means scenes from movies—whole and flawlessly recalled—play out continuously in his head, holding up confected celluloid realities against the harsh mundanity of daily life.

Now, unbidden, as he drives across the desert, the final scene of von Stroheim's *Greed* is projected onto the screen of his mind. For Conway, no other scene in movie history so confuses the real and the unreal. He knows that von Stroheim, in his near-insane drive for authenticity, filmed and refilmed the scene in Death Valley in midsummer, at midday. Actors and crew returned from the months-long shoot blistered and burned; one died, many were hospitalized, almost dead from heat exhaustion; co-star Jean Hersholt began vomiting blood when his insides ruptured in the heat.

But shit, thinks Conway, what a scene: the character McTeague under a blazing sun, keylessly handcuffed to the man he has just killed, the money he has schemed and murdered for lying just beyond his reach, the last of his water spilled and evaporating from his bullet-punctured canteen.

Tantalus in Death Valley.

Maybe *that* was the truth of the desert. The desert as death, as desolate judgment and arid purgatory.

Conway pushes the scene from his mind. He scans the road ahead for any landmark to indicate he's getting closer to his goal.

After several dust-fumed stops to check a map that refuses to yield to folding, he has all but given up when he finds the turnoff he's searched for, little more than a dirt trail opening like a dry, dead mouth at the side of the road. An ancient wooden sign, long separated from its post, lies on the ground, half propped up against a rock. The sign is so sun-faded and grit-scoured that if Conway didn't know the name he's looking for, he wouldn't be able to make it out. But he does know the name, and he mentally traces its faint outline on the sign.

SUDDEN LAKE

The desert growls and crackles beneath the Rambler's tires as he turns up the even rougher track. He sees it almost immediately, and it is a bizarre and intimidating sight: black and jagged, like some dark malignancy growing on the bleached skin of the desert. As he comes nearer, he gradually makes sense of it: a huge old house, tall and stark, with a jumble of mock-Victorian gables and mansard roofs stabbing the sterile pale-blue shield of sky. The house backs onto a long, wide depression, like a vast shallow crater, a mile wide and two long, paler than the desert beyond it and almost white in patches. The skeleton ribs of other buildings lie scattered around the depression's rim as if they have died of thirst at its waterless edge.

He slows as he approaches the house and sees that the wood of the roof shingles, the deep eaves and clapboard siding has been stained dark and restained darker over the years, until the house has become an impossible black silhouette in the desert, impervious to the scalpel-sharp sunlight.

Christ, he thinks, it's like a movie set. He gives a small laugh at the weird appropriateness of the thought, but at the same time it sits uneasily with him, as if he struggles to decide to which of his universes the scene should belong.

He now realizes that the building is too big for a house. A hotel? Out here in the middle of nowhere? Whatever it is, nothing could look more out of place in this setting.

Outside the house itself, an old Packard of indeterminate vintage stands rusting on rotted tires; a newer Airstream trailer blade-gleams in the sun. An even newer sedan is parked in the shade of a lean-to port.

She is waiting for him.

As he pulls up outside, she stands at the top of the steps in the main doorway, her shoulder holding the screen door open, her face in the shadow of the dark-tanned blade of hand she uses to sun-shield her eyes. He guesses that she must have followed the cloud of dust the Rambler kicked up all the way along the half-mile access road to the house. Why, he thinks, would a woman of her age choose to live so far away from anything, with no neighbor or help for miles? Then again, he pretty much knows the answer to that.

Conway steps out from the air-conditioned cocoon of the car, and the heat hits him instantly: dry and sharp and relentless. He takes a step toward her, and a dog—a huge, dark beast of a dog—emerges from doorway shadow and sniffs the air as if it has caught the odor of fresh meat.

"It's okay," she says. She makes the slightest of hand gestures, and the dog sits. "He's harmless."

"Hello, boy," Conway says nervously as he approaches the foot of the steps. The dog sits unresponsive, looking down at him impassively. "What's his name?" he asks.

"Golly."

"Golly?"

"Short for Golem."

"Oh, I see. . . . He's your protector. . . ."

"Of sorts. I named him for an old friend."

"A friend from back then?" Conway asks.

"Come in." She ignores his question. Another hand gesture: the dog follows her, and both are swallowed by the black mouth of the doorway. Conway, like the dog, follows her command.

He slips his sunglasses into the breast pocket of his shirt, and it takes his eyes a moment to adjust to the inner gloom. When they do, a large lobby is revealed. It's now clear that this *is* a hotel, or at least it has been at some long time past. There's a pervading sense of desuetude in the lobby, but it is nonetheless scrupulously clean. He imagines it must be swept daily to remain free from the constant, importunate probing of the desert's dusty fingers.

"This is quite a place," Conway says at last.

"It was built in the early Twenties," she explains dully. She has her back to him as she leads the way across the lobby. "The big salt pan out back was Sudden Lake back then."

"So there *was* a lake?"

"For about thirty years. It was called Sudden Lake because it sprung up out there over a few months in 1910."

"A lake just appeared?" he asks.

Her back is still to him and she shrugs. "A river changed course after a freak heavy rainfall. They say the basin was ready-made, from some prehistoric lake, waiting to be refilled. I guess it's waiting to be filled again in another million years."

"And the hotel was built because of the lake?"

She stops and turns to him. He sees her features clearly for the first time, and a thrill of recognition runs through him. There remains a faded magnificence to her. Her hair is bright white against the dark tan of her face, but he realizes that, were she to dye it, she could pass for a woman twenty years her junior. What fascinates him most is that hers is a face he knows so well—not aged, as it is now, but in bygone, camera-captured flawless youth. Looking at her now, he can see the fundaments of the beauty that had distinguished her younger self. It is, he thinks, like looking at some classical monument—like the Acropolis, or the Sphinx of Giza—where hints of the original, long-distant splendor shine through the ravages of time.

"It became quite the attraction back then," she answers his question; her tone is detached, as if discussing some distant place she'd read about, rather than the architecture around them, the home she occupies. "A New York financier moved his family out here about '20 or '21 and built this hotel and a whole lot of lodges around the lake. He was sure Sudden Lake was going to be the next big thing—that and the movies—so he built the hotel with a movie theater."

"What happened to the lake?"

"A small earthquake up north redirected the river's course again. The lake became landlocked and started to evaporate. It got saltier and saltier, until anything living near was poisoned. The last brine pool dried up sometime during World War II. Come on, I've set everything up in the parlor," she says, turning once more from him and leading the way across the lobby.

"What about the financier?" Conway asks her back.

"The '29 Crash and the lake drying up bankrupted him. He went out into what was left of the lake and stood in the midday sun, drinking the brine to kill himself."

Conway looks through the archway that leads from the lobby to a large hall. Beyond the hall's picture windows he can see the vast waterless lakebed, lying as white and dry as sun-bleached bone.

"The sludge he drank didn't kill him as quick as he thought it would," she explains in the same passionless tone. "It took hours, and he went mad before he died, his brain all swelled up from the salt and the heat. He came back into the hotel burned scarlet, raving, and bleeding out his ears and nose. Then he murdered his wife and four kids"—she nods through the arch—"there, in the dining hall, before the salt poisoning finished him off. Or so the story goes."

She leads him into a medium-sized, neat parlor, the walls of which are lined with books. A hall leads off to a small kitchen and another door that Conway guesses is to a bedroom. He gets the feeling that this is the only regularly used part of the building and has, at one time, been staff quarters of some sort.

"This was the night porter's accommodations," she says, as if she has read his thoughts.

The slats of the parlor's plantation shutters are angled against the severe desert sun. There's a red leather chesterfield sofa, two club chairs, a coffee table. Next to the window, a mahogany bureau sits with its top rolled up to expose a forty-year-old Remington portable type-writer that gleams like new. The books sit ordered and neat on dustless shelves.

Everything is scrupulously clean, but nothing is new. Conway senses a discordant lack of proportion: that these pieces, all items of quality, have been made long ago for a much larger, much grander room. She must have had to select just a few things to bring with her, he thinks, all those years ago. Back then, when it all happened.

But there is something missing in the room, an absence that he can't pin down, and it nags at him.

"Sit," she says, and Conway isn't sure if she is talking to him or the dog, but both obey simultaneously. He places his briefcase on the floor next to his chair.

"Sorry I'm late," he says. "I got a little lost. You're quite a ways from anywhere here."

"Yes," she says, and the subject of her remoteness closes.

"I can't believe I've found you." He waves a hand to indicate their surroundings. "I would never have believed it. I just don't understand why you gave it all up, back then, at the height of it all—why you went to such lengths to disappear."

"I had my reasons." Another conversational door slams shut. "I've made some lemonade."

She leaves to go into the kitchen. Beneath his shirt he feels a trickle of sweat run down between his shoulder blades, like a tepid fingertip tracing his spine. He examines the room more closely while the dog in turn examines him with coal-black eyes. In the absence of air condi-tioning, a ceiling fan rattles ineffectually above him. He thinks of ris-ing from his chair to examine the books on the shelves, but the black gaze of the huge dog keeps him pinioned.

What, he thinks, has he gotten himself into? And still the absence in the room tugs at him, like an impatient child on a parent's sleeve. Then it strikes him.

There's no television.

That's it: no television. The thought hits him with a sense of relief. But it's more than that—or less than that. He senses a greater absence: no photographs grace the walls or punctuate the bookshelves; no painting hangs from the picture rail. This is a space without images. There are no similitudes of reality. The harsh, hot, bounded here-and-now of the room and the harsh, hot, boundless desert beyond is all there is.

She returns carrying a tray laden with a pitcher and two glasses already filled with lemonade. She sets it on the coffee table and hands Conway a glass before taking her own, then sits in the chair opposite.

He sips the lemonade and winces slightly at its tartness.

"Thank you for seeing me," he says.

"You left me little choice." There's no bitterness in her statement.

"I'm sorry," he says, though he isn't. "I know you've tried so very hard to stay . . ." He struggles for the word. ". . . lost."

"You've told no one else where I live? *That* I still live?"

"As we discussed on the phone, no, I haven't. I understand why you have sought solitude and I respect it." He pauses. "Because you're the last. You *are* the last, aren't you?"

"You're the one who's researched all this. You must know."

"I do," says Conway. "All the others are dead. Dead or disappeared. Everyone connected to the movie, to the screenplay, to the book that inspired it. Victims of the *Devil's Playground* curse, as they call it in Hollywood. I thought you were dead too, everyone does, until I tracked you down. But don't worry, your secret is safe with me—and it will remain safe."

"So you think that's why I'm here—that I am running from some curse? That I'm hiding from a demon brought back to the world because we told his story?" She gives a small, scornful laugh. "You can't seriously believe all that—*mythology*? It was just a movie. It was magnificent, it was beautiful, but it was a movie. Just a movie."

"It was much more than just a movie," he says. "As for mythology—that's what Hollywood is built on, what it trades in. It has its gods just like Olympus; its devils and monsters, just like Hades."

"And why is it so important to you, Mr. Conway?"

"Dr. Conway," he corrects her. "I have a Ph.D. in film history."

"Why did you come looking for me, *Dr.* Conway?"

He pauses before answering, brushing the sweat-cabled red-blond hair from his eyes. "According to the few, the very few, who saw the film before it was lost in the studio fire, *The Devil's Playground* is the greatest horror movie, sound or silent, of all time. But it's a lost film. The most significant loss in movie history, along with the missing footage of Stroheim's *Greed*."

"I know all that," she says, impatiently. "But when the studio burned down, the master and all other prints were lost. I really can't see how I can help you."

"There is a rumor—again, a legend, almost—that a single copy, just one print, of *The Devil's Playground* survived. Every piece of research I have done suggests that only one person could possibly know where that print is—the only person to have survived all the mishaps, on-set accidents, and mysterious deaths and disappearances that have given the movie the reputation of a cursed production. There's only you. The only one left living."

She sips at her lemonade. "Well, all I can say is you're looking in an odd place for your lost masterpiece." She nods to the window, its tilted slats muting the dazzle of the sun. "This time of year, it hits a hundred twenty out there. No moisture in the air. You know what happens to old nitrate film if it goes above seventy degrees?"

"Believe me, I'm aware how hot it is." Conway pauses for a moment, mops his freckled brow with his pocket handkerchief. "But the rumor is that the surviving nitrate print was transferred to safety film in the Forties. I'm here because someone has asked me to track down that last surviving print of the movie. The person who has hired me is willing to pay a very large sum of money for that print."

"Who is this *someone*? And why did he pick you to be his ferret?"

"I can't disclose my client's name. Confidentiality. Let's just say it's someone with a special interest in these things."

"These things?"

Conway shrugs. "Lost movies. Lost classics. This lost classic in particular. As you've pointed out, cellulose nitrate film is notoriously unstable and flammable. What with stock degrading, rotting, spontaneously combusting, studios harvesting the silver from it, or reels just being dumped in the trash over the years, countless epic silents have been lost. And what is rare becomes valuable—like I say, there are those willing to spend fortunes on securing any surviving prints, especially after the 20th Century Fox vault fire back in '37, and everything in the MGM vault going up in flames a couple of years ago. One buyer—a different buyer—has offered me fifty thousand dollars if I can find a print of Tod Browning's *London After Midnight,* starring Lon Chaney. The last known print of that went up in the MGM fire."

"And for *The Devil's Playground*?" she asks, her face impassive.

"More. A lot, lot more. And as for my ferret skills—my buyer is aware of my knowledge of the industry and the era, and of my expertise as a researcher." He holds his hands out in a gesture to indicate their surroundings. "It would appear that I was the right choice."

"This last and only print of the film," she says. "You think I know where it is?"

"It took a long time to find you. And I nearly didn't. But when I do, I find you in the middle of nowhere in an abandoned hotel that happens to have a cinema screening room. Maybe you have the print here; maybe you don't. Either way, you're my best bet for someone who might know where it is. Like I say, that's information I'm empowered to pay a small fortune for. Actually, not that small a fortune."

"And what use would all that money be to me now?"

"I'm sure you could find a use for it," says Conway, and casts his eyes around the room.

She gives a small laugh. "And you're not at all afraid? Of the mythology? Of the curse?"

"I believe there is a masterpiece of cinema that isn't lost, like everyone thinks it is. A masterpiece directed by an Expressionist genius who surpassed Lang, Murnau, Dreyer, Leni—all of them. Those few who saw the movie said they had never seen or experienced anything like it. And that's something that should not be hidden from the world." He pauses. He looks from the woman to her dog and back again. The impotent rattling of the ceiling fan's blades fills the silence. For that moment, he is unsure if he is going to say what is in his mind. He commits. "I don't think it was the curse that made *The Devil's Playground* so dangerous."

"Oh?"

"There's this other theory that one scene in the movie—perhaps only a few frames—captures something."

"Captures what?"

"In the mid-to-late Twenties, there were murders in Hollywood, young women who were supposed to be connected to important people, big names. Those few seconds of film are supposed to give a clue to the identity of the murderer—someone connected to the movie and connected to the kind of weird secret stuff that was going on in the background."

"And you believe this?"

Conway shrugs. "It's more believable than crazy conspiracies about the movie bringing a demon back to life."

He takes a notebook and pencil from his briefcase and scribbles a note. He tears off the page and stretches it out to her. The dog makes a low, deep noise, and he drops his arm, setting the note on the table. She picks it up and looks across at him inquisitively.

"That is the sum my client is willing to pay. That's the figure to you, after my commission. With this you could stay lost, but lost in a hell of a lot more comfort."

She sits and watches him for a moment, and he is aware of the dog's eyes on him as well. After a while she says:

"Please, Dr. Conway, drink your lemonade—I have something to show you. . . ."

2

1927
Hollywood

It is just after 8:00 p.m. The sun has already almost set, backlighting a silk screen of sky, crimson fading to rose, fading to indigo. Even at this height, the air hangs heavy and orange-grove-scent laden, like a perfumed cloak draped around the shoulders of the Santa Monica Mountains.

A Packard 533 coupe pulls up at the curb behind a parked police wagon, and the driver, a woman of about forty, steps out onto the sidewalk. She is medium-height, slim and narrow waisted without being meager, her bust and hips fuller than the prevailing trend prefers; her dark hair beneath the navy felt cloche hat, too, is longer than is the current fashion and falls almost to her shoulders. She is wearing a blue, well-tailored jacket-and-skirt suit that is expensive without being extravagant.

There is an economy and purposefulness in the woman's movements as she makes her way to the house. As she passes, she looks into the parked police wagon and, seeing it is empty, walks on through the open gates and up to the house. An expensive, foreign-made, sand-colored sporting coupe sits at an angle on the driveway as if abandoned in haste, its top down, the driver's door flung open.

The house sits in the foothills, elevated enough to offer an unbroken twenty-five-mile view across the city to the ocean. The architectural vernacular is a mix of Spanish Colonial Revival grandness and poured-concrete amenity. The white stucco and terracotta-tiled house itself is large and sprawling, set on a proportionately generous lot dressed with acacia, palms, and olive and fruit trees; a kidney-shaped swimming pool glitters under suspended lanterns at the rear.

She knows the house and its scattered half-dozen neighbors are all less than a decade old, the blossoming of recently sown seeds of sudden wealth and confidence. After the war and the post-Armistice economic chaos that followed in Europe, the until then dominant French, German, and Danish film industries had been all but wiped out. The way had been cleared for a small Californian orange-growing town to expand its horizons, metaphorically and, as the house and its neighbors attest, literally.

A young policeman stands at the door of the house and moves to check her entry as she approaches.

"I'm Mary Rourke," she says to the officer. "Pops Nolan called me. . . ."

The young officer looks at her face. It is impassive, cool; its architecture is high-cheeked and strong-jawed beneath a glitter of blue-green eyes. In any other town in America, in the world, it would be considered a beautiful face. But this is Hollywood, and beautiful faces abound. Faces that are a decade or two younger; eyes whose glitter is more dew and less flint.

"Yes, ma'am." The patrolman, no more than twenty-one, stands to one side. "Pops said you'd be here."

She steps through the portico and doorway, into an entrance hall that is wide and white, the ceiling ribbed with Spanish arches. The white shields of wall are broken by vibrant modern paintings and pieces of hacienda-style furniture, the jacaranda wood twisting and rippling like dark muscle and sinew. There is a row of Spanish Colonial armchairs, the seat and back of each thick-padded and dressed in tooled blood-red leather, the naked wooden armrests lion-clawed. On one of the chairs sits a small older olive-skinned woman in a servant's outfit. Decades of labor have wrought her hands as dark and sinewy as the chair's carved wood, and they sit on her lap in a nervously clutched knot. Her face is creased with grief and stained with tears. Mary Rourke walks across to her, placing a hand on her shoulder to restrain the maid's habit of subservience as she starts to rise from the chair.

"¿Oye madre, estás bien?"

The maid looks up. She gives a small, tense nod, her resolve not to cry a fragile dam straining against the weight of shock and grief. The dam breaks, and the maid starts to weep again, tears refinding dried tracks like a fresh fall of desert rain. She nods.

"Did you telephone anyone else about this? Or just the police?" Rourke asks. The maid looks confused.

"*¿Llamaste a alguien más? ¿O simplemente telefoneó a la policía?*"

The old Mexican woman frowns. "*Sólo la policía, señora.*"

Mary Rourke comforts the maid some more but is interrupted when an older man in a patrolman's uniform, double chevrons on his sleeve, descends the grand sweep of white marble stair into the hall.

"Hi, Pops," Rourke says, turning from the Mexican servant. "Thanks for the call. Have you notified the medical examiner yet?"

"Nope. When I saw who it was, I phoned you straightaway. I guessed you'd want to see what the story is." The patrolman's voice is haunted by the not-too-distant ghosts of Kerry ancestors.

"I appreciate it. And . . . ?" She indicates the front door. Pops Nolan takes her meaning.

"Prentice? He's okay," he says. "The kid knows the score. You'll take care of him too?"

"Of course. Like I say, we appreciate your consideration." Rourke pauses; then she says, with purpose: "Where is she?"

The policeman nods in the direction of the upper floor. Rourke turns to the maid and speaks comfortingly to her in Spanish for a moment before following the policeman up the marble stairs.

The bedroom he shows her into is high and wide. Everything here is ornate, extravagant—dissonant with the style of the rest of the house. The walls are adorned with hangings, arcing swathes of silk in peacock hues.

A single, huge painting dominates: an overscaled full-length portrait, painted in luxuriant colors, of a woman standing on the steps of some ancient temple. A breathtaking, dark beauty and a potent sensuality radiate from the woman, who is dressed in a figure-hugging, diaphanous cloth-of-gold kalasiris. She wears the Vulture Crown of ancient Egypt, topped with a golden Uraeus cobra, its rearing head in turn sun-disk crowned. The bright dazzle of her eyes is accentuated by Egyptian-style black kohl and emerald grepond makeup. The slenderness of her neck is emphasized by an ornate gold-and-jewel collar that completely encircles her throat, from under her chin to where it fans out over her chest and shoulders as an Usekh necklace.

Rourke looks down from the painting to the bed beneath it. It too is oversized, twice the width and length of a double bed; Rourke guesses the mattress and the bedclothes were made to special order. It is dressed in satin and silk, again peacock blues and emerald greens.

A woman lies on the bed.

She is dressed in a full-length gown, the silk of which has an iridescent pearl sheen to it. Her arms and shoulders are bare; slender hands rest on her stomach. The woman's face is tranquil, the closed eyelids dark with mascara, the lips deep red. Her hair is a dark-auburn halo around her head.

"Beautiful woman," says Nolan.

Mary Rourke nods without comment. Considered by many to be the most desirable woman in the world, the woman on the bed is indeed very beautiful. She is also, Rourke has been told, very dead. The woman on the bed is the woman in the painting.

Norma Carlton, the movie star.

Such is Carlton's serenity that, for a moment, Mary Rourke can believe she is asleep, rather than dead, and expects to see the chest rise to take a dreamy breath. But it doesn't. Rourke places her fingertips against the side of Carlton's neck. The skin is cool, but not yet cold. And there is no pulse.

Rourke sighs as she straightens up. She makes a mental inventory of the rings, bracelets, and armlet that bejewel Carlton's body: it totals more than most people will earn in a lifetime. However, the most striking piece is the ornate collar necklace that completely encircles her slender neck—exactly the same necklace as in the portrait—splaying out across her shoulders. Despite being more striking, it does not match the other pieces in color or value: painted wire substitutes for gold, glass and paste imitate jewels. Yet Mary Rourke immediately recognizes the piece: part of the costume for Norma Carlton's most famous role, the one captured on canvas above the bed.

Hatshepsut in D. W. Griffith's historical epic *Queen Pharaoh*.

Rourke crosses over to the bedside nightstand. She picks up three empty medicine bottles; all three carry the name LUMINAL. A handwritten note, a still-uncapped silver fountain pen resting upon it, sits beneath the bulky table lamp. Mary Rourke picks up the pen and sees an inscription on its side: "*To NC from HC.*"

She reads the note:

I cannot live with it all anymore. I cannot bear it

There is no signature or initials. The two sentences sit at the top of the page, the second sentence without a period, as if Carlton had intended to write more. Rourke sighs. The Luminal, the note, the wearing of a memento of her most famous role: it all points to suicide, and suicide is scandal for the studio.

Rourke places both pen and note in her beaded clutch bag.

"How long before you have to call it in?" she asks Nolan when she is finished.

"It depends on what we're talking about, and whether the detective branch gets involved." Nolan shouts the word "suicide" without uttering it. "The maid called the station house, so the time is logged. She barely speaks English, so all that's recorded so far is there's some kind of emergency. But I have to call in with some details. I can give you another twenty minutes. Half hour, tops." He pauses. "There's a wrinkle."

"Oh?"

The patrolman leads her back out into the hall and along to the next bedroom door. Mary Rourke looks in and sees a tall man sitting on the edge of the bed, holding his head in his hands, slim fingers clutching thick brunet hair. He becomes aware of their scrutiny and looks up. His absurdly handsome face is drawn, his expression desperate.

Rourke recognizes him instantly, as would a quarter of the population of the world. She sighs, stifling a curse.

"When did he arrive?"

"Just after us," says Nolan.

"After, not before?"

"After."

"Is that his automobile in the drive?"

The patrolman nods.

The tall, handsome man speaks. His accent is clipped, British. His voice a little high and reedy. "I didn't think she would go through with it. . . . I can't think what to do. . . ."

"Well, she did," says Mary Rourke. "And leave the thinking to me, Mr. Huston."

"Who are you?" asks the Englishman.

"The cavalry," says Rourke flatly. "How did you know she'd be dead? The maid phoned nobody but the police."

"I . . ." Huston looks up at her. "She said she would. I mean, she threatened to do it, like she'd threatened to do it before. It just seemed . . . it just seemed talk." Rourke fixes him with her gaze. She knows Huston's type. He's a man in a man's world; a man women want to have and other men want to be. The type of man who glides through life, charming and beguiling his way, because nature accidentally gave his features particular proportions and a certain symmetry. But there is no guile in him now. No charm. No gliding.

"So why tonight?" she asks. "Why did you come charging to her rescue tonight in particular?"

"Because we had a row. A bad one. I told her I wouldn't leave my wife. We'd talked about it before, but things . . . things are complicated."

Sure, they are, thinks Rourke. Robert Huston, heartthrob star who is known worldwide for buckling his swash in a number of historical epics. He is also known within the closer circles of Hollywood as an equally accomplished bedroom swordsman. More than occasional and more than enthusiastic drinking buddy of John Gilbert and John Barrymore. He is married to Veronica Stratton, the glacial beauty whose star shines even brighter than his, and they are Hollywood's darling couple, second only in popularity to the Fairbanks-Pickfords. Rourke knows that a divorce would be disastrous for them both.

"I told her today that Veronica had found out about us," Huston continues, "and that we had to break it off. She took it badly."

Rourke nods thoughtfully. She knows—as everyone in Hollywood's inner circles knows—that Norma Carlton and Veronica Stratton are—*were*—bitter rivals. A rivalry that their respective studios had had to play down with picture articles of the two socializing, playing tennis, doing good works together—anything other than clawing at each other's faces, which was how one photo session nevertheless ended up.

Rourke examines Huston and makes an instant assessment that the beefcake Brit is short on brains and long where it counts, and that any possessiveness either Carlton or Stratton felt was to deprive the rival, rather than possess the object. Something that doesn't fit with a suicide. Nothing Rourke knows about the cool, assured Norma Carlton fits with a suicide.

"You say Miss Carlton threatened this before?"

Huston nods.

"When did you and she start the affair?"

"Shortly after we started shooting *The Devil's Playground*. She approached me; I didn't start it." He looks up at Rourke, as if he needs her to believe him.

"Well, you joined in. From what I remember, that's the way these things work." She turns to the patrolman. "Keep an eye on him." She goes out to the hall and picks up a telephone, gives the operator a number, and is connected. There is no conversation; she simply gives a series of instructions, then hangs the earpiece back in its cradle.

"I need an hour," she says to the patrolman. "I have people on their way."

"I . . ." Nolan begins to protest.

Rourke reaches into her bag and takes out a roll of bills. She peels off one hundred dollars in fives and tens. Nolan's eyes widen. She has bought herself her hour.

"You've done us—done me—a huge favor, Pops. This really is important to us. . . ." Rourke hands him the hundred. "I'll leave it up to you how much you give the kid, but we need everyone to keep this quiet. Before we leave, you'll have the official line, okay?"

The patrolman nods absently, hypnotized by the bills in his hand.

Rourke goes back into the bedroom where the Englishman sits. "Who knows you're here?" she asks.

He looks puzzled for a moment, his thoughts sluggish as they wade through the swamp of his shock. "I . . . Nobody. I didn't tell anybody. I telephoned and couldn't get an answer, so I came over."

"The maid was here," says Rourke.

"Norma didn't allow her to answer the phone. Her English isn't good enough."

"She did just fine calling the police."

"I don't know about that. All I know is that I rang and couldn't get an answer. As I said, Norma and I had a beast of a row over lunch, after I told her I'd have to break it off, and she stormed out."

"You were in a restaurant? This row was public?"

"No. We kept things discreet. I have a sort of retreat—this seafront lodge, down in Santa Monica. We had lunch there." He frowns. "Are you from the studio?"

"Yes. I'm from Carbine International," she clarifies for him: Huston is on loan to the studio from First National Pictures.

She is interrupted by the sounds of the young patrolman protesting as someone makes their way in through the main door downstairs. She goes out to the hall, leans over the banister, and calls out: "It's okay, they're with me."

Mary Rourke trots down the stairs. Four men wait for her in the hall. Of the four, there is no doubt who is in charge. The Golem. Sam Geller is a giant of a man: six and a half feet tall, barrel-chested, heavy-featured. When he speaks—which is seldom, and never without purpose—his voice is a rumbling baritone. His bright and intelligent eyes hide in the shadows of both his heavy brow and dark-gray fedora.

"Hi, Sam," says Rourke. "Usual drill. Anything sensitive about the studio, any narcotics, anything sex-weird, anything linking her to one of our names. There are three bottles of Luminal on the nightstand that need to disappear." She remembers the Brit. "Any notes or letters from Robert Huston, too. By the way, he's upstairs and in shock. You'll need to get him away from here without being seen. That's his chariot abandoned on the drive."

Geller nods, then sets the other men their tasks. "Luminal, you say?" he asks in his deep baritone. "The boss won't like suicide."

"I'm on it. Got Doc Wilson on his way. Wilson's been behind more medical fictions than Sonya Levien at Famous Players-Lasky. I'm guessing when he's finished our girl will have nursed a diseased heart instead of a broken one." She frowns.

"What is it?" asks Geller.

"Norma Carlton. Suicide," Rourke says. "I just can't put the two together. Norma Carlton and a broken heart neither. Norma Carlton even having a heart, from what I've heard."

"Three bottles of Luminal is a lot of beauty sleep," he says. "Not something you do by accident."

"Just didn't think she was the type, is all." She shakes off the thought. "You and your boys better hustle. Pops Nolan is watching the clock."

Geller barks orders at his men. The younger patrolman, Prentice, watches them at their work with an expression of unease. He protests to the senior cop, and Nolan leads him back out of the hall and onto the main drive, where he simultaneously delivers a brief lecture on the reality of being a cop in Hollywood and a neatly folded wedge of some of the bills Mary Rourke gave him.

Inside, Rourke is talking in Spanish to Renata, the Mexican maid, about the sin of suicide and the need to spare the señora's family the shame. She explains to the maid that, in any case, the señora was seriously ill, something she'd kept from her adoring fans, and she had taken too much medicine by accident, not on purpose. She asks the older woman how much the señora pays her. Five minutes later, the maid is in a cab heading for home, the edge of her grief blunted by the more than a year's pay in the pocket of her apron, and a telephone number to give as a reference for her next job.

A middle-aged man arrives. Heavyset beneath an expensive three-piece and matching homburg, his complexion is ruddy to the point of livid, and his glasses rest on a bulbous nose. Mary Rourke greets him in the hallway.

"Hi, Doc, your customer is upstairs."

"Suicide, you say?" Wilson's voice is deep and cultured, his breath fumes expensive brandy.

"Looks like she had a one-woman Luminal party. Sam Geller's gathered up the bottles. You got the ambulance outside?"

"And a driver and orderly. They can stretcher her down and we can get her off premises. Are the cops tame?"

"As puppies. But I don't want the detective branch getting involved. We've got half on the payroll, but the rags have got the other half. And I can hear a headline screaming."

"Then I suggest you get them to report it as a suspected heart attack, and that she was still alive when we came and took her to the Appleton Clinic. I'll nudge the time of death on the certificate to suggest she died in the ambulance. Cardiac failure caused by a heart weakened by childhood rheumatic fever."

Rourke makes a face.

"I know it's an old chestnut," says Wilson, "but it's the path of least resistance. I'll *revise* her records at the clinic to match the story, do an autopsy tonight, sign the cert, and we can have her casketed tomorrow. Otherwise, you may need to sweeten the county medical examiner's disposition. And that takes a lot of sugar, from what I've heard."

Rourke nods and directs Wilson to the body. "I've inventoried the jewelry," she says. "Safe it up for me at the clinic, and someone from the studio'll pick it up tomorrow."

"Fine," says Wilson. "I recommend a private family funeral. Ideally, a cremation, and as quickly as possible without arousing suspicion."

She leads Wilson to the bedroom where the dead star lies. The two ambulance orderlies follow with a stretcher. Rourke leaves them to it while she steps into the other bedroom and talks the Brit through the fiction.

"I'm telling you this, but you don't know any of it. When someone tells you that Miss Carlton has died of heart failure—I'll arrange for the news to be broken on-set tomorrow—make sure you look shocked. Got it? Devastated that your co-star has been taken so cruelly by ill-health. It would be good if you could mention that she had referred to heart problems in the past."

"I . . ." Huston frowns. "I don't know if I can pretend that—"

"Sure, you can," interrupts Rourke. "It's called acting. I'd give it a try if you want to keep your career."

She leaves him and goes back downstairs. The Golem and his men work their way methodically from room to room, meeting up again in the main hall. Between them, they have three carryalls filled with paperwork, letters, photographs, address books, and a diary. Most of the contents, they know, will be innocuous; but they have done this often enough to be aware they don't have the time to be too selective.

When they're finished, Mary Rourke gives Geller further instructions and the men depart, taking the Brit actor with them. One of Geller's men gets behind the wheel of Huston's sports coupe. She expresses her thanks to Pops Nolan and the younger cop. She talks through Norma Carlton's having a history of a weak heart—"illness in childhood"—and that she was barely but still alive when she was taken into the ambulance. She explains that Dr. Wilson, Miss Carlton's personal physician, has said she's unlikely to make it through the night.

She tells the fiction with such conviction and certainty that the younger cop looks disconcerted, as if he is no longer sure what really happened. She smiles at him.

"Don't worry, Prentice," she says. "This is Hollywood. Things are never what you think they are. You can call it in," she tells Nolan, and waits while he makes the call.

"Who's duty detective?" she asks him when he replaces the earpiece in the cradle and sets the phone down.

"Kendrick," he says. "But with natural causes they'll probably just go with my report."

"Good." She pauses as the ambulance men bring the stretcher-borne dead star down the stairs, followed by Doc Wilson. "If Detective Kendrick decides to take an interest, ask him to phone me. I know Jake."

The policemen leave, and she is alone in the house. After forty-five minutes of quick and deliberate activity, it is quiet, almost serene. She leaves, closing the heavy wooden door on the house and a tragedy that has left no trace there, and heads out into the evening air. Mimosa mixes in with the faint orange scent. At the curb, she finds Geller still waiting in his car, parked behind hers.

"Problem, Sam?"

"No problem," says Geller. "Just a message. The boss wants to see you tomorrow morning. Because of this, I guess. Asked me to tell you, is all."

She nods. "Good night, Sam."

Geller's heavy face breaks into a grin. "Good night, Mary," he says as he drives off.

Rourke looks up at the sky, then back at the house. She climbs into her Packard and eases it down the decline toward the city that glitters in the night.

3

Other than the rattle of bleakly illuminated, near-empty late-night streetcars, the roads are quiet, and it takes Mary Rourke only fifteen minutes before she pulls up outside her bungalow in Larchmont Village.

A creeping weariness seeps through her. She sits in the dark and the quiet of the Packard for a moment and sighs at the thought of having closed a door on one empty house, only to open a door to another. Some tragedies, she thinks, are more easily erased than others.

She hears the phone ringing inside her house as soon as she steps out of the automobile. She checks her wristwatch: quarter after ten. She walks briskly to the door, but the phone stops ringing as she puts her key in the lock. Letting herself in, she throws her keys onto the hall stand and hangs her hat and jacket on the rack in the short hallway.

Rourke slips off her shoes and pads her stocking-soled way to the wall cabinet. She pauses, as she always does, to look at the photograph sitting on the cabinet shelf, and she feels a faint stab of sorrow. As she always does.

Tossing her clutch bag onto the coffee table, she pours brandy into a Collins glass, topping it up with soda from the syphon. Prohibition is an abstract concept here: while the rest of the States buys overpriced gut-rot from gangsters or waits for the Vino Sano or Vine-Glo dehydrated grape bricks to ferment in their bathtubs, the real stuff is always available in Hollywood if you know the right people.

Mary Rourke has made a career out of knowing all the right people.

She sinks into a leather club chair and sips her brandy and soda, easing her head back. With her free hand she reaches into her bag and sets the note and initialed pen on the coffee table.

Something nags at her: some itch in her mind refuses to yield to scratching. Nothing Rourke knows about the dead woman fits with suicide. Nor does the idea that she would kill herself over a clearly weak and dim Brit.

Norma Carlton was a star, one of the brightest. She had a reputation for being determined—ruthless, even. Her numerous affairs were well known, but—despite post-Arbuckle morality clauses—no one at the studio much cared so long as her sexual adventures never made the papers. Rourke didn't know much about Carlton's entanglements, but what she did know was that they tended to be sexual, rather than romantic. Many had been used, then cast aside by "the most desirable woman in the world." Her only marriage—to Theo Woolfe, one of Hollywood's most successful directors—had been blink-and-you'd-miss-it brief and swiftly annulled. Some say she'd dumped her besotted groom when she heard he'd cast Janet Gaynor instead of her as lead in his next movie. Whatever happened, the rejection had driven Woolfe insane, and he had threatened her at a press gala with a gun. It had all been beyond a studio fixer's fixing, and Woolfe ended up in the booby hatch in Downey.

Norma Carlton also had a reputation for driving hard bargains and ruthlessly campaigning for the best roles. It was said that D. W. Griffith, pressured by Joe Kennedy, had wanted Gloria Swanson to play Hatshepsut but, somehow, Carlton had persuaded the director to offer her the leading role in *Queen Pharaoh*. Carlton's beauty, more than her acting talent, had captivated audiences around the world. Headlines had proclaimed that she possessed all the mystique and class of Greta Garbo, but also all the smoldering sex appeal of Theda Bara. "The Girl Who's More 'It' Than Clara Bow," one headline had declared.

A star had been born.

The phone rings again. She crosses to the sideboard and answers the call.

"Mary?" asks a cultured baritone. "It's Dr. Wilson. I need you to come over to the clinic morgue."

"Now?"

"Yes, now. There's something you need to see."

4

Sleek-lined and soft-angled in the streetlight, the three-story Art Deco building looks like a scaled-down ocean liner, roadside-anchored and sitting in its own bay of manicured gardens. Less than a year old, the clinic has all the equipment and resources of a small hospital, Mary Rourke knows. She also knows that, although Wilson runs it, and it's his name on the expensive letterhead, he doesn't own it. The holding company that has the majority share in the clinic is also Wilson's landlord, owning the real estate. In turn, it wouldn't take much investigation to trace the holding company back to its parent, Carbine International Pictures.

The studio's exclusive contract with Doc Wilson means Carbine International owns him almost outright. All the actors and actresses signed to the studio are contractually compelled to register Wilson as their personal physician.

More than anything, Wilson is a doctor for the unexpected and inconvenient. In the fantasy factory of Hollywood, it's easy to lose your grip on reality, on the rules that guided you till now but that you'd checked at the door with your winter coat when you arrived in town. Stars burn bright, and frequently burn out. Every studio needs people like Mary Rourke, Sam Geller, and Doc Wilson to deal with the inconveniences of mental breakdowns, unwanted pregnancies, sex scandals, drunken brawls, automobile wrecks, attempted suicides, syphilis and gonorrhea infections, morphine and cocaine addictions, booze benders. . . . The smooth cream stucco walls of the Appleton Clinic have drawn close around some of Hollywood's darkest and most sordid secrets.

The old security man, whose blue uniform and pistol on his hip are pale reminders of his days as a beat cop, beams a smile at Rourke as he unlocks the clinic door to admit her. It was she who got him the job on his retirement from the police. No doubt, she'll get Pops Nolan a similar job at the clinic or the studios when it's his time.

"Doc said you was coming," he says. "I'll take you to the morgue."

"It's okay, Frankie," she smiles at him. "I know the way."

The morgue is dimly lit, other than the overheads that shine down on the two white-tiled dissection tables. Her nose wrinkles at the smell of the place: antiseptic and bleach wrapped around something else; something less clean.

Doc Wilson's complexion is even more livid in the harsh downlight. He wears a full-length pale-blue rubber apron; his hands sheathed in white latex. She can tell from his face the news is bad.

"We've been had, Mary."

"Had?"

"Duped. Look at this. . . ."

The body of Norma Carlton lies naked on one of the dissecting tables. Rourke notes that her perfection has already begun to fade. Her flesh now looks gray and mottled, as if wax-coated, against the white porcelain tiles. Not yet wiped clean from her face, the eye and lip makeup stand out starkly. All her jewelry has been removed, except for a single piece: the costume collar necklace from her role in *Queen Pharaoh*.

"I put this back on her to let you see. As a movie costume piece it is very striking, but as an everyday item of jewelry, totally impractical. The steel-wire framework is almost completely rigid, allowing her to move her head from side to side, but that's about all."

"Doc, I—"

"It hides a multitude of sins," interrupts Wilson. He leans forward and unfastens the collar and eases it from the dead actress's neck and shoulders. Its removal exposes an angry red mark circling her neck. It is shadowed on either side by a small purple-crimson bloom of bruising, in turn run through with a fine tracery of spidery blue-black lines, like an inky filigree where capillaries have ruptured.

"Shit," says Rourke. "She's been strangled?"

"It's as sure as hell not the result of Luminal intoxication, Mary." He switches the overhead light off, surrendering Norma Carlton to the darkness. With an extended hand, he guides Rourke from her body. "Let's step into my office."

Rourke pauses for a moment, still looking down at the body now shrouded in shadow. Something nags at her, but she can't pin it down.

"Shall we?" asks Wilson. Rourke follows him out of the morgue.

Even in times of medical need, movie stars and studio executives need to feel they have not stepped out of Hollywood's luxurious cocoon: Doc Wilson's office is a grand affair of burnished maple, expensive art on the walls, bronze sculptures punctuating the lavish set of medical texts on the bookshelves. There is a door that leads off to a more clinical-looking examination room. Wilson takes a decanter and two glasses from a cabinet and pours them both a drink. "Medicinal purposes," he jokes darkly, and they both sit. "Like I say, Mary, we've been had. Putting the necklace on her wouldn't fool a homicide detective for long, and certainly not a coroner."

"But it fooled us."

"Long enough for us to remove her from the scene of crime and start covering up the cause of death—or at least the cause of death we were misdirected to believe was suicide. We've been played."

Rourke nods. "And played by someone who knows how we operate. He knew if he staged it to look like Carlton killed herself, we would move quickly to remove evidence suggesting suicide. Bastard. He's had us do his dirty work for him."

"That's what I think."

"And he knew we would end up here, having this conversation," says Rourke. "Your license is on the line because you've signed off on heart failure, and I've bribed two cops to accept the story. He knows we can't go back to the police now—a movie star committing suicide is a dream compared to admitting the studio has been involved in covering up a murder."

"So what do I do?" asks Wilson.

Rourke chews her lip for a moment, her brain shuffling through the new hand she's been dealt. She thinks back to the Englishman, Robert Huston. A movie star with everything to lose if his marriage broke up. And Norma Carlton had the lever to crack it wide open. If the police were involved, then he'd be at the top of their list, but somehow Rourke can't see it.

"Who else has seen the marks on her? Your assistant? The ambulance crew?" she asks.

"Only me. Jewelry of that value is too much of a temptation, so I removed it myself in preparation for an autopsy. The rest of it is in the safe. I'm guessing that when I take blood there won't be a whisper of Luminal in it."

"Okay. Go through the motions of an autopsy—tonight. Write up her cause of death as we agreed, then get her into a casket."

"I'll do it on my own," says Wilson. "I don't think it's a good idea to get an orderly to help. The fewer people who see her body the better."

Rourke nods, but her thoughts are elsewhere, and they've raced to get there. "You know what this all makes us?" she asks.

Wilson nods resignedly, pouring himself another brandy. "Yes, I do." He raises his glass as if in toast. "You and I, Mary, have just become accessories to murder."

5

1897
Kansas

It was night, the dark sky pressing down on the broad, flat prairie like a black-leaded flatiron. Breezes were emboldened by the treelessness of the landscape, and the dark air they carried into the small town was fumed with distant, artificial cheer: sweet cotton-candy odors and waves of reedy calliope tones.

Boy felt something else carried on the warm night air: an electric charge he was convinced was borne there for him alone. He had been waiting for the arrival of the show for so long, had played and replayed it out so often in his imagination, that his excitement now had him fit to burst. No one else here, no one in this dull, small town set on a dull, vast prairie, understood what it was that had come to the edge of their world. Sure, they would thrill at it, their small minds would swell momentarily with awe, but then all would return to flavorless normality.

But Boy—Boy knew he was different. It was as if he had been born with senses stretched or amplified: as if, unlike the others, he could hear, smell, and sense the world beyond the wide, flat circle of horizon; that he could see far past the featureless now, to where the lights of the future glimmered beyond. Around the world a new century was about to be born—around the world but not here—and he ached to be part of it. He sensed all the dark ages past and all the bright ages to come, while those around him were confined in the gloom of the perpetual present.

It took him half an hour to reach the field on the edge of Olsen's farm. Old man Olsen had rented it out to the carnies who had set up several stalls and one huge tent. A line had formed at the kiosk, itself a garish intruder in the monotone of the landscape, where a barker ushered people forward with promises pregnant with wonder and awe. A woman took rube coin in exchange for tickets, which she handed out with a fixed, phony smile. Boy had never seen a woman like her—her cheeks and eyes daubed with makeup, her teeth white behind dark-crimson lips—and her exaggerated femininity provoked a strange stirring in him—urges that were at the same time tender and violent.

Fizzing with eagerness, he followed the crowd into the big top. A huge, painted wooden sign arced over the opening, declaring in vivid colors that this was, indeed:

THE DAHLMAN AND DARKE

MAGIC LANTERN PHANTASMAGORIA

He entered. After the prairie night, it was dazzlingly bright inside the tent as he took his seat on one of the serried benches. He saw Nancy Stillson—about whom he had had *those* thoughts, but who in return had never paid him any heed—sitting two rows in front of him, and he imagined her with the same makeup as the woman in the ticket kiosk. Again he felt that deliciously dark carnal tingle.

The desire she provoked in him was equaled by his contempt for her. He hated that he has such thoughts about a girl who was as simpleminded and dull as everyone else there. Who seemed to have no response to anything, empty of all passion or energy or imagination. He shook the thoughts from his head: he had waited too long for this and wanted to devote every fiber and nerve to the experience.

But nothing happened. Minutes went by in silence, then were filled with the increasing rustling restlessness of the audience. Expectation yielded to exasperation. The limelight still shone as bright as day, revealing irascible faces. Voices rose in complaint. Even Boy became agitated, impatient for spectacle.

Still nothing, except for the eye-hurting brilliance of the limelight. Now the audience was loud; some began to rise from their places, gesturing annoyance.

Then it happened.

Darkness. Sudden and total. The flatiron night outside filled the tent and, after the limelight brilliance, weighed even heavier, even darker.

For a second, the darkness was all there was. Then an organ tone, deep-fluted, resonant, ominous, filled the space.

Silence again. The voices were quieted, seats were resumed, restlessness was stilled. Another urgent, imperative organ tone filled the near-total darkness. A dark-crimson glow was cast on the rear curtain of the tent.

A voice, so deep and resonant and rich that Boy felt it reverberate up his spine, tingle in the nape of his neck.

"Ladies and gentlemen, you have come by your own free will into this place. Here lie your darkest fears, your greatest terrors. The tales you were told as a babe, the cautions delivered at Mother's breast, the monsters and demons that have vexed your sleep into nightmares . . ."

The voice, which seemed to come from everywhere and nowhere, paused. The air between the rows of benches and the curtain screen began to ripple and fume with pale smoke that dulled further the crimson glow.

". . . all these things, and more, will now be brought to life. To life before your eyes—eyes you will no longer trust nor believe. For this is the Dahlman and Darke Magic Lantern Phantasmagoria, where all things are possible, where all history is to be seen. Behold!"

Mechanical sounds. A confusion of lights. Then, impossibly, the ghost of a beautiful woman, her form diaphanous, her silk gown fluttering in an unfelt breeze, hovered before them all, some five feet above the ground, as if she had taken form in the gathering smoke. The audience gasped.

"The beautiful Beatrice," resumed the voice. "Cast into the Inferno, into an eternal purgatory." The female figure pressed the back of her hand to her brow in an exaggerated gesture of despair, then disappeared. She was replaced by a flutter of crimson-and-yellow silken flames, then by the image of a male, muscular and fierce-browed, holding aloft a sword that blazed white fire.

Boy heard the audience gasp again, as if collectively drawing a single breath.

"Here is our hero, come to rescue her from the depths of hell. But first he must descend into the fiery pit, endure ordeals unimaginable.

And you, my audience, must make that terrible descent with him. But beware, for you know who waits in the pit: he who must be overcome—he who was first cast down. He who seeks to steal your very soul. . . ."

With that, the image of the hero disappeared. Pitch-darkness and the sonorous, ominous organ tone filled the tent again. In turn the darkness yielded to a vermilion glow, rippling in the smoke as if illuminated from below by some great unseen fire. Suddenly, in a great upward sweep, a shape took form. The shape—vast, dark, shadowlike, and more than twice the size of the figures that preceded it—was for an instant unrecognizable. Boy frowned as he, like the others, struggled to make sense of it.

The shape opened out. Spread itself wide. Revealed its true form.

The tent filled with screams. One man tended to a wife fallen in a faint.

Boy felt an electric thrill as he beheld Satan himself towering menacingly, terrifyingly over them all, his crimson bat-wings spread wide, massive ram's horns curling from a broad forehead, his eyes red flame, his taloned fingers reaching out to clutch at the crowd.

It was in that moment that everything changed for Boy. It was then that he saw the path laid before him. In the flickering colors, he caught sight of his neighbors, his acquaintances, most of all the girl whose body he craved but whose mind repelled him. They were *transformed*. Almost unrecognizable in their dark passions. He saw terror in their faces, and in that terror their transformation.

With absolute clarity, he knew this was his calling. His destiny.

He would bring people fear.

6

1927
Hollywood

There are conventions to wealth, especially new-money wealth, and Harry Carbine follows them all. The entrance hallway of his Santa Monica mansion is self-consciously grand: broad, high-ceilinged, the oak-paneled walls decked with paintings bought from the Paul Reinhardt Galleries, most of them personally selected for Carbine by Albert Eugene Gallatin. Burr-walnut furniture smolders in the light of the wall-mounted Tiffany lamps.

The butler's faux-English accent, snooty manner, and failure to be ruffled by the late hour—or early hour now—similarly obeys the conventions. He directs Mary Rourke into a reception room off the hall. It must be nice to be so rich, she thinks, that you can have a room just for seeing the help.

She doesn't have to wait long.

Rourke has never seen Harry Carbine anything other than appropriately and immaculately dressed, whatever the occasion. When a small, neat, handsome man of around fifty enters the room, his face set hard, he is perfectly dressed for a surprise 4:00 a.m. visit. His wide-shouldered, narrow-waisted satin dressing gown is better tailored than many Savile Row suits; his salt-and-pepper hair, despite the hour, is immaculately combed and lightly brilliantined.

"Thanks for seeing me, boss," says Rourke.

"That's okay, Mary." Harry Carbine indicates two low-slung club chairs facing each other on either side of the huge marble fireplace. Rourke takes one while he sits in the other. "I could tell from your call that this couldn't wait till the morning. If there's one thing I know about you, it's that you don't cry wolf. What's so serious that you couldn't tell me on the telephone?"

She tells him. She tells him everything.

When she finishes, Carbine is quiet for a moment, his face immobile; Rourke has known the movie mogul long enough and well enough to recognize that behind the temporary silence and expressionlessness is a large mind at work, processing information, shaping strategies. This time, however, there is something else, something in his eyes, and she senses the sharp edge of Carbine's grief cut through him.

"Who else knows?" he asks at last. "I mean, who knows it wasn't suicide, that she was murdered?"

"Me, Doc Wilson, you—that's it for now. Obviously, I'll tell Sam Geller when he gets here."

"I haven't called him," says Carbine.

"But I said on the telephone—"

"I know. But let's keep this as tight as we can for the moment. What about the limey?"

"Robert Huston? Unless he killed her himself—which I'm pretty sure he didn't—he has no reason to believe anything other than she committed suicide."

"You sure he didn't kill her? You said they'd had a row."

Rourke shrugs. "As sure as I can be. If he got away with it unde-tected, then why would he turn up afterward and make a scene? Any-way, I don't think he has it in him." She pauses. "I just don't get why you don't want me to let Sam Geller know."

"I trust Sam with my life, you know that. He's been at my side since we were making two-reelers on New Jersey rooftops, Sam pushing the turntable stages around whenever the sun changed and throwing Pat-ent Trust heavies down tenement stairs when they tried to muscle us out. So don't think that this is about me not trusting him. . . ." He flicks open a hunk of gold and holds it out to Rourke, who shakes her head. Carbine takes and lights a cigarette from the case before snapping it shut and slipping it back into his dressing-gown pocket. "This is dif-ferent. This is something we've never had before. You've cleared up some pretty messes for us, Mary, but we've never had one of our names murdered. I need to think it through before sharing with anyone else."

"You're the boss, Mr. Carbine."

"Between you and me, I've put just about every free penny I have into this movie, as well as borrowing heavy. Our last two didn't wash their faces at the box office, and I can't afford for *The Devil's Playground* to crash because of Norma's death. That's why we've got to keep control of who knows what.

"The way I see it is that there are three circles here, Mary. The outer circle—the public, the press, the general studio staff—who are completely out of the know. For them it stays that Norma succumbed to a long-standing heart complaint. I have to make sure that people like Clarence Van Brenner at Consolidated Californian, as well as the other investors, are kept in that first circle and out of the know. I'll book a call with Van Brenner and explain that the movie is all but done and that Norma's death is a tragedy, but a manageable tragedy."

"And the other circles?" asks Rourke.

"The second circle is the studio insiders, like Sam, like Clifford, like Brand the director, like Huston, who *think* they are in the know when they're not, and they believe the big secret we've got to hush up is that she killed herself. The third circle . . . well, that's you, me, and Doc Wilson. Let's keep it at that for now. As far as everyone else 'in the know' is concerned, it was suicide; for those not in the know, it was heart failure."

"There's someone else in the third circle, of course," says Rourke. "And that's whoever choked her to death." Carbine winces, and she regrets her choice of words.

"Oh, by the way," she says, and reaches into her bag, "I thought you'd want this back. . . ." She hands Carbine the engraved pen she found on Carlton's nightstand.

Carbine stares at the pen bearing his and Norma Carlton's initials in his hand. In that moment, Rourke sees the same sharp knife-tip of his grief momentarily cut through to the surface. Then it's gone.

"Thanks," he said. "She was a great kid. I gave her her first break, then I pushed Griffith while he was at United Artists to cast her in *Queen Pharaoh*. When she got the role, I gave her the pen to celebrate. . . ."

"There's no need to explain—"

The sentence is cut off by the sharp edge of his look. "I wasn't explaining. I was just telling you."

They talk for another half hour before Carbine signals the audience is at an end by tugging the tasseled bellpull to summon the butler.

When he shakes her hand, he holds it for a moment. "We're way past the point where we can bring the police into this, Mary. I don't want Sam Geller involved at this stage, but that may change. In the meantime, I'm depending on you."

"To keep this quiet?" she asks.

"To find out what the hell is going on. Everyone in this town knows that no one is more connected than you are."

"I think Eddie Mannix at MGM might have something to say about—"

Carbine's impatient shake of his head silences her. "You know more people, at more levels, in this business than even I do. I want to know what was going on in Norma's life that could have led to this. And if you can point to who did this to her, there's a big bonus coming."

"Boss—I'm a fixer. . . ." Rourke's tone is wearily apologetic. "I nursemaid them when they don't know the score, clean up after them when they do. I dry them out when they get drunk, get them out of sight when they're doped up, bail and bribe them out when they get busted . . . but I'm no detective. Like I say, Sam Geller's your man—"

"I've explained myself already." Flint now in Carbine's tone. "I don't expect to have to do it again." His expression eases. "Sometimes I think you're the sharpest mind I've got at the studio. And the most discreet. That's what I need at the moment. A gentler touch. A subtler approach."

"Harry, really, I wouldn't know where to start. If there's anything I know about Norma Carlton, it's that she was closed off. Private—or as private as you can be in this business."

"I'm sure you'll find your way. Like I say, I'm relying on you. You can maybe start with some of her strange ideas."

"Strange ideas?"

"All the occult nonsense she believed in. Fortune-tellers and the like. She—"

They are interrupted by the arrival of the butler.

"You look beat, Mary," says Carbine. "Get some sleep. I'll get everyone together on the lot at eleven this morning and break the news. We'll talk it over some more after."

"Okay, boss," says Rourke, and she turns to go.

"Do you know what I ask every writer who brings me a script?" he asks as she walks to where the butler waits by the door.

She turns back to him, frowning, and shakes her head.

"I ask them, 'Where's the hero's journey?'" He answers his own question. "I tell them, 'Don't bring me anything unless you can tell me the hero's journey.' It has driven every great narrative since ancient Greece, since before. If you want a big story, a great movie, there has to be the hero's journey."

"I don't understand . . ." she says.

"The hero's journey always starts the same way: the hero is given a quest, which he refuses or is reluctant to undertake. But something happens to change his mind, and he always ends up accepting the challenge, and it invariably takes him out of the world he knows and understands to some new world he doesn't. But you know what? It always works out for the best in the end. The hero always comes through." He smiles. "Let's talk tomorrow. See you at eleven. . . ."

7

She walks through another time, another country. The street she makes her way along is rough-paved; the dark gables of timber-framed, rough-plastered buildings seem to tilt menacingly toward her, the black, vacant gaze of their windows predatory. The cobbled street is littered with stained straw, horse manure, even the occasional dead rat. She has to step around stagnant puddles, like viscous ink blots, glistening darkly in the sunlight. The insufficient roadway gutters are stained black with sunbaked soil and effluence. The air should fume pestilently with the acrid stench of insanitary medieval living. But it doesn't.

There is no smell.

The street Mary Rourke walks is a thing of illusory substance. The clustering gables are façades, lacking any dimension other than the immediately visible. The cobbles, the stonework of buildings, the fountain she sees ahead of her in the town square, and the enormous cathedral that soars above it are all rendered from gypsum board and plaster, the manure and dead rats conjured from straw and paste.

The effect would be totally convincing were it not for the fact that to get to this movie set she had to walk through an equally credible facsimile of a New York City street lined with brownstones.

Rourke reaches the main town square. Up close, the cathedral looms even more menacingly, towering above her. Yet it is another, smaller structure that dominates the square, and demands her attention. A massive stone effigy sits in squat defiance immediately in front of the cathedral steps. A demonic doorkeeper to the house of God. The effigy, Rourke knows, depicts the Prince of Hell and Lord of the Flies: Beelzebub. He sits upon a throne, goat-legged and cloven-hoofed, his torso that of a heavily muscled man. Rourke is drawn to the eyes: insect eyes set into a horned ram's head, overlooking the town square. Crude wooden scaffolding frames the half-sculpted demon—supposedly unfinished by the inhabitants of Ouxbois—and prop stonemason tools lie scattered at his feet.

Again, the counterfeit convinces. She almost believes if she were to touch the statue she would feel stone, cold and solid, instead of insubstantial plaster, and for an instant she is convinced by her surroundings. But the industry and technology of twentieth-century Hollywood intrude into the verisimilitude of fourteenth-century France. There is no far side to the square. Instead, Klieg lights cluster like black crows on a jangle of scaffolding and gantries, their Fresnel-lensed gazes directed toward the steps of the cathedral and the unfinished stone idol. Stilt-legged platforms tower for elevated shots; short sections of rail stretch in all directions for tracking shots. Stand-mounted cameras present black mouse-eared profiles.

The ringing blows of carpenters' hammers and the whine of electric Skil saws echo throughout the set. In a far corner, a small group of musicians sit smoking, cellos and violins set to one side until called to perform by the director. No theater audience viewing this silent film will ever hear their accompaniment to the scenes: they are there solely to enhance the dramatic mood and tone the emotions of the actors.

Rourke spots a group of actors gathered around a tall blond man. Even at a distance, she can see that the director, Paul Brand, is talking to the crew calmly, assuredly, accentuating points with restrained gestures. She also sees that one of the actors in his thrall is Robert Huston. Beside Huston stands an equally handsome man. He is tall and copper-skinned, dressed in a flowing black cape. From a distance, as through the medium of silver nitrate, he is a man of ambiguous race. Rourke recognizes him as the actor and writer Lewis Everett, who considers his race anything but ambiguous.

An electric bell rings loud and harsh. A tall, lean man wearing riding britches and leather puttees mounts the broad steps of the cathedral, elevating himself above the assembly. Mary Rourke recognizes him as Clifford J. Taylor, Harry Carbine's deputy and production chief. Carbine runs the business, Taylor runs the studio. He calls for everyone to be quiet, and it takes a few moments for the buzz of voices to die down. The sound of hammering and sawing continues behind the set scenery.

"I need everybody to gather on-set," he calls out in a Locust Valley lockjaw accent. "That means actors, grip crew, gaffers, everybody." It takes a few minutes for all the grips and technicians to gather from their various corners of the lot, and for the sound of set work to subside. They gather behind the front-row arc of actors and the second rank of crew chiefs. Mary Rourke stands near the back, behind Larry Schneider, the chief grip. Everyone stands in front of the cathedral, while the demonic effigy gazes disinterestedly over their heads, out toward some imagined horizon.

Paul Brand, the director, takes his place on the raised cathedral steps, next to Taylor, his expression serious.

"Is everyone here?" asks Taylor. "I need everyone here—this is something that affects us all." He surveys the assembled crowd and nods. "All right. Mr. Carbine has something important to tell you. Mr. Carbine?"

Harry Carbine mounts the wide cathedral steps and stands between the two much taller men. There is a renewed buzz from the crowd, which he stills with a raised hand.

"Everybody, I need your full attention, please. I'm afraid I have some very sad news to share with you all. The saddest news. It is with the heaviest of hearts that I have to inform you all that our beloved star, Miss Norma Carlton, has succumbed to a long-standing heart condition. Being the professional, and the woman, that she was, she carried herself in the shadow of this condition with dignity, never revealing it to anyone other than her physician. I am so sorry to say that Miss Carlton passed away late yesterday evening en route to the Appleton Clinic."

Voices rise from the assembled cast and crew. Rourke sees genuine pain on some faces, feigned on others. A few brows are creased in self-interested concern as the consequences of the news are considered. She sees Robert Huston's overdone expression of grief; he catches her eye, then looks away. What she also notes is the raw shock on Lewis Everett's face. From the cathedral steps, Carbine once more stills the hubbub with a gesture. He is distracted for a moment by a loud bang, somewhere above and behind the cathedral set.

"I want you all to know, all to be reassured, that this tragedy, great though it is to bear, does not in any way mean that this great movie of ours . . ."

Carbine is again distracted by more noise, this time a metallic creaking, from behind the set. Rourke sees Larry Schneider lean in to his carpenter foreman and say something. The foreman nods and eases his way through the crowd and disappears behind the set, to investigate the source of the sounds.

". . . this great movie of ours," continues Carbine, "will not fulfill its destiny to become a screen masterpiece. Miss Carlton was devoted to her role as Adelicia and to the vision behind what we are creating here. As always, she gave nothing but the best of herself, and we should give nothing but the best of ourselves to making *The Devil's Playground* the greatest movie we're capable of creating."

The studio chief looks gravely across the gathered crowd. "I know Miss Carlton would want, more than anything, for this great vision to be realized. And that's exactly what we will do. Obviously, the shock and pain of our loss is still raw, but I will keep you apprised of all developments through the studio and production chiefs. I—"

Another sound, much louder this time, like a metallic snapping, halts Carbine's address. Everyone looks up at the fake towers of the cathedral. The top section of one of the towers tilts forward alarmingly. There is a collective gasp, as everyone, for a moment, forgets that it is set scenery and not real stone that threatens to fall onto them. The flat section jams, caught in cabling, but dislodges pieces of fake plaster masonry that rain down onto the steps and square below.

There are screams—from the crowd and from the figure everyone now sees falling from the buckled tower, along with chunks of the set. Rourke feels frozen, taken out of time: it seems to take an age for the man to fall.

She sees Sam Geller rush forward from where he's been standing in the front row of the assembled cast and crew. He slams into Carbine and thrusts him backward under the arch of the cathedral doors, out of the way of falling debris. A piece of the set hits Paul Brand, but he remains on his feet, leaning forward and cradling his injured head in his hands. Blood oozes from between his fingers, and Clifford Taylor guides him into the shelter of the archway.

The last of the debris clatters down onto the set floor, and there is a moment of shocked silence.

All eyes, including Rourke's, turn to the statue idol.

While the insect eyes of the demon continue to gaze out with cold impassivity, a body, like some received sacrificial offering, lies broken and bloodied across its lap. Rourke recognizes the foreman sent by Schneider to investigate the noises.

The screaming begins again.

8

They had always left the witch alone. Until now. Until the child. Until what happened.

No one knew for sure, or they had forgotten, who first gave this place the name Leseuil, or why. The Bayou Leseuil was a wide, sweeping, loitering body of water that writhed cottonmouth-snake sleek through the forests so indolently and slowly that it couldn't decide if it was a river or a swamp. It lingered dark and sluggish around the swollen feet of the bald cypresses, black willow, and tupelo gum trees; seeped thickly beneath its cloak of duckweed and alligator weed into the silty, peaty Louisiana soil.

Maybe the settlement got its name from the bayou, or the bayou got its name from the settlement. Again, no one knew or remembered.

Leseuil lay on the border of two parishes—they didn't call them "counties" in Louisiana. Perhaps some French bureaucrat, sitting in Baton Rouge way back before the Purchase, arbitrarily decided that the bayou should form the border between the parishes and named the crossing-point village "the threshold" in his own language.

But maybe—and more likely—it was someone who fully understood the true nature of the place who gave it its name. It *was* a threshold—or many thresholds. Leseuil was a liminal place where what you believed was one thing turned out to be something else; where you thought you'd arrived in one place, only to find yourself crossing into another. The edge between land and water was muddied and weed-and-moss-smudged, between both and the sky blurred by mist. The people who lived there knew their grasp of the land was tenuous, shifting, mutable; their way of life was *'n pied sec, 'n pied mouillé*. Even the way people talked—the people themselves and the blood in their veins—was on a threshold: constantly crossing from New World to Old, from one race to another. Most in the parish were Cajun, but here, in the thresholds of things, blood had mixed. The Creole they spoke blended Acadian with Haitian French; Choctaw with Chitimacha and Biloxi; Fon and Igbo with English; Dominican with Isleños Spanish. Even the name itself was on some kind of threshold: the older ones still pronounced it *le soy*, the younger ones *le sooel*, like the Anglos would say.

But everyone who lived in this place suspected, knew somewhere deep in the part of them where the shadows of their ancestors hid, that the real reason that this place was called Leseuil was because it was a threshold between worlds. The bayou as the Styx.

And that is why they had left the witch alone.

The witch came to the bayou back in the spring of 1889, steering herself downstream in a shallow chaland laden with three grand trunks and a huge, black-eyed dog. A steam-driven flat-bottom arrived about a month later, carrying what looked to those who watched from the bayou shore like tarpaulin-draped furniture and a couple of crates.

No one knew what brought her to Leseuil, no one knew where she had come from, but she had come with legal claim on the property she now occupied.

The witch's cabin was far out in the backwaters, ten miles from its nearest neighbor, and sat tall and dark and moss-bound like something grown out of the swamp. It was built with rot-proof cypress made fast with Spanish-moss-laced mortar and was not the fashioning of her hand alone. No one ever admitted to having helped in its building, but someone must have. More than one must have.

Out there, where the witch lived, was the other side of the threshold. Out there, in the backswamp, the water slid sleek and black into darkening mists; pale wraiths of Spanish moss hung shroudlike from the cypresses; the shadows were denser, fuller. At twilight and into the night, balls of light flitted through the swamp. The Cajuns called them *fifollets* and believed each light was the soul of a sinner, or an unbaptized child, locked out of heaven and eternally vengeful against the living; the Choctaw had a similar belief, calling them Hashok Okwa Hui'ga, and believed the lights were the shining hearts of shadow people intent on confusing unwary travelers, disorienting them until they became hopelessly and eternally lost in the swamp.

But there was worse still waiting out there. According to Choctaw legend, the Nalusa Chito, or Impa Shilup, a great, black shadow-being and the eater of souls, lurked in the darkest shadows, out in the depths of the swampland. The Cajuns too believed there were monsters hidden in the dark waters: the Letiche, again an unbaptized child, made monstrous by being brought up by alligators and with a taste for human flesh; the Rougarou, a soul condemned to walk the earth as half man, half wolf for 101 days; and, worst of all, Père Malfait—Daddy Do Bad—the eight-feet-tall father of all evil, who stalked you in the swamp and whose cloak and cowl of ragged Spanish moss allowed him to conceal himself until you were too close, and it was too late.

All these myths and legends served one purpose—to keep Cajun and Creole, Isleños and Indian alike away from the real dangers that lurked in that deep, dark-shadowed part of the swamp.

Out there, where the witch lived.

The witch—no one called her that to her face, though few exchanged words of any kind with her—was Hippolyta Cormier. She was tall and lithe and sensuous and dark-bronze-skinned, her hair a tumbling cascade of sleek black coils, her eyes emerald-bright. She carried herself with imperious grace. Her French, to the ears of the bayou, was more cosmopolitan than Cajun. And most striking of all was her beauty. Her beauty struck deep.

Rumors abounded about her origins. Her allure, some said, came from being part Chitimacha Indian, a tribe famed for the beauty of its women. Almost all agreed that she carried Haitian blood. There was a story that Hippolyta's grandmother had been one of the ruling mulatto elite in South Haiti, her grandfather the wayward son of a noble French family bewitched by dark beauty and vodou. Some suggested, more prosaically, that her mother had been a high-priced concubine in New Orleans's French Quarter, or a low-priced Storyville whore, depending on the telling and the teller. Another rumor, this one whispered, was that Hippolyta was related to the New Orleans Queen of Voodoo herself: Marie Laveau.

Some speculated that Hippolyta had chosen to live so deep in the swamp forest because she was a member of the voodoo cult who worship the *lwa* of the Grand Bois, and therefore had to be near the source of the dark nature needed for her potions. She had grown, they said, an herb garden out there, deep in the wetlands. There was talk that some of the womenfolk consulted Hippolyta to obtain folk cures for female complaints or family ails, where Doc Charbonnier had failed—although no one admitted to it.

None of these speculations and rumors were substantiated; sources were always someone who heard it from someone in Bayou Cane or Thibodaux, who was told by someone in Morgan City or Houma, who heard it from someone else in Baton Rouge or New Orleans. All were contested and debated.

However, everyone was agreed—without any basis for their assumption—that the beautiful mulatta in the bayou backwoods was a voodoo witch. Proof, they said, lay in the single, small blemish in her beauty. On her left cheek, just above the strong line of her jaw, a birthmark stained her copper skin darker. It was the size of a fingerprint, no more, and there lay its significance. On first sight of it, old Mama Bergier, the Cane River Creole, said it was the *anprent dyabla*—the devil's fingerprint.

"You'd better watch yourself," mothers would caution misbehaving children, "or the Swamp Witch, she put a *gris-gris* on you."

The truth of it though, as they all knew but never admitted, was that they feared her because her magic was the oldest known to man, the spell she cast the most commonplace. Which was why, on those rare occasions when Hippolyta Cormier came to town, women kept close watch on their menfolk. Even Madame Thibodeaux accompanied her husband, who was seventy if he was a day, when he took the store's chaland out into the swamp to make deliveries.

But there were more whispers, this time of nighttime pirogues being rowed or punted sleekly and silently through the swamp out to where the cabin waited. Who among the menfolk made that furtive passage—and whether they went in search of voodoo cures and resolutions, or whether more carnal transactions were sought—was again a matter of dark speculation.

In the meantime, the witch settled into her place in the swamp and at the edge of a mildly suspicious and mistrusting community—suspicion and mistrust that, for the most part, went unvoiced. But then there was old Élodie Faucheaux. The widow Faucheaux was a small, pinch-faced woman of seventy who lived in a cabin on the bayou, and who considered it her God-given right to speak her mind and to have others pay heed. Generally disliked and avoided because of her sharp tongue and malicious gossipmongering, she nonetheless found an audience for her complaints about the number of lamplit pirogues passing at all hours by her cabin and into the backwaters. And all since Hippolyta Cormier had come to Leseuil.

The arrival of the beautiful stranger and the draw she seemed to have on the community's menfolk made many in Leseuil more receptive to the old widow's bile. Encouraged that she was for once being listened to, old Widow Faucheaux heaped insult on accusation and accusation on insult.

She happened to be in the settlement one day when Hippolyta Cormier made her regular visit for supplies. The old woman began to hurl invective at her in the street, in front of a number of the locals. She accused Cormier of being a whore and a witch and disparaged the mix of races in her blood. Cormier, standing tall and erect, listened calmly to the widow's diatribe. Then, wordlessly, she walked over to her with such purpose that the old woman drew back, as if expecting a blow. Instead, Hippolyta Cormier leaned in to Faucheaux, her lips to the old woman's ear. She spoke for half a minute, straightened up, and walked on with the same purpose.

Whatever it was she had said, it went unheard by the bystanders. What they did see, however, was that the color had drained from Widow Faucheaux's face. She stood shocked for a moment, then opened her mouth as if to complain to the others. Instead, she turned on her heel and bustled out of the settlement.

Time passed, and no one thought much about the incident, but it was noted that Madame Faucheaux's diatribe about the beautiful newcomer ceased. About a month after the incident in the street, the old woman missed her regular weekly visit to the Thibodeaux store. After another two days had passed, Père Martin and Doc Charbonnier called out at her cabin on the bayou.

As they stood on the porch, Doc Charbonnier found it odd that the old woman, not known for her vanity, had fixed a mirror to the outer wall, in such a way that any visitor would be presented with their own reflection before knocking on the door. He turned questioningly to Martin, only to find the priest frowning.

"I didn't think Madame Faucheaux was the type to go in for this kind of thing."

"What type of thing?"

"It's an old Cajun superstition," explained Martin. "Surely you've heard of it? The devil is terribly vain, they say. This"—he nodded to the mirror that captured both their reflections—"is a protection against him. The belief is that the devil will be so enamored with his own image that he'll stand admiring himself until the sun comes up to banish him from the door."

When there was no answer to their knocking, they found that the widow Faucheaux had locked her door, which was contrary to local Cajun habit. Sensing something wrong, the two men forced their way in.

They discovered the old woman in her bed. Dead.

When they returned to the store, Doc Charbonnier passed on the news of Madame Faucheaux's death.

"Completely natural," said the doctor. "All the indications are that she died from a massive stroke while asleep."

What neither physician nor priest mentioned—because they had agreed before they returned from the old woman's house—was that Madame Faucheaux had covered the walls and windows of her bedroom with pages torn out of the Bible and fixed with flour paste. Nor did they mention that she had roughly fashioned wooden crosses and nailed them to the woodwork of each door, every window, and that she had lain clutching a crucifix. Nor that she had worn a drilled-through dime on a string around her neck—an old Cajun talisman to ward off evil.

Despite their omissions, Leseuil burned with intense speculation about why the old woman had died so soon after publicly insulting Hippolyta Cormier.

It was perhaps partly for that reason that they had left the witch alone.

Until now. Until the child. Until what happened.

9

1927
Hollywood

Mary Rourke turns off Ventura Boulevard and up the short access drive to the entrance. The gold lettering—embossed into a white stone arc above the gates and bright in the morning light—announces with sunny optimism that she has reached THE CARBINE INTERNATIONAL STUDIO RANCH. A uniformed guard smiles and gives her a casual salute as he swings open the gates. She pauses, looking in the rearview mirror, watching as a pale-gray sedan slides by. She's sure she's seen the sedan before but dismisses the thought with a shake of her head as she drives through the gates.

Ahead of her, a hacienda is arranged around a wide piazza. The windows of the white stucco, terracotta-tiled buildings are bracketed by sienna-colored shutters, the upper floors dressed with colonnaded balconies.

Behind the rancho buildings stretch seventy acres of backlot, which are home to simulations of New York brownstones, Wild West towns and ranches, Egyptian palaces, Roman forums, and, as she knows from her walk through it the previous day, the medieval French city of Ouxbois. This is a place where all types of fictions take solid form.

She parks the Packard and sits for a moment. She gazes at the name sign that marks her reserved spot, as she wonders exactly what "M. Rourke" is supposed to do now. She has made a career of diverting questions, covering up facts, bending truths to fit the studio's image and narrative. Now Harry Carbine expects her to ask the questions, find the facts, unbend the untruths surrounding Norma Carlton's life and death. While still keeping them hidden from the world.

She makes a brief stop at her office in the publicity department before heading into the more impressive central building that houses Harry Carbine's suite of offices.

The reception area is a grand affair of pale marble-tiled floors and white stone walls, the air sliced silently into cooling eddies by the blades of an array of ceiling fans. Carbine's secretary smiles at Rourke when she comes in and tells her the studio boss has someone with him but will be free soon. Rourke sinks into the white leather of one of the low modernist couches and waits in the stone-walled cool, taking in the framed posters that bedeck the walls. Most prominent of them all is the three-sheeter for the current production: *The Devil's Playground*. An entire city blazes in the poster's background, painted in vivid colors, the flames sinuous and writhing, orange, red, and gold, surging upward into black-and-silver smoke. Against the blue banner of the sky, the smoke coalesces into a vast, monstrous figure that stretches dark bat-wings wide, the flaming red eyes the only feature discernible in the black silhouette of the horned head. In the foreground, her back to the burning city, stands Norma Carlton. Her sensuous figure is sheathed in virginal white silk, her head held high, her expression noble and defiant, one hand clutched to her breast, the other reaching out to the viewer in righteous entreaty, while the smoke-demon looks down rapaciously upon her with fiery eyes.

Rourke is struck by the poster artist's skill in capturing Carlton's mix of cool nobility and dark sensuality. But it is the sky-filling demon that dominates.

"It gives me the heebie-jeebies." The secretary jolts Rourke from her study of the poster. "Stuck here behind the desk, I just can't seem to help looking at it."

"That means we got it right." Rourke smiles. "We got Karoly Grosz to do it, and he did a fine job. The artwork is excellent."

"I guess," says the secretary. "But it scares me. I swear those eyes follow you when you—"

An electric buzz interrupts her, and she answers the internal telephone.

"Yes, Mr. Carbine, she's here," the secretary says, and hangs up. She turns to Rourke and smiles. "Mr. Carbine is free now, Miss Rourke."

"Thanks, Lucy."

Rourke heads along a hall lined with photographic portraits of Carbine International's stars, her eye drawn to that of Norma Carlton. The door at the far end of the hall swings open, and a smartly dressed man steps out of Carbine's office. The man isn't tall—five-seven tops, Rourke reckons—but powerfully built and agile in movement. Despite his size, he fills the hall space with a sudden and intimidating presence. His deep-creased, craggy face is like something rough-hewn from stone, the eyes hard and glittering.

He catches sight of Rourke. In that instant, his face undergoes metamorphosis, lit up with a smile like the rising sun on a rugged cliff. Rourke has never known anyone else whose face can be so utterly transformed by an expression.

"Hi, Mary," he says, beaming. His warm, friendly tone is delivered through gravel. "Haven't seen you in ages. How are you?"

Rourke returns his smile. She likes the small man. Everyone in Hollywood likes him. The rest of the world is terrified by him and rejoices in its terror.

"It's good to see you, Mr. Chaney. I'm just fine. You?"

"Busy, as ever. But good. You going in to see Harry?"

"I am."

"I've just been asking him for a favor, but I don't think he's forgiven me for turning down the Archambeau part in this new horror picture of yours."

"I heard you'd been offered it. It would have been perfect for you. Or you perfect for it."

"Thanks, Mary—it is a shame—such a great part. Truth is, I would've taken it, but Metro wouldn't release me. Irving the Boy Wonder had me tied up for *The Unknown* and *London After Midnight*. Plus, I think he sees your movie as competition." Another profound change in expression, this time grave. "I'm so sorry to hear about Norma. That was terrible. Just terrible. Bad heart, they say."

"Yes. It's a great loss to us. To everyone."

"I only met her a few times," says Chaney, "but she was such a beautiful woman. Intelligent too. Very smart."

"So I believe," says Rourke.

"Do you know, Norma once quizzed me for over an hour about my makeup techniques?"

"Oh?"

"Yeah—she came by the lot I was working specially to ask me. She was really interested in it all. I had to go through my case and tell her what each paste, powder, and prop was for." Chaney laughs. "I started to worry she was stealing my trade secrets. But that was Norma, from all I've heard about her—she wanted to understand every aspect, every craft involved in moviemaking." The scenery on the face changes again. "So sad. So very sad."

Harry Carbine's expression when she walks into his office suggests he has been waiting impatiently for her. There is something about the readability of his usually unreadable demeanor that disturbs her.

"Sorry, Mary, I had an unscheduled visit. You bump into the Man of a Thousand Faces?" asks Carbine.

"I did. He's one of a kind," says Rourke. "If everyone in this town were like him I'd be out of a job. When he's not working, he simply goes home to his wife and family and lives quietly. Like he said himself, 'Between pictures, there is no Lon Chaney.' Can you imagine how little I'd have to do if every Hollywood star was like that?"

"Life would be a lot easier, that's for sure," says Carbine. "He's one hell of an actor. Did you see him as Blizzard in *The Penalty*? One day I'll get Thalberg to loosen his grip on him. Anyway, he just stopped by in passing, looking for a favor."

"Oh?"

"He wants me to see if I can get a part for this young guy." Carbine waves a dismissive hand. "I figure Lon sees him as some kind of protégé. Thing is, I'm being hit with it from both sides."

"I don't follow," says Rourke.

"Acting is apparently good enough for this youngster Lon's pushing, but not good enough for his own son. Lon's told him to stay out of the business. Problem is, I had young Creighton Chaney in this office last week, begging for a screen test—and begging that I keep the whole thing quiet from Pops."

"Are you? Giving him a screen test, I mean?"

"He's a good-looking kid, and a full head taller than his pop. Normally, I would, but I'm not going to come between father and son. Old Lon would have a fit if he heard what Creighton was suggesting—that he could be billed either under his own name or as Lon Chaney, Jr."

"So you turned him down? What about this other kid?"

"No use. Kid's as deaf as a post. You know about Lon's parents?"

Rourke nods. She knows the story: Lon Chaney had grown up with parents who were both deaf-mutes and he ascribed his whole acting talent, his ability to communicate emotion and thought with expression, to the fact he'd had to pantomime since childhood.

"Anyway," continues Carbine, "Lon's parents were teachers at the Colorado School for the Deaf, and that's where this kid graduated. He says the kid is so good at reading lips you wouldn't know he was deaf, but he can't talk that well."

"Maybe work as an extra?" suggests Rourke.

Carbine shakes his head. "You saw what happened on-set the other day. Accidents happen all the time. What if this kid is on a set and something goes wrong and he can't hear the set boss yelling a warning? Anyway, Lon reckons that, because movies have no spoken sound, the kid not being able to speak well isn't a problem, so long as he can mouth words—but Lon knows as well as you and I do that that's all about to change. You heard about this project Zanuck at Warner's got coming out in October?"

"I heard something about it," says Rourke.

"Full sound. Synchronized Vitaphone all the way through."

"Like *Don Juan* last year?" Rourke asks.

"No, this time there's going to be synchronized dialogue—actual spoken scenes—not just a musical soundtrack and sound effects. Word is, it's getting as big a budget—near half-million, like *Don Juan*. Or so Sam Geller's been able to find out. God knows where Jack Warner gets the funds. Al Crosland is directing again."

"Is it another musical?"

"I don't know, but it would make sense. They've signed up Al Jolson. But it must be Jewish-themed, because it premieres in New York first night of Yom Kippur. Griffith says it'll kill the movie business, kill Hollywood, because it'll kill the universal language of pantomime in movies, and every country will start making sound films in their own language."

"But you don't?"

"No, I don't. The microphone won't kill the movie business, but it *will* kill a lot of careers. Maybe even Lon's. But, sure as God made little green apples, there's no place in sound films for a deaf-mute." Carbine sighs, as if under the burden of weightier matters waiting to be dealt with. He waves Rourke to a seat, which she takes. "You dealt with the press?" he asks.

"Yes," says Rourke. "I told them the truth—that it was an accident caused by a badly secured piece of scaffolding. I've said that the foreman who was injured is in the hospital recovering. I didn't tell them the extent of his injuries, but I didn't lie either. If we could have gotten him to the Appleton Clinic, it would have made things easier, but spinal injuries like that are bigger-league, and they transferred him to Cedars of Lebanon. I dare say no one is interested in tracking down an injured set hand; it would be different if it had been one of the lead actors. But, coming like it did on the back of Norma Carlton's death, they're beginning to come up with their own take on the accident. Quinlan at the *Examiner,* specially, is all worked up about a new angle on Norma's death."

Carbine raises an eyebrow, his expression apprehensive.

Rourke holds up a reassuring hand. "It could work in our favor. Quinlan asked if I thought it was because *The Devil's Playground* is a cursed production."

"What?!"

"He read somewhere that the guy who wrote the original book a hundred-odd years ago was a defrocked Jesuit priest. That he was some kind of devil worshipper or warlock or something like that—and he ended his life raving in an insane asylum. The yarn being spun is that there's a legend he didn't really write the book at all but was some kind of amanuensis for a demon who dictated it. And there's all this stuff going on with this guy Nathan Milcom, the screenwriter, who nobody has ever seen except his agent. Have you met him?"

Carbine shakes his head. "I have to admit, it's an odd working relationship. All contact—including rewrites—go through Margot Drescher."

"Margot Drescher—as in, Norma Carlton's agent? She represents Milcom too?"

"Yep. She's our only means of communication with him."

"And you accepted this arrangement?" she asks incredulously.

"You haven't read the photoplay, Mary. Or the excerpts from the book. They're"—he frowns—"they're *exceptional*. I've never read anything like it. As soon as I read it, I knew we had to make the movie, no matter how oddball the setup. You know how professional Margot is—she makes sure it all runs smoothly."

Rourke shakes her head. "It's your business, boss. But all of this cloak-and-dagger stuff has the newshawks elaborating this cursed-production angle. Like I said, it could work in the picture's favor—add a little weight to the claim it's the greatest horror movie ever made. That's still the publicity angle we're taking, isn't it?"

"It is—but it's more than an angle. Between Milcom's photoplay and Brand's direction, it's not going to be an empty boast. Let the press run with the cursed-production malarkey; it's the least of our concerns right now. And no one's asking awkward questions about Norma's death?"

"So far, no. I've been trying to track down family so we can get her cremated, but there's none that anyone knows of. I'm going to see Hiram Levitt to see if he can point me in the right direction."

"Levitt? The Resurrectionist? He rebuilt Norma's backstory; he won't let any cats out of the bag. You know that unwritten code of his."

"It's worth a try. Specially if you want me to get something on what was going on in her life. I'm going to speak to Margot Drescher too, see if she can shed some light. What about Norma Carlton's ex-husband, Woolfe—whatever happened to him? He did get busted for waving a gun in her face. It might be worth talking to him if I can track him down."

"Theo Woolfe?" Carbine frowns. "He won't do you much good. But he's easy enough to find. Take the trolley to Downey."

"He's still in the nuthouse?"

"Last I heard. Even if he's not a babbling loony, I don't see what light he could cast."

Rourke sighs in frustration. "I guess not—but I really need a way into all this, boss. Is there anything you can tell me that could get me looking in the right direction?"

Carbine thinks for a moment. "Norma was like no other woman I've known. And I guess part of that is that I didn't really know her at all. All I can tell you is, she had almost every man she encountered wrapped around her little finger. There was something hypnotic about her, I suppose you'd say. I suspect Norma was connected in some way to just about everyone of any importance in Hollywood, but she kept those connections separate from each other."

"There's got to be something else," Rourke says impatiently. "The other night, you started to say something about weird beliefs."

"Norma was a levelheaded type, you know? Very clear-thinking and practical, I'd say. But she had this odd fascination—really odd, given everything else about her—with spiritualism, the occult, that kind of esoteric hogwash. I wouldn't have known about it myself, but it became clear when she started pushing me for the lead role in *The Devil's Playground*. Like she was obsessed with it. The fact that she felt the need to push me at all was strange—she was my first choice for the role. But she seemed to know so much about all of the occult side of the story. Just something I didn't expect."

"Did this fascination go any further than that, as far as you know?"

Carbine shrugs. He smooths his mustache with forefinger and thumb. "I don't know—everybody in this town, everybody outside it too, seems obsessed with all kinds of hocus-pocus. But here we've got everything from fortune-tellers and spiritualists to May Otis Blackburn and her mad cult. I know Norma was friendly with Rudy Valentino before he died—and his wife, Natacha Rambova. They were both into spiritualism. Someone told me once that Norma regularly consulted a fortune-teller—some voodoo priestess type."

"Who told you?"

"I honestly can't remember. If it comes back to me, I'll let you know. But it wasn't a real name—you know, a regular name. It was *Madame* something-or-other. The usual hoo-hah."

"Is there anyone else you know of connected to Norma?" asks Rourke. "Anyone who seemed in any way close to her? I need *something* to go on if you want me to get to the truth of what happened."

"Everybody connected to her who I know about tend to be movie connections. Business." Carbine thinks for a moment. "You know how the Negro actor Lewis Everett is playing the demon role? Well, he's also a writer and sometime director. He has a novel—his own novel—that he wants to make into a movie. It would actually make a good movie, but I can't back it. Or back it officially. Everett has his own small studio, and he's also worked as a photoplay writer and actor with Oscar Micheaux. I've heard that Noble Johnston over at Lincoln is something of a mentor to him. His novel is called *Silas Torn* and its protagonist's also a Negro. It's set in the Reconstruction South, and there are themes of miscegenation and 'passing' in it. Hollywood's a place where people maybe don't worry much about facing up to stuff like that, but it'll never play in Peoria. And nowhere in the South. I can't touch it. Or, more to the point, I can't be seen to touch it."

"But?"

Carbine smiles. "Everett didn't want to play the part of the demon. He thought it was trading on his 'darkness,' when every picture he's made has been a socially responsible drama trying to show the truth of Negro life—and go some way to undo the massive damage Griffith did with *Birth.* But I sent some of his scenes over to Paul Brand, who agreed Everett's got a lot of presence, and the camera likes him. Brand's enthusiasm gave me the excuse to offer him more money than the part warrants."

"A back-door way of funding his picture . . ."

"Or helping fund it."

"What's this got to do with Norma Carlton?" asks Rourke.

"That's the thing—it was Norma who persuaded me to meet with Everett. Set the whole thing up. And she kept on at me until I told her he had the part."

When they finish going through all the contacts and relationships Norma Carlton had—or at least the few that Carbine knows about—the studio chief escorts Rourke out to the reception area. They both stop in front of the poster for *The Devil's Playground,* silent in the thrall of a dead woman's beauty and a painted demon's gaze.

"Are you still going to use it?" asks Rourke. "This poster?"

"Almost all of Norma's scenes are in the can," says Carbine. "I really don't want to recast the part and reshoot. And as director, Paul Brand has made it clear he doesn't want anyone else either. You'll see why when the movie's ready for prescreening at the studio. Norma is . . . she was . . . *exceptional.* So, yes, I want this three-sheet in the foyer of every movie theater in the world. It's quite a poster, isn't it?"

"It sure is. Grosz is a hell of an artist. The whole thing with the devil taking form from the flames and smoke really is quite something," says Rourke.

"I know what you mean. But that element wasn't Grosz's idea."

"Oh?"

"No, Clifford Taylor described it to Grosz," says Carbine.

"Taylor?" Rourke frowned. Carbine's deputy and studio chief didn't strike her as the creative type.

"Yeah," said Carbine. "In fact, Cliff insisted it went in. Said it was based on something he saw at a magic-lantern show when he was a kid."

10

It is hot and sticky on Hollywood Boulevard. The noon hour slouches indolent and insolent into its place in the day. The fog that fumbled its blind way from the ocean into the morning city still lingers as a diffusing veil over the blank face of the sun.

Inside the restaurant, it is oak-paneled cool and dark and quiet. When Mary Rourke enters, she feels she has stepped into some fresh, shaded glade, the foliage of window shutters cutting the light in parallel shafts through the pale-blue mist of cigarette smoke. Hiram Levitt, a small, neat man in a sober dark-blue suit that gives him the mien of a bank official, sits in his usual booth, eating his usual appetizer. Levitt has strikingly dark and intelligent eyes, fine-drawn features, black hair, and a pale complexion. He sees Rourke and prepares his lips for a smile by dabbing them with his napkin. He rises as she approaches, extending his hand.

"How nice to see you, Mary. Is this a happy coincidence?"

"I knew I'd find you here, Hiram."

"Of course you did." His smile widens. "Everyone knows they can find me here at this time of day. I am nothing if not a creature of habit, that's for sure. Please, join me." With a gesture he invites her to sit in the booth, which she does. "Can I get you something? Some lunch?" He beckons a waiter.

"I'm fine, thanks, Hiram."

He waves the waiter away. "What can I do for you?" he asks. "Although I can guess . . ."

"You heard about Norma?"

The smile fades. "I did. It's awful, just awful. She was one of my first clients. One of my best and most loyal. She was more than that, she was a friend." He leans forward, lowering his voice. "Norma didn't have a heart condition. I would have known that. I've heard rumors. . . ."

"What rumors?"

"That it was suicide. That she killed herself over Bob Huston because he wouldn't leave Veronica Stratton for her."

Rourke sighs resignedly, as if caught out. "We're keeping it under wraps, but, yes, it was suicide. Enough Luminal for a hundred-year siesta. I know I can trust you more than anyone to keep that to yourself."

"I see, I see. . . ." Levitt nods thoughtfully, his dark gaze on the tablecloth for a moment. When he looks up, his face is rearranged into something hard-edged and cold. "You gave that up too easy, Mary. Way too easy. It's a crock and you know it. Norma is the last—the very last—person on this planet to kill herself. How long have you and I worked together? All the truths we've covered up and fictions we've spun? I never thought you'd try to spin one on me. So why don't you cut the bull and tell me what happened to Norma? What really happened . . ."

Rourke holds his gaze for a moment. Levitt's eyes are dark violet, almost black, the iris and pupil merging into one unreadable darkness. She's never been able to read him; and she's disconcerted by how easily he's read her.

"I don't know," she says, and the lie sinks into the darkness of his eyes without a ripple. "But I'm trying to find out. That's why I've come to see you."

"Old man Carbine ask you to do this?"

She nods.

"You, not Golem Geller?"

"For now."

Levitt leans back into the leather-upholstered booth, his dark eyes still fixed on Rourke, still unreadable, still reading hers.

"There's quite a buzz about this picture you're making over at Carbine," he says at last. "The word is that Harry Carbine has hocked every asset, called in every favor to make it happen. Only now everybody's talking about how it's a cursed production. First Norma's death, then this accident on-set. The word is that the source material for the movie—this old book nobody's ever heard of—is cursed itself."

"It's all baloney," says Rourke. "Norma's death, whatever was behind it, has nothing to do with the movie. And the accident the other day was just that: an accident."

"But the guy's dead, isn't he?"

Rourke shakes her head. "Busted back, but still alive. If he makes it, he'll be in a wheelchair for the rest of his life. All because somebody didn't secure a pin bolt in the scaffolding. Nothing supernatural about any of it."

"Doesn't hurt, though, does it?" Levitt offers Rourke a cigarette from his case before taking one himself. He lights them both. "Getting people talking like that about a movie—it's a publicist's dream. And let's face it, any movie needs an angle if it's going to compete with Paramount's *Wings*. After Clara Bow's performance, from what I've heard, both Norma and Veronica Stratton were worried about their places."

Rourke angles her head and impatiently blows a stream of smoke into the air. "Listen, Hiram, I came because I need your help. I know you and Norma were close, and I need you to give me some kind of handle on this. I don't know what drove Norma to suicide, but, like you, I can't see it being blind love for Robert Huston. It must have been something else. Something going on out of sight."

He sighs. "You're really still going to push that suicide fairy tale at me?"

"Nothing to suggest it was otherwise. What about it, Hiram, can you help?"

"Help in what way?"

Rourke sighs. "You know exactly how you can help. Norma Carlton's life was like an iceberg: all that majesty and beauty for the world to see, but ten times more—a hundred times more—going on beneath the surface and out of sight. And not just hidden from the public, hidden from everyone around her. I need to see what was under the waterline."

He doesn't answer, the dark eyes unblinking.

"Like you say," Rourke breaks the silence, "you and I have worked together for a long time now. I've put a lot of business your way. All I'm asking is for you to tell me anything about Norma that might help me understand what happened to her."

"You know what everyone calls me, right? That I know everyone calls me?"

"The Resurrectionist," says Rourke. She has never said it to his face before, but it is, as he says, what everyone in the business calls him.

He nods. "The Resurrectionist. It's what they used to call a body snatcher, a grave robber. A sort of euphemism, I guess. Maybe it's partly because people think I look like a mortician, or there's something about my sunny disposition they find funereal. But you know the truth of it: They call me that—*you* call me that—because I *resurrect* people, the people you and the other studios bring me. I make it possible for my clients to put whatever lurks in their true pasts behind them, and give them new lives, a new reality of themselves. You've brought God knows how many to me over the years. And out of all of those reinvented people, how many times have I told you about the truth of their pasts?"

"Never," says Rourke. "But, Hiram, Norma Carlton is—"

"When I resurrect a prospect into a star," he cuts her off, "I know that the fiction I create has to be taken for fact. For others to believe the fiction, my client has to start believing it themselves, at least in part. I rebuilt Norma. I renamed her, remolded her. I told her what books to read, what music to listen to, what wine goes with what food. I *resurrected* her. But, like all my resurrections, I was working with raw material that already carried the shape within it. The defects in that material were eliminated; the positives were emphasized. I tore down her real-life experiences and background, but I kept their foundations to rebuild her in her new image. That means I know all there is to know about the woman, the girl, that Norma Carlton was before she became Norma Carlton. Every secret." Levitt inhales and holds the smoke in his lungs, keeping Rourke in his dark gaze. He exhales. "And I won't tell you a single one of those secrets, Mary. You know that. You know it's a rule I never break."

"With living clients, yes. Norma is dead. You telling me now can't hurt her. All it can do is help me get to the bottom of what happened."

"I would say you clearly don't get it, but I know you do. You're too smart not to. Whether she's dead or not, I can't betray her confidences. If word got out, no client would ever trust me again. These people are, above all, egotists. They delude themselves into believing they have some kind of legacy to leave behind. When they confide in me, they expect their secrets to be taken to the grave—*my* grave, not theirs."

They are disturbed by the waiter, who sets a lunch plate down in front of Levitt.

"Are you sure I can't get you something, ma'am?" asks the waiter. "A coffee?"

Rourke looks up at him. He is young, strapping, and ridiculously good-looking. She remarks to herself how Hollywood is brimful of young, strapping, ridiculously good-looking young men, and young, svelte, ridiculously beautiful young women, all seeking their spot, but in the meanwhile waiting tables, washing cars, cutting lawns, cleaning washrooms, polishing cuspidors. And many even less elevated forms of employment.

"No thanks," she says. Once the waiter is gone, she turns back to Levitt. "This is different, Hiram."

"How is it different? You came in here ready with your half-assed half-truth—to insult my intelligence with this suicide applesauce. Now, without being open with me, you expect me to unpack all Norma's dirty linen for you to sift through."

"I've told you all I can. All I know. And, believe me, I don't like playing detective. I just want to try to understand—"

Levitt cuts her off with a gesture. "If Norma's path out of this vale of tears was unnatural, and she didn't commit suicide, then she was murdered. I suspected it as soon as I heard about her death, and you confirmed it when you walked in here. And that means Carbine has taken a step too far in covering it up. The cops have got sensitive about this kind of thing, Mary, ever since they turned up at William Desmond Taylor's murder scene to find Paramount execs warming their tootsies at a bonfire of personal papers. After Taylor, Ince, and Arbuckle, there's a limit to how much blue uniform studios can pay off. That's why you're here. Norma Carlton was murdered and necks are on the line because you covered it up. How am I doing?"

Rourke watches him for a moment. He has knife and fork in hand and begins eating his lunch, as if what they've been discussing was the most matter-of-fact thing in the world. She sighs.

"I swear we thought it was suicide, Hiram. I didn't lie about that. That's why I was there at her house—cleaning up what we thought would be an embarrassment for the studio. It wasn't until Doc Wilson examined her in the morgue that we realized it wasn't suicide."

"Sloppy . . ." says Levitt without looking up from his lunch.

"No, not sloppy. Whoever murdered Norma deliberately staged it to look like she killed herself. Not staged enough to pass close scrutiny, but enough to convince us we should clean up the scene."

Now she has his attention. He crosses knife and fork on the plate and leans forward, rests his elbows on the table, interlocks his fingers. "You think the killer *deliberately* got you to clean up?"

"My guess is he knew that it's studio policy to sanitize suicides, junk or booze overdoses, or sex-related deaths, but not murders." She pauses, leaning into the violet-black eyes. "Hiram, the sonofabitch choked Norma to death. Strangled her with a cord or a tie, Doc Wilson thinks. Only Harry Carbine, Doc Wilson, me, and now you know the truth. I'm sorry if you think I was holding out on you, but I'm sailing uncharted waters. I need to find a compass. Now will you help me?"

He stares unwaveringly into her eyes. "I need to think about it."

"Why?"

"Because of everything I said before. And because there's stuff that went on in the background. Bad stuff. There are some very dangerous people out there. Stuff going on that is way beyond the pale. I think Norma was involved in some of it."

"This hasn't got anything to do with the occult, has it? I heard she was interested in that kind of thing," Rourke urges impatiently.

"Don't push me, Mary. Like I said, I've got to think it all over. You know Salvaggi's Deli?"

"With the basement and the cheese password? Yeah, I know it."

"Meet me there tomorrow night at seven. I've got to think what I can and can't tell you. And I need to go through Norma's file first."

"Why can't—" she starts, but sits back and lets her shoulders drop resignedly. "Okay."

"I'll do what I can, Mary. But don't expect too much. People who've put their past behind them don't like it being hauled up again, even dead people. And if there's anything you can say about this town, then nothing and nobody are what they seem. Even you, Mary."

"Me?" Rourke laughs. "I promise you, Hiram, there's a lot less to me than meets the eye."

"Really? I have an ear for accents—part of my job, I guess—even when those accents are being suppressed, like the one you keep a lid on. Somewhere in the South, I'd say."

Rourke smiles and stands up. "I'll see you tomorrow night. Maybe we can trade backstories then." She pauses for a moment. "I need your help, Hiram. I know you thought a great deal of Norma—I need you to do it for her, not just for me."

11

This is the engine room of moviemaking. The production office is a no-frills affair. There are desks piled with paperwork, pieces of equipment and even film cans heaped in corners. The walls of the office are blackboarded and covered in notes and numbers. To Rourke's eyes, it looks somewhere between a bookie's alleyway office and a mathematician's laboratory.

But the numbers on the walls aren't calculus or winning odds—or perhaps in a way they are. These are the production slates. This is the music of film creation. Every department—technical, costume, makeup, set design and construction, even the director himself—dances to the tune of deadlines and dates, of the shooting schedules and requisition calendars, chalked up on the walls of this office.

The usual population of production staff have been temporarily evicted from the office so that this meeting can take place, and when she enters, three men turn in Rourke's direction: Paul Brand, the tall, wraith-like, and careworn German director, the wound on his high-domed head covered with a white square of gauze dressing; Clifford J. Taylor, Carbine's deputy, who regards Rourke with studied disparagement; and Harry Carbine, the only one sitting behind a desk, his expression dark.

Carbine invites Mary to sit, which she does, pulling a chair out from one of the desks.

"Mary is dealing with the consequences of Norma's suicide," explains Carbine, "and is trying to keep a lid on the whole thing. She has my complete confidence and we can speak freely in front of her. In fact, it's essential that Mary gets all the information she needs. So, gentlemen, if Miss Rourke asks you a question, I expect you to give a full and honest answer."

Paul Brand nods almost absentmindedly, as if he has bigger worries with which to occupy himself. Taylor regards her with an indistinct yet nauseating mix of lust and contempt. It is, she knows, a look that many young starlets have had to endure. And they've had to endure worse. Mary Rourke has always maintained a cynical detachment in her job, but when she had to use threats and payoffs to keep one of Taylor's worst incidents out of the papers—and potentially the courts—she had seriously considered changing to a more edifying career, like cleaning sewers.

She casts her eyes over the interwoven complexities of the production slate. "Where does this leave you?" she asks the room generally. "What I mean is, where does Norma Carlton's suicide leave you? Mr. Carbine tells me you may not have to recast the role of Adelicia. But how much of the movie are you going to have to reshoot?"

It is Paul Brand who answers, his voice thickened by a German accent. "We got just about all of her scenes in the can. The only major scene still to be shot—and it is *the* major scene in the movie—is the burning of Ouxbois. The whole set has to go up in flames, and it's a one-shot deal. Twenty cameras will be running from various different angles and elevations, but it will all have to go down in one take. And, obviously, because the whole set will burn, it's the last scene we'll shoot."

"And you needed Norma for that?"

"Technically, no," says Brand. "We have a scene showing Jean and Adelicia fleeing from the city—but the way it is described in Nathan Milcom's photoplay is as a panoramic, followed by a wide two-shot of them on the mountaintop, looking down, but the focus on the city burning. We still have to film that, because, obviously, we have to wait until the set is on fire. There is also a full-two-close-up of Jean and Adelicia holding each other, lit up by the glow of the flames, but even that's in the can—we filmed it with Norma last month, using special lighting." Brand shakes his head sadly. "It's almost as if she knew we had all her scenes—and the ones we didn't could be done with her stand-in."

"Is the stand-in convincing enough?" asks Rourke.

"From the distance we're talking about, yes," says Brand. "She is the perfect height and figure; no one would know it isn't Norma."

"I'd go so far as to say the similarity, from a distance, is quite startling," Carbine adds. "Her name is Carole Ventris. She's just a girl. Much younger than Norma. But there's something about the way she moves, the way she holds herself, that is strikingly reminiscent of Norma. She's not Norma, and never will be, but she's such a close match that we're screen-testing her for the lead in the next movie we have planned."

"What is it?" Rourke asks when she notices Carbine's expression. He looks troubled.

"Nothing . . . It's just strange that it was Norma Carlton who brought Carole Ventris to us and suggested she could be her stand-in. In fact, it was Norma who arranged Carole's screen test. . . ." Carbine shakes the thought off. "I wanted to talk to you about the shooting of the city-burning scene anyway."

"Oh?"

"We have it slated for the end of next week. I thought it would be good to invite the press along. It will be one hell of a spectacle and will maybe get them past Norma's death. Could you get your publicity team to sort something out? I'd want to invite some of our investors as well."

"Sure, Mr. Carbine," says Rourke. "I'll get on it." She looks across at Brand. The German director still has a distracted, faraway expression. For a moment she wonders where that faraway is—what it is that has him so preoccupied. Perhaps it is just the fact that the star of the movie he was brought over from Germany to direct has died.

"Mr. Brand," she asks, "you worked very closely with Miss Carlton. You're perhaps the closest person to her, other than Mr. Carbine. You worked with her almost every day for five months—was there anything you noticed about her? Anything troubling her?"

"No . . . No . . . I don't think so. Nothing in particular. But she was very focused on the film, on the story. She was a consummate professional, you know. She knew every page of the shooting photoplay script, including those she did not appear in. She often seemed very preoccupied with the film, but other than that it was impossible to tell what was going on in her mind—she was such a private person."

"Yeah," Rourke says dully, "so everybody keeps telling me. But you didn't ever get the feeling that she was in some kind of trouble? That she was worried about something, or that she was anxious or afraid?"

Brand turns and stares at Rourke. She notices his eyes are a bright, piercing blue, undulled by the weariness that seems to have possession of the rest of his body.

"No. I cannot say that I noticed anything of that nature. She simply seemed consumed by the film we were making. Almost to the point where it seemed that was all that mattered to her."

She nods, then addresses all three men. "Did any of you notice anything strange in the lead-up to her death? Anything unusual happen on set? Or even socially, after shooting?"

"Norma didn't hang around much after shooting," answers Clifford Taylor. "And, like Paul said, when she was working she was totally focused on the job. I certainly didn't get any hint that she was suicidal."

"There was one thing," says Carbine. "I was at my office window one day about three weeks ago when I saw her talking to a man in the parking lot. They were not exactly arguing, but I got the feeling that their exchange was getting heated. She drove off and left him standing there. I thought it odd at the time."

"Did you recognize him?" asks Rourke. "Was it someone from the studio?"

"That is the thing," says Carbine. "He wasn't a movie type. He looked like some kind of chawbacon—you know, like a rube passing through town. He would be older than me, in his sixties. Big man, but fat with it."

"You ever see him again?"

Carbine thinks, then shakes his head. "No. Can't say I ever did."

12

1897
Kansas

The night was dark and moonless, empty of light but, for Boy, full of wonder. He had lain awake since the sun went down, staring into a screenlike blackness against which his imagination projected a disorderly cavalcade of images. What he had witnessed at the magic-lantern show now replayed itself, tangled and jumbled with images of even greater, even more spectacular ambition.

A fire raged through him, as if throughout his childhood and youth some great store of ideas had lain within, undisturbed and tinder-dry, waiting for that single night and the bright spark of the magic-lantern show to find it and set it aflame. This, he knew, was his destiny; this, he knew, was what he was made to do, meant to be. Everything that made Boy who he was, was somehow bound indissolubly to creating images that stirred others. Images that delivered the sweet, dark ecstasy of fear.

He had always known he thought differently, saw things differently. He had always seen significances in things, saw meaning in what others would consider commonplace: in the sky, in the changing shape of clouds; or how the change of seasons or a particular dance of sunlight could make you feel. At school he did well despite his disinterest in the process. The one thing that stood out for him more than anything else was when the teacher had brought in that large art book. He had wondered at the color prints of great paintings, had been hypnotized by the craft of the image makers. For the first time in his life, Boy had seen proof that there were others like him: kindred spirits out there in the wider world. He had marveled at how an artist's eye could find majesty in a simple landscape or the arrangement of a still life. They saw the world in the same way he did, he realized.

But a bigger-yet realization was that, although everyone else around him would look at the sky or the land or a face, and not marvel at it, they would marvel at a painting or etching or photograph of the same thing. If they were to find wonder in the world, he realized, people—ordinary people—needed to see through the eyes of another. Through eyes like his.

But Boy's ambitions were not solely creative: there was money—a lot of money—to be made from images. Particularly when those images portrayed something bigger, something grander, something more frightening, than real life.

And still, as he lay there in the night theater of his bedroom, he felt that delicious dark tingle in his groin whenever he thought of the animation he had seen on Nancy Stillson's face as she had watched the devil spread great bat-wings above her. A deep, visceral terror running through her like an electric current.

There were, he knew, other ambitions to be fulfilled. Other ways to bring people, bring women, the ecstasy of pure fear. Fulfilling those ambitions would bring danger, and he made a decision to hide that part of himself from the world. For now. Until he had the power and wealth to do what he pleased.

For now, Boy lay in the dark and, with a cold, calculated patience ahead of his years, put together his even darker plans.

He knew that the Dahlman and Darke Magic Lantern Phantasmagoria had packed up equipment and tents and had already left town. He imagined the caravan of carriages moving quietly in dark procession across the empty prairie, ready to unpack wonder in a new village or town. From the flyer he had picked up that night, he knew their itinerary, the next three places the show was due to appear.

The next day passed painfully slowly, his ambition and impatience an itch he forbade himself to scratch. His father, tall and lean and meager of flesh and mind, kept Boy back from school to help on the farm—a not infrequent event. Boy knew that his help was often needed, but he had been certain for some time that his father was suspicious of Boy's clear aptitude for book learning. Today, Boy would make sure he gave no reason to provoke his father's ire or suspicion and acquiesce to every demand without complaint. Nonetheless, he still felt his father's pale-blue Norwegian eye on him as he undertook his assigned chores.

At least there had been no beatings. Today.

By the time Boy was again in bed, he was bone-tired. His lack of sleep from the night before and the arduousness of the day seeped lead into his limbs and eyelids. But he knew he must not sleep. If he surrendered to his tiredness, then he would never be able to make his way across country in time to catch up with the traveling show. He knew the next three stops they would make, but nothing beyond that.

He waited.

It was the small hours of the morning when he stirred from his bed, slowly and silently. Careful not to waken either of his brothers, who shared the room with him, he slipped out of bed and scooped up his clothes from where he left them on the chair. He eased open the door and stepped out into the hall. He considered dressing there, on the stair landing, but a sound from his parents' room caused him to freeze for a moment. His heart pounded as he considered whether to slip back into his room or to proceed and risk discovery. He stood motionless and cursed his indecisiveness, waiting for the bedroom door to open and his father to emerge. But the door didn't open, and his father didn't emerge.

Resting his weight on cautious toes, he made his way downstairs. He paused in the kitchen to wrap some bread and cheese in oilcloth. He dressed hurriedly but silently, pulling on his boots at the door before heading out to the barn.

The night waited for him outside like an impatient dark accomplice; above him a sheet of cloud drawn across the moon and stars made the sky's blackness complete. He crossed to the barn and retrieved the knapsack he had hidden under the hay and slipped the oilcloth-wrapped bread and cheese into it. Now he had all he needed—all he wanted to take with him from this place. The note he had left on the kitchen table, explaining his departure but not his destination, would satisfy his parents. He imagined his father's fury, not in despair of having lost a son, but at being down a pair of hands for working the farm. Maybe, he thought, his father would be less likely to beat his brothers lest he encourage them to follow Boy's footsteps.

The dog stirred in its kennel and whimpered. Recognizing the prelude to a bark, Boy crossed over swiftly and whispered a few words of farewell to the dog, who settled down again to sleep.

Without a backward glance, Boy crossed the yard, climbed the fence into the south field, and was swallowed by the night.

13

1927
Hollywood

Mary Rourke always puzzles as to why, in Hollywood, people at the very top of their careers, earning more money than they could spend in several lifetimes, and with nothing left to prove to the world, feel the need to make architectural statements. When she arrives outside Mount Laurel, the home of Veronica Stratton and Robert Huston, the architecture doesn't so much make a statement as yell at her.

This is a lofty place. The ascent up a snaking side road from Laurel Canyon Boulevard has been so steep it threatened to overheat the Packard's engine. Rourke imagines that deliveries must be charged at a premium—not that an extra cent per mile would trouble the Stratton-and-Huston household.

On arrival, the first thing that strikes her is that Mount Laurel isn't so much a house as a complex: a vast, sprawling mansion sitting atop a towering bluff looking out over Laurel Canyon, with smaller buildings neatly arranged, but suitably distant, at its flanks, like servants patiently attending a monarch. To Mary Rourke's eyes, it all looks more like business premises than a home; it is, however, a hugely impressive piece of architecture, perched on the bluff's edge and with views extending in every direction. A literal expression of careers having reached dizzying heights.

Like Pickfair, the ridiculously lavish mock-Tudor mansion of Mary Pickford and Douglas Fairbanks, this is the modern-day equivalent of a medieval castle. Instead of a moat and drawbridge, the walls and iron gates make an unequivocal statement of detachment from the world of the ordinary man and woman.

It is no wonder, thinks Rourke, that these people lose their grip on what is real.

There is a high wall surrounding the estate's ten acres, and when she arrives, she finds the gates closed to her. A guard, dressed in a uniform styled to look coplike, steps out of the gatehouse and approaches her window. He is early-middle-aged, that generation who saw action in the war. He has small, hard eyes and an ugly scar—more a deeply indented crease in his left cheek where substantial flesh has been lost, twisting the corner of his mouth up slightly to suggest a permanent sneer. Rourke recognizes it as the kind of damage serious munitions do, suggesting a battlefield history. He is unsmiling and brusque as he asks her her business and makes her wait while he phones the main house. Only then, and still unsmiling, does he open the gates for her.

"Park there, on the left." He points to a paved square parking lot ten yards along the drive. "No automobiles other than the owners' beyond that point."

"Sure thing, handsome," she says flatly. She does what he says, leaves the Packard on the lot and walks up the drive to the main house. And it is quite a walk—and steep.

At the top of the drive there is a large, paved courtyard in front of the main house. Rourke sees two cars parked there, one is a brand-new Rolls-Royce Phantom, its deep-blue paintwork, chrome, and burnished walnut all gleaming in the California sun. Next to it is an expensive foreign-made sand-colored sporting coupe. She recognizes it instantly as the automobile Robert Huston had abandoned on Norma Carlton's driveway that night. The car Golem Geller's boys got off scene—a Mercedes Supercharged Type-S, Geller had told her later, as if it would mean anything to her.

She crosses the courtyard. Less than a year old, the house and its outbuildings are pristine whitewashed stone and in a mix of styles: vaguely Mission Revival mixed with Art Deco—the brand-new style from some French exhibition a couple of years back that everyone in Hollywood now seems to want.

Reaching the vast double doors of the main house, she takes a moment to take in the view behind her before tugging at the door pull. Unlike at Norma Carlton's home, there is no single Mexican maid here, taking care of the household. A tall, blonde girl who seems to be modeling a maid's outfit, and who walks in a way that would make a cat look graceless, leads Rourke to a circular reception hall, all Egyptian-style colonnades and black-and-white-checkered marble floor.

"Mr. Parsons will be with you in a moment." The maid turns to leave.

"Mr. Parsons?"

"The butler," replies the maid flatly, and leaves Rourke in the hall.

When the butler arrives, Rourke has a déjà vu flashback to her small-hours visit to Harry Carbine's mansion. The butler—presumably Parsons, though he doesn't introduce himself—has an effeminate accent from the same part of mid-Atlantic-shire as Carbine's valet. His manner is equally aloof and patronizing.

"You don't have a brother working in Santa Monica, by any chance?" she asks.

Parsons looks confused for a moment, then, suspecting he is the butt of a joke he doesn't get, recovers his aloofness. "No, madam, I do not. This way . . ."

The room he shows her into isn't so much grand as grandiose, the scale and proportions too overdone for a habitable environment. Again the floors are marble, and the plasterwork of the cornicing and ceiling roses is ornate. Oil paintings from another century and another continent hang on every wall. It has, Rourke thinks, the cozy homeyness of the first-class waiting room in La Grande railroad station.

"Miss Stratton will be with you shortly."

"Thank you, Parsons," she says airily, and he fires her a look as he leaves.

She finds herself alone for nearly half an hour before Veronica Stratton sweeps into the room theatrically, as if she expects a film crew to be waiting for her with cameras rolling. Despite herself, and her experience of dealing with the beautiful people of Hollywood, Rourke is struck by Stratton's presence. She is dressed in a beige-and-gold flapper-style geometric-patterned dress. The dress's straight-lined simplicity sits uneasily with Stratton's classical curves. Rourke also notices the movie star's hair isn't a radiant silver blonde, as it appears on black-and-white celluloid, but more a rich golden tone. Similarly, she notices that Stratton's complexion is darker than she had thought it would be, suggesting that the glory of her hair is perhaps less natural gift and more hairdresser's artifice.

"Thanks for seeing me, Miss Stratton," says Rourke. "I appreciate you taking the time."

Stratton shakes her head dismissively and waves a crimson-nailed hand in a vague gesture that Rourke should sit. She does.

"What is this all about?" Stratton asks. Her voice has an unnatural accentlessness. "You work for Carbine International, don't you?"

"Yes, Miss Stratton, I do."

Stratton's eyes take in Rourke's face and figure slowly and disarmingly, as if appraising her from head to toe.

"I would have taken you for an actress," says Stratton, almost abstractly. "You have the looks. Or had them, probably. Maybe you were one when you were younger."

"I prefer working this side of the camera. Always have."

"What is it you want from me?" asks Stratton. Her gaze remains fixed on Rourke, her crimson lips slightly parted over white teeth. "I have no connection to Carbine International."

"No, Miss Stratton, you don't. But your husband is on loan to the studio from First National. I'm sure you're aware of what happened to Mr. Huston's co-star, Norma Carlton."

"She's dead. What of it?"

"Are you aware how she died?"

"I'm *aware* that you are pushing to the press that she died of a weak heart." Stratton continues to hold Rourke in a gaze that seems to smolder and chill at the same time. Rourke recognizes it as the practiced, trademark look from her movies. Rourke is used to dealing with people who confuse emotions with performances, but there is something about Stratton's gaze that discomfits her. "I'm also *aware* that she killed herself. And before you ask, I'm *aware* that Robert went up to her house that night, after she was dead."

"And what, as far as you're concerned, was Mr. Huston's relationship with Miss Carlton?"

"Relationship?" The movie star gives a small, derisive laugh. "There was no relationship."

There is a chunky box on the coffee table, green onyx marbled with cream. Stratton dips crimson-tipped fingers into it and, without offering one to Rourke, pulls out a cigarette. Rourke waits while she uses the matching green onyx table lighter.

"If there was no relationship, what was he doing up there that night?"

Stratton blows a jet of smoke into the air. "I didn't say they weren't fucking. They were. But, like I said, no relationship."

"And you told Mr. Huston to stop?"

"Me?" For an instant Stratton looks genuinely taken aback. "Why would I do that? No. Robert and I have an arrangement. We both do what we want so long as it doesn't cause embarrassment. And in any case, that's why the studios have people like you, isn't it? To deal with embarrassments?"

"Your husband told me that the reason he went up there that night was because Norma Carlton had threatened suicide. And the reason was because he'd had to break it off because you'd found out and told him to stop seeing her."

Veronica Stratton gives a small laugh. "I couldn't stand the woman. Hated her, even. But I have no interest in where Robert dips his English wick, like I said. It wasn't a topic that came up in conversation."

"Then why did Mr. Huston tell me that?"

"You had better ask him."

"But you knew he was involved with Norma Carlton."

"I had reason to believe so, but not the interest to confirm or deny that belief. I certainly didn't put pressure on Robert to end any of his liaisons."

"Then why would she commit suicide?"

"Certainly not over Robert." Stratton paused for a moment, taking time over her cigarette and her appraisal of Rourke. "Listen, Miss Rourke, you're clearly an intelligent woman. I'm an intelligent woman. In my opinion, Norma Carlton was, to be frank, a total bitch, but she was also an intelligent woman. The idea that she was so besotted with Robert that she took her own life because of him is absurd."

"You're saying she wasn't in love with him?"

"Norma Carlton had her choice of men. Sure, Robert's pretty, but that's about the extent of it. There's no real substance to him, not that it matters in this town. If anyone was besotted, then it would be Robert."

Rourke takes a moment to think over what Stratton has said. "So why did she commit suicide?"

"Don't ask me. But if you *are* asking, then I'd say Norma Carlton didn't kill herself. She's the last person I can imagine doing herself in."

Rourke doesn't comment that Stratton is not the first person to say that to her. If Stratton knows more about what happened to her rival in love and on-screen, then she's playing her hand dangerously faceup.

"So, if she didn't commit suicide, then what happened to her?" asks Rourke.

"I don't know. Maybe she took too much stuff by accident. It happens all the time here, as I'm sure you know." Stratton shrugs, leans forward, and crushes the half-smoked cigarette in the bowl of a chunky crystal ashtray big enough to serve punch in. "If that's all, Miss Rourke, I have things I need to attend to."

"I was hoping to talk with Mr. Huston while I am here."

"Robert's not here at the moment. He's in town."

"Oh? It's just that I saw his automobile outside. The German sports."

"I didn't say his car wasn't here. I said he wasn't."

"Of course." Rourke stands up. "Well, thank you, Miss Stratton."

She is surprised when Stratton stands up and walks with her to the door. As Rourke makes to leave, Stratton places herself in her way.

"Are you sure you weren't an actress? You do have the look. You remind me of Louise Brooks—without the bob, of course, and older."

"I screen-tested a couple of times, back in the old days," says Rourke, trying not to follow her instinct to take a step back. Stratton is deliberately close to her, too close, and Rourke can smell the faint fuming of perfume and body heat. "But it didn't work out."

Stratton smiles. Catlike. "I heard something of the sort. I heard you didn't play game with the director, and when he became insistent, you broke his nose. I admire strong women. Women who don't give in to men. There's not enough of us about."

Rourke is taken aback that Stratton knows her background. She senses that the movie star is about to move even closer when Parsons, the butler, appears at the door.

"Could you show Miss Rourke out?" says Stratton, her voice laced with a thread of amusement. "Miss Rourke, if I can be of any further help, please do call."

Parsons leads Rourke out through a million dollars of marble and stone. When he holds the front door open for her, the heat and brightness of the day outside flare like a reporter's flashbulb. Once her eyes adjust to the sunlight, she notices that Huston's sports coupe is no longer there.

"I believe Mr. Huston is in town today . . ." she says to Parsons.

"I wouldn't know, madam."

"Really? I thought you would. I thought telling people 'Master is at home' or 'Madam is indisposed' is the main part of your job."

"My responsibilities are manifold," replies the butler with studied flatness. "Good day, madam."

For a moment, Rourke doesn't make a move to leave, instead smiles as she examines him. The butler remains patiently unfazed.

"Toodle-pip, Parsons, old bean." Rourke affects a gratingly over-done faux-English accent, steps out into the sunlight and walks down the driveway to where she parked the Packard.

The main gates wait open for her, and she glances toward the gate-house as she drives past. From behind the glass, the guard with the scarred face watches her.

He is talking with someone on the telephone.

14

At least the descent won't overheat the engine again, thinks Rourke, but she decides to keep the Packard in low gear all the way down. The ribbon of roadway, which serves no other adjoining properties, loops around from the gatehouse at the rear of the Mount Laurel estate, before steeply declining through a gully, then snaking its way across the front of the bluff. Once on the face of the cliff, the road becomes edged with a precipitous drop. It is not, she thinks, an ideal drive home for someone like Robert Huston, with his affection for powerful liquor and even more powerful automobiles.

She has an idea that she could perhaps find some concealed place to park and watch out for Huston's return, or other comings and goings from the mansion, but the narrowness of the road and the sparsity of cover make that impossible. In any case, she is unsure what could be gained from surreptitious surveillance. She curses Harry Carbine under her breath: why has she been stuck with a task that she's not in the slightest qualified for?

Nevertheless, aware that the road leads only to and from Mount Laurel, she watches out for Huston's coupe passing on the return climb. She thinks back to Veronica Stratton, and the whole wrongness of the love-triangle story she's been fed. Stratton more likely than not has the same taste in sexual partners as her token husband. It isn't anything that shocks or surprises Rourke—she doesn't care about that kind of thing—and, anyway, it isn't that unusual in Hollywood. Everyone knows that Tallulah Bankhead and Garbo have bedded each other and, between them, as many women as men—so much so that the rumor is that John Gilbert sees Marlene Dietrich as his main rival for Garbo's affections. The freemasonry of sapphic female stars is known in Hollywood as the "Sewing Circle." It is common knowledge that the Russian movie star Alla Nazimova, whose Garden of Alla hotel is said to be the heart of "Lavender Hollywood," has had affairs with both Garbo and Dietrich; Nazimova's film *Salomé*, from three or four years back, had been cast exclusively with lesbian and homosexual actors.

What bothers Rourke is the hogwash she's been fed by Huston about Norma Carlton being distraught over the end of their affair—and that it had been Stratton who had caused its end, despite her not giving a damn. Rourke begins to think she's been too quick to dismiss Huston from any involvement in Norma Carlton's murder.

She has nearly reached the point in the road where it horseshoes back on itself before descending into the gully. It is a blind bend, and she suddenly finds herself faced with Huston's oncoming coupe. He has taken the corner at speed and has come round the bend in the center of the road. Rourke slams her foot on the brake and swings to the right, the wheels of the Packard shuddering over rocks and kicking up a vast cloud of dust. Huston's automobile, still in the center of the road, barrels past, only just missing the Packard.

Rourke has only just collected herself when she realizes she has not slowed down. In fact, the Packard has picked up speed. She stamps on the foot brake, but there is no response. Already on the bend, she is forced to do what Huston did and steers into the center line. The decline's gradient becomes steeper as she enters the short gully, and the Packard picks up speed, hurtling toward the sharp, cliff-sided bend around the face of the bluff. Still her urgent slamming of the footbrake has no effect.

The road dips deeper, but she can see ahead where it takes a slight incline at the end of the gully before looping around the bluff. Rourke realizes that if she hits that corner at any speed, she will career over the white picket edging the road, and plunge down into the canyon below. Even if she makes the corner, the gradient declines still more, and she will hurtle uncontrolled down the road until the next bend or curve sends her to the same fate.

The image of the scar-faced security guard, watching her leave while he spoke on the telephone, flashes through her mind.

Her only hope, she realizes, is to use the slight incline rushing toward her at the end of the gully, but before the bend, to slow the Packard long enough for her to jump from it.

But not at this speed.

She works the column gearshift, double declutching. There is the grinding protest of tortured metal, but she manages to come down a gear. She reaches down and grabs the parking brake, pulling it on and releasing it in short spurts. Still too fast. Much too fast. She repeats the action and drops to the lowest gear; the engine screams, and she feels the grinding spasm course through the gearshift and up her arm. She pulls on the parking brake hard but has to release it when the Packard starts to career out of control. She hits the short upward gradient, and the automobile slows some more, but not enough for her to stop it before it hits the bend.

In rage more than fear, she screams an obscenity and flings open the driver's door and hurls herself from the automobile.

Mary Rourke feels the rush of air, for an instant, then feels nothing more.

15

1893
Louisiana

Officially, Leseuil was a township, though it was too scattered and loose for the definition. It was more a collection of properties, ranging from semi-itinerant shanty boats and tumbledown shacks standing stilt-legged in the swamp, to more substantial cabins scattered desultorily along the bayou. There was a setback levee, untended and broken in parts, behind which sat the two grand houses that had once been the hubs of plantations. The windows of one of the houses gazed out with the blank death-stare of abandonment while nature slowly, ineluctably, stretched prying dark-green fingers into masonry and timber and pulled earthward. The other house was still occupied by the Trosclair family, but in circumstances much reduced from their slave-owning ancestors.

There was no defined center to the community, the closest thing to a civic hub being the arbitrary cluster of the Thibodeaux's store, the parochial house and chapel run by Père Martin, Doc Charbonnier's office, the schoolhouse where Père Martin taught three days a week, Dupont the blacksmith's forge and yard, and the Lagrange barn that served as a communal hall. But this was Cajun and Creole country, and no matter how spread out the community, there was a cohesion to it: a combination of respecting everybody's territorial rights while looking out for one another—and finding any excuse in the Lagrange hall to indulge the communal Cajun imperative of *"Laissez les bons temps rouler,"* and make music, dance, and have a *boucherie* all day or a *fais do-do* all night.

And still they left the witch alone. And she them.

Yet, even though Hippolyta Cormier was never part of the community, she was connected to it. She came into town once a month for supplies, sometimes more often if she had a special need. And every time she came into Leseuil, her presence stirred something: her grace and her beauty struck so very deep, and all the while stirred a dull resentment and mistrust, especially among the community's women. Everyone knew that certain of the village's men continued to navigate the ink-black night swamp out to the witch's cabin, but which of the men was never clear. Some of the women began to talk of voodoo ceremonies out in the backswamp.

And, of course, after the death of the widow Faucheaux, the mistrust and unease that Hippolyta stimulated bordered on fear, so many were careful in their accusations, while others fell silent.

And then there was what happened to Jacques Fournier.

Fournier was a huge man: at age fifty, he was tall and strapping with the kind of build that came from working lumber since he had been a boy. He was unmarried and known to have a dark and dangerous temperament that swelled easily with drink. Like the Swamp Witch, he was someone the others did not exactly shun, but kept a distance from, particularly when he came into town to collect his order of two quarts of whiskey. He too lived in the swamp—not as far out as Hippolyta, but on a stilted cabin and workshop in the cypress-pillared wetlands. He came into town seldom, but when he did, the women kept their distance and the men kept their tongues.

On this particular occasion, Fournier had come into the Lagrange hall, where the townsfolk were having a *boucherie*—a day-long roasting of pigs, dancing, and drinking. Fournier began to make a nuisance of himself, pestering some of the younger women. Père Martin's quiet diplomacy fell on bourbon-deafened ears, and when Fournier shoved the old priest away, the blacksmith Dupont—Fournier's only physical equal—stepped in. The ensuing struggle galvanized the other men into collective action, and they managed, with difficulty, to eject the lumberman.

As Fournier staggered away into the gathering twilight, he announced with drunken defiance that he was going to get what he needed from the *putain* witch in the swamp.

It had been noticed that certain of the men had exchanged looks on hearing Fournier's threat, but no one made a move to check him.

The swamp woodsman was not seen for three weeks. Communal relief turned to dutiful concern, and it was decided that a party should go out to Fournier's cabin to check that he had not fallen victim to drunken mishap. The blacksmith Dupont, Doc Charbonnier, and Père Martin set out while the blanket of morning mist still lay unfurled across the slumbering slow waters.

The cabin was like something out of a folktale, standing on long timber stilts, like the legs of some giant wading bird. A larger stilted platform with a work shed and a rack hung with saws stood in attendance to one side. They tied up next to a wide, flat-bottomed chaland, the boat Fournier used to transport timber, in turn securely moored to the foot of the ladder that reached from water to cabin.

Calls out to Fournier went unanswered.

Led by the blacksmith Dupont, the three men climbed, Père Martin with some difficulty, up to the cabin. When they entered, they were hit with the overpowering stench of rotted flesh. All expected to find the lumberman dead; instead, Fournier was sitting in a heavy wooden chair by the stove, staring at his visitors. He was mumbling incoherently, but what struck the others most was that the eyes staring directly at them were crimson, set into a livid yellow face.

The old priest retched as he spotted the source of the stench. Fournier sat with a handsaw streaked with blood resting on his lap. On the floor next to the chair lay the woodcutter's left forearm. It took them all a moment to recognize it as such, as it was discolored yellow-gray and distended, swollen to three times its natural size. For a moment, Père Martin thought he was looking at a rotting ham, until he discerned the shape of a swollen hand, like a puffed-up glove, at its end. The flesh where the forearm had been severed was ragged, indicating that Fournier had taken the saw to it several times before succeeding in his task.

In an attempt to stanch the flow of blood, the lumberman had wrapped the stump in layers of rags and had tied a belt tourniquet around his upper arm. Despite his precautions, the rags were sodden with dark blood.

"What the hell is wrong with him?" asked Dupont.

"Get rid of that," ordered Doc Charbonnier, ignoring the blacksmith's question and nodding toward the putrid amputated limb. "And fetch my bag from the boat."

Charbonnier scanned the room, grabbed Fournier's discarded jacket and threw it over the arm. Using the jacket to pick it up, he took the severed limb outside and threw it into the swamp waters. When he came back into the cabin with the physician's bag, Père Martin was starting a fire in the stove while the doctor tightened the injured man's tourniquet.

"Find an ax," ordered the doctor. "As clean as you can. Anything with a heavy, flat metal surface. I'm going to have to cauterize the wound before he bleeds to death."

And all the while, Fournier stared out with blood-red eyes and mumbled incoherently. He remained detached from the world, seemingly unaware of the urgent exchanges and actions of the intruders in his home. Even when the blade of the ax, heated in the stove until its edge had begun to glow, was pressed, hissing, against the wound, he did not flinch, and was oblivious to the smell of burning flesh mingled with that of putrefaction in the cabin's air. Once Doc Charbonnier bandaged the stump, the three men maneuvered Fournier out of the cabin. The doctor and the priest waited in the boat below to receive the injured man while Dupont lowered him by a rope tied around his chest.

"What the hell is wrong with him?" The blacksmith repeated his question as they rowed back to town.

"I don't know," said Charbonnier. "I can't say for sure. The jaundice and the conjunctival suffusion—I mean the blood in the whites of his eyes—point to leptospirosis, Weil's disease. You see more cases of it when there's a high water, like there was a couple of weeks ago. You get it from contaminated swamp water through cuts and the like. My guess is that he got it through a cut in his arm and it got infected, which is why he performed the self-amputation."

They were temporarily distracted by Père Martin's recitation of the last rites as he leaned over the injured man.

"So why do you say you're not sure?" asked Dupont.

The doctor shook his head, frowning. "I've never seen anything like this before. It fits with Weil's but it doesn't. And it's so severe. Whatever it is, there's poison in his blood." He shook his head again, this time in frustration. "I just don't know. . . ."

When they got back to town, they put Fournier in the back room of the parochial house, the three men each taking turns to sit with him. It struck the priest that, despite his faith, the deep dark of night, especially when one is listening to the ravings of a dying man with the eyes of a demon, can be a place where it is difficult to feel the presence of God.

Fournier began to cough up blood, which Charbonnier seemed to think confirmed his diagnosis. His breathing became a wet and viscous rattling.

At about four in the morning, the lumberman sat upright in the bed. He stared at the priest with eyes now so red and a face so yellow that he looked like a demon. "Father!" he cried out wetly when he saw the priest sitting by his bed, as if seeing him for the first time. "Father! Save me! Save me from her!"

"What happened, my son?" Père Martin stood up and leaned over the bed. "Save you from whom?"

"She . . ." he said. "The scratch . . . my arm . . ."

"Tell me what happened, Jacques. What—who—did this to you?"

Fournier was about to say something, but his mouth simply gaped, silently. There was a sound from within him, from his chest, like the crackling of green wood on fire. A great convulsion coursed through him. The eruption of blood from his mouth was sudden and violent. There were two pulses of it, covering the bedclothes, some striking Père Martin.

The priest could see that Fournier was dead even before he collapsed back onto the bed.

Charbonnier and Dupont both rushed into the bedroom. They saw the blood soaking the counterpane, splashed dark on the priest's clothes, streaming in gouts from the dead man's mouth.

"Did he say anything?" asked Dupont. "I thought I heard him speak."

"No," said the priest. "He was delirious."

16

After Fournier's funeral, if anyone in Leseuil suspected some connection between the lumberman's death and the Swamp Witch, they didn't give their suspicions voice. But they were there, those suspicions. Nevertheless, everyone continued to leave the witch alone.

Until the child.

The first sign was when Hippolyta Cormier came into town to place her regular order at the Thibodeaux store. It was clear that she was expecting a baby. With no husband or known suitors, the question of paternity became energetically and comprehensively debated. Attitudes in Leseuil hardened.

Then the child came.

No one saw the child for a long time, but the calculations of the womenfolk led them to believe the baby must have by now come into the world. As time passed, speculations turned darker. Père Martin was canvassed by parishioners concerned that not only had a child gone unbaptized, but it may also have fallen victim to some dark voodoo ritual. The old priest was reluctant to get involved: in his long custodianship of this flock, he had learned that the absolutes of faith tended to lose clarity in the dense, rich air of the bayous.

Eventually, he yielded, but insisted that he needed no escort to reinforce his authority and that he would travel out to the cabin alone. Which he did.

The sky was the color and weight of iron on the morning he chose to venture into the backswamp. The air was even more heavy and oppressive than usual, and the bayou's sweet odor had taken on a cloying quality. By the time he reached the cabin, the enfolding stretch of the black-willow trees had filtered out what meager light the overcast day offered. To emphasize the unnatural dark, the whinnying call of a screech owl pierced the midday. Père Martin found himself leaning on his Christian faith, putting out of his mind that the Choctaw believed that, if the *ofunlo* was heard in the day, it presaged the death of a child under seven.

It was as if the witch was waiting for him, the huge dark dog by her side. She was wearing a work dress, but one of quality, unpatched material. Père Martin saw that a substantial area of ground around the cabin had been cleared to make room for an herb garden, a large plot for growing vegetables, a small area devoted to flowers, and a patch brimming with kale. Beyond that, there was a fringe of naturally growing bayberry trees, the fruit of which Martin knew was used in folk medicine. Outside the cabin, fish hung gutted and salted on an upright wooden rack-frame, a veil of muslin protecting them from the swarming swamp bugs. The priest recognized them as warmouth, black bullhead, and pirate perch—fish that thrived in the acidic, oxygen-poor blackwater of the deep swamp. A tethered goat grazed listlessly on a patch of kale at the far side of the cabin, a cockerel and a dozen or so chickens roamed, and a flat-bottom and a pirogue sat tethered to the short jetty. It was a small oasis in what the priest realized with apprehension was one of the most noxious parts of the swamp. The air itself was dense and mephitic; the edges of the clearing were crowded by the burgeoning growth of poisonous white snakeroot, creeping spotflower, water hemlock, and buttonbush. The waters of the slough were a darker brown, almost black, and oil-sleek beneath the carpet of alligator weed.

Hippolyta and her hound watched Père Martin tie up on the jetty.

"Bonjour, Madame Cormier," he said with a smile. "I hope I'm not intruding."

"What can I do for you, Father?" she asked.

"Ah." He made a resigned and semi-apologetic gesture. "I am here to offer my services. I believe you have a child—one in want of baptism."

"My child is in want of nothing," she said. "And I have no need for a priest." She held him in her emerald-green stare and he was, for a moment, discomfited. "But, please, come in," she said with resignation. "I have made fresh lemonade. . . ."

Père Martin was taken aback by the interior of the cabin. Were it not for the rusticity of the timber walls, and the incongruity of the small cooking stove and the pans suspended above it, he would have taken the room he stepped into to be a New Orleans parlor. There were books everywhere, and a handful of paintings, some very fine indeed, graced the walls. There was only an armchair, a couch, and a small table with two chairs, but the furniture was of quality. The priest could see the cabin comprised only this room and one other, which was shielded by a heavy brocade curtain instead of a door.

He could see no sign of a child.

When she poured the lemonade, the priest noticed the large brooch at Madame Cormier's throat. Cast in gold, inset with small emeralds and rubies, the brooch described a circle. Now that Martin could see it up close, he realized it represented some form of serpent that sealed the circle by clamping its jaws onto its own tail. There was nothing particularly remarkable about the brooch, but the old priest was nonetheless disturbed by it, for reasons he could not fathom.

"That is indeed an interesting piece of jewelry," said the priest. Hippolyta's hand moved instinctively to it, and the expression on her face was, for a moment, dark. Then she smiled.

"It was my mother's," she explained. "And her mother's before her."

"It is an interesting design."

"It represents a cottonmouth snake." Hippolyta handed him a glass of lemonade. "The most common snake out here in the swamp, but a fascinating animal. When it needs to, the female can reproduce without having a male to mate with. The daughter snake is a simple but perfect reiteration of the mother. A beautiful thing. The cottonmouth consuming itself in an eternal circle is an old, old belief, hereabouts. Not *your* kind of belief, perhaps, Father, but a strong one nevertheless."

They talked generally for a while, she somewhat reluctantly. He noticed that her French was cultured and more metropolitan—she used the contractions *du* and *des,* where Cajuns maintained *de le* and *de les*—but her accent sung to the music of Louisiana rather than Paris.

"Do you not find it difficult?" he asked. "Out here, so far from everything?"

"No," she said. "I have all that I need. I am here because I seek solitude. And if I ever need company, I find that there are many glad to give it."

The old priest colored slightly.

"But, madame, this is so far, so very far, from the world. This part of the swamp is so remote, so dangerous. It is no place for a child. . . ."

"You are a man, Père Martin," she said, almost with sympathy for his condition. "You have no understanding of the strength those of my sex possess. Or perhaps you do, which is why the Church has for centuries suppressed that strength with such enthusiasm and vigor. But believe me, I am from a family of women who have always expressed their fortitude and independence. No father or husband, no priest or even slaveholder, has ever been the master of that which they considered to be theirs. I am more than capable of living my life here without the interference of men."

"But I speak of more than men," protested Martin. "There are women-folk in Leseuil who would be a great support to you."

"Greater still than the arrogance of men is the ire and malice of sub-jugated women. And, if I need anything, I am within reach of it. The swamp sustains me, and that which I cannot find here, I have the means to acquire from the store or from the city. As you can see." She pauses, holds him disconcertingly in her frank gaze, then says: "But you have come here to settle your curiosity, and that of your neighbors. I want no interference in my life, so let us settle the matter now. My daughter—yes, a daughter, and another in the line of women who will not be oppressed—is healthy and well. I would ask you to take my word for it, but I can see that would serve only to fuel suspicions further."

She rose and left him for a moment, stepping through the brocade curtain. When she came back, she had a baby in her arms, swaddled in fine, fresh linen. She handed the child to the priest and he caught his breath. The baby was beautiful. The most beautiful child he had ever seen. Her skin was several tones lighter than her mother's and a soft gold. He guessed that the father must have been white. Though just a babe, she had a shock of black hair tinged with auburn. The blue eyes that gazed up at him inquisitively already glittered with sparkles of emerald, promising the same striking hue as her mother's in the future. He was captivated. The only feature that caused him to frown was the presence of a birthmark similar to that which Hippolyta bore—like an impression of a fingermark on the left cheek. It was faint, but more noticeable than her mother's because of the child's compara-tively lighter coloring.

"All the women in my family have the birthmark." Hippolyta had read his expression. "Some more noticeably than others. No doubt there will be speculation about some supernatural cause among the locals."

"They're good people, Madame Cormier. Simple people, perhaps, but decent, and the warmest you'll find if you give them a chance." He looked down again at the baby. She returned his gaze with huge, bright eyes. He had never seen a baby with such dazzling eyes before.

"I take it you've satisfied your curiosity, Père?" asked Hippolyta, not coldly. "You can see the welfare of Anastasie is not at issue."

"Anastasie?" Père Martin echoed. "That is indeed a beautiful name for a beautiful child. It means 'resurrection.'"

"I know what my daughter's name means."

"Then do you not see that its meaning makes baptism all the more pertinent? Through the sacrament of baptism we accept a new life purified of sin."

"My child has no sin from which to be purified. And in any case, I am not of your faith, Père Martin."

"Of which faith are you?" he asked, almost cautiously.

"That is between me and my beliefs, and of no concern to any other."

"I see," he said. "That is a pity. It would be nice to do a baptism. All I seem to be doing these days are funerals."

Hippolyta Cormier made no comment, simply continued to regard the priest with her disconcertingly bright emerald eyes, empty of emotion or interest.

"I buried Jacques Fournier recently," said Martin. "Terrible case of swamp poisoning. Did you know him?"

"I can't say I did."

"And before him, the widow Faucheaux. You would know her, of course?"

"No, I didn't. Other than when she took it on herself to insult me in the street. But, then again, I'm not the only one she has insulted over the years. I don't believe she will be much missed."

"Sad nonetheless." Père Martin shrugged. "Are you sure you do not want Anastasie baptized? To bring her into the care of the Lord?"

"I'm sure."

Père Martin nodded resignedly and again looked at the baby, as if irresistibly drawn to those huge, bright-blue eyes glittering with the promise of emerald green. He smiled, but could not rid himself of a powerful feeling of foreboding.

Perhaps it was the oppressive weather, he thought. Perhaps there was a storm coming.

17

There is confusion. Consciousness, but confusion.

Everything is solid and bright, and has been waiting for her eyelids to part like stage curtains to reveal it. But, for a moment, this place has no meaning.

Then she makes sense of the room but not of herself. She is filled with growing panic as she realizes she doesn't know where she is or why she is there. She doesn't know her own name.

There is pain, she can feel it, but something in her veins has made it distant and abstract. She turns her head slowly. A window, bright but muted by a bleached muslin roller blind. Chrome pipes, porcelain washbasin. The ribs of a radiator painted ivory. A mirror reflects a geometry of light across the opposing wall. A woman in a nurse's uniform.

Memories come back to her. A cluster of tumbling fragments, sudden and scattered, but within seconds they gain coherence. There was an automobile. A steeply declining road. A sharp bend ahead that meant death. A leap.

She is Mary Rourke and she is alive.

The nurse has been busying herself at the sink by the door. When she turns and sees Rourke awake, she crosses the room with professional swiftness and purpose. The nurse checks her patient, tells her she is in the Appleton Clinic, and asks her if she can remember what happened. She can and she tells the nurse so, but her mouth is dry and her voice cracks. The nurse cups the back of Rourke's head with one hand and gives her some water from a sipping cup with the other.

"I'll get the doctor," the nurse says with a smile, easing Rourke's head back onto her pillow. "I'll be right back."

Rourke is alone. The room smells faintly of floor wax and antiseptic. There is the sound of footsteps in the hallway, and the door swings open. Rourke turns her head slightly to see the nurse return with Doc Wilson. He wears a white medical dust-coat that accentuates the floridity of his face. He smiles.

"How are you, Mary?" he asks. He doesn't wait for her to answer and crosses to her bed, leans over, and pulls open one eyelid, then the other, shining a penlight in each to check her pupils. The ghost of a fine brandy faintly haunts his breath.

"I'm okay," she answers redundantly. "How long have I been here?"

"Not long. Couple of hours. You came around earlier but were pretty confused. I gave you a sedative."

She reaches her right hand up to her face and head, expecting bandages. There are none.

"Your head's fine," says Wilson. "You took a knock but nothing too serious. In fact, you've done remarkably little damage, considering your little adventure. We've X-rayed your head and chest. No fractures. But you've bruised your ribs badly. And tomorrow you're going to hurt like hell all over."

"How did I get here?"

"Ah . . ." Wilson grins knowingly, crosses the room, pushes open the door and calls into the hall, "You may come in now."

Doc Wilson steps to one side, and a tall, handsome man enters. Handsome enough to be a movie actor; when he crosses the room he does so with a slight limp, which is why he isn't. Detective Jake Kendrick takes off his hat to reveal a thick mop of dark-blond hair, pulls up a chair, and sits next to Rourke's bed. She feels glad to see him. She generally does.

"What's to do, toots?"

"What have I said about calling me that?" she protests weakly. "If I don't let Golem Geller call me that, I don't see why I should let you."

Kendrick smiles. "I thought maybe you forgot about that. You know, like you forgot you're supposed to stop a car before you step out of it."

"You found me?"

"Not quite. Your Packard went over the edge and made a mess. A Highway Patrol motorcyclist tracked back up the Stratton residence road to where they thought it must've gone over. That's where he found you, napping at the side of the road."

Rourke frowns. A memory, vague and inchoate, comes back to her of dark uniforms and bright pain.

"They got you in an ambulance and you were coherent enough to tell them you worked for the studio and you knew me—so they gave me a courtesy call."

She frowns, trying to mold her memory into some shape. "The motorcycle cop—did someone from the Mount Laurel estate telephone the police about the accident?"

"Not that I'm aware. Nobody there but you when they arrived. Why?"

She is about to explain her near miss with Huston's coupe, but checks herself. "So a Highway Patrol motorcycle cop just happened to be passing on a road that only goes to and from Veronica Stratton's mansion?"

"I guess. Not my department. But remember, you sent your automobile on a shortcut down to Laurel Canyon Boulevard. Maybe that's where he found it."

Rourke nods, unconvinced. She turns to Doc Wilson.

"When can I get out of here?"

"You better stay overnight, Mary. You're likely concussed."

"But nothing came up on the X-ray?"

"No, but that doesn't mean—"

"I've arranged to meet someone tonight," she interrupts. "It's important, Doc. Can you give me something to kill the pain?"

Wilson looks as if he is about to argue the point, but Rourke's set expression makes it clear that protest would be fruitless. "Very well, Mary. But I want you back here tomorrow for a checkup. And absolutely no alcohol."

"As if I would." Rourke makes a mockingly petulant face.

Wilson returns with a stern look. "Seriously. I'll give you something that packs a punch. If you mix it with alcohol you'll have real problems. . . ."

"I get it, Doc. I promise Andrew Volstead will be proud of me."

"And the condition is that I want you to stay for at least a couple of hours first so I can check up on you. That's the deal."

"That's the deal, Doc."

Wilson and the nurse leave Rourke and Kendrick alone.

"Is there something in all this I should be concerned about, Mary?"

"What do you mean?"

"I've seen you drive. I know you can handle an automobile well. For a woman, I mean." He grins mischievously. Kendrick has a face hardened by the world, but when he smiles he looks boyish, she thinks. "It don't make sense that you get flung or jump from a car because you couldn't make a corner."

"I didn't realize having a penis was essential to steering a car, but I'll accept your compliment in the spirit it was intended. No, I didn't panic or lose control. The brakes failed."

"The brakes?" Kendrick's smile fades.

"Yeah. Must've been a fault. Unlucky, I guess. I should sue my mechanic."

"You drive a Packard, don't you?"

"Yeah?"

"Packard's got direct drum brakes to each wheel. That means you were unlucky times four. Have you been pissing someone off? Again?"

"Maybe it was something to do with the pedal. The linkage or some whatever-you-call-it. I don't know. All I do know is the brakes didn't work." She winces as pain stabs through her ribs.

"I'll get out of your hair," says Kendrick. "We can talk later. I'm working this weird case right now, but I'll come back in a couple hours and take you home. Try and get some sleep." He hesitates. "You sure you don't want to call off whatever you have going on later and let them keep an eye on you overnight?"

"I'm sure. Thanks, Jake—I appreciate you coming in."

"No problem." He stands up and replaces his hat. He smiles. "You've helped me out often enough. See you in a couple hours."

"Oh, there is one other thing," she says apologetically. "I'm trying to find the name of a spiritualist."

"A what?" Kendrick frowns.

"Not for me," Rourke says. "Just someone who might be fleecing one of our stars. She goes by the name of Madame something. I think she's got a place out on West Sunset."

"Okay, I'll see what I can find out."

—

There is a slow blooming of pain as whatever it was that Doc Wilson gave her begins to wear off. She sleeps fitfully, dreams flitting through her brain like the windows of a passing train. In one, she sees a child, a young girl who looks a lot like her, laughing in the sunlight.

Eventually, Wilson comes back and gives her another, final check. When the physician is grudgingly satisfied with her condition, he gives her a bottle of pills with strict instructions on their use. After he leaves her, Rourke gets out of bed and showers in the bathroom attached to her room. She palms two pills from the bottle into her mouth and swallows them with some water.

Standing naked in front of the mirror, she sees the dark blossoming of bruising on her left shoulder and upper arm, and the left side of her ribs. The skin on her left elbow has been abraded into an angry red graze. A scythe-shaped bloom of crimson and purple arcs beneath the curve of her breast, and she is aware of a current of pain when she draws a breath. Her face looks drawn and paler than usual, and it accentuates another bruise—smaller and less livid—on her right temple.

Rourke's own powder compact, and the handbag containing it, took the drop into Laurel Canyon along with her Packard. So, once she is dressed, she asks the nurse for some foundation—this is the Appleton Clinic, after all, where stars are restored to full brightness and where cosmetics are as much part of the restorative process as medicines.

The nurse returns, smiling. "Here's a first-aid kit for you," she says, and hands Rourke a collection of makeup.

"Thanks," says Rourke. "You're a lifesaver."

After the nurse has gone, Rourke takes the makeup into the bathroom. She flips open the disk-shaped tin of Princess Pat Olde Ivory and uses the velour pad to dab the foundation onto her face, lightening the natural tone of her skin. She applies it more thickly to the bruise on the side of her head. It is the way of the world, she thinks without much bitterness, that men bear their scars and blemishes with pride, while women must always conceal evidence of their having lived a life. She applies lipstick and eyeliner, adding a dab of rouge and rubbing it in beneath the angle of both cheeks. Men don't have to hide their true colors, either, she thinks.

She pulls on the white toweling gown, covering up her bruises. The memory of her leap from the car flashes into her recall, and she finds herself shaking. In colorful language, she admonishes her reflection in the bathroom mirror to pull herself together.

The nurse returns with a change of clothes draped on a hanger and wrapped in cellophane. "Your stuff is pretty much beyond cleaning or repair," she explains. "Dr. Wilson asked me to find something in your size. I think I got it right."

"You went out for these?" asks Rourke as she takes the clothes.

"Oh no." The nurse gives a small laugh. "You know who our patients are—they bring stuff in with them or have it ordered in and don't bother taking it with them when they're discharged. The clinic's basement looks like Paul Poiret's or Jean Patou's storeroom."

Rourke unwraps the cellophane and whistles when she sees the skirt suit and blouse. She dresses well, and expensively, but this outfit would be beyond the reach of her bank balance, far less her pocketbook. "You sure this is okay?"

"Doctor's orders." The nurse smiles. "Oh—your shoes are in the wardrobe. They just needed a cleanup."

After the nurse leaves, Rourke changes into the outfit: a lightweight linen suit of straight-cut navy-blue-and-white-piping jacket and knee-length skirt, a hip-length satin blouse with a large, loose neck-bow, and sheer silk stockings.

She is ready by the time Jake Kendrick returns.

"Hospital wear suits you." He looks her outfit up and down appreciatively.

"Oh, this old thing? I keep it just to change into when I jump out of cars. Thanks for picking me up. How's your weird case?"

"Oh, that . . . Weirder by the minute," says Kendrick. "Some old guy found dead last week in his hotel room. A pilgrim a long, long way from home—he'd driven all the way from Louisiana in a battered old Ford. To start with, it seemed he'd simply had a heart attack, but now it's beginning to look like he was poisoned. When we went through his stuff, we found an old Colt Police Positive Thirty-eight, and it turns out the old guy's a retired sheriff from Louisiana. Anyway, that's why it took me a while to get back. You ready to go?"

Rourke nods. "Can we make a stop on the way home?" she asks. "If you've got time."

"No problem." Kendrick smiles. "I'm a public servant, after all, and you are the public."

His smile fades when she tells him where she wants to stop off.

"Sure thing, Mary," he says. "Are you sure you're okay?"

"Little shook up, is all."

Rourke crosses the grass of Forest Lawn. She stands in front of a white marble grave marker for several minutes, her back to where Jake Kendrick waits in the parked Ford. She always has plans to say something when she's here, to open her heart, to somehow fill gaps in a conversation that never happened. But it always ends the same way, with her realizing that all that's here is chiseled stone set into manicured grass. There's no one here to hear her.

For a while, Kendrick remains quiet when she returns to the automobile.

"It's fine," says Rourke eventually. "Like I said, I'm okay. Just been a while." She shakes the thought off. "Can I ask you something?"

"Sure."

"You've done me—done the studio—a lot of favors over the years. And I know you'll have done other studios favors. I'm not asking you to betray trade secrets, but have you ever been asked to turn a blind eye to anything with either Robert Huston or Veronica Stratton?"

He turns to her, frowning, a hint of suspicion in his expression. "What *were* you doing up there at Mount Laurel? Has this all got something to do with Norma Carlton?"

"Carlton? Why would you ask that?"

Kendrick makes a "Really?" face. "Because, generally, I *don't* ask questions if I'm asked not to. And I haven't been asking about Norma Carlton suddenly having a lifelong heart condition that no one was ever told about. But if there's something going on that has something to do with your brakes suddenly failing on one of the most treacherous roads in the Hollywood Hills, maybe now's the time for you to level with me."

"Listen, Jake, this movie we're making is very important to the studio. We've lost our leading lady and had a near-fatal accident on set. I'm just trying to make sure there's nothing going on with our leading man that we need worry about."

"You must have thought about this before you hired him for the role."

"We did, but things are different now. I—*we*—need to put this movie to bed with as little extra scandal or drama as possible. So what about it? Is there anything we need to know about Huston?"

"Nothing that's going to surprise you." Kendrick shrugs. "He's a boozer. He's been picked up a few times well and truly ossified, once when he got behind the wheel and took out a fire hydrant. The studio—I mean First National Pictures—seems to have a lid on him, but since he started hanging out with Barrymore and Gilbert, things have gotten a little more . . . *visible,* I would say. He and Gilbert had some trouble with a couple of girls of a professional disposition, if you catch my drift. Mannix at MGM and Jordan at First National worked a double act on the department, and it all went away. But I got the impression both studios have just about had enough. And I have heard that the juice isn't his only weakness. . . ."

"Yeah, I know, women."

"There is that," says Kendrick. "But that's not what I meant. I heard Huston is a serious gambler. And that he's gotten himself into company that's much heavier-weight than Barrymore, Fields, Gilbert, et cetera."

"You're talking gangsters?"

Kendrick shrugged. "He's not running a book with Aimee Semple McPherson and the Foursquare Church, that's for sure."

"Anything else?"

They have reached Larchmont Village, and Kendrick pulls the Ford to the curb. He turns to Rourke. "Anything else . . . No, I don't think so. I can ask around if you want. Why do I get the feeling you've got something particular in mind?"

"I talked to Veronica Stratton for a while. She wasn't what I expected. I think they have a lavender marriage, as it's called in the industry. Except lavenders are usually arranged between lesbian women and homosexual men, and Huston doesn't fit that bill."

"But Stratton does?"

"That's my feeling. Sewing Circle member, I'd say, and Huston is her beard. Could you check her out as well? Just in case there's something with her I'm missing."

"Okay," he says, and she climbs out of the car. He leans across and speaks through the open door. "You sure you're okay, Mary?"

She smiles, weakly. "I'm fine. We'll talk soon."

18

It takes another shower, this time at home, for Rourke to feel clean of the day's drama. Again she feels shaken, and again she mutters a curse and pushes down the fluttering in her chest. After a moment's hesitation, she dresses again in the outfit supplied by the hospital. She is going out, after all. And you can never overdress for visiting an Italian grocery.

It's seven-thirty when she gets there. From the street, and indeed when you go inside, there's nothing about Salvaggi's Delicatessen and Grocery that would strike you as unusual or different. Outside the shopwindows, wooden crates and wicker bins laden with fruit and vegetables stand on the sidewalk, under an awning striped green, white, and red. In the brightly lit windows and beneath a pelmet of hanging cured meats and sausage, large Italian-labeled cans of olive oil sit posed into pyramids, straw-jacketed wine flasks are arranged into rows, wheels of cheese have been stacked into columns.

If you watch long enough, though, you might notice that Salvaggi's attracts a particularly well-dressed enthusiastic clientele, or that once a customer goes in they seem to spend an inordinately long time choosing their eggplant or tomatoes.

Mary Rourke steps out of the cab and makes her way into the store. Inside, the walls are dry-goods-shelved from floor to ceiling. There are more rows of fresh produce arranged in front of the broad oak counter, behind which stand two men in white shirts and aprons.

"*Buona sera, signora*," one of the attendants greets her, smiling. "Can I help you with something?"

"Yes, please," Rourke replies. "I'm looking for some advice on Tuscan pecorino."

"Certainly, *signora*. If you go through to the back of the store, my associate will help you."

She does as she is told, walks to the far end of the store and steps through the beaded curtain that hangs in the doorway. She is now in the storeroom, where another aproned attendant, this time very heavyset and with the face of a boxer, unsmilingly raises an eyebrow in question.

Rourke repeats her Tuscan-pecorino request. The attendant nods and leads her over to a small freight elevator, more like a large dumbwaiter, and indicates she should step inside. Once she does, he presses a button and she feels the floor jolt slightly, then descend.

Immediately before the Volstead Act was enacted and the "noble experiment" of Prohibition passed into law, there had been fifteen thousand licensed bars and other establishments serving alcohol in Los Angeles. Now, seven years later and with Prohibition in full swing, there are over thirty thousand unregulated and illegal speakeasies in the city. Some are huddled, dirty drinking-den hovels tucked up some back alley; others are glitzy and glamorous. The drink served also varies, from "blister booze"—laced with benzine that manifests itself, a week after drinking it, as large, puffy, oozing white scabs in the mouth and on the skin—to the best-quality wines and spirits smuggled down the Pacific Coast from Canada by the currently on-the-run Tony the Hat Cornero, and other creatively business-minded individuals.

Il Paradiso is one of the glitziest and glossiest speakeasies on the West Coast. It serves, at a premium, everything from aged Scotches to the finest champagnes, and not a drop of benzine in sight. It has two bars, a dance floor, plush wall booths, and a stage for a band. It is to Il Paradiso, in the soundproofed basement of Salvaggi's Deli and Grocery, that Mary Rourke is dumbwaiter-bound.

At the bottom is another, smaller storeroom with a heavy door off it. She is met by another attendant, this time tuxedoed and brilliantined, who beams a smile at her, greets her by name—this is not her first visit—and leads her across to the door. As soon as the door, which is quilted on the inside with thick crimson-satin-dressed padding, is opened, there is an urgent burst of music, laughter, and general hubbub. She is conducted through, and the door is closed behind her.

To Rourke's eyes, it is like some red satin and leather-upholstered anteroom of hell. The space is too small for the number of people in it. Clearly in an effort to disguise the poverty of legroom, the furnishings are lavish and expensive: One wall is dedicated to a full-length bar of gleaming mahogany and chrome, the opposing wall has a row of a dozen horseshoe booths, either sealed off with velvet rope stanchions or occupied by famous faces. The VIP booths are served by their own, smaller, bar. The floor tables, for the not-so-famous, are clustered with too many chairs and so close to one another it creates a crammed, elbow-bumping claustrophobia. An array of ceiling fans labor to mitigate the accumulations of tobacco smoke and body heat. Rourke notes that the cramped square of dance floor is so dense with bodies it would give a canned sardine anxiety. A Negro jazz quartet occupies the stage by the door and plays swing music with solemn-faced vivacity. The wall at the far end is mirrored floor to ceiling to create the illusion of greater dimensions, but merely reflects back the hectic hell.

There was a time, Rourke remembers, when she sought out excitement and buzz: when she was young and feisty. When the world seemed full of promise and light. But this clamor is desperate, manic. There is light here, but it is the falsely bright shadow of recent war and epidemic.

She is greeted by a girl no more than nineteen, dressed in a flapper dress, her bright-blonde hair bobbed and heat-curled into a yellow-silver helmet and ringed with a forehead band of pink pearls. She introduces herself as Aimee, which Rourke decides is as genuine as her hair color.

"Mr. Levitt is waiting for you, Miss Rourke," she says. Navigating the narrow straits between the tables like a log-rafting lumberjack dodging river rocks, Aimee leads the way to the booths at the far side. As they pass the booths, famous heads nod in recognition of Rourke; others turn imperiously away. Gloria Swanson, sitting in a booth with a glum-faced Joe Kennedy, beams a grin at Rourke and waggles bejeweled fingers in a schoolgirlish wave. At the next, the *Ben-Hur* star and Latin heartthrob Ramon Novarro sits in huddled, conspiratorial conversation with his press agent—and lover—Herbert Howe. Aimee unclips the velvet rope at the next booth. Hiram Levitt stands up and shakes Rourke's hand. His smile fades to a frown.

"Are you all right, Mary?"

"I'm fine," she says wearily. "Been one of those days. I see you rank among the elite—I've never been able to get a booth here. It must be all those secrets people are afraid you'll spill."

"What will you have?" asks Levitt.

"A Brandy Highball."

He turns to the young hostess. "A Bee's Knees and a Brandy Highball." He turns back to Rourke. "Seriously, you look shook up. Something happen?"

"An accident, that's all," Rourke replies. "I wrecked my car. I'm not hurt, but I'm a little shook up, like you say. Have you had time to think about what I asked?"

"I have. No can do on Norma's background. Like I said, I have rules. But there are some things I might be able to help you with. Why don't you ask specific questions and I'll either give you specific answers—or no answers at all. Sound fair?"

Rourke is about to say something when the hostess returns to the booth. She places paper coasters on the mahogany and sets the drinks down.

"Okay, let's go with that," says Rourke once the hostess has left. She lifts the Brandy Highball to her lips, pauses, then puts it back down, untouched, with a sigh.

"What's up?" asks Levitt.

"I forgot. I'm sworn off the booze. Doc Wilson's given me horse tablets and I can't mix them with alcohol."

"I thought you said you weren't hurt."

"Banged up a little, nothing more. Nothing broken. Bruised ribs and bruised pride, mostly."

Levitt frowns, then beckons to the hostess. He has her take the Highball away and bring Rourke a soda.

"First question," says Rourke. "I'm guessing Norma Carlton wasn't her real name?"

"Technically, that's protected information, but in this town nobody much goes by the name they were born with. Natacha Rambova wouldn't have the same exotic European allure if Joe Blow knew she was good ol' Winnie Kimball Shaughnessy from Salt Lake. And Harry Warner rolls off the tongue easier than Hirsz Wonsal. For that matter, your own boss left New York as Herschel Karabin and arrived in California as Harry Carbine. Mind you, Clara Bow has always been Clara Bow, I suppose. And you know that the first thing I do to resurrect a client is to separate them from their pasts by separating them from their birth names—so, yes, you're safe to assume Norma changed her name."

"From what?"

Levitt makes a "You should know better" face.

"Okay," says Rourke. "Where did Norma come from? I'm guessing she wasn't an Angelino."

"Can't say. Next?"

"Okay, putting her past to one side, what about her ex-husband? He already threatened to kill her."

"Theo Woolfe?" Levitt gives a small, scornful laugh. "He's still funny-farming in Downey Asylum."

"You sure he's still there?"

"Yep, he's still there, in a padded cell, for all I know. More likely, his own private padded suite. It was one of the first things I checked out after we last spoke. A few years ago, his psychiatrist argued at a review that Woolfe should be let out, and nearly succeeded. But a couple of days later, the hospital ran a screening of *Dark Passions*—which so happened to be the last movie Woolfe directed."

"Oh," says Rourke. "Not a good choice."

"For so many reasons. When one of his loony chums started yelling at the screen and complaining that the movie was dull, Woolfe obviously took exception to his fellow patient's aesthetic sensibilities. He used a pencil to blind him in one eye—and would have done the other eye if the orderlies hadn't got to him in time." Levitt smiles wryly. "I get it—no one likes a critic. Anyway, that incident closed the gates, quite literally, on his bid for discharge. So, no, Theo Woolfe can't have killed Norma. And I don't see him having the connections—or even the capacity for organized thinking—to have arranged for someone else to do it for him."

Rourke sighs and nods. "You said she was involved with shady people. Who?"

"I don't think I used the adjective 'shady.' I'm nothing if not meticulous in my choice of words. Half—more than half—of the people in this whole city are shady. I was talking about *dangerous* people."

"Okay," says Rourke impatiently. "Dangerous people. What kind of dangerous people?"

"It's the curse of stardom," says Levitt. "And maybe partly my fault. I give people like Norma new identities, but they're paper identities—stories made up for them that are no more substantial than the photoplays they act out in front of a camera. They start to believe in their own exceptionalism, but remain insecure and vulnerable—so they seek out other *exceptional* people. People whose own stories are as big and loud as their own."

"Hoodlums?"

"Hoodlums, gangsters, crackpots." He pauses for a moment, his dark eyes briefly scanning the room, before turning back to Rourke. "This city is unique. New York has the Cosa Nostra and the Kosher Nostra, Chicago has Polack and Italian mobs, Boston's run by the Micks. And in each of these cities the powers that be—the elected officials and the police—fight these organized crime groups. This town? In this town the mob *is* the powers that be. Los Angeles is the only place that has a 'City Hall Gang'—Mayor Cryer is a stooge for Charlie Crawford, and the Los Angeles Police Department is run by Kent Parrot, not the commissioner. The population of Los Angeles has doubled in the last decade—and that's all because of Hollywood. That means that studio bosses and others behind the scenes have almost unlimited power. Some are tied in with the City Hall Gang. Basically, there are people here who get to do whatever they want, to whomever they want, providing City Hall gets its beak wet."

"And you think Norma was involved with some of these people?"

"I didn't see her as much of late as I used to. Although I get used to that with clients—I'm very often the only person in town who knows who's got what skeletons in what closets. They get nervous, I guess, knowing I've got the key. But I thought Norma was different."

"So what about the other stuff?" asks Rourke. "The weird stuff. Spiritualism and occult shenanigans."

Levitt doesn't answer for a moment. There is no perceptible change in the reflecting windows of his violet-black eyes, but Rourke senses unseen shutters being pulled down.

"You mentioned that the other day," he says eventually. "I can't say I know anything about that. Norma didn't so much have her circle, but several circles, none of whom knew about her other involvements. Me included, especially of late. If she was involved in that kind of thing, then it was with a different crowd. But I did hear worrying stuff."

"Worrying how?"

Levitt frowns as he taps his cigarette against the edge of the ashtray. "Rumors that she was mixing with people involved with *this* kind of stuff." He waves a hand to indicate their surroundings. "Rumrunners, hoodlums, and other variously naughty types with friends in City Hall. Like I said, dangerous people. If you're looking for who's more likely to have done her harm, then they're who you should be looking at. Not table tappers and spook conjurers." He pauses. "Although, if I were you, I'd be pretty circumspect about whose doors you knock on. The only connection to the afterlife that these people have is that they tend to hasten others into it. If you want my advice, you should drop the whole thing, Mary."

"Norma wasn't involved with spiritualists and the like?" Rourke ignores his warning. "I heard she'd gotten mixed up with a strange crowd—the sort with screwball beliefs. And that she seemed obsessed with the occult."

Levitt shrugs. "Half this town is into that kind of hokum. Norma was drawn to the *Devil's Playground* role because it had supernatural elements, but that's as much as I know."

"You know nothing about a fortune-teller-psychic—some kind of voodoo priestess type who owns a huge mansion somewhere out on West Sunset?"

Levitt paused, absently blowing a plume of smoke into the air. "The kind that fleeces the rich and gullible? Norma was rich all right, but she was most definitely not gullible."

"Well," says Rourke, "Harry Carbine mentioned that Norma consulted her. Often. But he didn't really know much more. Couldn't even remember her name."

Levitt offers her a cigarette, takes one and lights them both. "That's a pity. So you don't have a name for her?"

"I didn't say that," Rourke replies. "I have a friend in the LAPD, he did a little sniffing around for me. The spiritualist goes by the professional name Madame Erzulie, Maîtresse des Ombres. Mistress of the Shadows."

"Never heard of her," says Levitt with a disinterested shrug.

Rourke sips her soda, wishing she had kept her Brandy Highball. She feels like celebrating: for the first time ever, she has seen through Levitt's defenses, and knows with absolute certainty that he has just lied to her.

19

1907
Louisiana

The years passed, largely without incident. The child grew.

As she did, she was seen more often in Leseuil, and the people wondered at her. By age thirteen, Anastasie Cormier was becoming tall and lithe like her mother, and the promise of an even greater beauty stirred. The boys of the village itchily bided their time, while the old women reignited the debate over Anastasie's fathering. Some said the father of the child was the devil himself, or that Hippolyta Cormier had invited the demon of the swamp, Père Malfait, to put off his cloak of Spanish moss and lie with her. Others suggested that it had been the Rougarou who sired her, while under the spell that condemns him to stalk the bayou as half man, half wolf for 101 days.

These superstitious explanations sat more comfortably with the community than the suggestion that the child was the result of surreptitious visits into the backwaters and clandestine union with one of their own menfolk. All the men of the area still seemed to fall silent whenever Hippolyta was in town. All the women continued to become watchful.

And then there were the specific rumors about Dupont. The muscular, handsome blacksmith was a childless widower. His young wife had died suddenly from swamp sickness two years back, and he seemed to dote on Anastasie as if she were his own. It was noted by all that, if it were indeed the case that Dupont was the father, it would have meant that the blacksmith had lain with the Swamp Witch while his wife had still lived.

Despite all this, despite rumors of supernatural sires and suspicions of adulterous unions, the child remained an object of wonder. Despite themselves, all were beguiled by Anastasie: by her beauty, by her spirit. This child of nature, who carried great beauty and grace so lightly, who moved through their landscape with such carefree ease that it seemed gravity itself held her with a gentler grasp. Old Mother Thibodeaux, in particular, was besotted with the child she called *p'tit joyau d'marais*— the little swamp gem—and every time Anastasie visited the store, Madame Thibodeaux would give her a *lagniappe*—some small extra gift.

And as affection for the daughter grew, suspicion of the mother waned. But never disappeared.

Père Martin persuaded Anastasie's mother, with some difficulty, to allow her to attend the village schoolhouse three days a week. It was then that it became clear to the cleric that the girl's education extended beyond the bounds of both the timber schoolhouse and his abilities as instructor. Anastasie's clear intelligence, her literacy, and the sheer breadth of her knowledge soon made the confines of the rustic curriculum redundant. He admitted defeat and released her from the school, on the understanding that she accept individual tuition from him, and that her mother seriously consider his appeal that Anastasie be sent to high school at Terrebonne.

"With Anastasie's gifts," he said, almost with the pride of a father, "she is a natural to go on to Louisiana Normal School, where she could study for a degree."

Père Martin did indeed wonder at Anastasie: at her child-of-nature grace, at her profound beauty, most of all at her intellect. But while the priest found so much wonder in his protégée, he found himself inexplicably fearing her. The child was so bright with beauty and intelligence—dazzlingly so—but he sensed a shadow made yet darker, more intense, by that very brilliance.

He would think about that a lot, later, when he looked back to those days; when he would question his own actions and whether there could have been something, anything, he could have done to prevent what was to unfold. Whether there had been some presage, some subtle hint, of the darkness that lay hidden behind the light of Anastasie's bright eyes. But there had been none.

Père Martin was not the only soul in Leseuil with an interest in Anastasie Cormier. And not all interest in the girl was innocent.

The German Coast of Louisiana, north of New Orleans, was heavily settled by immigrants from the German Rhineland, many of whom became part of the land- and slave-owning classes. Over time, almost all became assimilated into Cajun culture, and names changed. One such name was Troxler, which became Frenchified to Trosclair. The Trosclairs had left the Côte des Allemands three generations before, after their plantation there had been razed in the 1811 slave revolt. They had moved south to Leseuil and had owned the plantation behind the levee ever since. The plantation still produced just enough cane to keep the Trosclairs in the house, though most of the fields were now lost to the wild, and there were only two families of workers left living in the old slave quarters.

Despite their much-reduced circumstances, the Trosclairs maintained a superior and distant attitude toward their neighbors, white and, particularly, Black. It was no surprise to anyone that the son of the household, Paul Trosclair, had grown up with an attitude of entitlement. He was a vain young man in his early twenties, with little to be vain about. He was tall and thin, permanently stooped, his black hair lank and oil-sleek. A hooked, beaklike nose and small dark eyes gave him a vulturine, predatory mien.

The Trosclairs and their superior attitudes were tolerated—even laughed at—but they remained part of the web that held together a sense of what Leseuil was. Paul Trosclair, however, was observed, noted, regarded with unspecific mistrust. There was something about his behavior around children that sat uneasily with the folks of the bayou, particularly his behavior around girls on the verge of womanhood.

Girls like Anastasie.

It happened—whatever it was that happened—one day while Cormier mother and daughter were in the village. Once they had done their marketing at the Thibodeaux store, it was Hippolyta's custom to visit the feed store and blacksmith for her other needs. It was at this time that she allowed Anastasie to play with the other children, all of whom, since their shared schooldays, seemed drawn to her and inclined to compete for her affection.

It was one of those gray-green bayou days, when the heat of a diffuse sun fumed the sluggish waters into a thick, clumping mist. Anastasie was walking back to meet her mother where the pirogue was moored when she encountered Paul Trosclair. A disused cabin perched on the flank of the bayou, half concealed by a set-back levee overgrown with scrub. Somehow, Trosclair enticed Anastasie into the cabin. Whatever happened in that cabin, Trosclair emerged bleeding and half blind, his face ripped by scratches, one of which had seriously injured his right eye. Anastasie ran to her mother and told her what had happened. Hippolyta, grim-faced and silent, took her daughter home to their backwater cabin.

What happened over the next weeks was unclear to those outside Leseuil. Even those who survived the events could not give the sheriff clear details when he arrived from Houma.

Doc Charbonnier patched up Paul Trosclair's wounds, securing a dressing and bandage over his injured eye, voicing concerns that, should it become infected, he might lose his sight or even the eye itself. Despite the urgings of Wilhelm Trosclair, Paul's father, the youth refused to explain what had occurred in the cabin.

There were whisperings along the Bayou Leseuil. Accusation and counteraccusation became the currency of huddled exchanges. Madame Thibodeaux complained to her elderly husband, "Something has to be done about that boy." In the meanwhile, Cormier mother and daughter remained sequestered in their backwater cabin.

Then, a week and one day after the incident, when midday came without Paul's stirring from his bed, a servant was sent to waken him. As expected, he found Paul Trosclair still in his bed. But dead, not sleeping.

There were no signs of injury, other than the still-raw scratches on his face and the bandage over his eye. His parents were distraught at the loss of their son and sole heir to their shrinking, damp-dirt empire. Doc Charbonnier examined the dead youth but was at a total loss as to why such a young man had died so suddenly and inexplicably.

"But these things happen," he said with resignation, as if that should suffice.

In a landscape where inundation was a frequent and inescapable fact of life—and death—Paul Trosclair was laid to stone-coffined rest on the plantation, in the aboveground family mausoleum, elevated on marble blocks and above the reach of potential floodwater. The Trosclair scion's death occurring so close to the incident with Anastasie blew life into the still-smoldering embers of suspicion in Leseuil, though few had sympathy for the dead man.

Nonetheless, memories of the Fournier and Faucheaux deaths were stirred, and once more there was talk of voodoo, of witchcraft out in the black backwaters. That Cormier mother and daughter shared some dark knowledge of the planter's son's death.

Wilhelm Trosclair, more than anyone, became convinced that his son had fallen victim to the dark arts. He traveled up to New Orleans, and a friend put him in touch with "someone who knows about these things." His friend took him to a parlor on the wrong side of Canal Street, where, to Wilhelm's distaste, he was introduced to an old Negress known as Mama Dubois. The parlor he was conducted to, with its burning essence and unholy shrine bedecked with garish offerings, was the kind of affair his father had described when telling Wilhelm about the slave days, when Hispaniola Blacks had brought with them their stew of Catholicism, Igbo Odinani, fetish magic, Fon Vodun, and Haitian Vodou.

The Louisiana Voodoo that had evolved from this stewing, his father had said, was a thing to be feared by everyone, white or Black.

The parlor was dark, which was clearly of no matter to Mama Dubois. The old woman was all but sightless behind the cataracts that had made glaucous globes of her eyes, gray-white against the ebony of her skin. Trosclair noted with irritation that there was a certain nobility about the old woman; that Africa still asserted itself defiantly in her features. Her scalp was bound tight in a scarlet head-scarf; her throat and wrists dressed with countless beads and charms.

She listened intently, her pallid eyes unblinking, her head nodding, as Trosclair related his son's fate, and his suspicions about the cause. There was a moment's silence; then Mama Dubois said: "You best get back and check on your son. Get back as soon as possible. You say he's not in the ground?" Her French, too, defiantly carried the rich tones of Africa.

Trosclair became agitated, angry, but his friend rested a hand on his forearm, and he swallowed his ire.

"No, he isn't. He is in our mausoleum, aboveground."

"That's good," she says and nods. "That's good. You've got to go back and check on him."

"Check on him? Why?"

"Because he's going to rise. He's going to rise up soon. You say this woman in the backswamp is a *caplata*—a voodoo witch. If she is, and if she wants revenge, she made your boy a *zombi*."

Trosclair lost the grip on his anger. He stood up abruptly. "This is a waste of time. I knew it would be. Zombies . . . You're telling me that my son is going to come back from the dead?"

"No, monsieur, not from the dead. No such thing as the undead. Your son has never been dead. That's not what a *zombi* is. Voodoo got two hands—right and left, good and bad. If this woman really is a *caplata,* and if she's out there in the swamp to be close to the Gran Bwa, then she's working with her left hand. Back in Haiti, they believe in resurrection in all its shapes. They believe they can make their own slaves by resurrecting them. I never saw it done, but they say that it's done by a special poison—*coup de poudre.* It makes people go into the death sleep. Some use a special mix of plants to do it, but most use puffer-fish poison. They give it to the one they want to be their zombie slave. They look like they're dead—no breathing, no pulse that you can feel. Then they bury them like all dead. But they're never really dead and they don't bury them deep. When they come out of the death sleep the poison put them in, they dig their way out of the ground. Then they're *zombi.*"

"I don't believe it . . ." said Trosclair, but he felt his heart beating faster.

"You don't have to believe me, monsieur. It's done so much back in Haiti that they put down a special law against it. They made it a charge of attempted murder if you give someone the potion that makes them go into that death sleep, like a coma. All there in the law books if you don't believe me. And it's not magic—it's chemistry. You ask me and I tell you: your son's not dead, he's in the death sleep, and he's going to wake up soon. Maybe damaged, maybe not, but you better get back there."

She hadn't finished speaking before the thrown dollars clattered on the table before her, and the parlor door slammed shut behind Wilhelm Trosclair as he rushed out into the night.

Convinced her husband had lost his mind, Marie Trosclair sent one of the servants to find Doc Charbonnier. Trosclair's horse was close to collapse, its withers whip-scourged and its flanks sweat-frothed. Trosclair had not even come back to the house when he returned but had gone straight to the mausoleum in the rose garden. He yelled and bawled for someone to bring him tools—a lever, anything.

His wife came running with the mausoleum key, but he had already taken a hammer to it in his haste.

"What is it, Wilhelm?" she asked desperately. "What is wrong with you?"

"It's Paul," he said, his eyes wild. "We gotta get Paul out! He's still alive!"

"Wilhelm . . ." She seized Trosclair by the shoulders and turned him to face her. His eyes were wild; his expression tortured. "You're not making sense, Wilhelm. . . ."

One of the servants came running with an iron lever. Trosclair pushed his wife to one side and pulled open the white stone door. The servant followed him, but eyed his employer anxiously.

"Come here, man!" shouted Trosclair impatiently. "Help me budge the lid."

It took them all their combined strength, and the benefit of the lever, to slide the heavy marble lid off the stone sarcophagus.

"Paul!" yelled Trosclair. "It's Papa. I'm here, Paul. I'll get you out!"

With a final, desperate shove, Trosclair and the servant dislodged the lid, and it slid off, its edge slamming into the ground and resonating through the mausoleum.

"Oh Jesus," said the servant. "Oh sweet Jesus."

There was a moment of silence as Trosclair and the servant gazed into the cavern of the sarcophagus, and the horror it contained.

Paul Trosclair lay dead in his tomb, but not in the attitude of repose in which he had been put to rest. His dead eyes, injured and uninjured, were wide, frozen in his terminal terror. His hands were bloodied, the fingernails torn from them, several of the fingers broken from his furious clawing at the stone lid. His mouth gaped wide, unnaturally wide, in a silent scream.

His mother rushed into the mausoleum and looked down at the twisted limbs and contorted features of her only son.

The scream was no longer silent.

20

1927
Hollywood

Everyone in Hollywood knows the legend of the Golem. Not because they are particularly well read, or especially well versed in Jewish history and mysticism. Like everything in the studio town, their knowledge comes from there having been a movie made about it. Or three movies, to be precise. Paul Wegener's trilogy of Golem movies, and the visual drama of his German Expressionist sets and lighting, has inspired so many directors, including Paul Brand, to develop their own version of the form.

In any case, everyone knows the story of the Golem, and some wiseacre, inspired by Sam Geller's height, bulk, brutish appearance, and Jewish background, fitted the epithet to Harry Carbine's head of security.

Someone, she can't remember who, once told Mary Rourke that above the old synagogue in the Jewish Quarter of Prague there is an attic that can only be accessed from the outside of the building. Iron step rungs on the outer wall lead to the attic door, but the rungs stop twenty feet before they reach the ground. The legend is that the attic is where the Golem, the demonic protector of the Prague ghetto, sleeps. They also say that if you take a ladder to reach the rungs, then climb into the attic, the ticket price for entry is your sanity, your life, or both.

It had been one of those stories you are told at a Hollywood party by someone who is somebody or nobody in the studio system but who thinks that seeming so incredibly deep and interesting will win them a ticket to your bed. The face behind it has faded, but the story has stuck with Rourke, and every time she visits the small office occupied by Sam Geller, tucked away at the end of a corridor at the back of the main Carbine office building, she feels her feet ringing on those iron rungs.

This is the Golem's lair.

It's not that Rourke dislikes Sam Geller. There is a lot she admires about him. He has an honesty, a forthrightness, that she finds refreshing. Geller is unpolished, untouched by the glitz of movieland. He has lived and worked in Hollywood for over a decade, yet still carries the Lower East Side around with him like a well-worn winter jacket he is reluctant to discard in the California sun. He is also, she knows, very, very smart. Rourke senses that Geller disguises his deep, wide, and penetrating intelligence behind the smart mouth of the New York street. Maybe, she thinks, Sam Geller is just like everyone else here after all, playing a part and hiding his true self.

Whatever the script he plays to, Rourke senses that something, some hard whetstone of experience, has honed in him a severe, bright edge. Something about Sam the Golem Geller stirs unease in Rourke.

It's midafternoon when Mary calls at Geller's office. She has spent the morning at home, resting ribs that protest every moment in defiance of the tablets Doc Wilson gave her. When she arrives, the air in Geller's office is eye-stingingly thick with cigar smoke, the sunlight through the blinds slicing it into angled stripes of light and shadow. When he sees her enter, Geller beams a broad grin, carefully extinguishes his cigar in his desktop ashtray, stands up, and opens the window to ventilate the office.

"Hi, Mary, what's to do?" He rumbles New York vowels amiably. He invariably addresses women as "toots" but, as she pointed out to Jake Kendrick, Geller learned the inadvisability of using the form of address with Rourke some time back. "Hear you had automobile trouble."

"Sure did. Brakes were busted. It's halfway down a gully in the Hills, but I've got one of the company's pool cars."

"What can I do for you?" He indicates she should sit, and Rourke is happy when he does the same, easing the stress on her craned neck.

"You got the stuff we took from Norma Carlton's place?"

"Sure. But I ain't had time to look through it. Didn't see much to worry about when we were cleaning the place out. Say, did you hear about John Gilbert?" He hands her a newspaper.

A headline glares. The picture beneath is an unflattering press snap-shot of Gilbert, not one of his studio-supplied publicity portraits. She finds it depressing and sad: John Gilbert had been as massive a heartthrob as Rudy Valentino, before he got on the wrong side of both Louis B. Mayer and a whiskey bottle.

"Apparently, he tried to climb up the side of the Miramar Hotel in Santa Monica to get into Greta Garbo's second-story apartment. Quite a feat with a quart of whiskey in you," Geller says with mock admira-tion. "Ten days in L.A. County Jail for drunk-and-disorderly."

"I know Mannix and Strickling have had their hands full with him lately." Rourke is referring to MGM's two fixers. "The studio didn't step in this time?"

Geller shakes his massive head. "Nope. In fact, I heard that Howard Strickling put the word out for the press to have a field day with it. Mayer's told the studio to hang him out to dry. If 'dry' is a word you can use when talking about Gilbert. Thank God it ain't our problem. We've enough of our own to deal with."

"I wouldn't go so far as to say it isn't our problem." Rourke drops the paper on Geller's cluttered desk. "I heard Robert Huston is a drinking buddy of Gilbert's. I have a feeling Huston is cut from the same cloth— and, like Gilbert, his stitching is ready to come apart."

"Oh?"

"I spoke with Veronica Stratton. It seems that she and Huston are more business partners than their public image of the perfect mar-riage. I get the feeling that Huston was involved with Norma Carlton as much because his wife, like Garbo, plays both sides of the fence. Or maybe just her own side."

"I see. . . ." Geller's massive brow creases in a frown. "Veronica Strat-ton is one of Hollywood's baritone babes? Ain't heard that before. And you know word like that gets round."

"That's the impression I got. Whatever the domestic situation, there's more going on with Huston—and Stratton—than we know. Normally, that would be First National Pictures' concern and not ours, but Huston's our male lead in a movie that's already had too much off-screen drama. Norma Carlton's death has pushed this production to the edge; then there's the accident on-set. Robert Huston getting into press-visible trouble could give it that last shove over the edge. I'd appreciate it if you could find out anything you can about him. Including what he's been up to with Gilbert. And with John Barrymore—I heard Huston learned how to raise hell from the master."

Geller looks at her for a moment, something like vague suspicion in his eyes. "Sure, Mary, I'll see what I can find out. You know, if I didn't know better, I'd sure think you were running your own investigation into something."

"Thanks, Sam. And no, not really—that's your domain. Just trying to keep a lid on stuff after the Carlton thing, that's all. The press smells blood, and I don't want them to follow Huston's trail if it brings them back to our door. One more thing—Huston and Stratton live up at this place called Mount Laurel. I guess you know that?"

Geller nods. "Everybody does."

"They've got this security guy on the gate. Looks like an ex-soldier. Big scar on his face from a war wound, I'd guess. Any way you could see if you can find out anything about him?"

"I'll see what I can do. Is someone giving you trouble, Mary?"

"What? No, nothing like that. Just a hunch that may be something or nothing. Thanks, Sam, I appreciate it," says Rourke. "Could I see it now?"

Again, he frowns.

"Norma Carlton's stuff," she explains.

"Oh yeah—sure, Mary," he says again. Slowly, as if his mind is processing the significance of the request. "I got it in the storeroom here. . . ."

21

Geller leads Rourke along the corridor to the storeroom at its end. It is small and windowless, and he switches on the single pendant naked lightbulb, which fills the space with hard-edged brightness and shadow. He points to where the three studio carryalls sit next to an expensive-looking valise on one of the shelves. Rourke, despite herself, feels a sense of relief when Sam Geller's vast bulk disappears from the door frame it has been filling and leaves her alone in the storeroom.

Something troubles her about her exchange with the Golem, but she can't pin it down. Between Jake Kendrick and Sam Geller looking into the same things, in their very different ways, she should get something worthwhile. The cost, she realizes, is that both are beginning to suspect Rourke has a bigger interest in recent events than simply keeping the lid on potential bad press.

Lifting it down from the shelf, she examines the small alligator-hide valise, embossed with the initials "NC." Its contents are of no interest, so she empties it before going through the carryalls and transferring anything she feels may be worth looking at later. She selects the diaries, notebooks, receipts, and letters the team removed from Carlton's home and places them in the valise. She also lifts down a locked jewelry box from the shelf. Geller had explained that it contains the jewelry retrieved from the house, plus that which had been picked up from the Appleton Clinic.

"What about the Egyptian necklace, the stage piece from *Queen Pharaoh*?" she had asked.

"The boss has got it," Geller had replied. "He asked for it special."

She leaves the storeroom carrying the valise and the jewelry box.

On the way past his office, she leans in through the door of Golem Geller's office and thanks him again.

"Sure thing, Mary," he rumbles.

Outside, she crosses the hacienda courtyard to her office in the studio's publicity wing. When she arrives, Sylvie, Rourke's assistant, gives her an update on who's called to see her and who's been on the telephone.

"A cop called in to drop your bag off."

"My bag?"

"Yeah—he said they recovered it from your car."

"Oh, right, I see."

"He said he was Detective Kendrick and asked if you could telephone him when you got back. Oh—and Mr. Carbine asked if you could meet him in the parking lot in an hour."

"The parking lot?"

"That's what he said."

Rourke goes through to her office. The beaded clutch bag she had had with her when she went up to Mount Laurel sits on her desk blotter. There is nothing about it that suggests it has been in an automobile wreck, yet it looks odd, alien to her—like an artifact from another time, an intrusive reminder of a history she has tried to put behind her with painkillers and a determined focus on the present. She picks it up and goes through it: her wallet, her compact, and, most important of all, her notebook and address book are still there.

They are important to her because anyone prying into them would get too much of an insight into her personal and professional life. And what is true for her was perhaps true of Norma Carlton. The thought spurs her, and she pushes her bag to one side and replaces it with the valise.

Taking them out one item at a time, she goes through the contents. There are receipts from hairdressers, couturiers, spas, and restaurants; ticket stubs from the Hollywood Bowl. She spends nearly an hour going through Norma Carlton's address book: she guesses that the numbers and addresses listed include the famous and the infamous, the well-known and the anonymous. She has to guess because Norma Carlton has taken great care to identify them all only by their initials, not their names. Where two or more sets of initials are identical, Carlton has put a number next to each. Rourke can identify many of them by their street names: some of the most recognizable addresses in Hollywood are listed, including "RH" next to the Mount Laurel address, as well as one in Santa Monica, which she guesses is the beachside getaway Huston mentioned.

But some of the addresses don't give Rourke a clue to who is behind the initials. And, oddly, some initials have no street name or even location attached, only a telephone number. She sets the address book to one side and looks through Carlton's diary. The diary is full, but the same cryptic approach has been taken with the daily entries. Rourke recognizes that "TDP" refers to *The Devil's Playground,* as the initials appear next to times, durations, and locations that correspond to the filming schedule. "HC" appears next to the word "party" in one entry, and she recognizes the date as one of Harry Carbine's press galas. The thing that intrigues Rourke the most is that every few weeks a day is marked without initials but simply with a star, drawn in red ink, whereas all other entries are in blue. Whatever the stars denote, Carlton thought it so secret that she deemed her usual initials system not secure enough. On the other hand, thinks Rourke, it could be something insignificant.

She is interrupted by her assistant, who leans in through the office door.

"Miss Rourke, just to remind you that Mr. Carbine will be waiting for you."

"Thanks, Sylvie, I'm on my way," says Rourke, and she leaves the scant sketches of a movie star's life lying on her desk.

Outside, the sun is lower in the sky and has already dipped into a richer palette. When she reaches the parking lot, she finds Carbine waiting for her, smiling. Behind him is a brand-new Packard 426 roadster. Its burgundy paintwork gleams like dark wet blood in the late-afternoon sunlight.

"I feel it's my fault that you had that accident," he explains as he hands her the keys. "I felt this was the least I can do."

"Thanks, boss. I really appreciate it. It's a beaut," she says with a weak smile. "But I have a funny feeling my accident wasn't an accident."

Carbine frowns. "You can't be serious."

"I don't know. . . . I just get the feeling that someone doesn't like me sniffing around Norma Carlton's death. If it's her killer, then he already knows that we know he murdered her, and maybe he thinks putting me out of the way is the smart move. Are you sure you still don't want Golem Geller involved?"

"Sam is best left out of this for the moment."

"Why do I get the feeling that there's something you're not telling me? About Sam Geller?"

"I've told you all I know about everything to do with this mess." His smile has faded. "Listen, Mary, I'll give you a bonus, as well as the car. Five hundred dollars in expenses."

"Boss, I'm not looking for—"

"I know. But, again, it's the least I can do. And if you have any hint again that someone is out to get you, then let me know. I'll get Sam involved. But, in the meantime, I'm sure you have your own contacts you can call on. I'll foot the bill."

"How well do you know Veronica Stratton?"

Carbine looks mildly taken aback by the question. "Veronica? Not well. I've never cast her in anything, because she's on an exclusive to First National Pictures, and they famously don't loan her out. That may change, of course. Why?"

"Nothing—just that she was the last person I spoke to before I nearly took the scenic shortcut off a mountainside."

"You think she had something to do with that?"

Rourke shrugs. "I don't know. Maybe. Maybe not. I've asked Geller to do some digging into Bob Huston and Stratton. He doesn't know the real reason—I've told him I want to make sure Huston isn't a further liability to the production, which isn't far from the truth. I take it you're okay with that?"

Carbine thinks for a moment. "I guess. Just don't share any more—and if you need him involved in any way, run it by me first."

"Sure thing, boss," she says. "And thanks again for the new wheels."

Back in her office, she gathers Norma Carlton's things and starts to replace them in the valise. She'll go through the jewelry later, she decides. The last thing she picks up is a small rectangular silver case, smaller than a cigarette case. She flips it open and discovers it contains visiting cards—not Norma Carlton's own, but a selection of others. There are cards for everything from high-class French caterers, hairdressers, and couturiers to an auto shop in West Hollywood. Two cards stand out for her. On one, expensive gold lettering embossed into thick, creamy velum declares that Madame Erzulie, Maîtresse des Ombres, is available for séances by appointment. Rourke dismisses the thought that ghosts and visitors from the otherworld obviously schedule their appearances according to Madame Erzulie's diary.

The second card doesn't look like a personal visiting card at all. There is no address, no telephone number.

J. K. Armitage
SUDDEN LAKE

22

1967
Sudden Lake

She leads Conway through the hotel, and he is amazed at how clean everything is. The rich, dark wood of the floors is brushed and polished, the light fixtures dusted, the brass furniture of the doors burnished to a gleam. It is only when they pass a door that has swung partially open that he sees into one of the hotel rooms. It is exactly as it would have been forty years before: the bed is an impressive four-poster; a Biedermeier chaise sits under the window; a vast mirror, framed with Baroque gold moldings, sits on the wall above an ornate dressing table. But here time and the desert have claimed long-term occupancy: The window is almost opaque with grime, one of the panes broken. The tapestry hangings on the four-poster bed are rotted and thick with dust and the fresher weavings of desert spiders. The rich wood of the floor is sun-dulled and coated with a pale soot of desert dirt and grit.

Again, the thought occurs to him that this is all like a movie set: that beyond the presented façade lies nothing of substance.

She steps deliberately in front of him, grasps the polished doorknob, and closes the hotel-room door. It takes two attempts for the latch to engage, and Conway guesses he only got an insight into what lay beyond courtesy of a faulty lock spring. Without comment, she turns and continues along the corridor, and Conway follows.

They pass the empty dining hall, where, four decades before, a businessman—transformed into a scarlet demon by desperation, sun, heat, and salt—had cried tears of blood as he murdered his wife and daughters. And still the corpse of the lake mocks with its bone-whiteness from beyond the picture windows.

She leads him down a long corridor and into a large, dazzlingly bright space, like an atrium or a conservatory. Along one wall, huge convex windows bulge outward, stretching from the conservatory's marble floor to its opaque glass ceiling. The view through the windows is obscured by a forest of plants and flowers. It should cheer, but there is something about the dark vividity of the flowers, the fleshiness of the tonguelike succulents, and the almost-black green of much of the foliage that Conway finds nauseating. Something akin to ivy coils dark green, waxy-leafed, and snakelike up one of the metal columns supporting the conservatory roof. There is an incongruous sound of water babbling where a small fountain spurts and splashes into a stone basin at the center of the conservatory.

"My little indoor garden," she says in explanation, but still without any passion. "I'd go mad without at least something green and living around me. The water comes from a deep spring under the hotel." She gives a small laugh. "Ironic, isn't it, that the lake dried up half a mile away while clean water trickles through some subterranean crevice under our feet. This way . . ."

He follows her. As he does, his eyes are drawn to the only painting he has seen since arriving in the hotel. It hangs on the atrium wall facing the conservatory; it is large, painted in vivid oil colors, and Conway can't decide if its style is modernist or primitive. It depicts an almost abstract figure of a snake, its skin multicolored, rippling and writhing until it forms a circle, the jaws of the head closing on the tail, as if the snake is consuming itself.

"That's an interesting piece," he says. She stops, turns, and looks up at the painting.

"Yes," she says. "It is. This way, Dr. Conway . . ." She turns back and walks on.

They reach a small square hall. Two sofas against facing walls give the impression of a waiting area. An ancient wheelchair, dust-free, sits beside one of the sofas. To their right, a wide, doorless access yawns darkly. She leads him to it, and he sees a set of stone steps, flanked by a ramp, decline into darkness.

For some reason he cannot fathom, Conway feels ill at ease. There is something about this place, about the situation he finds himself in, that feels unreal. Dreamlike. The darkness at the foot of the steps yawns threateningly.

"A basement?" he asks.

"The movie theater. They built it underground so it kept cool, especially for storing film stock when showing movies to the guests. They installed a ramp alongside the steps for rolling equipment and film carts in and out. Also, one of the owner's daughters was put in a wheelchair by the 1916 polio epidemic and they used the ramp to wheel her in and out."

"You have it, don't you?" says Conway. "I was right all along; you do have the only print of *The Devil's Playground*."

"Please, Dr. Conway . . ." She extends an arm to indicate he should go before her. He looks down into the darkness apprehensively, and she sighs, reaching for a wall switch. The lower reaches of the ramp and steps are illuminated. "I think you'll find this most interesting."

He descends the stone steps and feels the temperature drop. At the foot of the stairs are double doors fashioned from expensive cherrywood. He looks back at her, and she nods. He pushes the doors wide.

The theater is bigger than Conway expects, and particularly impressive given that it has been hewn out of desert rock. It is also higher—or deeper—than he had anticipated. Conway sees that the theater has been dug out—probably dynamited first—from the bedrock.

They must have done this first, he thinks; they must have created the theater, then built the hotel above and around it.

There has been no attempt to hide the nature that contains the theater: the rock that forms the walls has been cut and polished by masons, but left exposed, and the variegated seams of red, umber, and gray stone sweep across them as if painted on. There is something cathedralic about this place: a solemnity that makes Conway feel he should speak in hushed tones.

"Do you have it here?" he asks. His patience is wearing thin. He is tired, and in the comparative cool of the stone theater suddenly and paradoxically feels sapped by the desert heat he's had to endure all day.

"Please, Dr. Conway, sit. You will see for yourself. If you are right, then you'll be the first person in forty years to see *The Devil's Playground*. If not . . ."

He sits down three rows back, in the center, a lifetime of movie watching making his choice automatic. The woman leaves him and enters the projection room at the back.

Conway, his mouth dry, his head pounding, a dry nausea tickling unpleasantly in his throat, gazes at the screen. The silver screen. Unlike newer versions, this one is a classic from back in the day: thick fabric given a lenticular surface and painted with reflective silver paint.

Without warning, the lights go out, and Conway tries to push the thought from his mind, and the rising panic it brings, that he is in total blackness in a place beneath the ground.

There is the sound of a cooling fan from the projector room; then the screen bursts into silver life. The opening credits. All Conway's feelings of discomfort and vague nausea are forgotten as he reads:

Harry Carbine and Clifford J. Taylor Present
A Carbine International Pictures Production . . .
THE DEVIL'S PLAYGROUND

PART TWO

23

1967
Sudden Lake

The opening titles fade from the screen. There is a moment of blackness, laden with electric expectation.

The story begins.

Conway sits transfixed. He forgets he is confined in a tomblike space hewn out of desert rock and fashioned into a movie theater. The desert, the strange hotel on a dead lake, the old woman and her black-eyed hound, the buyer in Santa Barbara who sent him on this quest—none of them exists anymore. Nor is there any duality of universe: all that is real for Paul Conway now is the light-and-shade celluloid realm before him, haunted by its silver-nitrate ghosts.

Like a dissipating shadow, the dark screen fades into a street scene of clustered gabled houses and a soiled, littered cobbled street in a medieval French city. The contrast of light and dark is jarringly severe. The slumlike buildings are exaggeratedly sharp-angled and menacing, and tilt and lean through age and neglect. From the crooked chimneys, wraiths of ink-black smoke writhe upward onto the parchment of a pale, graphite sky. Conway, already completely immersed and absorbed into the screen's chiaroscuro universe, can see this is a place of great poverty.

There are only three or four peasant citizens to be seen on the street, and they make their way with hurried, fearful purpose. It is clear these people do not wish to linger out of doors. In the distance and looming above them, however, is a great twin-towered cathedral. Its grand proportions and harshly angular structure are also menacing, oppressive. It is clear the cathedral dominates the city more than just architecturally.

An intertitle card declares that this is:

> *The city of Ouxbois, France.*
> *The year, 1348*

Another intertitle card follows:

> *A city living in Fear.*
> *That greatest Fear of all . . .*

The card is replaced with an interior scene. Inside one of the dilapidated houses, in a small room, plaster peeling from walls, an anxious mother huddles in a corner, cradling her infant, who cries as if hungry or fearful, swaddled in rags. Their faces are illuminated by the stark light from the windows, which carves hard-edged geometries into the hovel's gloom.

A cut to the street outside again. It is still day, but something vast is casting its night-black shadow across the front of some of the buildings. The shadow moves slowly, menacingly, swallowing first one house, then its neighbor, then the next, in inexorable progress along the street, consuming more housefronts, and turning day into night.

He feels his thrill at what he is watching turn to a visceral unease. The shadow that progresses along the walls is an impenetrable black slab of darkness—yet Conway gives a small start when he thinks he sees something still darker shift and shimmer in the shadow, like rippling obsidian. As if the shadow is alive.

"How did he do that?" Conway mutters to himself. "How did Brand do that with the shadows?"

The scene moves to the ramshackle stairway of one of the tenements. The shadow is cast onto the soiled, crumbling plaster of the wall, moving upward as if climbing the staircase.

Now the mother and child in the small garret room. The mother is struck by terror, her eyes wide, her hand raised to shield her child as . . .

The shadow creeps across the bare and broken wooden floorboards, like a dark tide heading toward the huddled mother and child.

There is a sudden cut to an intertitle card. Only one word, so large it fills the screen:

... PLAGUE!

The card is replaced by the image of the terror-stricken mother and child as the shadow is cast over them, now taking the shape of a clutching, clawlike hand.

Back in the street, the metaphorical shadow of the plague is now shown as the actual shadow of a large cart, being cast upward onto the buildings by the sinking sun. The cart's grim cargo is a jumble of a dozen or more rough sacks, each the size and outline of a human body. Ahead of the cart walks a tall, thin man clad and hooded in black. He is a civic official, yet his appearance calls to mind images of the Angel of Death. He wearily swings a heavy bell, and we see that he calls out in all directions.

An intertitle card gives his words form:

"Dead! Bring out your dead!"

There is a slow fade to black, followed by a slow dissolve into a new exterior scene: the balcony of a grand house, dressed with statuary, urns, and pots; bedecked with flowers.

Despite looking out over the stark poverty of the city, this is a place of wealth and comfort. The sun is setting over Ouxbois. Alone on the balcony stands a young woman. Beautiful, virginal, yet darkly sensuous.

Conway catches his breath as he looks upon the face and form of Norma Carlton. He has watched and rewatched all her movies, and to see her now as he had never seen her before sends a thrill up his spine. The set, the art direction, the drama of lighting and angle—all the hallmarks of Paul Brand's Expressionist genius. But Conway realizes he is not only watching the work of a genius but watching his masterwork. Even these thoughts pass only fleetingly through Conway's brain, as he remains captivated by the story that plays out.

She gazes out over the clustered city below to where the cathedral soars opposite. The young woman's face is as sad as it is beautiful. A card announces that she is:

The pious and kind ADELICIA,
beloved of the city's people,
pure-of-heart daughter
of Ouxbois's Mayor.

As Adelicia continues to gaze at the city below, an older man, expensively dressed, wearing a fur-trimmed cloak and feather-decorated hat, steps onto the balcony from the windows behind her and sets a hand upon her shoulder. His expression, like hers, is careworn. He is:

FRÉDÉRIC MARQUAND,
Mayor of Ouxbois.
Doting father of ADELICIA.

He frowns with concern as he speaks to his daughter. It is clear he asks what troubles her. She extends a graceful arm and sweeps it to indicate the city below them.

"Father, why do the people suffer so? This was once the happiest place on God's Earth. The finest artists, artisans, and craftsmen in all of France. Creators of great images . . ."

There is a fade to the same city street scene as before, but seen through Adelicia's memories. The sun shines brightly, the street alive and bustling. A lively market is under way: the camera pans across the same houses seen before, but now they are bright, clean, and cheerful. Outside each building, artisans sell their wares to buyers who throng through the street: painters sell canvases, sculptors chisel and polish stone, weavers display fine tapestries. Players of all kinds perform on raised stages at intervals along the street: jugglers juggle, acrobats tumble, actors pantomime dramas, tragedies, or comedies. All art is to be seen here on this single street.

The scene opens out as the viewpoint is raised to a rooftop-level wide shot that shows the same burgeoning creativity taking place on every other street. All is bright and cheerful; only the looming cathedral seems to look down, with a disapproving, architectural glower.

A cross-fade dims the scene and replaces it with a view, from the same vantage point, of the city as it is now: deserted, desolate, and forbidding; a place of fear and harsh shadows. Again Conway is astonished by the purity of image; he feels that Paul Brand has engraved these scenes rather than filmed them—using light itself as his etching mordant to bite into the solid black shadows.

He sees it again. Conway feels his pulse quicken as he once more senses movement, dark life, in those shadows. This time he believes he caught sight of eyes, of some monstrous, black-etched face in the darkness.

"How *did* he do that?" he asks himself silently. His excitement is tempered with an inexplicable fear. This, he feels, is more than cinema. Whatever this art is, it is a dark art.

The scene returns to Adelicia and her father on the balcony. Adelicia's expression is now one of desperation. Suddenly, they are both drawn to the balcony's edge, as if something has caught their attention simultaneously. They look across to the towering cathedral opposite, at the far side of the square.

There is a cut to a scene at the steps of the cathedral. Conway once more marvels at the artistry of the mise-en-scène: the architecture of the cathedral is impossible yet credible; the clutching huddle of the city's buildings seems the fanciful conjuring of an artist's imagination, yet Conway can believe these people really live there.

There is tumult. A rabble has gathered, armed with torches; the mob shouts and gestures angrily at the cathedral doors. Their leader springs forward and mounts the steps, turns to the rabble, and gestures to them. Conway recognizes the actor as Lewis Everett. Clad in a black velvet cloak and cowl, he is tall, dark, and wickedly handsome. A card reveals he is:

ALBAN ARCHAMBEAU,
Master Alchemist and Black Magician . . .

Archambeau is appealing to the assembled rabble, alternately ranting in fury, beseeching in sorrow. His gestures indicate the thrust of his entreaty: outstretched arms signaling the suffering of the people, his contorted features and shaking, black-gloved fist, raised first toward the mayoral residence and then the cathedral that looms above him, indicating those he feels are responsible.

Archambeau's exaggerated gestures and expression are a panto-mimed symphony of despair and fury, malicious incitement and dark exhortation. The rabble responds to him as an orchestra would its conductor.

He looks slyly to the side, then assumes a pained expression as he clutches both hands to his breast. An intertitle card gives words to Archambeau's gestures:

"Citizens of Ouxbois . . . Brothers and Sisters in the Arts. How long have we toiled to bring beauty to the world? Created image and lyric to inspire and soothe the souls of others? Look how much light we have brought to the world."

He flings his arms outward and looks heavenward beseechingly. Conway thrills as he watches Archambeau's expression turn night-dark as he leans forward to the crowd.

"But look also at how our King and Mayor, our Bishops and priests thoughtlessly extinguish that light. How easily they forget our labor and relinquish us to the darkness of Plague . . ."

The mob is now in an ecstasy of outrage. Heads turn to one another and nod, fists are raised skyward in fury.

"It is time to break the shackles, let loose the chains of convention that church and state have imposed on us. It is time we find a stronger God, a more powerful Magic, with which to free ourselves . . ."

There is a fade to the future and the city that Archambeau describes. It remains Ouxbois, but the buildings are dressed in marble and gold; people in the streets are luxuriously if immodestly dressed. Wine flows, behavior is wanton, uninhibited. And overlooking it all is a monstrous, towering idol: on a throne sits a cloven-hoofed demon with the body of a man and the horned head of a monstrous ram or goat. Insect eyes bulge hideously from the head and gaze down malevolently on the city.

There is a sequence of two intertitle cards:

The Dark Master Alban Archambeau secretly serves . . .

Prince of Hell and Lord of Flies . . .

The scene cuts back to the stone idol. Suddenly, the camera pulls back to reveal the sky above the city. Impossibly, a thousand feet tall and materializing as if out of the air itself, the demon takes living form. It turns its heavy goat-head from side to side, as if surveying its domain. From behind its back, vast bat-wings unfurl and turn day into night.

There is a third intertitle card, and the screen is filled with a single name:

BA'AL ZEBUB!

Conway presses back in his seat as he involuntarily shrinks from the screen. Awe and fear mingle as he again asks himself:

"How *did* he do that?"

24

1927
Hollywood

The next two days bring little in the way of enlightenment, but much in the way of discomfort, as the bruising from her tumble settles in for the long haul. Mary Rourke sits in her office, dressed in black. A skull-hugging cloche hat with a half-face veil sits like a black dome on one side of her desk. On a hanger hooked on the back of her office door, a long black velvet coat trimmed with a broad, pale fur-stole collar hangs waiting for the appointment she has to keep in a few hours.

Rourke has twice telephoned the West Hollywood residence of the mystic-cum-psychic-cum-spiritualist Norma Carlton had consulted. The first time, the telephone rang out unanswered. The second time, she was given the brush-off by a male voice that informed her that Madame Erzulie was unavailable without an appointment, even on the telephone. Rourke had arranged a day and a time to call back. Today was the day and now was the time. She gets the operator to connect her and is put through to the same male voice who answered before. Am I the only one in Hollywood, she thinks, who doesn't have a butler?

"Madame Erzulie cannot take your call at the moment." At least this one doesn't have a faux-English accent.

"But I arranged that I would call this morning. I arranged it with you. Today, eleven-thirty," protests Rourke.

"I'm aware of that, Miss Rourke," he replies in an "I couldn't care less" tone. "Unfortunately, Madame Erzulie has had to go out of town unexpectedly and at short notice."

"Unexpectedly? Really? I thought she would have expected it—her being clairvoyant and all."

Rourke's witticism is met with a click and the deep purr of a vacated telephone line.

Next, she calls the Everett Motion Picture Company and asks to speak to Lewis Everett. She's luckier this time—at least insofar as Everett takes her call—but he seems ill-at-ease when Rourke starts asking him about his relationship with Norma Carlton, and her championship of the movie adaptation of his novel, *Silas Torn*.

"I really don't understand why you're asking me these questions," says Everett. Rourke notices that his voice is cultured, velvet-rich and deep. If the future really is in sound films, she thinks, Everett's voice is his ticket, even if his skin tone will mark that ticket third class. "In any case, I don't like talking about this kind of stuff on the telephone."

"Okay, then, can we meet to discuss it?" she asks.

He pauses, and she hears a sigh on the other end of the line.

"Things are a little tight right now. I've got a lot going on."

"Do you have any more scenes to do for *The Devil's Playground*?" persists Rourke. "If you do, we could talk at the studio."

"No, I don't have any more shooting to do. Let me get back to you once I've had a look at my schedule."

Again Rourke is left with the receiver purring in her ear. She winces as she hooks it back on its cradle: the pain in her side is now less sharp and more a diffuse aching, as if it has grown bored of its habitation in her body and has lost its focus. Once in a while, as now, it delivers an ill-tempered jab to remind her of its tenancy.

Rourke has been weaning herself off the tablets Doc Wilson gave her and now only takes one at a time, and less often. She has just palmed a painkiller and is washing it down with the water Sylvie brought her from the cooler when Jake Kendrick steps into her office. He grins and nods at the bottle of pills.

"Should I be looking for a Jones-Miller Act warrant? I believe 'breath mints,' as they call them in flapper circles, are all the rage at the moment." He tosses his hat onto Rourke's desk, next to her unworn cloche, and sits across from her.

Rourke smiles. She knows all about "breath mints" through her experience with errant starlets: hashish or cocaine pellets carried in handbags and stirred into bootleg cocktails. She examines the half-full pill bottle.

"God knows what Doc Wilson has in these, but he could make a fortune on the street with them." She puts the bottle down.

"And what's with the dark duds?" he asks, nodding to Rourke's clothes.

"Funeral. Norma Carlton's, to be precise. I have it this afternoon. A memorial service at the chapel in Forest Lawn before they inter her ashes."

"She's been cremated already?"

"Happening now. Private ceremony for family and close friends." She doesn't mention that the family and close friends extend only to Doc Wilson, two orderlies to carry the coffin, and the crematorium director. "The main event's out at Forest Lawn this afternoon."

"That was quick with the cremation." There is now a hint of suspicion in Kendrick's tone.

"I guess." Rourke shrugs, then, to deflect him from the subject, asks, "You find out anything about Hollywood's dream couple?"

"Surprisingly little. I tapped a few shoulders and dropped a few nickels, but nobody had anything much to say about your Englishman. And less about his ice-maiden bride. His record's as clean as a whistle, despite his carousing buddies, various scrapes, and his gambling itch."

"That's nothing new in Hollywood, Jake. You know that. Between them, Alma Rubens and Barbara La Marr have kept the Hollywood cocaine industry in business and no one is any the wiser, despite it killing La Marr a couple of months back; and that's twice now that a dash across the border and a hasty Mexican wedding has saved Charlie Chaplin from thirty years for statutory rape, but he's still the public's favorite. I could fill a century's worth of front pages with the stuff we've kept a lid on. That's why they call us fixers—we fix it so records stay clean as a whistle."

"I guess."

"What is it, Jake?" Rourke has read something in Kendrick's expression.

"It's just that I smell fish, Mary. A lot of fish and none of it fresh. You've got to watch your step with this."

"Why?"

"I get the feeling Robert Huston has an angel on his shoulder. And I don't mean a studio fixer. You know the head of LAPD Vice, McAfee?"

"Yeah . . ." Rourke knows all about Captain Guy McAfee of Vice. Everyone does. McAfee had been an iron fist brought down hard on Los Angeles's streetwalkers and brothels, sworn to clean the city of sin. Except that all the streetwalkers, brothels, and sins that felt the full force of his wrath were the few who did not work for McAfee himself, or his wife, LA's preeminent madam.

"Well," says Kendrick, "he dropped by my desk yesterday, all smiles and menace, which is his big suit. I got the hefty nudge from him to quit sniffing around Robert Huston. You know me, Mary, I work quiet, especially when I'm doing stuff off the books for you, so God knows how he got wind of it. But McAfee ain't a real copper but a mobster wearing tin. He makes a corkscrew look straight, and he's got fingers in every pie and connections in every sewer. Somehow he got wise to my sniffing around and has suggested that I drop it."

"You think McAfee is the angel on Huston's shoulder?"

"Could be. Maybe not—McAfee's rackets are liquor, pro-skirts, and can-houses. Although I hear he's getting into the gambling racket big-time—on the Strip legally and elsewhere less so. Maybe he's warning me off because Huston owes him heavy."

"But you don't think so?"

"McAfee is all wrapped up with the City Hall Gang. They play for even bigger stakes, and if you ask me, they're more likely to have their fingers in the biggest pie of them all."

"Hollywood," says Rourke.

"That's my feeling. I got the idea that McAfee was maybe just the messenger. You studio people clean up the messes made by your sheikhs and Shebas, as well as the odd producer or director—but only when those messes are going to spill into the public eye and when keeping them under wraps is manageable. I'm suggesting that some people in this town get into much worse fixes out of sight. Stuff they can't afford the studios to find out about."

"And you think Huston is one of these people?"

"I don't know, but they say gambling is riding the tiger—you can never dismount. Get into debt with these bozos and the juice they apply is at a rate you can never pay off. That means they own you and can ask for all kinds of payment in kind. I just don't know what the game is with Huston." He frowns. "Truth is, Mary, this is all beginning to feel a whole lot heavier than it did to start with. And it's made me pretty uneasy about what happened with your car. You sure you're telling me all there is to tell?"

"I've told you all I can, Jake. Are you saying you're dropping it?" asks Rourke. "I understand, and thanks for doing what you could."

"I wouldn't say I've dropped it—let's just say I'm being careful before I pick up the next rock to look under. And maybe I'm just being paranoid, but I think you gotta be more careful if you continue digging into this. Especially as you ain't sharing all you have to share with me. So I got you a present." He reaches into his inside jacket pocket and hands Rourke a folded piece of buff paper.

"What is it?" asks Rourke as she takes it from him.

"A license," he replies.

Rourke grins darkly. "A marriage license, Jake? I thought you'd never ask."

"Sorry to disappoint, toots, but this is for something less deadly than marriage—this . . ." He reaches into his coat pocket and places a small rectangular box on the desk. Rourke flicks the lid open and stares at the box's contents for a moment in silence.

"Jake, I—"

"It'll put my mind at rest, Mary. Do you know how to use one?"

She considers lying but changes her mind. "Yes. Yes, I do."

"But you don't already have one?"

"No." She takes the palm-sized pistol from the box and examines it. It is black and silver and looks too small to be a weapon. She looks up at him. "But there's one thing you ought to know before I accept this."

"What?"

"Don't ever call me 'toots' again when I have a gun in my hand."

Kendrick laughs and holds up his hands. "It's a deal." Again she thinks how boyish he can look when the weight he habitually carries is temporarily lifted. She knows herself that history can weigh heavy. There had been a Mrs. Kendrick, she knows, just like there had been a Mr. Rourke. Past-tense spouses: cancer had taken one, and a German artillery shell the other.

And, of course, history has given Mary Rourke another load to carry. One that nearly broke her.

She places the box with the gun in her desk drawer.

"I think the place for that is your purse," says Kendrick. "At least until you sort out whatever it is you need sorted out. The permit is for a carry."

"I won't leave home without it. Thanks for the information, Jake. Anything else you can get on Huston and Stratton would be good. So long as it doesn't mean you running foul of McAfee."

"Sure thing, Mary. Can I ask a favor in return? Could you cast an eye over something for me?"

Rourke leans back in her chair and is rewarded with a dull jolt of pain. "Sure, Jake."

Kendrick reaches into his inside pocket and places four photographs on the desk in front of Rourke. Head-and-shoulders publicity shots of four women, more girls than women, each heavily made up and each smiling coquettishly over a raised shoulder or with finger coyly lifted to dimpled cheek. They are the kind of cheesy publicity shots that cross studio desks every day. The girls are unexceptionally pretty, and Rourke recognizes the work of a second-rate photographer.

"What's this all about, Jake?" she asks.

"I just want you to take a look at these girls, Mary. Tell me if you've seen any of them around. You know, looking for screen work, that kind of thing."

She leans forward and examines each of the girls. "Can't say I do, Jake. Why? Are you moonlighting as a talent agent now?"

"Take a good look at them, Mary. Please."

She frowns and looks again. "Sorry, Jake, I don't recognize any of them, but I'm not the best person to ask. I can see if anyone in Casting has come across them. What's the deal with them?"

"Something that came across my desk almost by accident. Four girls, all aspiring actresses, at least one also an occasional pro-skirt."

"It happens, Jake. You know that. A lot of girls come looking for stardom, run out of cash, and have to turn to prostitution to make ends meet. I wouldn't have thought that makes them a priority for Hollywood Division."

"They're not. And, like I say, maybe only one turned pro. The reason I'm asking is because they've all gone missing."

"That happens too, Jake. Girls try their luck with the studios, strike out, then get the late-night bus back to Sticksville in Alabama or Dakota or Kansas or wherever they came from."

Kendrick places another photograph on the table. It is another head-and-shoulders shot, but this time against the white porcelain of a morgue dissection table. Her eyes are half open, her lips dark and parted. The photograph brings back to her recall the image, briefly illuminated under the stark mortuary light, of Norma Carlton lying in the Appleton Clinic.

"This is the only one to be found. Lucille Quimby," explains Kendrick. "She went missing the same way as the others, except this time she was found dumped. She had been strangled."

"Strangled?" asks Rourke, keeping her expression blank.

"Narrow ligature," says Kendrick. "Maybe a tie."

Again the image of Carlton on the morgue slab, an angry, bruise-edged red mark around her neck, flashes into Rourke's mind. She shakes her head. "You know, Jake, this town can be the best place in the world to be a woman. Or the worst. Why did you bring these to me?"

"Like you say, so many girls like these pass through Hollywood, and most of them try out for a studio. You're the most connected person I know in Hollywood."

"That's not the first time someone's said that to me," she remarks glumly. "You have no other leads?"

He shakes his head.

"Okay, Jake. Let me see what I can find out. But I can't promise anything. Girls come here to become famous and often end up more anonymous than when they arrived. But I'll ask around."

"Thanks, Mary." Kendrick picks his hat up from the desk, smooths back his thick dark-blond hair with his free hand, and puts on his hat. "Oh, one other thing. The guy you asked about—the one who works the security gate up at Huston and Stratton's place, Mount Laurel."

"The guy with the scar? You got something on him?"

"His name is George Blevins, out of Kansas. He seems a tough cookie. You were right about that mess on his face being a war wound. It would appear he was quite the war hero, by all accounts. Served with distinction in France with the AEF. Came back with a chest-full of medals and a face-full of shrapnel. I had a quiet word with Jimmy Delgado, who works the patrol car for Mount Laurel. He does a drive-by a couple of times a week and sometimes makes a stop at the gatehouse for a coffee and a smoke with the security guys. Two of them are ex-cops. But Blevins seems to be a bit of a loner, keeps himself to himself. He works general security, but both Huston and Stratton have used him on occasions as a bodyguard. The closest he's come to being busted in L.A. was when some drunk took a swing at Robert Huston. Blevins gave him a smacking that was a little too enthusiastic and a little too professional. Apart from that, he has no criminal record that I can find. What's the deal, Mary? Why are you interested in this lug in particular?"

"Just let's say you're right, Jake, and that my brakes quitting on me wasn't a mechanical failure—or at least a mechanical failure that wasn't helped along some. The brakes were working just fine on the way to Mount Laurel; then they weren't on the way back. In between, the car was left unattended on a lot next to gorgeous George's security cabin."

"If that's a serious accusation," says Kendrick, "then I think I should go up personally and have words with Blevins. Maybe bring him in for an hour or two and discourage him from his ways."

"No," says Rourke emphatically. "I could have it all wrong. Even if I am right, I don't want him to know I suspect him. In any case, from what you've said about his background, he's not the kind to be discouraged by a roughing up from the police."

Kendrick sighs and shakes his head. "You're holding out on me, Mary. You don't get spooked easy, and people don't go about sabotaging other people's brakes for no reason—"

"If that's what happened . . ."

"If that's what happened. But let's face it, the fact that you think it's a possibility means there's a hell of a lot more going on than you're admitting. I could help you a lot more if I saw the whole picture."

Rourke regards him for a moment, the confession sitting itchily behind her lips. She swallows it.

"Listen, Jake, you're right—there is more going on. But I can't tell you. If I were to tell you, it would put us both in a difficult position. But I still need your help."

"When you say 'difficult position,' I take it you mean we'd be on opposite sides of the law?"

"If that were the case, then I need you to believe that it would be by omission, not commission. Someone has played the system—played me—is all I can say at the moment. It's a mess I'm trying to straighten out, and, to be honest, I don't see how I can without your help."

Kendrick frowns and holds her in a steady gray gaze. Eventually he says, "Okay, Mary, what can I do?"

25

The chapel is already almost full to capacity. Everyone who is anyone has turned out to applaud Norma Carlton's final curtain call. Director Paul Brand, producer Clifford J. Taylor, and all the principal cast and crew of *The Devil's Playground* are there, and the remaining seats are occupied by Hollywood's most famous faces. There's nothing like a good funeral, thinks Rourke, to get your face back in the public eye.

Rourke takes in the constellation of stars that dress the body of the chapel: she sees Clara Bow, Lillian and Dorothy Gish, Gilda Gray, and Louise Brooks. Douglas Fairbanks is there with his wife, Mary Pickford; Norma Talmadge with her studio-exec husband, Joe Schenck. Greta Garbo is there, pointedly distant from John Gilbert, who sits next to John Barrymore and Barrymore's co-star and current inamorata, Dolores Costello.

The moon-pale complexions and kohl-shadowed eyes of Pola Negri and Theda Bara compete for the greatest drama as they gaze out in studied sorrow; Gloria Swanson uses her thousand-dollar black mourning dress and matching turban as a contrast backdrop for a dazzle of platinum and diamonds.

The powerful are as well represented as the famous: Rourke notices the small, squat frame of Louis Mayer squeezed into a pew next to the aristocratic lankiness of D. W. Griffith. The Lasky-Paramount partners—Jesse Lasky, Adolph Zukor, and Cecil B. DeMille—sit together, though Sam Goldwyn is two rows back, next to Jack Warner and Darryl Zanuck. King Vidor has his head tilted in hushed conversation with his wife, Eleanor Boardman. Across the aisle from Rourke, she sees a thin, older woman dab her eyes with a handkerchief. Rourke recognizes her as the talent agent Margot Drescher, who had represented Norma Carlton.

She scans the rest of the assembled mourners and is surprised that she can find no trace of Hiram Levitt.

"Everything in place?" asks Harry Carbine, drawing Rourke from her who's-who inventory. He is dressed in a double-breasted suit: black wool threaded through with fine dark-red pinstripes, a black silk tie shimmers at his throat. He is, as always, perfectly dressed for the occasion. He sits with Rourke on one side, his wife on the other.

"Don't worry, boss—this little operation makes Black Jack Pershing's battle planning look shoddy," answers Rourke. "Sam Geller and his boys are outside, keeping the press far enough away so they can see everything but not get a good look at anything. They're more interested in getting pictures of famous faces arriving than anything else, so we've got the newsies and the photographers corralled where the limos make their drops."

"I see you managed to track down Norma's folks." Carbine nods to the front row of mourners, separated from the rest of the congregation by a barrier of silk rope. An older woman sits weeping, two younger women, on either side, comforting her. The faces of all three are concealed by mourning veils. "Hiram Levitt point you in the right direction after all?"

"No. Not at all. It's a staged setup. Again for the press to see from a distance. Interring Norma Carlton's ashes with no relatives to be seen might attract the wrong kind of press interest. So the 'sisters' are Sylvie, and Nancy from Publicity; the mother is Betsy Colman."

"Betsy Colman? The same Betsy Colman I cast in *Eternal Sorrows*?"

"That's her."

"Christ, Mary," hisses Carbine. "Betsy Colman's a complete lush. She could drink Bill C. Fields under the table. No one's cast her in five years because she was permanently hammered on set—"

"Well, she's sober today. And this is the best-paid job she's had in years. I told her to stay off the sauce for a day and to make sure she never lifts her veil. She'll be whisked away immediately after the service because she's 'too overwrought.' Had to do it, boss. I need to throw the press something to photograph. Like I say, from a distance."

Carbine is about to reply when all heads turn at the sound of the chapel doors opening again. Like the rest of the congregation, Rourke and Carbine turn to see Robert Huston and Veronica Stratton as they make their way in. And it is a real entrance—for a second time, Rourke feels like Stratton believes she's under studio lights, playing a part.

"Perfect timing," she whispers to Carbine. "I bet she had her chauffeur do the circuit a couple of times so she could make sure everyone was seated before she came in."

Robert Huston solicitously ushers his wife into a pew. As he does so, he looks in Rourke's direction. Their eyes meet for the thinnest sliver of a second; then he looks away, but there is something about that look, something in his expression, that troubles Rourke.

"I'm talking to First National about her," says Carbine.

"What?" Rourke frowns, confused as her thoughts are brought back to the moment.

"Veronica Stratton. I have a new movie ready to go into the works, and it was conceived entirely as a Norma Carlton vehicle. Norma had a beautiful voice, and I was thinking of going talkie with it. Clifford Taylor wants me to sign up Carole Ventris, the stand-in we've got for Norma, but she's too green and too unknown. Without Norma, I need a star—a big star, to fill the slot. If it goes ahead, I mean."

"You didn't tell me about this before."

Harry Carbine turns to her, clearly taken aback by her tone of admonition. No one admonishes Harry Carbine.

"I have to clear studio decisions with you?"

"Did Veronica Stratton know about this new Carlton vehicle?" persists Rourke.

"We've talked about it, yes."

"Before or after Norma's death?"

"After." Carbine frowns. "Of course after. Why?"

"Nothing."

Their hushed conversation is stilled by the entrance of the pastor.

Rourke doesn't listen to the service. Instead, as she sits in empty-eyed and bruised discomfort on the chapel pew, she thinks of what Carbine has just told her, the strange look she got from Robert Huston, and tries to work out why she again has such an uneasy feeling in her gut.

—

After the service, Rourke steps out with the others into incongruously bright sunlight. Scanning the departing crowds, she spots several stars being ushered into their limousines. The well-oiled machine of studio publicity and star management runs smooth and quiet. She catches sight of a small older woman behind everyone else, slowly walking down the chapel driveway. Rourke recognizes her as Renata, Norma Carlton's Mexican servant; the one she had paid off at Carlton's house the night the movie star was found dead. When she sees the maid begin to leave on foot, Rourke turns to Carbine and his wife and excuses herself. She has to trot to catch up with the maid.

In Spanish, they speak for a while about the service and how sad an occasion it is. The maid explains that she was not able to come inside the church, but that she had wanted to pay her respects. Rourke feels sorry for Renata, whose sadness is refreshingly genuine—but she also feels glad that she's run into the maid, given that she hadn't known she was dealing with a murder when they last spoke. Now is her chance to ask unasked questions.

"Do you know what I think we both really could do with right now?" asks Rourke with a smile. "A strong cup of coffee."

Rourke's sympathy for the maid increases on the short drive into downtown Glendale. Renata seems ill-at-ease in the expensive automobile, dark hands kneading the black leather handbag on her lap. Rourke parks on Brand Boulevard and guides her into the small café next to the Central Hotel. It is clear that Renata feels even less at ease in these surroundings, despite the café being none too glitzy. Her unease is probably compounded by the close-to-indignant scrutiny of the middle-aged waitress who comes to serve them. Rourke notices the waitress cast an appraising eye over her as well, obviously assessing the origins of Rourke's dark hair and complexion, and the fact that she speaks to Renata in fluent Spanish.

She orders two coffees and some cakes, and the stone-faced waitress turns wordlessly from the table.

Rourke spends the next five minutes making small talk, trying to put Renata at her ease. After the coffee and cakes are placed before them unceremoniously, she notices the maid's reluctance to help herself to the cakes; she holds the plate out to her. "Go on, have one. If I eat all these it'll ruin my waistline."

Renata mutters her thanks and takes one. Not for the first time, it strikes Rourke how this town can elevate women beyond anything they could know outside it, yet also crush them into subservience and worse. She asks Renata if she has found another position, to which she says she has, but Rourke can see that the older woman is not at all happy with her new employment. She does, however, make a point of thanking Rourke again for the money and the references.

After Rourke has eased into the subject, she begins to discuss the days before Carlton's death.

"I was surprised that Miss Carlton only had you working for her. With a house that size, I would have thought she would have had other staff. You know, with parties and suchlike—wasn't that too much for you to manage on your own?"

"Oh no, señora—Miss Carlton was very easy to work for. Very good to work for. She did have parties, but not very often at all. And when she did, she hired in a company to cater them—but she always left me in charge." The tired sadness in Renata's face is temporarily replaced with pride. "But she was a very private person. People don't understand that—that she liked to keep herself private, keep her home private. She went to a lot of movie-business parties and events, but hardly ever hosted anything in her own home."

"So it was just you and her most of the time in the house?"

"Mostly just me. Señora Carlton spent most of her time at home when she was filming, but other than that, she would be away a lot. It meant that I could clean all the house without needing anyone else to help me."

"She was away a lot?"

"Yes. And sometimes for a long time."

"Where did she go?"

"I don't know. She told me that I didn't need to worry about callers, because her agent, Miss Drescher, would take care of all that." Renata frowns. "Maybe I should have asked more. But she was the best employer I ever had, and the work was not so hard. Miss Carlton was very happy with my work."

"I'm sure she was, Renata." Rourke pauses to sip her coffee. "Did she ever talk to you about her past? About where she had come from?"

"No. She was very kind and friendly, and we would talk often, but I knew there were things she wouldn't talk about. Like I said, she was very private. Even with me."

"What about gentleman friends? She must have entertained them?"

Something approaching prudish disapproval flits across Renata's face.

"It's all right, Renata," says Rourke. "This is between us. It's important I know these things, and the señora would want you to answer me honestly."

"You don't understand," she replies. "There were men came to the house. Often. But none of them . . ." She struggles for the best description. "None of them spent *private* time with her. I think they must have been connected to the studio, or to some other business."

"Did you ever hear what kind of business was discussed?"

"No. Not really. But . . ." The maid frowns.

"What is it, Renata?"

"Sometimes it was strange. Sometimes I got the feeling that the men who came were—well—*afraid* of her."

"Was there anyone in particular you remember visiting? I mean, someone who came more than the others."

"There was one man came often. He had very dark hair and very dark eyes—but very pale complexion. Always very smartly dressed. He looked like a businessman. Not film business, but business, like a lawyer or something."

Rourke frowns as the description strikes a nerve. "This dark-haired man, what was his name? Was it Levitt? Hiram Levitt?"

"I don't know. No one gave their name. If I asked, they just said that Miss Carlton was expecting them."

"But this man came more than others?"

"Yes. Sometimes once a week, which was a lot, because Miss Carlton had so few visitors to the house."

"So you would say he was a special friend of Miss Carlton's?"

Renata shakes her head emphatically. "No, no, señora. Not at all friends. I always thought it was business. He and Miss Carlton talked often, in her study. But I don't think that she liked him."

"Oh? Why?"

"Just the way they talked to each other. Sometimes I would hear like an argument. One time I heard their voices really raised."

"Did you hear anything that was said?"

"No, señora. My English, like you know, is not very good. I missed things that were said. Anyway, I did not want to intrude. I have been a maid in Hollywood for twenty-five years, I have learned it is best to know when not to see, when not to hear. And in any case, Miss Carlton trusted me, and I never betrayed her trust." The thought seems to sit ill with Renata; she places her coffee cup back in the saucer and looks at Rourke with something like suspicion conquering her habitual subservience. "You said it is very important for you to know all these things— why? Why are you asking so many questions about Miss Carlton?"

"It's very simple, Renata," says Rourke with a reassuring smile. "It's the same reason we went through everything at the house the night Miss Carlton died. When someone like her dies, someone important, a big star, there are always people who want to say bad things about them. Make accusations that they can no longer defend. It's like all of the things that people were saying about Rudolph Valentino after he died last year—even Pola Negri claiming to be his fiancée, when there was no proof. My job is to make sure I can defend Miss Carlton's memory. Do you understand? I just want to make sure no one says bad things about her or starts bad rumors or spreads lies. It's like what I said to you that night: that Miss Carlton's death was a misadventure, an accident, not suicide. There are people in the press and elsewhere who would love to say it was suicide and make up all kinds of stories about why she did it. If you had seen how distraught Miss Carlton's mother was at the funeral service, you would understand—we really don't want her to suffer more by having her daughter's name dragged through the mud. Now do you understand?"

"I understand," says the maid, but Rourke can see she still has suspicions.

"Was there anyone else who visited regularly?"

"There was Miss Drescher, Miss Carlton's agent. I knew who she was. She would come over every now and then. Not as much as the businessman, but often. And they talked on the phone a lot. I liked Miss Drescher, she was very nice."

"No one else?"

"No . . ." Renata frowns. "Not visited, but a young woman would telephone. I could always tell by the way Miss Carlton spoke to her. Like they were very close."

"How do you know it was a young woman?"

"I could tell from her voice. I answered the telephone to her once. I asked who was calling, but she just said it was a personal call."

"But I thought you weren't allowed to answer the phone, Renata. . . ."

"It was after that. After I spoke to the young woman. Miss Carlton said it would be better if I didn't answer the telephone because my English was not so good. She was very nice about it. Said I had enough to do and she knew it was difficult for me. She said if anyone telephoned when she was out, they would always call back."

"And this was all after you answered the phone to this young woman?"

Renata nods.

Rourke thinks for a moment. "But there are no other visitors you can think of? What about Robert Huston? He must have visited often."

"No, señora—just once, maybe twice before that night. I knew who he was, of course."

Rourke's eyebrows rise in surprise. "Really? I thought he was around more often than that."

"No. I'm sure of that."

"Did Mr. Huston telephone that night?"

"Like I said, Miss Carlton told me not to answer the telephone because my English isn't good enough. I struggled to tell the police what had happened when I telephoned them."

"Okay—but did the telephone ring that night, whether you answered it or not?"

The maid frowns. "I can't remember, señora. I'm sorry—but you have to understand, I was very upset. But I don't think so."

"Okay, Renata." Rourke leans forward, resting elbows on the table. "I need you to think very carefully. Did you hear or see anything odd in the house that night? Anything out of the ordinary before you found Miss Carlton?"

"No . . . There was nothing unusual about that afternoon or evening, other than Miss Carlton said she didn't feel well. She said she was tired and had a headache and needed to lie down. She told me that she did not want anything to eat, and she was not to be disturbed until eight p.m. She asked that I wake her at eight and bring her some green tea." A tremor of emotion rumbles through Renata's voice. "I did what she said, and that was when I found her. I knew something was wrong when I saw she had changed into those clothes and that necklace. Why would she do that? If it's not suicide, why did she lay herself out like that? I tried to wake her, but—"

"It's all right, Renata. There was nothing you could have done," says Rourke. The maid's hand sits on the table, and Rourke places her black-gloved hand on it. "I promise you that."

Renata nods, struggling to hold back tears.

"But you didn't notice anyone else, anything else, that struck you as strange that evening?"

Renata thinks for a moment. "No, nothing at all that I can remember. I was surprised how quick the police arrived. Really within minutes of my telephoning. Then when señor Huston turned up at the door, all upset."

"That surprised you?"

"Yes."

"You didn't know that they were friends? *Close* friends?"

"Absolutely not. But I knew he was señora Stratton's husband. I thought maybe that was why he came round that night."

Rourke frowns, her expression confused. "I'm sorry, Renata, I don't understand. . . ."

"Señor Huston didn't visit often, but señora Stratton—she came round every now and then."

"Wait a minute—you're saying that Norma Carlton and Veronica Stratton were *friends*?"

"I don't know if they were friends, but she visited occasionally." Something lights up Renata's face. "I remember now: one time—just this one time—señora Stratton was there at the same time as the dark-haired man. The businessman . . ."

26

"Where the hell did you get to after the funeral service?" In a mountain-comes-to-Mohammed moment, Harry Carbine has made his way over to the publicity department and Mary Rourke's office. Now he stands in front of her desk. His expression and tone are more irritated than angry. "God knows, if I needed you anywhere, I needed you at the drinks function afterward. I got cornered by Frank Quinlan from the *Examiner*. That damned Mick's like an Irish terrier when he gets his teeth into you. He wouldn't let up with all this crap about *The Devil's Playground* being a cursed production, and kept asking for more details about exactly what kind of heart condition Norma had had and for how long, and had I known about it all along—all that kind of horsefeathers. Christ, Mary, that's the kind of crap I pay you to deal with."

"And that's the crap I'd be much happier dealing with, boss. But you sent me on this 'hero's journey' of yours, remember? I saw Norma Carlton's maid outside the chapel after the funeral, and I needed to ask her some questions. I didn't know the full deal with her death the night we moved her body—meaning there were questions I didn't have for her then that I have now."

Carbine nods thoughtfully. "Okay—so what did you find out?"

She runs through the conversation with him.

"So you think this dark-haired visitor was Hiram Levitt?" he asks.

"The description sure matches. And if it is Levitt, then he's been spinning me a yarn. He told me he hadn't been in regular contact with Norma for some time. But, then again, maybe it wasn't him. Although I found it odd that he didn't make an appearance at the service yesterday."

"So you going to follow this up with him?"

"That, boss," she says with a sigh, "was exactly what I was doing when you showed up. I telephoned him but got no reply. His routine is like clockwork, though—I'll try his usual places and times."

Carbine makes to turn and leave, but checks himself, frowning. "We need a distraction, Mary."

"A distraction?"

"Frank Quinlan won't let Norma's death go. If he starts looking into it seriously, he might get to the truth—whatever that is—before you do. After all, that's his business. And the *Examiner* isn't the only rag with a horse in this race—they all have the scent of something. A movie star's murder sells a lot of papers. And the headline 'Studio Covers Up Star's Murder' sells a hundred times more. At the very least, they've really got their teeth into the whole 'cursed production' nonsense. I agree that it's a good angle for the movie, but there's a real danger they're taking it too far. Maybe audiences will be afraid of being caught up in the curse and will shy away from the movie when we roll out. We need to get the press to point their cameras and aim their questions in a different direction."

"What do you have in mind?" asks Rourke.

"We're shooting the final scene next week. The one we discussed with you in the production office."

"When the whole set goes up in flames?"

Carbine nods. "The burning of Ouxbois. It's going to be spectacular. I'm going to invite some key investors over to see it. I thought you could pull in enough journos to get the kind of headlines we want for the movie."

"It's not a bad idea," says Rourke thoughtfully. "I'll get a team on it."

"Good. Are you going to see Hiram Levitt now?"

"Like I say, looks like I'll have to track him down at one of his usual haunts first."

"Then I'll let you get on with it. And let me know how it goes." He turns and heads out of her office.

"Harry . . ." she calls as he is framed in the doorway. He turns back. "What?"

"This is all getting a little heavy. The thing with my car . . . and there have been a couple of occasions where I've thought someone has been tailing me."

"You sure?"

"No, I'm not sure at all. But I've been more than a little jumpy ever since the accident. The point is, are you sure you don't want to turn this over to Sam Geller? Like you say, you pay me to deal with other stuff, not play Pinkerton."

"You want out?" Carbine frowns. "I'd rather you stayed with it."

Rourke thinks for a moment. "I'll stick with it for as long as you want me to—you know that. But Golem Geller is a professional at this kind of stuff."

Carbine nods thoughtfully, then leaves the doorway and comes back over to her desk.

"Okay, Mary, the way I see it is this: You're right, Sam is a professional. He's very obviously a professional, and he has a presence for it. But can you imagine how your Spanish maid friend would react to being quizzed by him? Or Veronica Stratton? Or any of the people you need to talk to in order to get to the bottom of this? We're navigating shallow waters here, Mary. I need someone who makes fewer waves. That someone is you. But if you want out . . ."

She sighs. "No . . . no, it's fine. Leave it with me."

He turns to leave again.

"And let me know how you get on with Hiram Levitt," his back tells her.

After Carbine leaves her office, Rourke goes over to the window, lights up a cigarette and smokes it in contemplation of a view she looks at but really isn't seeing. By the time she has finished smoking, she has a rough plan of her next moves. She goes back to her desk and tries telephoning Hiram Levitt once more, but again doesn't get an answer. She also tries for a third time to get hold of Madame Erzulie, but, as before, the connection rings out.

She grabs her jacket, purse, and keys and heads out of the office.

Margot Drescher's fourth-floor office has huge picture windows opening out onto Wilshire Boulevard, but she has her desk arranged so that her back is to the view, as if she is adamantly avoiding its distractions.

When Mary Rourke is shown into her office, the talent agent is in conversation; she has one thin hand wrapped around the telephone's candlestick body while the spider-jointed, crimson-varnish-tipped fingers of the other are pinched around the receiver she presses to her ear. Drescher is a thin, meager woman somewhere north of sixty with a face that is all hard angles and skin that has become leather-seasoned by more summers under the California sun than she would admit to. Her hair is dyed in what is now only a rough approximation of the red of her youth, her mouth an agile gash of crimson at the telephone's mouthpiece. Drescher is one of the most powerful agents in Hollywood, the type whose calls are always taken by studio executives, even movie moguls. She looks so much the part that she could have been sent up for the role by Central Casting.

As she talks on the telephone, however, her voice is soft and light, often spun through with laughter. Margot Drescher is indeed a tough and implacable negotiator; she is also known for her loyalty to her clients and for her keen, often biting, sense of humor. Mary Rourke has had only a few encounters with the actors' agent, but enough for her to come to like her.

Without breaking the flow of her conversation, Drescher nods vigorously to the chair across from her desk, indicating that Rourke should sit. As she does so, Rourke takes in the walls of the office, decorated with studio shots of the stars Drescher represents. She spots the same head-and-shoulders shot of Norma Carlton that Harry Carbine has commanding the corridor to his office. Rourke is beginning to feel haunted by the dead star's ghost.

"Hello, Mary," Margot Drescher says as she hangs the earpiece back in its cradle and beams a nicotine grin at Rourke. "It's been a while. I meant to talk to you after the funeral yesterday, but you took off somewhere." Her accent, despite those countless California summers, is pure Lower East Side. Rourke wonders if she moonlights giving Sam Geller elocution lessons.

"It *has* been a while, Margot. That's because you teach your clients well and they never get into the kind of trouble where they need me to intervene." She lets her smile dissolve. "I wanted to talk to you about Norma too—it's just I had to deal with something straight after the service. Her death has left everyone at the studio shocked."

"Me too—as you can imagine. Poor Norma. I still can't believe it.

Such a beautiful girl." Drescher stands up from behind her desk. She is five feet in heels. "You had lunch? We should have lunch."

Drescher doesn't wait for an answer but comes around the desk, fanning an impatient hand to indicate Rourke should get out of the chair. When she does, Drescher takes her proprietarily by the arm, and guides her out of the office door.

It seems everyone knows Margot Drescher, and likes her. The elevator man, people from other offices whom she and Rourke encounter as they cross the grand lobby of the building, even the news vendor they pass on the sidewalk—all exchange friendly words with her. She walks with a quick, electric energy that suggests her body is trying to keep pace with her mind.

They reach a luncheonette on the corner where, unsurprisingly, everyone again exchanges friendly words with Drescher.

"Counter or booth?" Drescher asks Rourke, and, again without waiting for an answer, says, "Booth. We should take a booth."

She guides Rourke to a bay by the window, and they both slide onto the glossy red leather bench seat.

"You're looking good, Mary. Real good. I could have gotten you parts you know, with looks like yours, back in the old days." She gives a sardonic laugh. "The old days . . . In this business that's anything before last week. No, I definitely could have gotten you parts. . . ." She shrugs one of her habitual shrugs, the thin crimson lips becoming an inverted U as she considers the idea. "But after you busted you-know-who's nose—after that, not so much."

"You're looking good yourself, Margot," says Rourke.

"Me?" She laughs. "Me, I look like something Lon Chaney's put together. But thanks—it's nice that you should lie."

They place their order. Once the waitress has gone, Drescher's smile fades.

"Why have you come across town to talk to me about Norma?" she asks. "Is there something going on I should know about?"

"No, Margot, I'm just trying to straighten a few things out."

"Mary, I know you and I know Harry Carbine—you didn't just stop by on a social whim to chat about Norma. So what is it? Are you trying to keep the studio clean of something?"

"No, nothing like that. It's just—well, there was some strange stuff going on in the background with her, and I'm trying to get to the bottom of it."

"What kind of strange stuff? I have to tell you, I don't much like what I'm hearing. I'll ask again, is there something I should know about?"

"Listen, Margot—I just don't want the press blindsiding us with stories we can't counter. The truth is, I'm hearing that Norma was caught up in some kind of weird occult stuff."

"Oh, that . . ."

"You knew?"

"I knew and I didn't know. I heard rumors. And Norma would come out with something every now and then. Norma was so very beautiful and so very smart—but she was also so very strange. Had a lot of weird beliefs—including all that mumbo-jumbo stuff. But that's not that unusual in this town. Rudy Valentino was obsessed with spiritualism, Clara Bow holds séances at her place, there are stories of black-magic covens in the Hills, every second movie star has a psychic adviser . . . It's all horse crap. I thought Norma would be too smart for that kind of thing, but I guess she wasn't."

"You hear of this Madame Erzulie woman?"

"She's an older woman. I heard she's stuck in a wheelchair, but I don't know if that's right. I knew Norma had something to do with her. So have a lot of the big names in Hollywood. When some of these bimbos and bimbas become fabulously successful and fabulously rich, it's such a strain for them, poor dears, so they go and seek meaning, whatever that is. A lot get involved in all kinds of supernatural nonsense. There's always some swami or spiritualist or theosophist or psychic fleecing the glamorous and gullible. From what I hear, this Madame Erzulie fleeces the best. I wish I'd gotten into the racket. It's an easier way to make money than being an agent."

"And Norma believed in spiritualism?"

"Not as such. She got into the voodoo nonsense that Madame Erzulie spouts. Especially about reincarnation."

"Reincarnation? I take it we're not talking about the Hiram Levitt kind?"

"No—Norma seemed obsessed with the idea of rebirth, transmigration of the soul, all that hoo-hah. Like I said, she never struck me as someone who would go for that sort of thing."

Rourke thinks over what Drescher has told her. "Thing is," she says eventually, "I really don't feel I understand Norma Carlton at all. And, from all the people I've spoken to who had any kind of connection with her, nor did anyone else. That's the real reason I've come to see you—to get a handle on who she was. Did you ever get to know anything about Norma's past? Like where she came from?"

"Well, you know the story: the daughter of a New York socialite, finishing school in Europe, some experience on the English and New York stage. . . ."

"Yeah, I know all that. I'm not talking about Hiram Levitt's fiction, I'm talking about fact: where she really came from."

Margot Drescher shrugs bony shoulders under silk. "In that case, your guess is as good as mine. I've always just taken her background at face value. Whether it's Levitt's fiction or not, I had to believe it and sell Norma to studios on the basis of it. And you know more than anyone that nobody in Hollywood is who or what they're made out to be. Theda Bara gets spat on in the street, you know. To the public she really is the 'Serpent of the Nile'—worshipper of ancient Egyptian gods, sex temptress, and wanton seducer of married men. No one wants to know that she's really Theda Goodman, daughter not of a tormented Italian sculptor father and passionate French actress mother, but of a Polish Jewish tailor."

Rourke laughs. "You mean Theda wasn't really raised in the shadows of the Sphinx and the Pyramid of Giza?" she asks in mock disappointment.

"Maybe she was—if the Sphinx and the Pyramid of Giza now happen to be located in Ohio, not Egypt. My point is, it's the fiction, not the reality, that sells. It's who Theda Bara is. For me, Norma Carlton was the backstory she gave me, whether that backstory was conjured up by the Resurrectionist or not."

"But you must have picked up on *something*," protests Rourke. "Some clue to her background?"

Drescher shakes her head. "The part Norma Carlton played best was the role of Norma Carlton. So much so that I believed in it completely. There were maybe a couple of times that the accent slipped, that there was something else there. But, then again, you know only too well that Hiram Levitt encourages his clients to take voice lessons. It's always seemed a bit much—after all, have you heard Clara Bow talk? She makes me sound like an English duchess. But with all this hubbub about speakies or talkies, or whatever they're going to call them, being the next big thing, Levitt getting them to do voice training isn't that bad an idea after all."

"So that's it? You represented her for ten years and that's as deep as your knowledge of her goes? You don't think there was something more to her?"

Margot Drescher again shrugs thin shoulders. "I didn't say that, Mary. The truth is, I knew all I *needed* to know about her. Sure, I would have liked to get to know her better, understand her better. But it's like you said about everyone else who crossed her path—all you knew about Norma Carlton is what Norma Carlton let you know. And if there is anything more, anything darker, lying hidden in her past, then either it's gone to the grave with her or it's all locked up in Hiram Levitt's files."

Rourke nods contemplatively. Their lunches arrive.

"What about Norma's only marriage? To the director Theo Woolfe?"

Drescher makes a scornful face. "You know, after the Santa Barbara earthquake in '25, I read that California has earthquakes all the time, almost every day, but most are so small and fleeting they barely register; no one notices them. That's what her marriage was like—brief, and so insignificant you'd miss it if you blinked. And take my word for it, the earth definitely did not move for Norma. Pity, he had something, old Theo—unfortunately, that something wasn't talent or personality. She got her divorce after he threatened her with a gun. She would have gotten it earlier if she could have proved he made her sit through one of his movies. Now, *that* would be mental cruelty."

"She had no contact with him afterward?"

"When he was in the nuthouse? No, definitely not. As far as I know, he's still locked up—unless he was moved to a home for the incurably talentless. But there's no way she ever visited him."

Rourke thinks for a moment. "Did you know Norma was involved with Robert Huston?"

"Bob Huston?" Drescher asks through a mouthful of Prosperity Sandwich. "No, I didn't. Doesn't surprise me much, though. Norma would often close in on a co-star if she liked the cut of his jib—or the length of it. But I didn't hear anything specific about Huston. I'd'a thought Veronica Stratton would have worn his balls for earrings if she found out."

"That's what I would have thought too, but apparently not. In fact, it seems that Veronica Stratton and Norma were well acquainted. Well acquainted enough for Stratton to make visits to Norma's house."

The talent agent's agile face takes the shape of disbelief. "Are you sure about that? I would be very surprised—everyone knows they hated each other."

"The more I learn about Norma Carlton's life, the less credence I place on what everyone thinks they knew about her," says Rourke disconsolately. "Was she involved particularly with any other men, that you know of?"

"Your guess is as good as mine. But if she was, then I doubt it would have been anything *particular*. Norma had affairs with all the usual suspects but no attachments, if you know what I mean. She swore that no man would ever control her, or think he was in a position to control her." Drescher frowns. "In fact, she was so vehement about that that it was like an obsession with her. She wanted men, but discarded them afterward. She treated them as if they were a habit that she hated but couldn't give up, like smoking. So there were men, all right—but specifics? Specifics I can't give you."

"But you saw her often? As her agent. You were up at the house frequently."

Drescher's large eyes narrow in suspicion. "How did you know that?"

"I talked to the maid," Rourke confesses.

"Renata?" asks Drescher. "Poor old girl, she was devoted to Norma. Is she okay?"

"I've made sure she's okay."

"I see. Good. Yes, I saw Norma at her house. I don't know, I felt responsible for her. I liked to check on her from time to time."

"Norma Carlton doesn't strike me as the kind of woman who needed a nursemaid."

"No . . . me neither. But there was . . . I don't know . . . There was something *missing* in her. Anyway, she seemed to tolerate my company. Not that she spent a lot of time in the house. You were in it; didn't you get the feeling it was unlived in?"

"When I saw it, it wasn't under the best circumstances. Renata also told me a man fitting Hiram Levitt's description visited often. In fact, he was Norma's most frequent visitor, she said."

"Really?" says Drescher. "I doubt it was Levitt. What would she want with the Resurrectionist now? He did his reinvention job on her a decade ago."

"That's if this guy *is* Hiram Levitt. But according to Hiram, he and Norma had stayed close. Old and close friends, was more or less the way he put it."

Drescher makes a face. "Now, that's complete *shtuss*, Mary—horse crap if ever I heard it. Norma never gave away much, but this much I do know, she couldn't stand the little shit."

"Yeah," says Rourke. "I got that impression. Renata told me she heard Norma and this guy arguing. So, if it was Levitt, why would he be around so much?"

"Beats me," says Drescher. "Maybe you should ask Levitt."

"That," says Rourke wearily, "is exactly what I've been trying to do."

They eat in silence for a while. When they're finished, Rourke leans forward.

"There's one more thing you can help me with."

"Name it." Drescher sips her coffee.

"Put me in touch with Nathan Milcom."

"The screenwriter of *The Devil's Playground*? The one who I've made sure even Harry Carbine and Paul Brand have never met?" She replaces her cup in its saucer and shrugs with overdone nonchalance. "Sure thing, Mary. Let me just write down his address for you."

"I'm being serious, Margot."

"So am I. There are very good reasons I am protecting my client. Sorry, Mary, it's a no-can-do."

"At least think about it."

"Why would you want to talk to Milcom? What's he got to do with anything?"

"He's got everything to do with this movie. And I can't shake off the feeling that this movie has got something to do with Norma's death."

"While we're on that subject, what version of Norma's death are we talking about, Mary?" Drescher smiles knowingly. "The Norma-committing-suicide version, or the Norma-having-a-secret-heart-condition version?"

"What version do you subscribe to?" asks Rourke.

"The one where the circumstances of Norma's death have gotten Harry Carbine getting his best fixer—his best brains—to do the kind of sniffing that he would normally have Golem Geller do. The version where there is more to Norma's death than meets the eye and a huge investment goes down the toilet if the truth comes out. That's my version—but I didn't push you on it. I don't know why you're having to keep things quiet, but I respect you enough not to push me."

"Okay, Margot. Forget it."

Drescher sighs. "There's no way you're ever going to meet Nathan Milcom, or find out anything about him from me. But I tell you what, I will ask him if there's anything he can tell me about Norma Carlton and all of the crazy stuff going on, and if he thinks the movie has anything to do with it. Sound fair?"

Rourke smiles. "Sounds fair. Thank you."

27

There is something wrong. Hiram Levitt is a creature of unbreakable habit, of rigid schedule—someone who builds structure and order into his personal and working life in an effort to separate himself from the chaos and excess that surround him.

Except now that unbreakable habit had been broken.

Rourke telephones him that afternoon and evening, again without success. She visits Salvaggi's later that night, but no one there has seen the Resurrectionist. It is when she calls into the Hollywood Boulevard restaurant the following day that someone starts ringing a fire bell in the back of her mind.

She recognizes the handsome waiter from her last visit and asks him when he last saw Levitt.

"Mr. Levitt is always here for lunch at twelve noon," he explains. "But this is the third day he hasn't turned up. I hope he isn't ill."

"I'm sure he's just fine," Rourke says in empty reassurance as she hands the waiter five dollars and a card with her number on it. "Please ring me at that number if he should come in."

Back at the studio, she calls into the office of Phyliss Morrow, who is Carbine International's casting director. It is she who supplies lists of likely candidates for audition to the producers and directors. Without explaining the background, Rourke shows her the photographs Kendrick had supplied her of the missing girls. Morrow, a tall, thin woman with putty-colored hair and the mien of a schoolmarm, looks at each in turn, shaking her head.

"No. 'fraid not, Miss Rourke," she says as she hands the pictures back. Then she frowns. "Wait a minute, may I see the last one again?"

Rourke hands her the picture.

"I'm not entirely sure, but I think she may be in the audition register. Do you have a name?"

"That one is Sadie Ehrlich. She may also go by Sadie Weston."

"Can you leave this with me?" asks Morrow. "Give me a couple of hours."

"Sure. Thanks, Phyliss. I'm going out for a while. I'll check back in with you later."

Rourke calls Kendrick from her office, but is told he isn't on duty for another hour. She holds down the receiver bracket for a couple of seconds, then dials Hiram Levitt's number. Again there is no answer. She telephones the main desk of his apartment block but is told rather snootily by the concierge that, no, he hasn't seen Mr. Levitt for a while, but, no, that doesn't mean he has not been in the building.

A third call is just as fruitless: this time an unsuccessful fifth attempt to speak to Madame Erzulie. No male voice this time; the call simply goes unanswered. Replacing the earpiece in its bracket, she stands up, checks the West Hollywood address again, picks up her jacket and heads out of her office.

"Sylvie—I'll be back in an hour or so," she calls to her assistant as she breezes through the main publicity office and out into the sunlight. In the lot, she sits in her automobile for a moment before starting it up. It smells new: burnished walnut and polished leather, vinegar-water-rinsed windshield and windows, the rich nutty odor from the newly waxed fabric of its convertible top, a hint of engine oil. Her own reticence to start the engine irritates her: she had promised herself to put the accident out of her mind. This is a new car, she tells herself, a different car. Different brakes.

She starts the engine and drives out through the studio's arched gateway.

Whatever Madame Erzulie's clairvoyant abilities are, she clearly has a talent for seeing where the money is, thinks Rourke as she pulls into the driveway. The medium's house is huge and Gothic, sitting on a lot of an acre or more of manicured gardens bounded by expensive stone-and ironwork. The house itself is over three stories and is all overblown oriels, latticed windows, and finial-tipped peaked gables. To one side of the house is a building that has been styled to be reminiscent of a nineteenth-century coach house but comprises a triple garage for automobiles with rooms above it.

She walks along a stone-chipped driveway to the front door, rings the doorbell and waits, but gets no answer. Going around to the back of the house, she finds another door and she knocks, again without success. Walking back around to the side of the house, she leans into one of the leaded windows and looks in, cupping her hands around her eyes. The room she looks into is crammed with dark furniture, sculptures, and art. Paintings lie stacked against the marble fireplace, and there are stacks of books and other objects sitting on the floor. Some furniture is already shrouded in dust covers, and Rourke sees packing crates sitting patiently waiting to be filled.

Madame Erzulie, it seems, has foreseen new pastures.

A painting leans against the wall facing Rourke and it captures her attention. Her view of it is only partly obstructed, and she can see it is brightly colored and almost abstract in style, sitting discordantly with the rest of the self-consciously Gothic items in the room. The painting shows a large snake, almost rainbow colored, describing a writhing oval shape. The snake's gaping mouth is sinking fangs into its own tail, as if eating itself. It troubles Rourke that she has seen something similar somewhere recently but can't place where or when.

"What do you think you are doing?"

The male voice behind her gives her a start. She spins around to see that a man has come up behind her. Tall and muscular, tough-looking, with a thick mop of butter-colored hair, and very pale blue eyes that are narrowed and fixed on her. The man is jacketless, his white shirt-sleeves rolled up past his elbows. He holds a rag, which he uses to wipe engine grease from his hands.

Mary Rourke recognizes his voice as the one who answered the phone.

"I'm looking for Madame Erzulie. I spoke to you before. I told you I needed to speak to her as a matter of urgency."

"I remember. Why?"

"Why do you remember? Maybe because I have an unforgettable voice."

He ignores the joke. "Why do you need to speak to Madame Erzulie?"

"I have questions."

"About what?" He looks from her face to his hands, which he continues to work at to clean of engine grease. The casualness of the gesture is overdone, and Rourke senses an insecurity.

"Maybe I want my tea leaves read."

"That's not the kind of thing Madame Erzulie does."

"No? Pity. Who are you, by the way?" she asks.

"I'm Jansen." Again, she senses his unease. "I work here. For Madame Erzulie."

"Then you should know where she is."

"Out of town."

"I see specificity isn't your strong suit," says Rourke. "Where out of town?"

"Back east. New York. She had some business to attend to. What is this all about?"

"When will she be back?"

"Hard to say."

"That a fact? Presumably, she'll mail you your paychecks. What about you, Jansen? You going out of town anytime soon?"

"What's that got to do with you?"

"Oh, nothing. I'm just a friendly and inquisitive kind of gal."

"That's the kind I don't like."

"Oh? Which? Friendly or inquisitive?"

"Nosy."

"Not like the girls back home, eh?" Rourke mimics a Midwestern accent. "Where you from, Jansen? Swedish name, prairie accent. Minnesota? Kansas?"

"I gotta get back to work. You should leave."

Rourke ignores him. "Say—I bet you see a lot of famous people here . . . movie stars and the like."

"I just do my work. . . ."

"But you must see people coming and going." She makes a face as if an idea has just come to her. "What about the movie star Norma Carlton? Did you ever see Norma Carlton here?"

That hits home. Rourke sees a reaction flit across Jansen's expression before it's suppressed.

"Like I said, I mind my own business and get on with my work. You said on the telephone you was from a studio. Why should I answer any of your questions?"

"If you prefer, I could get the police to drop by and ask them."

"The police? What's anything got to do with the police?"

"You know, it really is odd," says Rourke with an "Isn't it the darnedest thing?" expression, "but almost everything has something to do with the police if they look at it hard enough. Voodoo snake oil, like the type your employer peddles, doesn't stand up to too much of their scrutiny, I'd say."

"I got work to do," he repeats.

"Don't let me stop you." She looks beyond him to the coach house. One set of garage doors is open, and she can see an automobile inside with its hood up. A gray sedan.

Jansen's eyes narrow. "Maybe it's me who should call the cops."

"Maybe . . . But the way things are looking, I don't think your employer would want too much police attention."

"Now, it ain't right, you coming here and throwing around accusations and insults." He steps forward in an attempt to intimidate Rourke, but she stands her ground. "I've asked you polite to leave. I ain't going to be so polite the next time."

Rourke's expression hardens. "The Heidis and the Helgas back home go for that tough-guy thing, do they? You know something, I don't like chawbacon lugs who throw their weight around with women. Maybe we should just get the police involved and see what they say."

"I don't want no trouble," he says, and takes a step back. "But I just gotta look after the place, is all. Madame Erzulie ain't here, and I don't know when she'll be back. So I've answered your questions. Now, I'm asking you to leave. I got work to get on with."

"Like packing up some of those crates I saw in there? Madame Erzulie's trip permanent, is it?" He doesn't answer. Rourke regards him coldly for a while, then smiles brightly and waves a hand with exaggerated airiness. "Well, see yah, country boy."

She walks back to where she's parked her car, deliberately not looking back. She doesn't need to: she knows he's still standing there, watching her.

As she drives back into town, Rourke repeatedly checks her mirror to make sure she has no gray sedan shadow. She hasn't. At the corner of Sunset and Laurel Canyon, she pulls up at the curb and calls into the

Haverfield drugstore. She knows the Bell pay telephone at the rear of the store affords more privacy than most.

Her first call is to the studio, to Phyliss Morrow in Casting. Morrow confirms that she had been right: Sadie Ehrlich was on their books, registered as Sadie Weston. The address she had registered was one of those rooming houses set up to offer ingenues new to Hollywood a place of relative safety, and away from predatory types. Rourke thanks Morrow, but thinks to herself that this won't be anything that Kendrick doesn't already know.

"Did we cast her in anything?" asks Rourke.

"No . . . not that I can see," says Morrow. "She was called by the studio three times to do extra work. She either didn't call back or turn up for any of them, so she was filed inactive. You know, studio policy. Happens all the time—these girls get something else or go home."

"Thanks, Phyliss," says Rourke.

"One thing I noticed," says Morrow, "is that there was another girl at the same address registered with us at the same time. Maybe they came in together, if that's any help. Just a minute . . . Got it: Betty Dupris. Like I say, same address. Anything else I can do, Miss Rourke?"

"No, thanks, Phyliss, that's great. Appreciate it."

Rourke hangs up. She next calls the precinct again, and this time gets through to Jake Kendrick.

"I was just on my way out," he says. "You're lucky you caught me."

She tells him what she found out about the missing girl's friend.

"That's great, thanks," says Kendrick. "Could I ask you a big favor?"

Rourke sighs. "Okay, hit me. . . ."

"I'm tied up on this retired-Louisiana-sheriff thing. And, anyway, these girls' boarding houses are cagey about men visitors, even those with a badge. Do you think you could see this Betty Dupris? You got the connection to the studio and all—you could make it seem like you're following up the contact."

"Don't you have female detectives these days? Why don't you send Alice Stebbins Wells? Or are you going to give me a badge to go with my gun?"

Kendrick laughs at the other end of the line. "I'd appreciate it, Mary. It makes it unofficial for now."

"I've got a hell of a lot going on at the moment, as you know." She sighs her acquiescence. "All right, I'll see what I can do."

"Thanks, Mary, you're a peach," says Kendrick. "By the way, you asked me about the names Armitage and Sudden Lake."

"What?" Rourke is momentarily confused, then remembers the enigmatic card she had found among Norma Carlton's belongings. "Oh . . . yes . . . Sorry, Jake, my mind's all over the place. You find anything out?"

"Nothing of any interest, really. John Kenneth Armitage is some kind of Wall Street type. Or was. He's sunk a pile into this hotel in the middle of the Mojave Desert. You know, like that inn they've just opened in Death Valley. It's the same kind of thing—except this one is on the shore of a big desert lake and has a movie theater. All I can find out is that Armitage has been looking for movie-business investors. He has this idea of setting up a kind of second Hollywood out there. Any help?"

"Yes—thanks, Jake. Just something I needed to check out. Not important." From what he has told her, Rourke decides Norma Carlton was probably just handed the card as a potential investor.

"Anything else I can do?" asks Kendrick. Rourke is about to ask him if he knows anything about Jansen, working out at Madame Erzulie's mansion, when she checks herself. Kendrick is smart, and if she gives him too many dots, he's going to start connecting them.

After she hangs up with Kendrick, she tries Hiram Levitt's number once more, again without success. She looks at her watch. It's half an hour across town if the traffic's not too bad. She collects her change from the pay telephone and heads back out to her automobile.

It is fitting that Rourke saw the movie star Norma Talmadge and her husband, Joseph M. Schenck, at Carlton's funeral service. The couple were known as clever investors and had put money into real estate. One of their investments took the solid and prestigious form of an elegant building of deluxe serviced apartments on the corner of Wilshire and Berendo. The three-year-old red-brick-and-white-stucco edifice had been named the Talmadge after its glamorous landlady, and had instantly become one of L.A.'s most desirable addresses. The couple had moved into its tenth floor, leasing out the other apartments to style-and-quality-conscious Hollywood tenants.

One of those tenants, whose apartment is on the third story, is

Hiram Levitt. Rourke parks across the street, next to the neighboring lot, which is ring-fenced and from which a scaffolding-clad shape is beginning to emerge. The Talmadge, she can see from the painted construction-site sign, is soon to rub shoulders with a Presbyterian church.

The doorman at the desk in the marbled reception hall has a military air about him and seems immune to Rourke's usual application of charms. Nevertheless, as requested, he rings Hiram Levitt's apartment, but gets no answer.

"He must be out," he says blankly, hanging up the telephone's earpiece. "Perhaps you can try again later."

"Listen, I'm very concerned about Mr. Levitt. No one has heard from him for a couple of days. Couldn't you let me in to check on him? You'd be with me the whole time."

"I'm afraid I can't do that, miss," he says. "Like I say, perhaps you can try again later. Excuse me—" He breaks off to deal, smilingly, with two tenants who engage him with a query. After they go, he turns back to Rourke, the smile slipping from his face like a fried egg from a greasy skillet. "Was there something else?"

"Yes." Rourke smiles charmingly. "May I use your telephone?"

"There is a pay telephone two blocks up, madam."

"I see—but this is a very urgent matter. If you won't let me use your telephone, then can you place the call for me? It's to Detective Jake Kendrick at LAPD. Could you tell him that I will wait for him here and could he bring some of his men? As I say, this is a very serious matter."

"Police?" Now she has the doorman's attention.

"Detective Kendrick owes me a favor or two. And I'm not leaving here until I'm sure that Mr. Levitt is safe. I can understand that you aren't happy about accompanying me to check on him—I'm sure you'll feel happier if the request comes officially from the police." She smiles amiably. "But your guests might be a little alarmed when the foyer is teeming with policemen." She nods to the ivory-handled candlestick telephone. "Could you give Detective Kendrick a ring? I'll give you the two cents."

He sighs, picks up a set of keys, and comes round from behind his desk. "I cannot leave you alone, you understand. And if Mr. Levitt is not at home—"

"I'll leave quietly, I promise."

—

The doorman's knuckles rap loudly on the white-painted wood. He turns the bell twist, and there is an angry buzzing ring from inside the apartment.

"Mr. Levitt?" he calls. "Mr. Levitt, are you all right?"

No answer. He looks at Rourke for an indecisive moment. She nods to the keys in his hand. After one final, fruitless knock and ring of the door buzzer, he relents and uses his master key to open the door.

"Hiram?" Rourke calls into the empty hallway. They make their way into the apartment. It is small but bright, with white walls and burnished maple floors. As she expected, everything is clean and meticulously ordered.

Which is why the scene that awaits in the living room is such a shock to them both.

"I think you should make that telephone call to the police now," she says to the doorman.

28

1907
Louisiana

Père Martin sent word to the sheriff's office in Houma. In the meantime, the priest did his best to calm things down, but old man Trosclair, insane with grief and fury, had infected many with his madness. Like some medieval feudal seigneur, he summoned the smallholders, shrimpers, and fishermen to the Lagrange hall and demanded they rally to his banner. Most ignored him, though all were shocked by Paul Trosclair's death and unnerved by its bizarre manner. Doc Charbonnier assured them that it must have been simply some kind of catalepsy or neurological condition that profoundly mimicked death.

"Such things happen," he once again announced with grave, impotent authority.

Wilhelm Trosclair reacted aggressively, manically, to any denial of his claim that the witch Hippolyta Cormier had murdered his son.

"Have you all forgotten what happened to Jacques Fournier?" he fumed at the gathering. "Or to old Ma Faucheaux? Both crossed the Swamp Witch in one way or another, then both died of illnesses that Charbonnier here was too incompetent to recognize. I'm telling you, that bitch murdered my son."

"Why?" asked Dupont, the blacksmith, his tone laden with suspicion. "Why should she do that? What did your son do to her daughter in that cabin?"

"My son was attacked!" shouted Trosclair. "He was near-blinded in one eye by that witch's evil little bastard."

"But what was he doing in there with her? What did he do to make her attack him?"

"She must have—I don't know—she must have tricked him. Lured him in there."

"Lured him?" Dupont asked incredulously, scornfully. "He was *lured* by a child?" He shook his head disbelievingly.

"The fact is, my son was murdered." Trosclair was still shouting, his voice fractured with age, frustration, and grief. "He was given some kind of potion, some poison that feigned death. A voodoo potion. And I'm not going to let that quadroon *salope* get away with it."

"Now, Wilhelm," said Doc Charbonnier, his tone appeasing. "You know that there are a dozen things that could have caused that deep comalike state."

"What would you know? Why are you pretending to have the slightest clue as to what happened to my son?" Trosclair eyed the physician malevolently. "The only thing worse than a *couyon* is an educated *couyon*. If you were any good as a doctor, we wouldn't have half the folks here going backwater to get herb potions from that witch. What Paul suffered, what he went through—he went through all that because we put my son in his tomb because *you*"—Trosclair stabbed an angry finger toward the physician—"because *you* said he was dead. You couldn't even get that right."

"This is getting us nowhere. . . ." Père Martin held up his hand. "We should wait until the sheriff gets here from Houma. Then the truth will be pursued without all these passions."

"We have no need for sheriffs here," protested Trosclair. "We never have. We deal with our lawbreakers ourselves. That's what we've always done, and that's what we should be doing now."

The meeting degenerated further into a shouting match. Only a small group—mainly women—seemed open to supporting Trosclair's claims and agreed that the voodoo witch must have had something to do with the death, and that something needed to be done about her. The men reacted either with sly-eyed reluctance or dark, vengeful enthusiasm. Only Dupont countered Trosclair's claims with matching vehemence; others exchanged knowing looks whenever the blacksmith protested. Père Martin again called for calm.

The meeting ended abruptly with Trosclair condemning his neighbors' weakness and declaring his intent to deal with the matter himself. He stormed out—but was followed by a small group.

No one knows for sure how it all happened. No one knows for sure exactly *what* happened, out there in the swamp and the shadows at Hippolyta Cormier's cabin. The ones who came back—and they did not all come back—told the same story, but with inconsistencies that signaled a hastily assembled lie.

It all happened on the third day after old Trosclair had uncovered his son's terrible final torments. As the sun went down, a small, silent flotilla of three pirogues slipped into the moss-shrouded blackwaters of the backswamp.

Trosclair led them, sharing his boat with Franc Guillory, who owned the most land in Leseuil after the Trosclairs and saw himself as some kind of feudal lieutenant to the old man. Trosclair had a revolver tucked into his belt, and Guillory cradled his waterfowl twenty-gauge on his knees. They were followed in the second boat by Paul LeBlanc and Jacques Bordelon, both in their late twenties and known troublemakers when a drink was in them. Billy Fontenot and Henry Landry, older men who rented land from Trosclair, and the least convinced of the posse, brought up the rear. All were armed.

As they penetrated deeper into the swamp, where the night wore its darkest velvet cloak, the bourbon-fueled courage they had felt when they set out started to wane. They lit torches and set them in the bows of the pirogues, which seemed only to intensify the dark beyond the pools of light. Their torches seemed inadequate, like candles passing through the vaults of a vast cathedral, the black-trunked trees like the columns of an infinite colonnade. Around them, the blackwater glistened like oil-sleek obsidian. In the second boat, LeBlanc started with fright when he realized a sudden sparkle in the water, only a foot from his paddle, was the torchlight caught in the watchful eye of an otherwise submerged alligator. Bugs—some small, many huge—danced around the torches' flames in an unnerving clustering, fluttering pandemonium of silhouettes.

Twice they lost their way, despite Bordelon's boasting of his wetlands knowledge. Henry Landry called to Trosclair, two boats ahead, that they should perhaps turn back, think the whole thing over, and maybe come back in daylight. Trosclair snapped back at Landry, accusing him of cowardice and being afraid of a woman and a girl.

By the time they saw the glow of lamplight in the cabin's window, every nerve was stretched taut, all resolve loosened.

Only Trosclair remained grim-faced and determined. He told the others to keep quiet as the boats slid around the tangle of shrub and bush that concealed the cabin.

It would only be later, in confession, that old Landry would tell Père Martin what truly happened out there. But the first thing he would tell the priest was: "She was waiting for us. I don't know how she knew we were coming, but she was waiting for us. Maybe she seen the light from our torches. If only we had turned round, like I said. If only we had left them alone. Oh, God forgive me, Father. God forgive me for what happened. . . ."

29

1927
Hollywood

Mary Rourke has seen life from every angle, has looked around its sharp, ragged edges that tear and rip at people. She has taken just about as many knocks, kicks, and blows as the world is capable of throwing at her. She has been broken, and more than once. Some of the shattered pieces of her lie buried in an unmarked military grave in France, a lot more under a tree in Forest Lawn, and the rest lie deep within herself, in the deepest tomb of all. It's as if she's been bruised numb, and emotions are now muted and distant to her.

She knows it has made her tough. A toughness that, along with the cold-steel cynicism that seems welded to it, isn't something she admires in herself. In fact, she fears it, and is afraid that one day she might wake up and find that the numbness and the toughness are all there is left.

And in this moment, she finds it troubling that the scene facing her and the Talmadge concierge puzzles her more than shocks or disturbs her.

She stands next to the doorman, who is gape-mouthed and frozen by the vision they both share: Hiram Levitt sits in the middle of his living room, tied to a dining chair. He is in his underwear, which Rourke notes is a garish pink. Who would have guessed, she thinks, that under those sober business suits— She cuts the thought off, silently admonishing herself: in front of her a man sits bound, beaten, and clearly murdered. And the first thing she remarks on is the epicene nature of his undergarments.

Someone has gagged Levitt. Obviously sensitive to the decorum of a place like the Talmadge, they have stuffed his mouth jaw-breaking wide with a towel, clearly to stifle his screams while they went to work on him. And they really have gone to work on him. His undershirt is stained with blood. His wrists are bound tight to the arms of the chair, and there are cigarette burns on his forearms.

She hears the repeated crackling tick from the electric Victrola gramophone as the needle skips at the end of a record. Levitt's torture had an accompaniment, she thinks. Not so loud as to cause complaint from neighboring apartments, but loud enough to stifle what the Resurrectionist's gag had failed to contain.

This all took time, she thinks. And it had purpose. This wasn't brutality for brutality's sake—they wanted something from Levitt. He had something to tell his tormentor.

"Phone the cops," Rourke repeats her instruction to the doorman, and when he still doesn't move, "now!"

After the doorman has gone, she moves closer to Levitt. His dark eyes are open wide, but have become dull, lusterless, as the moisture has dried from them. She can see from its unnaturally wide angle that his jaw has been dislocated by the bulk of the towel and the force applied to stuff it into his mouth. She guesses that the Resurrectionist probably suffocated. The fingers of the bound hands are livid crimson and purple-black with pooled blood. Levitt's face is drained of color other than the inky web of ruptured capillaries under the skin. She's no expert, but she reckons he's been dead a couple of days. She looks around the room. Cabinet drawers lie open. The bookcase has been cleared of the books now piled on the floor.

They took their time, she thinks. This was no ransacking, this was a thorough, painstaking search. Levitt would no doubt have approved of their methodology.

Her thoughts are broken by the return of the doorman. With him is a burly middle-aged man in a dark suit who has the lumbering, weary look of an ex-cop.

"Did you call the police?" she asks.

"I wanted to see the story first," says the burly man.

"You the house dick?" asks Rourke. "They have a house dick here?"

"I'm Travis, the security officer, if that's what you mean. Just what's the story here?"

Rourke stares open-mouthed at Travis, then at Levitt's body, then back at Travis. "You an ex-cop?" she asks. "I'm guessing you weren't detective-branch. What do you think the story is here, Sherlock? That I caught him fiddling the gas meter?" She turns to the doorman again. "I told you, and I won't tell you again: go and call the cops."

The doorman looks to the house detective. "Don't look at him," shouts Rourke. "Call the Hollywood Division right now."

The doorman runs back to the main desk.

"There's no need to get antsy," says the house detective. "This is bad news for the building. We ain't had anything like this before. We ain't had any trouble of any kind before. You come in here demanding to see this guy, worried about his safety, then you find him here dead. I just gotta know what the story is."

"The story is that you have a pretty easy number here. All you need to do is to rattle a few windows, check a few locks, make sure there are no hookers or wild parties on the premises." She sarcastically feigns suddenly remembering something. "Oh yeah—and making sure the apartments aren't burglarized and your tenants tortured and murdered." She jerks a thumb in the direction of Levitt's corpse. "Good work, pal."

"No need for that kind of talk," he says disconsolately. "I don't know how this happened."

"You can explain that to the cops when they come. What I want to know is how anyone could have gotten in here to do this."

"There's the fire escape, I guess." He nods over to the side-wall window. Rourke goes over and, without touching anything, sees the window is closed and the catch is still in place.

"Think again."

"The only other way is if someone came in through the front door and the foyer. Maybe wasn't seen by Ralph or whoever was on duty if they was called away from the front desk."

At that moment, the doorman returns.

"You Ralph?" she asks.

"Yes, ma'am. The police are on their way."

"Did Mr. Levitt have any visitors over the last week or so?"

"Can't say he had visitors much at any time. Mr. Levitt was a quiet tenant, a good tenant." The concierge looks again at the dead man. Rourke can see he's reconsidering his breakfast as he does so. He turns back to her. "Never any trouble, and regular in his habits. But a lady did come by, a week or so past. I remember her. She was quite a looker, from what I could see."

"From what you could see?"

"She had this big hat on, and sunglasses."

"Any chance you recognized her? Was she someone from the movies?"

"No—I don't think so. Like I say, I really didn't get a good look at her. Leastways, I didn't recognize her, and her name wasn't one I recognized neither."

"What was her name?"

He tries to frown the name back into his memory, then shakes his head. "Sorry, I can't recall. I think the name was fake."

"Why so?"

"Because the hat and all—it was like she was making a real effort not to show her face. And if she was doing that, then she isn't going to give her real name. We see it all the time, and that's usually when I get Mr. Travis involved—you know, if I suspect it's a chippie trying to get into one of the apartments. But this was a dame, not a quiff. Anyways, she can't have had anything to do with this. . . ." He looks across to where Levitt sits, and swallows hard. "I saw Mr. Levitt alive and well after she left."

"Just a minute." Travis, the house detective, straightens up his posture and holds his shoulders back, as if the action draws some authority back to him. "Who are you to be asking all these questions? Just what has it got to do with you?"

Rourke looks at him expressionlessly, as if he's empty space, then turns back to Ralph, the doorman. "No one else?"

"No— Oh, wait, about a month back. There was this fat old guy came looking for him. He had a Southern accent. His name was Biggs. No, Briggs. But that was even before the woman, so he can't have done it." He frowns again. "Unless he came back later, that is." Ralph again looks over at the dead man. "Can we step outside? I don't feel so good. . . ."

"How come you remember his name but can't remember the name of the woman who came more recently?" asks Rourke.

"Ah, that's easy. Because he showed me a badge. Not a local police badge, but a sheriff's badge. I can't remember where from. To be honest, I thought he was far too old to be a sheriff. That's how come I remember his name. Briggs. Sheriff Briggs."

It is two days later when Mary Rourke visits Harry Carbine's Santa Monica mansion. Two days that have called on every trick in Rourke's fixer book. The butler shows her out to the garden at the rear of the house, where Carbine, dressed in cream linen pants and a white shirt muffled at the neck by a French-blue silk cravat, sits having breakfast.

"Coffee?" he asks. "You look like you can do with some coffee. It's nine-thirty, and already you look beat."

"Sure, thanks," she says. "It's been quite the time." She looks across the large garden and the pool that sparkles under the sun. "What I'd give for a view like this," she says.

Carbine nods to the butler, who pours a cup for Rourke.

"Where are we with this mess?" asks Carbine once the butler has returned to the house.

"The studio's clear of it all," says Rourke. "At least for the meantime, and maybe for good. Hiram Levitt worked for all the big studios, so there's nothing to link him that directly to us or *The Devil's Playground*. Nothing except me finding him, that is. The first cops on the scene were blues; then a couple of suits turned up who didn't know me. My famous charm made sure that the house detective gave me quite the glowing character reference when the cops arrived—and for a while they were more interested in what I was doing there than anything else. I got a real grilling until I persuaded one of them to call Jake Kendrick. Kendrick came over and oiled the waters a little. But there's a complication even in that."

"Oh?" Carbine frowns and puts his cup down. "Complications I don't like. What kind of complication?"

"Jake Kendrick—you know, the detective we keep sweet and who does the odd off-the-books for us—well, he's working this case. Some old retired sheriff from Louisiana was found dead in a motor-hotel room. It looked like a heart attack to start with—the guy was in his sixties and just shy of three hundred pounds. But something turned his blood to sludge, and the thinking now is that he was poisoned, but they're having a problem working out how."

"And this has to do with Hiram Levitt how?"

"This sheriff visited Levitt not long before he was murdered—before they both were murdered, for that matter. The problem is that Kendrick now wants to know everything I know. His off-the-books work for me and his on-the-books case are getting all mixed up together, and he wants to know why. Can't blame him. I'm meeting him for lunch today and I guess I'm in for another grilling. For a cop, Kendrick is smart. He'll see me coming if I try to pull the wool over his eyes."

"What does he think is going on? I mean with this retired sheriff?"

"He's still trying to get to the bottom of that. Briggs—that's the old dead guy—was sheriff in some Louisiana backwater for twenty years. Kendrick has this idea that the old guy had some unsolved case on his mind—or conscience. Cops can get that way when they retire, he says. He thinks that, whatever it was Briggs had going on, he had a lead that brought him to Hollywood."

"What's your take on it?"

"Hiram Levitt was the Resurrectionist. He polished a lot of country coal into Hollywood diamond. No one was better than Levitt at turning pedestrian real-life histories into glamorous backstories. He remade people so thoroughly that nobody—not the studios, not their co-stars, not their new friends or lovers or spouses—ever knew the truth of their backgrounds."

Carbine nods. "So you think that someone Levitt worked on had some kind of troubled history in Louisiana and a connection to whatever it was this guy Briggs was investigating?"

"That's my guess. Or something close to it. And that becomes a problem if that someone is connected to Carbine International Pictures. More than that, there is someone out there on the loose who's prepared to torture and murder to make sure that secret is kept out of sight."

"You think Norma Carlton was murdered because of this? You think there's a connection?"

"Well, what you and I know that Kendrick doesn't—though I'm pretty sure he suspects—is that Norma was also murdered. So, if there's a connection, then my guess is that Norma somehow found out the secret of whoever Briggs was looking for. Whoever killed Norma did a very professional job. Whoever killed Levitt and searched his place was highly professional too." Rourke sips her coffee, lights a cigarette, and looks out over Carbine's garden for a moment.

"The thing that worries me most," she says, blowing smoke into the air, "is that *if* Norma was murdered because she knew something, it's more than likely we are talking about someone connected to the studio. Maybe even connected to *The Devil's Playground*."

"So this could all come back to bite us in the ass," says Carbine dejectedly.

"To be frank, boss, if this is connected to Carlton's death, bad publicity is the least of our worries. Whoever is behind this is a stone-cold killer, and good at it. Plus, they are someone pretty close to the business to know we would jump to cover up a star's death if they dressed it up as a suicide."

"What about the cop? Can you sweeten him with a bonus to keep us out of it?"

"Before we do that and show our hand, I think we've got to make sure it is something we need to be kept out of. We're speculating here, and the whole Levitt thing could blow over without ever blowing in our direction. It could be that there's no connection to Norma Carlton, and I don't think we should be flagging it up that we maybe have something to hide. Anyway, Jake's on the payroll and has been for a while. I've bought some of our names out of embarrassment with the police by going through him. Problem is, there's definitely a limit to what he'll turn a blind eye to. I'm afraid Jake Kendrick has an annoying tendency to try to do the right thing."

"So we just sit it out?"

"That's my recommendation. In the meantime, the best I can do with Jake is to keep him sweet by doing him a favor with this other case he's running."

Carbine raises an eyebrow.

"Missing girls," explains Rourke. "And something the studio really doesn't have any connection to, other than one of the girls was on our books for a while. I'm hoping I can pull a quid pro if I need to. But let's just hope I don't need to."

Carbine nods, considering all the angles. "Anything else I need to know?"

"Kendrick gave me a gun and permit."

"What?"

"For my own protection. After my automobile brakes may or may not have been tampered with. And that's a wrinkle—another of the twos he might be putting together to make four."

Carbine remains quiet for a while, considering all he has been told. Rourke looks out over the gardens and again thinks how nice it would be to have a place like this. How nice it would be to be out of this business and your biggest worry was forgetting to water the begonias.

"Okay, Mary," says Carbine. "Let's see if we can ride this one out. The studio's whole future hangs on this movie, and nothing can get in its way. Are we fixed up for the city-burning scene? You got the press lined up?"

"Yeah, boss. Everything's organized. Let's hope the event lives up to the billing we're giving it."

"Good," says Carbine, and he stands up, announcing the end of the audience. Rourke puts her half-drained coffee cup down. "And don't worry, it will live up to expectations." He comes around the table, takes Rourke by the elbow, and walks with her to the open French windows. "One other thing, Mary," he says. "Keep an eye on Paul Brand. He's the nervy type, and he's gotten himself into a state about the shooting of this scene, and I don't want him spooking the investors."

"Okay, Harry," says Rourke, frowning. "But there's not a lot I can do to keep a director in line."

"Just keep an eye on him, and the press and investors at arm's length from him, that's all."

After she leaves Carbine's mansion, Rourke heads back into Hollywood. The mercury has taken a real boost during the morning, and she drives with the Packard's convertible top down. Resting an elbow on the doorsill, she tries to take a moment to herself and clear her mind of the tumbling, jangling thoughts that clamor for her attention. She knows Kendrick isn't going to let up on her to give him the full picture, so she's talked him into meeting her for lunch on neutral territory, rather than at the studio or the precinct.

But first, she wants to see if she can bring something to the table.

She is on Santa Monica Boulevard heading through Beverly Hills when she first sees it in her mirror. She knows she could simply look back over her shoulder to get a better look, but with the top down, it would give away that she has spotted him.

A gray sedan, making a big effort not to get too close.

She can't see it clearly enough to judge if it's the automobile she saw Jansen working on at the mansion in West Hollywood. At this distance, she can't even be sure of the make or model. The road ahead is clear, so she accelerates the Packard to fifty-five, and the air begins to rush cool and velvet-smooth past her, whipping dark coils of hair into life. The sedan shrinks to a dull spot in the distance.

But when she eases her speed a little, she notices the sedan has obviously accelerated to take up his position again. If it is the same gray sedan. Maybe she is becoming paranoid. There are lots of gray sedans. If she starts to imagine they are all following her . . .

As she passes through Beverly Hills, on an impulse she takes a sudden and unsignaled right turn. She knows the sedan is far enough behind that he will have more than enough time to make the turn. If he does make the turn after her, then it will prove he is on her tail. The street she's turned into is wide, lined with newly planted palms and newly planted Spanish Revival bungalows that gleam with the bright promise of new builds. The road is wide enough, and clear enough, for her to make a sweeping U-turn at some speed. It leaves her facing where the street opens out onto the boulevard. If he turns in after her, she will be able to get a good look at him. She waits. A large black truck passes by the road's end. Then a pale-blue Buick. There is a long gap before the next car, an old black Ford, trundles past.

No gray sedan.

A thought strikes her, and Rourke spins around in her seat and checks the street behind her: the driver of the gray sedan has either pulled over on the boulevard, or predicted her move and taken an earlier right turn. Or maybe, oblivious to her suspicion and the mission she believes he is on, the driver is just some Joe Blow who has simply turned off earlier to go home to wife and kids in a bright new bungalow on one of the other streets.

She sits for ten minutes, then eases the Packard forward to the junction. She checks in both directions: no sign of the gray sedan. With a sigh, she turns out onto the main drag and heads on to her first destination.

—

192 · CRAIG RUSSELL

Having closed the convertible's roof to make her presence less obvious, Rourke pulls the Packard to the curb opposite the large mansion in West Hollywood that has, until now, been the residence of Madame Erzulie, Maîtresse des Ombres. She watches for a while from across the street. Nothing moves. No curtain stirs, no shadow falls across a window. There is no sign of life in or around the house. More important, there is no sign of Jansen, or the gray sedan. The coach-house doors are closed.

There is something about that house, something about the brief through-the-window glimpse of its interior, that itches at her with dogged persistence. Most of all there is something about that strange painting of a snake. . . . She is determined to get a look inside that house. And soon, before it has been emptied.

She watches the house for another fifteen minutes; when there is still no sign of life, Rourke starts up the Packard and heads back to town.

She doesn't see the gray sedan that pulls out from behind the mansion's coach house once she has reached the junction.

30

There is a good reason the Hollywood Studio Club exists, Rourke knows. It, the Hollywood Women's Club, and the other establishments like them, are needed.

Hollywood offers women opportunities like nowhere else in the United States, like nowhere else in the world. The actresses Mary Pickford and Norma Talmadge, and the screenwriter-producer June Mathis aren't just some of the most powerful women but some of the most powerful people, male or female, in Hollywood.

That is why so many girls from all over the nation's heartlands pack swimsuits and summer dresses, head to the California sun, and dive into the shimmering bright pool of promise that is Hollywood. For a tiny few, the dream comes true. The overwhelming majority discover that all the bright California sun does is cast a longer, darker shadow.

Hollywood's twenty-five square miles is a small pool filled with a lot of fresh flesh. And fresh flesh attracts sharks. Studio men, talent scouts, pimps, and perverts circle with long-practiced skill. For many of the new arrivals, much easier to find than a studio contract is the rape, the forced prostitution, the sweatshop labor.

Even those who go on to things great or middling in the movie industry have generally experienced the always transactional and very often coercive sex exacted from a woman seeking to make it here. Roles aren't won at auditions, but in beachside chalets, hotel rooms, producers' offices.

After the very public Fatty Arbuckle spectacle, in which Hollywood's first million-dollar star had been tried and acquitted three times for rape and manslaughter, awareness of the vulnerability of young women in the movie industry had been raised. First Universal, then all other studios, started to introduce morality clauses into contracts. Various women's charitable organizations were set up to try to offer young female arrivals to Hollywood protection from predatory forces.

That's why the Hollywood Studio Club was set up, offering dormitory accommodation, sorority-like conviviality, activities, and strictly chaperoned safety to young women working, or seeking work, in the film industry. The club is subsidized by the studios and supported—and very often staffed—by the wives of the powerful. Rourke knows that Cecil B. DeMille's wife is a regular contributor of time and money.

The Studio Club sits just off Lexington in an impressive Italianate building. Rourke has been here a couple of times before on a mission to quiet a publicity storm by bribery or threat. Because of this, her presence is not always welcome—but, as Kendrick pointed out, she'll be more welcome than a man knocking on the door, even a man carrying a badge.

She's lucky. The matron she encounters at the club's Lodi Place entrance is a former script supervisor at Carbine International. While she goes to fetch the girl whose name Rourke has given, the matron directs her to a large lounge. Rourke sits and smokes a cigarette. She hears the main door clatter open and closed, followed by carefree laughter as a group of young women enters. The laughter swells, then fades, as the girls make their way upstairs from the foyer. When was the last time I laughed like that? she thinks to herself. Then she remembers, and she puts the thought from her head.

Betty Dupris is no more than twenty, thinks Rourke as she sees her approach. She has a round, unexceptionally pretty face framed with a short dark bob, and her figure is a little on the heavy side. Her eyes are large and attractive and suggest a keen intelligence at work behind them. Her expression is suspicious, and when Rourke stands up and offers her hand, Betty takes it as if she's being handed a questionable bill of goods.

Once they're both seated. Rourke explains she's from Carbine International Pictures, and that she knows Betty registered with the studio for work. The suspicion fades a little from the younger woman's expression.

"This is a nice place," small-talks Rourke.

"Yes, it is."

"Have you been here long?"

"A year, give or take," says Betty. "Not long after it opened."

"You happy here?"

"Pretty much." The suspicion lurks in Betty's tone, in the narrowing of the intelligent eyes. "I've got a new roommate. She's Russian and smokes these awful cigarettes. Other than that, it's just fine."

"You manage to get any parts so far?"

"A few. Extra and bit parts. But I'm concentrating on screenwriting now. That's what my roommate, Ayn, does. They have script classes here. Classes on all kinds of things relating to the business. I always say you have to be adaptable."

"That's true," says Rourke. She considers the space around them. The lounge is Italianate in design, like the rest of the building, with rose-pink and pastel-green plastered walls, run around with an elaborate frieze. "I've never been to Italy," she says. "I wonder how close this is to the real thing. You been?"

"To Italy? No."

"It's funny," says Rourke. "I guess architecture isn't so different from our business. The movie business. Both try to give people experiences of a different world."

"What can I do for you, Miss Rourke? Does Carbine International have a part for me? I would have expected just to get a casting call, not have someone come to me in person."

Rourke smiles. Betty is smart.

"You're right, Betty. I'm here about something else. I believe you know Sadie Ehrlich. Or Sadie Weston, as she goes by professionally."

"Sadie? What's this got to do with Sadie?" The suspicion's back in full bloom now. "I thought you said you were here because I'm on your books."

"You are—and so is Sadie—you came in together to sign up. I assumed you knew her."

"Maybe. Sadie isn't here."

"I know. She's gone missing."

"Maybe she went home."

"But you don't know that for sure?"

Betty shrugs. "Why are you looking for her?"

"It's the cops who are looking for her. I'm doing a favor for a detective friend of mine. He's worried that something's happened to Sadie and some other girls. I take it you know about what happened to Lucille Quimby?"

Betty nods curtly. "Why would the police get someone from a studio to help them?"

"It's a long story. But if you don't believe me, telephone Hollywood Division and ask to speak to Detective Jake Kendrick. He'll vouch for me."

To Rourke's surprise, Betty stands up, asks her to wait, and walks out of the room. Five minutes later, she comes back in and sits down.

"I checked," she says flatly.

"And?"

"And he confirmed your story. He asked if you could put lunch back a half hour."

"Thanks for passing it on," says Rourke, smiling. She wasn't bluffing, she thinks. She really did check. With her smarts, Betty should do all right here.

"I don't know where Sadie is," Betty says.

"Did you know Lucille Quimby as well?"

Betty nods. The tough exterior softens for a split second, then is reinforced. "I knew Lucille. She lived here too. Me, Sadie, and Lucille. Sadie and Lucille got into trouble for getting drunk one night and trying to sneak a couple of fellers in. They had to move out. They stayed in a boarding house farther up Lexington."

"You know that Lucille was found dead."

Another crack in the armor. Betty nods.

"Listen, Betty, I know you don't trust me, but you and Sadie were both on our books, and that makes me feel, well, a little responsible for you, I suppose. And I'm trying to help the police find whoever killed Lucille."

"I don't know what I can tell you to help."

"Tell me about the three of you. Tell me which studios you registered with, if there was ever any trouble with a guy—that kind of thing."

"Okay," says Betty, and she does. She runs through everything from their first meeting in the Studio Club to the other two moving out, to Betty finding out about Lucille's death. And in it all, there is nothing that helps Rourke.

She gets up and thanks Betty. She dips into her bag and hands her her business card.

"That's my number, if anything comes to mind. And I'll put a word in at the studio. See if there's a script-girl placement open."

"Thanks," says Betty.

Rourke dips into her bag again and hands the younger woman twenty-five dollars.

"There's no need to do that," says Betty.

"You've done your best to help. And I want you to look after yourself."

"Thank you," she says, looking at the bills in her hand. "Why?"

Rourke frowns. "Why what?"

"Why do you care?"

"I just do." Rourke looks at Betty for a moment, then sighs. "If you must know, I lost somebody. She'd be not far off your age if she had lived. And, anyway, I know what a cruddy town this can be for women. I've been through it myself."

"I see. I'm sorry. About your friend, I mean."

"She wasn't a friend," says Rourke. "She was my daughter."

31

The grill house started off as a place where the movie industry's writers would gather and bitch over chicken potpie or grilled tenderloin about the raw deal they got from the studios. The clientele is still mainly writers and deals are still raw and the bitching still goes on, although a handful of actors and actresses have discovered the place. But no big-name stars yet, and the scribblers console themselves with that, but they bemoan the coming day when this treasured place, too, will fall to the big names and the agents and the reporters and the limelight.

Rourke explains to the maître d', who knows her as a semi-regular, that she has business to discuss and needs a quiet spot. Bartenders and maître d's in Hollywood have a sense of discretion that would make the average confessional priest look like a blabbermouth, and he smiles and takes her to a booth by the window, looking out over Hollywood Boulevard.

Through the window, she sees a black Ford pull up on the other side of the street, and a tall man steps out and crosses quickly. It is his gait—a paradoxical blend of athletic grace with a distinct limp—that she recognizes before she sees his face clearly.

A minute later, a red-jacketed waiter directs Jake Kendrick to the booth.

"What's to do, toots?" He smiles, and again she sees the ghost of the boy he had been before the war.

"You do know I've got that gun you gave me in my purse?" she asks with a raised eyebrow.

He mimes surrender with held up hands. "Sorry. What's to do, *Miss Rourke?*"

"I spoke to Betty Dupris, the girl who came into the studio with Sadie Ehrlich."

"And?"

"Not much help. I mean, she tried to help—she's a good kid, and smart, too—but she didn't have anything useful to share. Sorry, Jake, I had hoped to have more to give you."

She picks up the menu and examines it. "What are you going to have?" she asks. He peruses his menu.

"Oh, I think I'll have . . ." He puts the menu down, rests elbows on the table, and leans forward. "A big plate of the truth and hold the applesauce."

"Isn't that a bit heavy for lunch?" she jokes weakly.

"I can spend the afternoon working it off. So how about it, Mary?"

"Remember I said that—"

"That it would put us on opposite sides of the law," he cuts her off. "Yeah, I remember. You also told me that if you've done something wrong it was because you were tricked into it. But let's just say that this booth is a confessional. Anything you say here stays in here, between us. You deal straight with me; I'll deal straight with you."

Rourke doesn't answer and, for a moment, she loses her way with it all. The woman who has all the answers is left scrabbling for one.

"Listen," says Kendrick. "I don't know what you were doing up at the Stratton place, but you nearly didn't make it down that hill with your hide intact. You talk to Hiram Levitt, and when you go back to see him, someone's used his throat as a laundry chute. I'm not kidding, Mary, I'm really worried that you're going to end up getting hurt. I'm talking to you as your friend, not as a cop."

"Is that what we are, Jake? Friends?"

He holds up his hands. "I like to think so. And I think you know that I do care about you. So, like I say, forget I'm a cop for an hour."

She watches him silently for a moment. "Okay. I will if you will. But when you walk out of here, your badge will be back on. I want you to promise that you won't act on anything I tell you unless we agree first."

"Mary, just tell me what the hell is going on."

So she does. It takes the whole meal for her to unpack it all.

He sits quiet for a long time when she's finished and it unnerves her.

"What I don't get," he says at last, "is why Harry Carbine has placed this all on your shoulders. Why not the Golem?"

Rourke shrugs. "He said he wanted a gentler touch. He thinks I'll make fewer waves. I get the feeling Carbine has hocked himself up to the eyeballs to finance this film. He's paranoid that any scandal will attach to Carbine International—not to mention word getting out that the studio concealed a murder."

"But you didn't know it was a murder."

"You *are* talking as a friend. But look at it with your badge on, Jake. It doesn't look too good, does it?"

He shakes his head. "It still ain't right that he's put you in danger."

She shrugs again, this time a little disconsolately. "It is what it is, Jake. Okay, I've shown you mine, now show me yours. . . ."

"I have a lot to show. Things are getting pretty mixed up, if I'm honest," he says. "By which I mean your business and my case. I can't help thinking that it's all got something to do with everything you've just told me."

"This about the retired Louisiana sheriff? The fact that he visited Hiram Levitt?"

"Yes. And there's even more to it than that. The guy who runs the motor hotel said that Briggs asked him how to get to the Stratton place in Laurel Canyon. Briggs told him he was doing a tour of the homes of the stars, all that malarkey. The hotel guy showed him on the map, but when he started to show him where Pickfair was, or Falcon Lair in Beverly Hills, Briggs wasn't interested. The hotel guy just thought that Briggs mustn't have been a Pickford or Valentino fan."

"Briggs went to Mount Laurel?"

"Looks like it. His brakes maybe didn't fail on the way back, but he still ended up dead in his bed a couple of days later. I'm going to take a little run up to Mount Laurel myself—because, you see, that's not the only connection."

"Oh?"

"The hotel owner saw Briggs talking to a guy in the hotel's parking lot. Not something he would normally have taken any notice of, except he said the guy was a real tough-looking character with a terrible scar on his face. Like a war wound."

"Blevins?" Rourke is taken aback. "Veronica Stratton and Robert Huston's security man?"

"And occasional and volatile bodyguard. When I go up to Mount Laurel, I'm going to come back with him in the back seat. Maybe that way I can be sure my brakes won't pack in on me. I can only bring him in for questioning at the moment, but it's a start."

Rourke thinks it all through. She imagines Blevins in Norma Carlton's home, dressing her body and placing the high-necked stage-prop Usekh collar around her throat. Something about it doesn't sit right with her.

"The problem I've got," says Kendrick, "is that I can only look at him for the Briggs murder. Other than they both talked to Briggs, I've got nothing to connect Blevins to Hiram Levitt, and I don't *officially* know that Norma Carlton was murdered. So I can't even discuss that without bringing you into it." He holds up his hands. "And don't worry, you won't be brought into it."

Their conversation is interrupted when the waiter comes with their coffees.

"What the hell could your backwater sheriff have to do with Hiram Levitt?" she asks when the waiter is gone.

"I don't know, Mary. But there's something else you should know."

She puts her coffee cup down.

"I took a good look at Hiram Levitt's apartment. Every drawer, every cupboard, wardrobe, and cabinet had been gone through. And, like you said, gone through very thoroughly. Whoever murdered Levitt was looking for something, and when they didn't find it, they turned on the charm with a sap and a lit cigarette. My guess is that he gave them what they wanted in the end; then they finished him off. Incidentally, the downtown office he rented got the same treatment. All—and I mean *all*—of Levitt's files have taken a stroll."

"Why, Jake? Why would someone do that to Levitt?"

"He traded in secrets. For every shiny new history he gave someone, he buried an old one. If there's anything I've learned over the years, it's this: the one thing that's sure to get you killed is a secret."

"So this goes back to your theory that he was murdered because someone wanted to keep their secret hidden." Rourke shakes her head. "I don't buy it. Levitt was tighter than a bank vault when it came to that. When I asked him for information on Norma Carlton's background, he gave me the brush-off, even though Carlton was dead. No one is going to murder him over a secret they know is safe."

"There's more," says Kendrick. "We've gone through Levitt's financials, as much as we can. It would appear he had a number of bank accounts under different names. He shifted money from one to the other, and we reckon we've only got some of them. I'm guessing Levitt was well paid for his expert service?"

"Well enough. He'll—I mean he *would have* never been short of money."

"But not Hollywood star money?"

"Of course not. Let me guess . . ."

"Yep. Over a million and counting. Like I say, some of it we may never trace."

"The little bastard," mutters Rourke. "Blackmail?"

"That's what we think. You're right that Levitt kept all these stars' secrets locked up like Fort Knox—but there was obviously a storage fee. If you didn't pay . . ."

"But that's all speculation, surely."

"Informed speculation—informed by the size of his bank balance. Unless he was secretly a European prince, a railroad tycoon, or a genius at backroom poker—I can't see any other way he could have put together that amount of dough."

Rourke thinks about Levitt's coal-black, unreadable eyes. As dark and impenetrable as bank vaults. Except his discretion wasn't motivated by professional ethics, the way he dressed it up; it was motivated by greed, by its turn-a-buck yield, like everything else in this shitty town.

"And there's something else, Mary," says Kendrick. "You're right that other studios have asked favors in the past, so I called a few of them in. I spoke to Dave Jordan at First National, and I made a couple of calls to Paramount, Fox, and MGM. The result is, I've got a list of stars that were 'resurrected' by Hiram Levitt. Nearly a hundred names, and some of them at the very top of the business."

"Why do I feel I'm not going to like what you're going to tell me?"

"Robert Huston was on the list," says Kendrick.

"Huston? But he's a foreigner, a Brit. Why would he need Hiram?"

"There was another name as well. . . ." Kendrick smiles, but there's nothing boyish in it. "Hiram Levitt created a new backstory for one of the biggest names in Hollywood today. Veronica Stratton."

32

Mary Rourke has no idea why, when sharing everything else with Kendrick, she didn't tell him about Jansen and Madame Erzulie's mansion—or the suspicion that Jansen's was the pale-gray sedan she imagined was following her. Maybe it's because she knows he is working on solid leads, and she doesn't want to distract him from them. But she knows it's not that. Maybe she's afraid he would think her stupid for believing some old voodoo priestess-cum-spiritualist has something to do with everything that's going on.

Or maybe it's because, friend or not, Kendrick is a copper. If she adds burglary to being accessory to murder, maybe that blind eye is going to become more difficult to turn.

It is dark, and the streetlamps are dim and infrequent, but she still chooses not to park anywhere in sight of the house. Instead, she drives on to the next block and parks around the corner. Again she finds herself cursing Harry Carbine for landing her with this job. This is the kind of thing the studio has Sam Geller for. The kind of thing Sam Geller is paid for.

Before she steps from the automobile, she slips off her heels and puts on a pair of navy canvas flats with rubber soles. She reaches into her shoulder bag and makes sure that she has the broad-bladed screwdriver she picked out, then checks to see that the small flashlight is working. Rourke pauses for a moment, taking time to consider that she is about to commit another felony.

With that thought in mind, she checks herself as she is about to step out of the car, reaches into the glove compartment and takes out the Colt .25 pocket pistol Jake Kendrick gave her. For an uncertain moment, she looks at it as it glitters darkly in the dim light, then slips it into her bag.

Closing the Packard's door quietly, she walks swiftly and silently along the street. The Gothicness of the mansion, which had looked almost comically overdone in the bright California day, achieves its full potential for menace in the dark. Rourke turns soundlessly in through the open gates. She steps onto the grass and off the gravel driveway that would announce every crunching step taken. She stands for a moment in the shadowed English-style garden and looks over at the coach-house-styled garage. There are no lights showing, either in the main house or in the windows above the garage. She looks up at the looming mansion. Rourke can imagine "Madame Erzulie" picking it as the ideal premises for a supernatural business in much the same way an accountant would choose a stolid stone office building on which to hang his shingle.

She again finds the door at the rear of the house. She jams the broad head of the screwdriver between the jamb and the door, just above the lock. There is a loud sound of wood cracking and splintering, and the door yields to her leverage. She freezes, checks the coach house one last time for signs of a light or movement, then slips into the house.

Using her flashlight, Rourke makes her way along a hall until the main entrance hall opens out to her. The main reception room, the one she saw into, is to her left. She sees that everything is still where she saw it when she peered through the window. A couple of the crates have been sealed, but she determines to crack them open if she feels it necessary. She'll start upstairs, she decides. But, before she does anything, she crosses to where the painting leans against the wall. It is completely covered by a dustcover, and she throws it back to expose the canvas.

The colors are vivid, disturbingly so, in the pool of brightness from her flashlight. The snake writhes with a strangely nauseating sensuousness. There is a pattern to the skin, an almost diamond pattern, but the colors are unnaturally exaggerated, and though Rourke looks at a two-dimensional oil painting, she is seized by the overpowering feeling that the snakeskin shimmers and ripples, and that there is movement in the body. Not just in the body, but in the dark leaves and vines that form the background. She shakes the thought from her head: it's the light from the flashlight, she tells herself.

What is it about this painting? she asks herself. What is it I see in it? What is it that it reminds me of?

The question goes unanswered.

Her mind is snapped elsewhere, and the question she now asks herself is how she could possibly know that the hard, imperative pressure she feels in her back, above her kidney, is the barrel of a gun.

33

1907
Louisiana

When Sheriff Briggs's skiff arrived in Leseuil, he found Père Martin waiting for him. Briggs was a tall, heavy-built man in his early forties, broad-shouldered but with a gut overhanging his belt. His complexion was florid, his hair reddish auburn. He wore civilian clothes; the only items of uniform were the pinched-crown campaign hat that bore his badge, front and center, and the revolver holstered on his hip. He had come with no deputy: Briggs was the kind of man who was confident in his authority and, when his authority was challenged, in his personal mettle. Père Martin did not know if the sheriff had any knowledge of French, but if he did, he made no effort to speak it. Briggs's power was not just state-invested or personal, it was linguistic: the sheriff was an Anglo, and English was the language of authority. There was even talk of the Louisiana Legislature passing a law that would ban Cajun and Louisiana French from schoolrooms and all other official places. English, Père Martin feared, would be the language of the Cajun future.

The priest told the sheriff all he knew, and they traveled together out to the cabin. Martin was unnerved by the sounds of the swamp—much louder and more layered than usual—as if something had disturbed the wetlands' balance. Like never before, he felt the swamp seethe and teem with life—hostile, dark-gathering life. From beneath its spiked black carapace, an alligator snapping turtle turned its heavy, vicious-beaked head and eyed them as they passed by. A ten-foot alligator slipped silently and with malevolent saurian grace from its levee into the blackwater. If it unnerved Briggs, he showed no sign of it.

As they rounded the brush-dense corner, they got sight of it. Père Martin felt his throat tighten and pulse pick up pace as he saw smoke drift upward from the property. They tied up on the small jetty and they could see death, even from there. When they disembarked, there was a flurry of coal-dark wings as a black vulture relinquished its meal.

A man's body lay dead on the grass, a bullet wound in his chest, and one in his head. A discharged shotgun lay at his side. His face had been ravaged by the attentions of the vulture and other carrion eaters. One eye, its luster dulled, stared up disinterestedly at the swamp's canopy and the sky beyond; there was a ragged, raw, red-black chasm where the other eye had been scavenged.

"It's Franc Guillory," said the priest, a tremor in his voice. "At least I think it's Franc Guillory."

Behind the dead man, the cabin was reduced to a charred skeleton: a tangle of blackened debris that still ember-glowed, smoke curling blackly like spilled ink into the gray mist. Outside what had been the door, the huge dog lay dead, one flank ripped open where a shotgun blast had met its target. The vultures and the carrion crows had feasted on the goat, which lay dead, still tethered to its post. The carcasses of chickens dotted the property.

They searched for Cormier mother and daughter, but there was no sign of either—alive or dead. Père Martin pleadingly called Anastasie's name into the fog-shrouded swamp but received no answer other than the indignant, reeling cries of the swamp birds.

"I reckon they're still in there." Briggs nodded over to the charred, smoldering remains of the cabin. "I'll bring some boys out to go through it once it's gone cold. My guess is, we'll find them there."

It didn't take them long to search the rest of the property. As they did so, Père Martin was once more aware of occupying a small oasis. Even now, he imagined that around them the constricting dark swamp was closing in on the property, like a Louisiana pine snake coiling around its prey. It brought back to mind the strange brooch he had seen Hippolyta Cormier wearing. These thoughts were broken by the sheriff calling him from the back of the property, behind the smoldering remains of the cabin. Briggs pointed to where a pirogue was half banked up onto the shoulder of the small levee.

"I guess this is our missing men's boat." Briggs turned from it to look back at the ruins of the cabin. "Looks to me like your boys tried to sneak around back of the property. Like the women were holed up in the cabin. From the look of the dead guy out front, it seems to me your boys bit off more than they could chew. Did you know that this woman Cormier had a gun?"

The priest, still looking down at the abandoned pirogue, shook his head.

"Well," said the sheriff, "the way I see it is this: These good ol' boys of yours came out here with ideas of teaching this Cormier woman and her daughter a lesson. God knows what other mischief they had on their minds. But when they get here, they get a reception they ain't been expecting. This Franc Guillory feller is keen to impress old Trosclair and comes charging up toward the cabin with a twelve-gauge, shoots the dog, and gets his change back in head and chest. The others are pinned down, so they send these two . . ."

"Paul LeBlanc and Jacques Bordelon," the priest filled in the gap.

"LeBlanc and Bordelon are sent around back to sneak up on the cabin. Maybe Ma Cormier picks them off, maybe they end up gator food. Whatever happened, their boat's here and they ain't. No way they made it outta here on foot. They're gone now, and we ain't gonna find them. Old man Trosclair gets impatient and tells the others to burn the women out, and they set fire to the cabin. Like I said, I reckon when they've cooled down enough for it to be safe for me to send in some deputies to go through the cabin, we'll find what's left of them."

Père Martin remained silent; the meager light of the swamp was dimming further, but he peered into it as if it still had something to yield.

"Yeah, looks to me like both women are dead," Briggs announced with finality. "Them two Cajun fellers too." He pushed the campaign hat back on his skull and wiped his forehead with a handkerchief. "Goddammit, Father, you're supposed to keep these people in line, and all they do is go burning each other out and shooting each other up." He sighed. "Best get the body back."

They made their way back from the swamp, towing Franc Guillory's body, which they'd laid in the recovered pirogue and wrapped in waxed canvas. As they turned the corner, Père Martin took a long last look at the small clearing with the black skeleton of the cabin still smoldering. An overpowering feeling burned on in the old priest: a conviction that Anastasie was still alive, perhaps her mother too, and the urge to find her was overwhelming.

That urge, he realized with disquiet, was not for her sake, but everyone else's.

Back in Leseuil, word of what had happened in the backswamp had burned through the township. There was shock, there was anger. There was even a little relief.

The sheriff surprised Père Martin by not immediately seeking out the main actors in the events out in the backswamp. Instead, using Martin as his introducer and occasional translator, he talked to various people along the bayou. Talked, listened, nodded his head.

"You say this blacksmith of yours was always speaking out for the Cormier woman and her daughter?" Briggs didn't wait for an answer. "Best we go have a word with him."

Dupont's yard wasn't far from Père Martin's parochial house, and the priest and the sheriff walked there. It was midday, but the sky had darkened and the air hung thick around them. There was a flash of brightness, then, seconds later, the rumble of thunder somewhere in the distance.

"You expecting a storm?" the sheriff asked.

Martin looked up at the sky. "Yes," he said sadly. "I've been expecting it. I've felt this storm coming a long, long time."

Dupont's cabin and work sheds sat shadow-black between the bayou and the main road. There was no sound from the blacksmith's, no ringing of hammer on metal, no smoke leaching from the forge stack. No response to their calling Dupont's name and, when they tried his cabin, no sign of him there.

But they found him. They found him in his work shed. As they looked at Dupont, there was another rumble of thunder, then the rattling sound of rain on the shed's corrugated iron roof.

A long horse-tether rope had been thrown over the crossbeam and secured. Dupont hung motionless from it. Tongs and hammers lay scattered across the wooden floor where they had fallen from the kicked-over table.

The priest crossed himself and shook his head mournfully. "Louis . . . Oh no, Louis . . ."

"I'm guessing the rumors about Anastasie Cormier being his daughter maybe have some weight to them," said Briggs as he looked up at the dead blacksmith. "A feller don't just go and do this for no reason. You best get that doctor of yours—Charbonnier—to pronounce life extinct. Though I believe he ain't always on the money with that, from what I hear."

Briggs seemed to see the blacksmith's suicide as a time-consuming interruption. Between them, the priest, the lawman, and Doc Charbonnier dealt with the body.

Old man Thibodeaux brought his buckboard and, after the four had loaded the body between them, transported the dead blacksmith to Charbonnier's surgery.

"Sad business," said Martin. "Very sad business."

"I think I'd better go visit old man Trosclair. Get his story," said Briggs. "I need someone to show me the way. Doc Charbonnier tells me he has to visit him anyway—check on his wound. He says it ain't necessarily life-threatening, but with an old man like that you never know."

"Do you want me to come as well?" asked Père Martin.

"I guess I'll need someone to translate, so I'd appreciate it. You mind? Or do you think Charbonnier would manage?"

"I'll come. I want to hear what he has to say for himself."

It took them a half hour to get out to the plantation. They rode crammed in together on Doc Charbonnier's buggy. The storm had hit hard and, though there were no strong winds, gray rain thundered down on them and seemed to wash the bayou clean of any color.

"This may not be a serious wound," Charbonnier said to Briggs, "but in a man of Monsieur Trosclair's age, it needs to be taken seriously. I would ask you not to overtax him with questions."

"Sure thing, Doc," said Briggs.

When they arrived at the Trosclair plantation house, to the doctor's annoyance, Sheriff Briggs completely ignored Charbonnier's instruction and questioned Trosclair for over an hour. The old man, clearly put out that his perceived position in the community failed to impress the sheriff in any way, remained steadfast and defiant in the face of the interrogation and repeated the same account as he had told the priest.

"She was waiting for us," maintained Trosclair. "With a shotgun. She fired a round and hit poor Franc Guillory square in the face and killed him. Then she gave me the other barrel but only caught me in the side, like you know. It was murder, what she did to Franc."

Briggs sat slumped in the chair by the bed, the exaggerated casualness of his pose a signal of who was in charge here. "It could be argued—in a court of law—that she was within her rights to defend her property. I mean, you fellers went out there all armed. Looks to me like you were intending mischief. If she thought that too, then she'd have the right to use force."

Trosclair glared at Briggs. "This is a part-colored we're talking about."

Briggs shrugged. "Still within her rights. Negro, colored, Creole, or Cajun. Anyways—you say she fired first."

"She did, and *I* was within *my* rights to defend *myself*."

"So you shot her."

"Yes. Or I shot at her, with my revolver. I don't know if I hit her or not."

"After both barrels of her gun were empty and she wasn't any threat no more. But you still fired at her."

"She had just killed Franc Guillory and shot me. I wasn't going to wait until she reloaded. Anyway, she ran back into the house. Her and her bastard holed up, and they were both armed. They both fired at us."

Briggs paused for a moment. "The cabin. How come that burned down?"

"It caught fire when we were shooting it out with that bitch. I guess the daughter knocked a lamp over or something. They must have gone up with the cabin. I don't know."

"Nor do I, but we'll find out soon enough. What happened to your other two compatriots?"

"They went round the back, through the swamp, to get in back of her when she started firing."

"So what happened to them? If you say you dropped the Cormier woman with your first couple of shots . . ."

"I don't know. We called for them, but they didn't answer. We waited for as long as we could, but with me shot and bleeding, we had to come back."

"You, Landry, and Fontenot?"

"Yes. Just the three of us."

"You just left your friend's body lying there? You could have brought it back with you."

"We couldn't go for Franc's body; those whores would have shot at us."

"Wait . . ." Briggs frowned. "I thought you said they were in the cabin and it was burning down."

"They could have still been alive. Still armed."

"Any *ideas* as to what mighta happened to the other two?"

"A lot of things can happen in the swamp. Maybe that little bitch of a daughter got to them. Maybe she was out back waiting for them."

Briggs shook his head, his expression impatient. "The girl? A thirteen-year-old girl killed two full-growed men?"

Trosclair shrugged. "Maybe it was her that killed my son, not her mother. They were both witches. Both whores."

"But you have no proof that either killed your son."

"Then who did?" Trosclair eased himself up in the bed and winced.

"Your son," said Briggs. "He wasn't exactly the clean-living type, if you know what I mean—now, was he, Mr. Trosclair?"

"No, I don't." The old man was angry now, his tone defiant. "What *do* you mean?"

"Well, from what I hear, your son liked to go into the big city regularly. Have some fun in Storyville, for example."

"What's that got to do with anything?"

"Mostly, nothing. But there are a lot of bad diseases you can pick up behaving like that. Now, I heard that your boy had a bad case of syphilis. And it had gone into his brain, his nerves. What do you call that, Doc?"

"Neurosyphilis," said Charbonnier, and Trosclair glared at him.

"Yeah, neurosyphilis." Briggs picked up the campaign hat that had been balanced on his knee and brushed the brim thoughtfully. "And from what I hear—and I'm no expert, mind—but from what I hear, once you got that rotting away your brain and nerves, you can go into a coma that looks like you're dead. People—doctors—have been fooled by it before. The person looks dead but they ain't dead. Sometimes they get buried, only to come outta the coma when they're six feet under. Couldn't that be a more reasonable explanation than all this voodoo mumbo-jumbo?"

Trosclair raised himself up slightly from his bed, again winced in pain and fell back. "I told you," he hissed. "It was that bitch Cormier. She poisoned him knowing we'd bury him alive."

The next morning, early, Père Martin saw from his window that Sheriff Briggs was preparing to leave from the bayou jetty. He pulled on his surplice and rushed out. The lawman looked up as he approached.

"I was just coming to tell you I was heading back to Houma," said the sheriff. "Ain't much more I can do here at the moment."

"Aren't you staying longer?" asked the priest in English. As his first words of the day, he felt the language sit clumsily in his mouth, like gristle. "There's so much left unanswered."

"And it'll probably stay that way, Father," said Briggs. "I don't know what happened out there in the backwater, but it sure as heck ain't the story we're being spun." He sighed. "I want you to organize a search of the swamp—see if you can find that girl and her mother—or them two missing fellers, for that matter. You've more chance of finding her than I do by the time I get back with deputies. In any case, you know this swamp better than I do."

"And that's it? You're finished with this matter?"

"I didn't say that. But there ain't no way I'm going to prove the woman Cormier and her daughter were murdered. The only witnesses to what truly happened are all bound up in the same lie."

"So what are you going to do?"

"I'm going to look into her background. There's gotta be a reason a woman like that hides herself away in the middle of nowheres." He stepped into the skiff and cast off. "You bury your dead, Father Martin—I'll be back soon enough."

Père Martin watched as the sheriff's skiff slid upriver and faded into the morning mist. He turned and looked along the bayou, at the small cluster of wooden buildings that looked so small and insignificant against the verdant, clustering mass of a million acres of swamp forest like a great green beast ready to swallow them up.

The anxiety he felt clutching at his chest seemed to be more than that caused by recent events. It was foreboding: he knew this dark business was far from finished.

34

When he returned to Leseuil a week later, Sheriff Briggs didn't come alone. In that week, he had learned a great deal about the nature of evil; so, when he came back, he brought three armed deputies with him.

It was early morning and a thick, yellow-gray mist covered the waters of the bayou, fudging, as it often did, the demarcations between air, forest, and water. They arrived on a twenty-eight-foot naphtha-vapor launch, and as they rounded the bend in the bayou, it was clear at first sight that something was wrong in Leseuil. In dark reflection of the scene that had awaited them in the backswamp, Briggs could see the blackened skeletons of the Lagrange hall, the schoolhouse, and Père Martin's small wooden chapel.

One of the deputies muttered a curse.

No one waited for them when they cast up by the village pier. The humid, cloying morning air was infused with a granular, sooty odor.

They found Père Martin at the Thibodeaux store, the only building in the central cluster of Leseuil left standing. Old Ma Thibodeaux stood behind the counter, her pale, knotted hands clenched as they rested on the counter, her expression one of grief riven with fear. The priest sat in a rocking chair by the door, his face ashen and weary. It seemed to Briggs that the old priest had aged a decade in the week since he last saw him.

"She came back?" asked Briggs.

Père Martin, still suffering from smoke inhalation, coughed thickly and darkly.

"She came back," the old priest echoed.

"Hippolyta?" asked Briggs.

"No, not Hippolyta—or at least I don't think she was there. Anastasie. It was Anastasie who came back and set fire to the chapel, the Lagrange hall, and the schoolhouse. No one saw her, no one heard her. The first thing we saw was the flames."

"Then how do you know it was her?"

"There's more," said old Ma Thibodeaux. "You best go right to the Trosclair plantation."

The priest held up a calming hand. "There's time enough for that. You see, the fires here were a diversion," he explained. "At least, I think that's what they were meant to be. It meant every able-bodied man in Leseuil was fighting the fires here, while she was long gone. One of Leclaire's horses is gone too. Anastasie set the fires, then rode to the Trosclair house. That's the only time she was seen. Mama Bergier saw her ride out, bareback, clinging to the mane of Leclaire's horse. You know what Mama Bergier's like—she described Anastasie silhouetted against the burning village, her hair streaming out behind her, and swears that she was the devil himself, or possessed by Baron Samedi. You'll see for yourself what happened there. . . ." The priest frowned, reading Briggs's expression. "There's more, isn't there? You know more."

Briggs nodded. He pulled a chair out from the wall—the chair usually used by the Thibodeauxes' customers to sit and pleasantly pass the time of day—and sat down.

"I ain't never come across anything like it. Maybe that old woman is right, and we're chasing the devil. Hippolyta Cormier's tracks were difficult to follow," he said, grim-faced. "But when you get on her trail, my God, you're up to your ankles in blood and tears. The police in Baton Rouge and New Orleans have been looking for her for years. Wherever she went, she left a trail of dead men—sometimes women—in her wake. Before she came here, she made a small fortune in Baton Rouge. Before that, I believe she was operating in New Orleans. Different towns, different names. She was Marie Brasse in Baton Rouge; Véronique Benoit, then Éléonore Duplantis, in New Orleans; and has gone by a good many other names, I would guess." Briggs paused, and leaned forward, resting his heavy forearms on his knees. "You wanna know something, Father? The Baton Rouge police have a name for her. They call her the Southern Black Widow. They call her that because she has made a fortune out of seducing rich men—sometimes even marrying them under a false name—then poisoning them. But here's the thing: they also call her that because there's a rumor goin' round that she uses the poison from Southern black-widow spiders to kill her unsuspecting mates, and make the whole thing look natural. And you know what that poison does to you if you get bitten enough? It paralyzes you. Even makes you breathe so low, and your heart beat so slow, that you can be taken for dead."

The priest looked shocked, disbelieving. "You don't mean you believe what Trosclair claimed?"

"I think she came here for a quiet life, and Paul Trosclair threatened that, or disrupted that. Maybe she fell back on old ways."

"That's if she is the same woman," says Martin.

"In each town, with each death, the description of the woman changes. But one thing stays the same: she has a fingerprint-type birthmark on her left cheek." Briggs stood up. "I think I better go up and see what happened at the Trosclair place. I can tell the old man his ideas ain't so crazy after all."

Père Martin exchanged a meaningful look with Madame Thibodeaux. "I'm afraid that won't be possible." He turned back to Briggs. "Wilhelm Trosclair is dead. Anastasie Cormier murdered him in his bed and burned the house down."

35

1927
Hollywood

It's still there: the pressure of something hard jabbing into her back, just above her kidney. She freezes; opens her mouth to speak but makes no sound. An unseen movement of a hand slips her bag from her shoulder. She hears it hit the floor some distance behind her, obviously having been tossed there. Another movement, and the flashlight is snatched from her hand.

"Over there." The voice is male, hard-edged, and cold. "The chair by the window. Sit down." The gun barrel prods her to move forward.

"Listen," says Rourke without turning. "Don't dig yourself deeper into—"

Another push of gunmetal, this time harder, more insistent. She moves across to the chair, turns, and sits. She is dazzled by the glare of her own flashlight in her face. Behind it she can see nothing more than the silhouette of a hat-wearing man.

Rourke feels her pulse throb in her chest. Her mind races to assess the situation. She knows the pocket pistol Kendrick gave her is in her bag and out of reach. She's going to have to talk her way out of this. If there is a way out of this.

"So, Jansen," she says, "what now? You going to fake my suicide like you faked Norma Carlton's? That'll take some doing—no one will clean up your mess this time."

He says nothing. The flashlight burns in her eyes; then he switches it off. Rourke squints as the sudden dark is filled with red and orange ghosts of the flashlight. The room fills with light when he switches on a table lamp. Now Rourke sees him. He is sitting cross-legged in the armchair beside the lamp table. With his free hand, he casually removes his hat and places it on the chair's arm. His other hand still holds the large-caliber automatic trained on her. Now she sees his face.

"Oh . . ." says Rourke.

"Not who you were expecting, eh?"

"No. You're not. So you're the gray sedan I keep seeing in my mirror?" She shuffles through a dozen confused thoughts as she tries to work out the significance of the face opposing her.

"This ain't my hometown; otherwise you would never have seen me," he says without emotion. "So Norma Carlton's death wasn't a busted ticker, and it wasn't suicide. Ain't that a turn-up?"

"Well, I'm guessing you know all about that," she says. Her voice is calm, her tone confident. The truth is, Mary Rourke is afraid, truly afraid in a way she hasn't been for years, but she is determined not to show it, and she digs her fingers into the padded leather of the chair's arms to stop her hands from shaking.

"Now, now, Miss Rourke," he says in mock admonition. "You're being more than a little inconsistent. A moment ago, when you thought I was someone else, you were accusing him. Who's Jansen?"

"The chauffeur here. Or at least I think he's the chauffeur. Some kind of general factotum for Madame Erzulie, I guess."

"And you think he has something to do with Norma Carlton's murder?" His face is impassive, unreadable. The light from the lamp casts the ugly crease of the scar on his cheek and up to his eye in deep shadow.

"I did. Until now. What's the deal, Blevins? How does this play out now? I'm guessing you're planning to finish the job you tried when you fiddled with the brakes on my car. So there's no harm in you telling me who is really pulling your strings. Veronica Stratton or Robert Huston? Or are you just into this voodoo-hoodoo, like everyone else? I suppose it's the only way of getting your pipe cleaned—you know, with that handsome kisser of yours. The whole wearing-masks thing must work in your favor." She tries to keep the tremor from her voice. She tells herself to shut up, to quit smart-mouthing her way to a bullet. But the words, the vitriol, keep coming. "How's the whole Lon Chaney thing working out for you?"

"What can I say," says Blevins, blankly. "You're hurting my feelings.

By the way, I didn't touch your car. Or, at least, I didn't touch it before it went off the edge of Mount Laurel. I went down and had a look at it after, though. You're right, by the way—someone fixed your brakes, all right."

He stands up, the black eye of the pistol staying locked on her as he crosses to where he tossed her bag. He brings it back to the chair and goes through it. He gives a low whistle as he takes out the pocket pistol.

"That's some toy you got there," he says. "You shoot sparrows with it?" He replaces it in the bag. Rourke is taken aback when he tosses the bag back to her. It lands on her lap, and she catches it with both hands. Blevins's face is still impassive. He stands up. Reaching into his inside jacket pocket, he takes out a folded piece of card and tosses that on top of Rourke's bag. "Take a look," he says. Rourke unfolds the photograph to reveal a copy of the same poorly executed publicity shot that Jake Kendrick had shown her of the missing girl who had turned up dead.

"This is Lucille Quimby," says Rourke, frowning.

"Her mother's maiden name was Blevins, my sister. Lucille is— was—my niece. Can we play nice?" he asks, and tucks the automatic into his waistband. As soon as he sits back down, Rourke snatches the pocket pistol from her bag and points it at him.

"That ain't playing nice," says Blevins. "And I'm a pretty big sparrow."

"Think of it as my comfort blanket. Lucille Quimby was brought up in an orphanage. She has no family."

"Yes, she does. Me. Her folks died of the flu back in '19. I wasn't long back from the war, and pretty messed up. I tried to get my job back as a mechanic, but the price you paid for serving your nation was, you came home to find your spot had been given away to some soft stay-at-home Joe." He points to his scar. "And as you so kindly pointed out, I ain't no John Gilbert. No one wants a kisser like this serving tables or selling automobiles. I ended up driving for a local rumrunner for a while. There was no way I could have taken on a kid. But I did make sure she was looked after. Once I got a regular job, I paid for extras for her, and when she turned sixteen, I took her in from the orphanage. But she already had all these crazy ideas about Hollywood and being a star. After all those years she'd been on her own in the orphanage, I didn't have the right to stop her. She wrote me regular, but when the letters stopped coming, I came out here to find her." For the first time, there is a hint of emotion on Blevins's face. "And I did—but it was too late."

"I'm sorry," says Rourke. She stops pointing the gun at him, but doesn't return it to her handbag, instead letting it rest on her lap, her hand in turn resting on it. "So what's the deal with you working up at Stratton's place?"

"The last letter I got from Lucille said she had gotten a job—a good-paying job—at some club. She didn't give too many details, but from the little she did, I didn't much like the sound of the setup. In the same letter, she was all excited because she'd been asked to do a screen test. She said it was Robert Huston, the English actor, who had set it all up."

"So that's why, when you came to L.A., you got work at the Stratton place? You thought Huston had something to do with Lucille's disappearance?"

"I still do. Him or Veronica Stratton. But I can't prove it—yet."

"And you didn't think of going to the police?"

"The police?" he scoffs. "The police here in Los Angeles? You only get cop time here if you pay for it. And most of it's already bought up. You of all people must know that."

"They're not all bad," she says.

"What? Your tame detective Kendrick? He's on the take as much as anyone else. No, no cops—I knew when I came here I'd have to sort this out by myself."

"So you started following me around?"

"Sometimes, yeah. I didn't know how kosher you were. Still don't, really. But one of the days I followed you, your detective pal took you out to Forest Lawn Cemetery. I looked at the grave you visited."

"What the hell has that got to do with anything?" Rourke fights down a flash of anger.

"Gave me an insight, is all. People tell me you're a tough cookie, but when I saw the dates on that grave, I reckoned you might understand something of what I'm going through. They would have been the same age, more or less."

"I know. I can do the math."

"The fact that you've already done it says I'm maybe right about you."

"So you think I'm ripe to become a crusader for justice for your dead eighteen-year-old niece? Even at the expense of the studio's interests?"

"No, I know there are limits. But I also know that you're someone who wants to do the right thing. I'm guessing that, the deeper you've gotten into this mess, the more you feel like that."

"Yeah, sure," she sighs. "It's called 'the hero's journey.' I know all about it."

"Huh?"

"Never mind." She looks at him for a moment. The scar, the build, the cool attitude—nothing about Blevins fits with him being the hero of the piece. "There's a body in the morgue, and you're connected to it. Explain that to me?"

"You're talking about Briggs. . . ."

"Unless you're connected to other bodies in the morgue, yes, Briggs."

"He's a sheriff from Louisiana."

"That much I know," she replies.

"Did you know why he was here in Hollywood?"

"I'm guessing he was resolving some unsolved case, am I right?"

Blevins gives a small laugh. "In a way. It was more of a crusade, you might say. He was a big guy, tough, and he'd seen just about all there is to see in his time, but he thought he was getting close to his target, and he was as jumpy as hell. I mean, like, he was scared for more than his life."

"So how come you ended up talking to him at his motel? What was your connection with Briggs?"

"No real connection at all. He came up to Mount Laurel, and I happened to be on the gate. He asked to speak to Miss Stratton, but I told him she wasn't there. Then he asked to speak to Robert Huston, and I told him the same thing. Then he starts asking all these strange questions about Stratton, so I ask him what his game is. It was then he showed me his badge and told me he was looking for a missing person. A woman."

"What kind of strange questions?" asks Rourke.

"Like if Miss Stratton had a birthmark on her face. One about the size of a fingerprint."

"And does she?"

"Not that I've ever noticed."

"So how come you end up in the lot of his hotel?"

"Some cop—retired or otherwise—turns up from Hicksville on the trail of a missing girl. . . . You can see how I would start thinking he and

I have some common ground. So I asked him where he was staying so I could let him know when Miss Stratton would be available. To start with, he was real cagey about it, but then he gave me the address of the motor hotel."

"And you went to see him?"

"Yeah. I leveled with him and told him my story—Lucille's story. Showed him her picture. He told me that the missing-person case he was on was nearly twenty years old and not connected. Then he owned up that he wasn't a sheriff anymore, but he wasn't going to stop until he found this girl—a woman now—and her mother."

"Did he tell you why? What was it about them?"

"He told me that it was much more than a missing-persons thing—it was about murder. More than a dozen murders over decades. He reckoned both mother and daughter were involved. He said he saw an entire community destroyed by them. I tell you, Briggs was no shrinking violet, but I could tell he was just as scared as he was committed. He told me that the mother would be somewhere shy of sixty now, and the daughter in her thirties. Their names had been Hippolyta and Anastasie Cormier—Anastasie was the daughter—but God knows what they're called now. The thing with the birthmark he asked me about is the only thing he said he had to identify them."

"And he thought the daughter was Veronica Stratton?"

"He said he didn't know, but the leads he had followed had brought him to Hollywood, and he thought Veronica Stratton was possibly the daughter."

"Why? I mean, how did he end up here?" asks Rourke.

"He tracked the women to this traveling magic-lantern show that went bust about fifteen years since. There was a man worked there, a feller called Boy Lindqvist, got into some trouble. Lindqvist was the creative genius behind the show, apparently, but became suspected of attacks on women wherever the show traveled. The three of them took off about the same time, after a local mob got antsy and set fire to the show."

"And Briggs thought the three of them were together?"

Blevins shrugs. "At least the women. But he was sure that the mother and daughter had moved to Hollywood under new identities. And that brings me to right here."

"Here?"

"Briggs reckoned the mother was injured in some kind of swamp shootout. That she maybe ended up in a wheelchair."

"Wait—you mean Madame Erzulie?"

"Briggs said there were no clients. It was all a front, but a front for what, he didn't know. But one thing he was convinced about was that your friend—now dead friend—Hiram Levitt, the so-called Resurrectionist, had been involved in giving them new identities and backstories. What is it?" Blevins reads Rourke's expression.

"I have reason to believe that Hiram Levitt was blackmailing his former clients."

"Ah, I see. . . ." Blevins frowns. "Except, if he blackmailed the Cormier women and Lindqvist, he bit off more than he could chew."

"Quite literally—someone stuffed his mouth and throat with a towel," says Rourke. "So you think that Veronica Stratton is Anastasie, Hippolyta is Madame Erzulie, and Robert Huston is Boy Lindqvist?"

"That's what I think, but I could be wrong."

"Listen, Blevins, you can't lone-wolf this. Nor can I."

"That's my thinking. We should work together."

"No—I mean yes. What I mean is, this is way too big and way too dangerous for us to handle on our own. Jake Kendrick's a good guy. Honest and reliable, no matter what you think. And he has a horse in this race with Briggs's murder. We need to bring him in on this."

"I told you, I don't trust cops."

"Maybe so—but you ought to know that Jake Kendrick picked up your niece's murder, and has been trying to find the other missing girls, when no one else gave a damn. The other thing is, you saw what happened to Briggs when he tried to go it alone. Let me fix up a meeting with Kendrick. In the meantime, with Briggs and Levitt dead, and Levitt's files disappeared, Stratton and Huston think they're in the clear. Huston's got this movie to finish for the studio, so he's not going anywhere. So I'll set up a meeting with Kendrick. Sound good?"

Blevins shrugs. "No, but I'll go along with it anyway." He stands up and walks over to her. "Turn your face to the light," he says.

"What?"

He takes a firm hold of her chin and turns her face one way, then the other. Rourke pushes his hand away from her face and stands up abruptly.

"What the hell do you think you're doing?" she demands. They both look down at the same time to where she has jammed the pocket pistol into his belly.

Blevins's disfigured face approximates a smile. "Sorry, I just had to check. Another theory I thought might be possible."

"You're kidding me." Her voice is raised now. "You were seriously looking for this birthmark?"

He shrugs. "I had it down as a possibility. You can't be too careful."

"You think? Then I'd be a lot more careful before you lay hands on me again." She lets the anger subside. "By the way, what was it for?" she asks.

"What was what for?" He frowns.

"The screen test Lucille said Huston had set up for her? What was she testing for?"

Again, something like a smile, made lopsided by the ugly deep crease of his war wound, crosses Blevins's face. "Ah, that . . . that, Miss Rourke, is where our paths cross. . . ."

"*The Devil's Playground*?" she asks, though she already knows the answer.

36

The next day feels unreal, like when she walked through the Ouxbois movie set. Everything around her seems like an approximation of reality. Everyone she meets or thinks about seems a character pantomiming their emotions for an audience no one can see. Maybe, she thinks, she has been in the movie business too long.

She has the address of Blevins's boarding house and the times she can telephone and catch him there. First, she has to speak to Jake Kendrick, and she has no idea how that conversation will go, or even how she is going to begin to explain it all to him.

She tries to focus on the task at hand: the final details of the press-and-investor event tonight. Tonight, they are going to watch a city burn to the ground. Everything is more or less lined up, yet as she tries to focus on the typewritten details on the desk in front of her, all she can think about is what she has found out. Huston will be there tonight. Somehow, he was involved with Norma Carlton's murder—whether he is Boy Lindqvist or not. Maybe it's Stratton who is in charge, who wrapped a ligature around her rival's neck.

What was it that Norma Carlton knew that sentenced her to death?

Rourke's musings are interrupted by Sylvie calling through. "That's a telephone call for you, Miss Rourke."

"Who is it?"

"A Betty Dupris. She says you'll know what it's about."

"Fine—thanks, Sylvie." Rourke frowns and lifts the receiver to her ear. "Betty?"

"Hello, Miss Rourke, I wanted—"

"Just a minute," says Rourke. She waits until she hears the click of

Sylvie hanging up. "What is it, Betty? Have you thought of something else?"

"Yes—well, no. I need to meet with you. There's someone I think you should meet. It's important."

"Who?"

"It's best we meet. You'll understand then. Can you meet me tonight?"

"No, sorry," says Rourke. "Not tonight. The studio has something big going on and I have to be there. No way out of it. How about tomorrow?"

"Just a minute—" Betty says. Rourke hears the muffled sound of a hand over the mouthpiece. Betty is clearly talking to someone else there with her. The hand is removed. "Tomorrow night. Six-thirty. There's a café a few blocks from the Studio Club, on Lexington and Vine. It's called Armando's." There is a pause; then Betty says, "Please come, Miss Rourke, it's important."

"I'll be there."

At 8:00 p.m., everybody is gathered in the studio cafeteria. The sun is already almost down, and when it's full dark outside, Rourke calls for everybody's attention.

"Ladies and gentlemen, could you all make your way to the main entrance. We'll be leaving in five minutes," she explains. "Transportation is waiting outside. Thank you all for coming. I promise you, this is going to be a truly unforgettable experience for us all."

Rourke is pleased to see the press turnout. A dozen or more newsies have turned up to witness what has been billed by Rourke's publicity department as "the greatest dramatic moment in moviemaking history." There are, however, no photographers allowed in their number—no flashbulbs will ruin this one-take opportunity, no badly taken image will give away the spectacle. Besides the reporters, there are a handful of senior executives from Carbine International, as well as four of the investors in the movie, including a middle-aged balding man, with a suitably dyspeptic demeanor, whom Rourke recognizes as Clarence Van Brenner, the chairman of Consolidated Californian, the bank with a major shareholding in the company.

A Studebaker bus, dressed in the Carbine International colors and emblem, waits outside the main building. As they are conducted to it, Van Brenner seems put out that he is expected to share transport with the newsmen and studio staff.

The studio bus takes them as far as the back of the embankment. Golem Geller has security men all around the lot's perimeter, and stewards guide the bus to where it parks, next to half a dozen other vehicles. Above them, and between them and the Ouxbois set, the embankment looms steep and dark, like some medieval earthwork battlement topped with a chaos of scaffolding, bright lamps, and cameras: an armory directed toward an enemy Rourke and the others cannot yet see.

The flank of the embankment rises sharply, and Rourke and the others have to lean into it as they climb. More studio security guards wait at the top, directing the others to where there are seats arranged for them, safely distant from where Paul Brand's tall, thin figure stalks constantly and anxiously between cameramen, checking equipment, examining the vista below through a viewfinder, shouting German-inflected orders at gaffers and crew. Rourke has never seen the director so agitated. Then again, the studio's entire investment in his movie is about to go up in flames.

A security man's extended arm indicates the direction Rourke should take, away from the others. "Mr. Carbine says you and Mr. Van Brenner should sit with him to watch the scene, Miss Rourke," he explains.

"Thanks," she says, and she and the dour banker walk along the crest of the embankment to the row of canvas studio chairs where Carbine, his deputy Clifford J. Taylor, and Margot Drescher sit. Carbine stands up when Rourke arrives; Taylor, dressed in jodhpurs and riding boots, does not. Drescher smiles and waves.

"Here you go, Mary." Carbine indicates a vacant studio chair. "This is the grandstand view. Hello, Clarence," he says to the dour banker. "I'm so glad you could make it."

Everyone sits, Rourke taking her place next to Margot Drescher. As she does so, she notices Van Brenner and Clifford Taylor exchanging a look that strikes her as odd. A look that suggests something more than acquaintance.

"Who's the stiff?" asks Drescher under her breath, rolling her eyes to indicate Van Brenner.

"The money, apparently," says Rourke. Drescher nods knowingly.

From the elevated position where they now sit, Rourke can see the full expanse of the lot below them. There is a second bank of lights and cameras farther down and on the same level as the set and closer to it, and she knows that Brand's fellow German assistant director, Hugo Aschenbrenner, is in charge of that unit.

Rourke has the same feeling of conviction when she sees the set from a distance as she did when she walked through it: she really could be looking at a medieval French town. There are lights in some of the windows; torches flare insubstantially from wall stanchions to illuminate pools of cobbled street. Thready coils of smoke rise from chimneys as darker traces against the deep blue of the night sky.

Only the A-frame buttress supports she can see behind those façades that are side-on to her view, the coiling cables, and the cluttered camera tracks and light gantries of the second unit prevent the illusion from becoming total.

"I'm glad you could make it, Mary," says Carbine. The studio chief seems less assured than usual. "This is going to be quite the thing. Quite the thing indeed."

"I wouldn't miss it," she replies with a smile.

Paul Brand has two campaign tables set up side by side and centrally on the embankment's ridge. On one sits a simulation of a simulation: a scale model of the set, complete in every detail. On the other table, shooting plans and set diagrams are paperweighted to its surface; the inverted cone of a huge megaphone sits next to the crank-operated field telephone Brand uses to keep in touch with Aschenbrenner and the second unit.

Brand takes out his pocket-watch-sized timer and holds it ready. He nods to the assistants in charge of each camera unit, then turns to Carbine. "We are ready."

Carbine nods.

Brand lifts the megaphone and yells, "Positions!"

There is an excited buzz of chatter from the assembled reporters and other spectators. Rourke smiles to herself: this could work out just fine, after all.

Suddenly, everyone falls silent. Rourke hears Margot Drescher gasp at her side.

She turns to see what has stilled the hubbub, what has caught everyone's attention simultaneously. And she sees it: Robert Huston, dressed in peasant clothes and in character as the hero of the movie, Jean Durand, walks along the embankment ridge's path toward the section dressed to look like a mountainside. But it is the woman at his side who has stunned everyone, including Rourke, into silence.

There, at Huston's side as they make their way to take their places for the scene, is Norma Carlton.

"It can't be . . ." she hears Margot Drescher mutter with something like dread in her voice as she begins to rise from her chair.

Rourke watches as the movie star continues to make her way along the embankment's ridge path, her gaze down at her feet to guard against misstep. Rourke again thinks back to her brief sight of Carlton's dead body, cold and pale and mottled, lying starkly illuminated on porcelain in the Appleton morgue, before it was once more plunged into darkness by Doc Wilson's flick of a switch.

"It can't be . . ." she finds herself repeating Drescher's words. Thoughts fly through her head as she tries to make sense of what she is seeing. Thoughts of Norma Carlton's belief in resurrection.

It is only when the actress is less than thirty feet distant and illuminated by the stand lights that the truth is revealed. Nothing in Hollywood, Rourke once more thinks to herself, is ever what it seems.

The similarity is stunning. But now that she is closer, the actress is revealed to be considerably younger than Norma Carlton, her figure a perfect match, but her features, though sharing the same architecture as the dead star's, are slightly less sultry, less sensual. The actress is, Rourke realizes, the stand-in Harry Carbine and Paul Brand had discussed in the production office. Rourke is aware that Margot Drescher has retaken her seat, but when she turns to look at her, she sees the agent is still recovering from her shock.

Robert Huston and Norma Carlton's stand-in take their positions on the part of the embankment that has been dressed with rocks, trees, and shrubs to suggest a mountainside overlooking the city.

"My God," says Margot Drescher at last. "She's the image of Norma. For a moment I thought—"

"Me too," says Rourke.

Brand furiously cranks the handle of the field telephone, then, like a Prussian general commanding his infantry, barks an order in German down the line to Aschenbrenner. Brand then takes his pocket timer from his vest and clicks the button. Despite herself, Rourke feels an electric thrill run up her spine. It is beginning. She knows that a third of the cameras, covering the scene from all angles, will begin rolling simultaneously, the other third will start one minute later, the final third sixty seconds after them. It means that, between the reels, nothing of what is to follow will be missed.

Brand nods to the clapper boy, lifts the megaphone to his mouth and yells, "Action!"

The cameras begin to roll.

There are two minutes of nothing happening, merely the city sitting unstirred beneath the vault of deep blue. The stars twinkle brightly above the scene.

Brand turns in the direction of the chief grip. With a grim decisiveness, he raises his long arm above his head, then brings it swiftly down in an arc.

Down below, an orange glow illuminates the dark set. Like a river of lava, an army of extras charge through the streets, each carrying a flaming brand. The same extras, dressed in the surplices and the pointed, conical *coroza* hats of the Inquisition, have already been filmed weeks earlier from street level, performing the same purging surge. Now, seen from a distance and vivid in the night, thrown torches form bright arcs as the crowd throws them toward the buildings. But it is not these, Rourke knows, that will cause the city to burn: Brand's gesture to the chief grip of the engineering team means that the fuel jets, the timed incendiaries behind the façades, and the gullies filled with tar and petroleum are about to be ignited.

From where they sit, Rourke and the others can hear the bellowing fury of the mob. She thinks how strange it is that the extras give feigned anger a voice that no audience will ever hear. Suddenly, flames leap upward from several of the buildings. The face of the cathedral is illuminated by fire. Rourke can see a ripple of bright blue, then vivid red, as the trenches of fuel ignite. Still the extras make their way through the set, surrounded by towering flames. Carbine has already explained to her that the routes taken by the extras are actually safely away from any source of heat. Simple distance and perspective angle are what give the illusion of proximity.

The fire spreads. The facsimile city of Ouxbois burns bright and vivid. The façades of its buildings are thrown out as stark silhouettes. Again, Rourke knows that the flames they see don't touch the set scenery. The burning of the actual set will be the climactic third act of this spectacle, once all the extras are safely out of the way.

It is breathtaking. The flames surge upward, casting an eerie glow into the night sky. Rourke turns and looks along the embankment to where the reporters sit. All are transfixed and silent. She smiles.

From the simulation of a mountainside, with their backs to the cameras and spectators, the two principal characters stand watching the conflagration, their forms etched by its glow. Jean Durand puts his arm around Adelicia, and despite how hard she tries to remind herself of the reality of the situation, Rourke cannot help but see Robert Huston and Norma Carlton.

Paul Brand paces, calling out to crew chiefs through the megaphone, using the field telephone to check with Aschenbrenner and the second unit.

The spectators gasp collectively when a bright burst of flame shoots upward and across the face of the cathedral. There is a second, even more forceful than the first.

Rourke catches sight of Brand's face. There is an expression of genuine surprise, as if the last two flame bursts were unexpected, unscheduled. He frowns.

There is another gasp from the assembled spectators, this time with an appreciative tone, when a third, then a fourth burst of flame surge up from different parts of the set. Rourke turns again to see Brand waving over to the engineering grip.

She knows something is wrong. It is then that she hears it: a change of tone, of pitch, in the cries from the extras. It is no longer feigned anger. It is fear. Real fear.

"Something's wrong," says Rourke.

"What?" asks Drescher.

"What?" Harry Carbine echoes, turning to Rourke, frowning.

"Something's wrong," she repeats. "On the set—something's not right."

At Brand's instruction, Huston and the stand-in actress turn their backs to the burning city and slowly begin to climb up and away from it. Rourke realizes that Brand has issued that direction earlier than planned. He knows, she thinks. He knows there is something wrong.

She sees it, they all see it, before they hear it.

Even at that short distance, the flash dazzles them before they hear the deafening, percussive thud of the explosion. A massive fireball surges up from the heart of the set. Everyone on the embankment's ridge is lit up as if by the midday sun, as the huge, swelling, fiery dome wells upward, opening out like a blossom in the night sky. As the burgeoning fireball fades, it is clear that every part of the studio lot is now uncontrollably ablaze. Rourke, Drescher, Carbine, and the others are now all on their feet, gazing at the unfolding horror. From where they stand, they can hear the screaming of extras as they are burned alive. Small figures, bright with flame, run blindly into burning façades, into one another, before falling down.

The tall, thin figure of Paul Brand also stands in mute horror for a moment. Then he turns, looking from one camera unit to another, then back again.

For a moment, Rourke thinks the director is lost in shock. Then the realization strikes her.

He is checking to make sure the cameras are still rolling.

PART THREE

37

1967
Sudden Lake

The story unfolds before Conway: there, on the screen, in the slow unfurling of shadows, the black, glossy pooling of blood, the creaking stretching of bone. He knows he is watching the greatest piece of cinema he has seen in his career, in his life. It is wondrous—darkly, terrifyingly wondrous. His awe is matched only by the fear that blossoms within him, growing with every scene.

The tale has captivated him. The city of Ouxbois, a place famed for having the finest artists and artisans in France, has closed its walls against the Black Death that ravages the country, and the Continent, around them. When the city's population is nevertheless struck with the plague, Ouxbois's mayor turns to the alchemist and black magician, Alban Archambeau, to protect the city. In return, Archambeau demands the hand in marriage of the mayor's daughter, the pious and virginal Adelicia.

In a scene that leaves Conway breathless, Archambeau summons up the Lord of Hell, Ba'al Zebub, to protect the city from pestilence and provide an abundance of provender for the townspeople. In the alchemist's dungeon workshop, he mixes potions, incants blasphemous invocations, drains blood from animal offerings. Again, the film historian feels his pulse pick up pace as the shadows ripple and seethe around Archambeau. Inhuman faces leer and glower momentarily in the shadows and in the cauldron's smoke.

Then comes something else, something even more disturbing, that

Conway can't explain. In the character of Archambeau, the actor Lewis Everett's darkly handsome face transforms. The features stretch and sharpen. The eyes swell and turn inhuman. With no idea how the director Paul Brand has achieved the effect, Conway watches as the evil sorcerer Archambeau transforms into Beelzebub, revealing that is his true identity.

Meanwhile, as a result of rejecting good and embracing evil, Ouxbois is saved from the Black Death. The great pestilence retreats from the city, but rages on through the lands and settlements around it. Ouxbois becomes an oasis of plenty, and, increasingly, of excess. The city becomes for its citizens more than a sheltering haven in the storm of plague, it becomes their universe. But Ouxbois's life has been bought at the cost of its soul: the populace becomes ever more forgetful of the plague that afflicts their countrymen, and ever more hedonistic and lascivious.

God and the Church are abandoned for orgiastic worship of the three Lords of Hell: Belphegor, Lord of Sloth and Unearned Riches; Beelzebub, Lord of Gluttony; and Asmodeus, Lord of Lust. The city's artists and artisans continue to create their art, but it is ever more extreme, ever more libidinous and outrageous. Some pieces are magnificent, epic, if self-indulgent; others are vulgar and frequently pornographic.

In Ouxbois's main square, in the shadow of the once-dominant cathedral, a huge idol is fashioned. The city's finest stonemasons and sculptors hew a vast and monstrous statue of Beelzebub, Lord of Flies. The director has used lighting like a sculptor's chisel to carve harsh, angular shadows in the stone, and has created dramatic perspective by filming upward from the base. The result is that the graven idol has a towering, terrifying presence.

Only simple peasant painter Jean Durand, played by Robert Huston, remains untouched by the city's idolatry and lubricity. In one beautifully imagined scene, Jean looks out mournfully from the battlements of the city's wall to where smoke rises blackly into the sky from thousands of bright specks that dot the landscape beyond. These are the funeral pyres of those, in the harsh reality of the world beyond Ouxbois, who have died from plague.

Jean's heart remains not only pure, but devoted to Adelicia, whom he has long loved from afar.

Conway finds himself drawn ever deeper into the world on-screen.

THE DEVIL'S PLAYGROUND · 239

There is something strange in the way nothing else seems to exist for him anymore, as if his being is no longer anchored in flesh and blood but being pulled into the screen itself. So deep is his immersion that even that thought is vague and abstract to him.

In return for his saving the city from plague, Archambeau demands that the mayor, Frédéric Marquand, keep his bargain and give over his daughter to him as his bride. Hanging his head in shame and sorrow, the mayor agrees. Doughty Jean Durand overhears the conversation and despairs. Firm resolve, however, triumphs over his despondency, and he determines to save Adelicia, should it cost him his own life.

Adelicia is fitted with her bridal gown. It is a monstrous affair made of black silk, with flamelike details surging up from the shoulders. Her hennin headdress comprises twin towering black cones, draped in spiderweb veils. The impossibly long, ink-black train of her dress stretches far behind her and up the stone steps of the chamber like an elongated shadow.

It is clear that the pious and virginal Adelicia is to be married by Satanic rite.

What strikes Conway most about the scene is how, in the role of Adelicia, Norma Carlton's beauty itself becomes transformed from pure and virginal to something darkly voluptuous and sultry. The black silk of the gown clings to her form like a liquid sheen. He sees it now, in this scene more than any other he has seen her in: Norma Carlton truly is "the most desirable woman in the world."

On the eve of her wedding, however, Adelicia is saved by Jean Durand, who, after an epic struggle with Archambeau, pushes the necromancer to his apparent death from the balcony of the mayoral home. Jean has saved his beloved's soul, though he cannot save the soul of the city.

The couple make their escape from Ouxbois and its ruin.

The forces of the Inquisition, consumed with righteous fury, besiege Ouxbois and ultimately break down the great gate. Paul Conway is spellbound as he watches the *coroza*-capped and white-gowned soldiers of the Inquisitional Brotherhood surge through the town, setting it ablaze.

Conway had, of course, read about the filming of the scene—about the loss of life. It was part—a big part—of the mythology of *The Devil's Playground* curse. Along with the flood scene in Michael Curtiz's

Noah's Ark, where six hundred thousand gallons of water had been lethally unleashed on unsuspecting extras, the burning of Ouxbois scene was one of the most notorious examples of disregard for extras' safety in movie history.

Unseen for decades, the scene is uncut. Conway can see people burning—*really* burning. It is terrible. It is obscene. It is magnificent.

Adelicia and Jean escape to the mountains. In the most spectacular closing scene Conway has ever seen, Ouxbois is totally consumed by a fire so great and so fierce that it seems to have surged up from hell itself.

The great city of Ouxbois is brought down by the righteous rage of the Inquisition, and its own hubris.

Conway watches in awe as, in the final scene, the black, rippling smoke that rises up from the burning city coalesces into the monstrous, towering figure of Archambeau transformed into Beelzebub. The gigantic figure of the Prince of Hell opens wide his vast black bat-wings. It is the most awe-inspiring, darkly terrifying thing Conway has ever seen.

Two intertitle cards give voice to the demon's curse. The first:

"You put your faith in fire; that I can be burned from the world.
But fire is my natural climate; the flame the humor that sustains me,
the eternal furnace my abode.

"Rejoice, if you will, as the city of Ouxbois burns . . .
But have also this wisdom: I SHALL RETURN . . ."

The second card:

". . . for I merely slumber in Hell,
gone from this world only while you speak not my name.

"One day—when these events and glories fade into memory, with
your fears of them and of me—someone will retell my story.
And when my story is retold . . .
THEN AM I REBORN,
ONCE MORE TO WALK UPON THE EARTH!"

Conway's mind is a swirl of thoughts and emotions. It was all true, everything they had said about *The Devil's Playground*. And beneath his wonder is his dread that he has just watched the very retelling of a demon's story that would return it to the world.

Yet, strangely, having tracked down this masterpiece, achieved his goal, fulfilled the mission given him by his rich Santa Barbara client, all Conway's ambitions for his discovery, all his plans of books and documentaries, now seem vague and abstract, as if he is yet to return fully to the real world.

It is only after the film ends that Conway becomes vaguely aware again of that world around him. Of the reality of where he is. Of his own body.

And that there is something seriously wrong.

38

1907
Louisiana and Arkansas

Death itself, she realized, was the flame that illuminated the soul. In the fierce dazzle of that bright, burning instant, all truths lay exposed. All vanity and pretense were scorched into ash.

The old man had been so afraid. All of his bluster and arrogance had been stripped away from him when she turned up his bedside oil lamp. Opening eyes blinkingly, he had found Anastasie standing there by his bed. Wilhelm Trosclair had made to cry out for help, but she had silenced him by placing the sharp edge of the knife against his throat. He had whispered urgent pleadings for his life, made guarantees of silence, promises of freedom and money. Anastasie had been disgusted by his lack of shame or pride, and had been surprised at how desperately such an old man would cling on to the tattered and fading rag-end of his life.

Before she finished him, she had leaned in close and whispered in his ear; told him all she had to tell about the serpent that continually consumes itself and renews itself; told him about the eternal cycle of womanhood, of the dark glory of the swamp and its magic. She had rejoiced in his terror as she explained how she had learned from her mama all the dark, sweet art of poisons. How his son would have slowly woken up in the cold, airless, lightless prison of his tomb, how it would have taken a while for him to realize where he was, what had happened to him. How, when it came, his fear would have burned brighter than any flame of emotion he had ever experienced.

But that was not, she had told him, going to be his ending. The knife still at his throat, she took the kerosene can she had brought with her from the shed outside and with her free hand tipped it over onto his bed. Trosclair had whimpered as he felt the viscous liquid soaking through quilt, sheet, and nightclothes to rest against his skin.

No, she had explained, he was not going to be poisoned and wake in the stifling dark of his tomb. Instead, he was going to die in the manner he had chosen for her and her mother. The death they had escaped but that he would not.

With that, she snatched the knife from his throat. Before he could call out for help, the oil lamp described a bright arc through the dark of the room and burst onto the bed.

How the old man had burned.

Anastasie had listened to his screaming and noted how little like a man it sounded. More like an animal, as if the first thing the flame had burned away had been the tissue-thin wrapping of humanity.

She had left as she had come, by the window and down the trellis woven with dry, dead vines.

Before she faded into the night, she had stopped, turned, and watched the house burn like a bright watch-fire between the dark folds of the levees. As she slipped into the shadows to where she had hidden the horse and her mother waited, she could have sworn she still heard the animal-like screaming as that tattered and faded rag-end of a man's life burned briefly and brightly into ash.

The journey took twelve days. Twelve days and twelve nights. Despite Hippolyta's wound, they had made good progress, resting by day, traveling the bayou edges and levees mostly by night. The horse carried them both much of the way, and the rest, Hippolyta rode and Anastasie led the horse on foot.

The swamps only seemed to come fully awake after nightfall, filled with a symphony of dark life. Anastasie found she wasn't frightened, realizing instead that, like her mother, she was native to darkness, that the night was her motherland. Hippolyta spoke little during their traveling, and Anastasie knew the pain from her wound was biting through her mother's armor of resolve.

When they put sufficient distance between themselves and Leseuil, Hippolyta had said they could stop, set up camp, light a small fire, and rest.

"From now on," Hippolyta had said weakly, her beautiful face golden in the flickering firelight, "you are in charge. The circle is complete. You must use all that I have taught you."

And Anastasie did. Her mother had taught her all her skills not just of a *caplata*, but as a *traiteuse*: she knew how to heal using ancient Cajun and Creole folk medicine and her knowledge of the nature of the swamps. And Anastasie had been an eager and gifted student. She knew how to forage for the plants and fungi she needed to treat her mother's wound. In daylight, Anastasie gathered mamou, bristle mallow, and purple cudweed; she cut yellow witch's butter fungi from the limbs of trees; she mixed clay-rich red mud with Spanish moss to make a drawing poultice, brewed groundsel bush to make manglier tea to keep her mother free of fever.

It gave Anastasie some comfort that it was now she who was caring for her mama, that the circle was being completed. She was determined to use every one of her learned arts to take them to safety. But there had to be something else beyond safety.

There had to be a future.

The horse went lame on the seventh day, and Anastasie let it go on the edges of the Kisatchie Forest. It meant the rest of the way was slower, crossing country by foot and mainly avoiding towns. The journey was now, she could tell, really taking its toll on her mother. Hippolyta never complained, never uttered any plea for rest or diminishment of pace, but Anastasie knew she was having trouble. When Anastasie pushed her, all Hippolyta would say was that she had some numbness in her legs.

By the time they reached Pineville, their clothes were dirty and tattered, and they were hungry. A deep, primal hunger. Her mama had taught Anastasie how to forage for food, how to trap it, how to walk the earth independent of any man. But they had moved on too continuously and too quickly for Anastasie to weave and set grass-rope traps. She had had some success in catching crawfish, but other pickings had been meager.

Looking at her weakening mother, Anastasie knew she had to find more substantial nourishment soon.

Her mama had also taught her stealth. When they reached the edge of Pineville, she approached the town from the forest, watched, and waited for the darkness to fall. She found a provision store and waited until the owner locked up before finding a window that eased to her urging.

The raid yielded a canvas sack–full of dried food.

The next day, from the other side of the town, the pickings from unattended clotheslines gave both mother and daughter a change of dress. They bathed in a brook, and Anastasie again applied a drawing poultice to Hippolyta's wound. Feeling invigorated, they put on fresh clothes and continued their journey.

The days and the nights passed and placed even greater distance between them and the death and chaos they had left behind them in Leseuil. No one would be looking for them so far north. Few men had the imagination to think two women, one injured and the other a mere girl, would have the wherewithal to travel so far, so fast, without detection.

It was when they crossed the Arkansas border, and the landscape around them changed, that Anastasie realized that this wasn't a journey after all. A journey had a conclusion—a destination and an arrival. All they had was a point of departure: the place and event from which they were fleeing.

She thought back to that night. She thought about old man Trosclair in his bed, screaming in terror as his flesh, his house, his pride burned around him. How gloriously it had all burned, but it had illuminated only their departure point, and offered no beacon to guide their flight.

Their journey had no destination. No meaning or purpose or shape other than escape. They now crossed a landscape that held no lasting shelter or comfort, no connection.

A creeping dark despondency, black as the blackwaters of the swamp they had left behind, slowly engulfed Anastasie. For the first time in her life, she felt despair.

It was then, on that last night of their journey, when Anastasie had given up finding a destination, that their destination found them.

There was a smell, rich and deep, carried on the dark air—sweet cotton-candy odors—and with them waves of reedy calliope tones.

She left her mother to rest while she sought its source. She found their destination in the hollow of a field on the southside of Magnolia, Arkansas: a collection of carnival tents and booths. Above it a proud, bright sign:

THE DAHLMAN AND DARKE
MAGIC LANTERN PHANTASMAGORIA

39

1927
Hollywood

They talk it through until the early hours of the morning.

After the nonstudio guests have left, they hold a late-night inquest in the production office. Carbine, Paul Brand, and Clifford Taylor sit behind a campaign table like military judges at a court-martial. The production engineer, the armorer, the pyrotechnician, the chief grip— all are quizzed about what had gone wrong; none can explain it. All that can be said with any certainty is that, somehow, too much of the inflammable liquid had come in contact with ignition, and too quickly. There is talk of possibly faulty valves, of admixtures perhaps mismeasured, but no definitive answer is found.

The only certainties that face them are that two extras are dead; seventeen are hospitalized with varying degrees of burns. Some are blinded, many are disfigured for life. The worst cases are being treated at the Appleton Clinic.

"Where are we with the footage?" asks Clifford Taylor. "How much of it is usable?"

Paul Brand looks as if he's received an electric shock. He turns abruptly to Taylor. "What do you mean, how much is usable? It is *all* usable." He turns to Carbine. "I insist it is all used. Ouxbois *will* burn at the end of my film."

"It's not your film, Paul," says Carbine, his authority quiet but cogent. "It's the studio's movie. We can't afford to have it banned from distribution. But I do agree that the scene is too valuable to lose if we can avoid it." He turns to Rourke. "Where are we with containing the damage, Mary?"

"We've got the whole legal team on it," Rourke explains. "Every surviving victim, and every family of those who didn't survive, will have a visit from a legal representative from the studio by the end of the day tomorrow." She checks her wristwatch. "I mean by the end of the day today. We have strictly limited liability: like every other studio in Hollywood, the contracts we offer extras have preset limits on responsibility. Everyone involved will be offered a take-it-or-leave-it compensation package that includes a gagging clause. Like I say, by the end of the day."

Carbine nods as he listens. Like everyone else, Rourke knows that, although there has been talk about unionization, the studios have united in their suppression of any kind of representative body for actors or extras. There will be no class-action lawsuits, no collective grievance. The victims and their families will take what they are offered, which will be less than Harry Carbine spends on tailoring in a year. Not for the first time in her career at the studio, Rourke has to push from her mind that the collateral she trades in, and trades off, is real human suffering and real human lives. The career shift to cleaning sewers becomes ever more attractive.

"What about the press?" asks Clifford Taylor.

"We'll find out in a few hours," says Rourke. "It'll go big, and it'll go wide, but who'll take what angle we'll only find out when newsprint hits sidewalks. My guess is that we'll be okay—the line they're most likely to take is that this latest accident cements the movie's reputation as a cursed production. As we've discussed, that's something we can make work to our box-office advantage. The only real complaint I got from the reporters that were there was that they hadn't been allowed to bring photographers or cameras. It means there will be no pictures to go with their copy when they go to press." Carbine exchanges a look with Rourke. She is ashamed that she clearly is thinking the same thing he is. She gives the thought voice: "That means, if the press builds this incident up, and have no pictures to go with the headlines, the only way the public will get to see what happened is if they pay for a ticket at a picture-house box office."

"You really think we can turn this in our favor?" asks Clifford Taylor.

"All I can say is, the reaction of the assembled press and investors surprised me: they were clearly more impressed than horrified. They obviously saw it as a spectacle, rather than a tragedy. And, like I say, this accident has probably cemented *The Devil's Playground*'s reputation with the press as some darkly cursed production. I guess they'll imply the hand of some supernatural agency, despite both accidents' clearly being caused by some technical fault. The French have a name for it—*succès de scandale*. If we play this right, from here on in there really is no such thing as bad publicity."

Carbine asks Rourke to stay behind when the others have left. She slumps back in a chair and wearily pushes tired hands through thick, dark hair.

"What's to do, boss?"

"The Norma Carlton thing—"

"Oh, yeah. Sorry . . ." She straightens herself up. "With all of this drama, we haven't had a chance to discuss it. I think—"

"I want you to drop it." Carbine cuts her off.

"What?" Rourke frowns, confused. In her tiredness, she fails to keep the irritation from her tone.

"I want you to drop it. I need you on point to deal with what happened tonight. There's going to be all kinds of hoo-hah because of it. It and the other accident and what happened to Norma."

"*What happened* to Norma? You mean her murder?"

Carbine sighs. "Whatever it was, it's best left alone. I was right to get you to look into it when I did, but it's wrong now. We don't want people asking too many questions about Norma's death, and, discreet as I know you are, you looking into it will only draw attention to the fact that there's more to the whole sorry mess."

"Harry," says Rourke, "whoever murdered Norma knew how we operate, knew who would turn up and what we'd do. It could be someone right under our noses. It could be someone connected to the studio. I've found out things. Lots of things. About Veronica Stratton and Robert Huston. About missing girls. About another killing. There was this sheriff from—"

Carbine stops her with a held-up hand. "Forget it, Mary. For all our sakes. We need to focus on what's in front of us. For the meantime, the movie is everything."

"So what about the hero's journey?" she asks sardonically.

"I'm sorry, Mary. I shouldn't have asked in the first place. You were right."

"So that's it? I just drop the whole thing?"

"You've got more than enough on your plate." Carbine looks dejected, burdened, and Rourke senses some of his typical vigor sapped. He looks older. Maybe it's just the hour. Or maybe the angel that Robert Huston has on his shoulder has been keeping Carbine awake nights. It stinks, she thinks, it all stinks.

"Sure," she says with a shrug. "You're the boss. I'll drop it."

She surprises herself at just how convincing she managed to make it sound.

The next day is packed. There are meetings with department heads to make sure that every member of Carbine International's staff dances to the same tune. Then there are the endless telephone calls to reporters and editors, to gossip columnists and movie critics. Mary Rourke spends so much time on the telephone her voice turns husky.

She reports back to Carbine on progress. The "Curse of *The Devil's Playground*" is, as predicted, the direction taken by almost all of the papers. The *Examiner* goes into all the details, vague as they are, about the mysterious screenwriter and the dark history of the novel and its defrocked-priest author. It's the best result she could have hoped for, and she tells Carbine so.

When she gets up to leave, she senses Carbine is about to say something, but he thinks better of it. She says nothing more about the Norma Carlton affair, and she gets the feeling he had been ready with further defenses or justifications for telling her to let the whole thing drop.

She makes time midafternoon to call at the Appleton Clinic. Only five of the injured extras are being treated there, the most serious cases, out of sight of the press. Doc Wilson sees her in his office and breaks down the prognosis of the five. One, he says, isn't likely to make it through the next two days. The others will be hospitalized for a long time. Rourke makes no effort to visit the injured. She found out long ago that it's best to keep things abstract, depersonalized. It's the professional way, she tells herself. Even if it makes looking in the mirror a whole lot harder.

"Why do I get the feeling you've come about more than these patients?" Doc Wilson asks her as he pours them both a brandy.

Rourke tells him that Harry Carbine has told her to drop looking into Norma Carlton's death. For some reason she can't fully understand, she tells him nothing of the progress she has made, the things she's found out.

"Maybe it's best, Mary," says Wilson. "You and I both could end up in jail if this plays out the wrong way. It's been a strain. A real strain." He pauses and sips his brandy. "In fact, I'm thinking of getting out of Los Angeles. Of giving up my post here."

Rourke is surprised. "What will you do?"

"I'll get a place somewhere. I was even offered a position heading up a Brinkley clinic." He gives a small laugh.

"The goat-gland doctor?" Rourke knows of John Romulus Brinkley. He has set up clinics in every state, where men seek cures for everything from impotence and sterility to baldness by having goats' testicles surgically inserted in their scrotums. Recently, Brinkley has extended his miracle cure to female patients, implanting goat glands in their ovaries. Brinkley has made millions from the practice.

"Needless to say, I told him to take a hike," answers Wilson, taking another sip of his brandy.

"You still haven't said what you'll do."

"I'll get a place somewhere. Go part-time in some general practice or hospital away from Los Angeles. Might even retire. The Norma Carlton thing has me shaken up, if I'm honest."

"You told Harry Carbine?"

"Not yet. I will when I have my plans more final. I might take a few days out to think it all through, leave Davidson in charge. In the meantime, as far as Carbine is concerned, I'd appreciate it if you kept this under your hat."

"Of course," says Rourke. She tilts her glass in toast. "Here's to your future, Doc. . . ."

Despite the chaos of the day, she is there in time for her appointment. Armando's sits on the intersection, in a two-story white building with

Spanish-arch windows edged in cerulean blue, jostling shoulders with its larger, pool-hall neighbor. Hanging signs promise "Open All Day, Dairy Lunch," and "Coffee Only 15 Cents a Cup."

Inside, it is clean and bright. As soon as she enters, Rourke sees Betty Dupris sitting alone at a table in the far corner. Betty makes a gesture of recognition so slight that it suggests she is trying to avoid rather than attract attention, and Rourke crosses the café and sits opposite her.

"Thanks for coming, Miss Rourke," said Betty, but the bright, agile eyes scan the café behind her, the door, the street through the arched windows.

"I didn't bring anyone with me, if that's what you're worried about," says Rourke.

"I'm sorry," says Betty. "It's just we've got to be careful."

"Careful? Why?"

"You asked me about Sadie and the other missing girls. About Susie and Lucille. I couldn't tell you more then—I had to check first. But there's someone you need to meet."

"Who?"

"Wait here, I'll be right back." Betty stands up and leaves the café. While she is waiting, Rourke orders a coffee. As her back is to the door, she turns her chair slightly to give her a view of the street. She sees Betty coming back past the windows. Someone is with her.

When Betty returns to the table, the other girl sits beside her, both opposite Rourke. The new arrival is roughly the same age as Betty. Her cloche hat has a wide brim that hides much of her face, and Rourke gets the idea the choice of headwear is based on anonymity rather than style. Facing her, Rourke can see the girl is, like Betty, unexceptionally pretty, her complexion pale and drawn. Everything about her suggests weariness, yet her eyes are twitchily agile—unnaturally agile, thinks Rourke.

"Miss Rourke," says Betty, "this is—"

"I know who you are," says Rourke to the new arrival, cutting Betty off. "I recognize you from your photograph. Hello, Sadie . . ."

40

The car, a rental, is inconspicuous in make, value, and color, but very conspicuous by its sole presence in this strange landscape. Anastasie Cormier—though she has not been called by that name for such a long, long time, so long that the name now seems alien—turns in to the track off the main road and pulls the automobile over. It is not yet night, but the darkness is already gathering. This is, after all, a place where darkness literally seeps out of the earth.

She sits with the automobile's engine and lights off. And waits. It seems so alien here, so isolated and distant from anything, yet she can clearly see behind her the lights on Wilshire Boulevard. Los Angeles glitters so close by, but here the only light is the last bleeding of the dying sun.

And, as it always has, the darkness comforts her.

Another automobile pulls up behind her. The headlights dazzle in her mirror, then are killed. A man gets out and comes to the passenger door.

"Not here," she says as he makes to step into the automobile.

"Where?"

"Follow me," she commands. Commanding men comes naturally to her—as naturally as their willingness to obey. She steps out of the car and leads him deeper into the darkness. She stops when she gets to the edge of a small gully. The man follows, and for a moment they both stare down into the shallow depression in front of them. In the semidark, it almost looks as solid underfoot as the rest of the land around them: dusty, strewn with brush and tumbleweed. A large body of water, too big to be called a pool, too small to be called a lake, glistens malevolently, like black obsidian, at the center of the depression.

The true nature of the small lake's "shore" is revealed only when the thin skin of dirt and plant debris ripples and bulges upward with a large black, glossy bubble, which then bursts like a lanced boil, splashing viscous black tar. The water too bubbles intermittently, and foul methane odors mix in the air with the smell of asphalt.

The small dark lake is surrounded by an iron forest in constant breezeless motion, as a thousand clustered oil derricks nod their horseheads, dipping and pulling sucker-pump rods deep into the earth's bedrock flesh and tapping its deep, inky veins.

"Why here?" the man asks.

"Because it's quiet, and it's safe, and there's no one to recognize me. What has she found out?"

"Not much," he says. "And I think that's the end of it. Harry Carbine has told her to drop the whole thing, and I think she has."

"She doesn't know about Sudden Lake? About the gatherings?"

"I think she was getting close, she was asking around about the missing girls—but I don't think she connected them to anything else. So no. I don't think so."

"And she doesn't suspect your involvement?"

"No. Of that I'm certain. We've left no trail for her to follow."

Beneath them, another bubble of molasses-like asphalt, two feet across, swells up and bursts, again splashing black tar and releasing an odor like freshly laid roads into the dark air.

"They've found all kinds of animals down there, in the pitch," she says, gazing blankly into the tar pit. "Animals that don't exist anymore. Dire wolves, mostly. Mammoths. Huge saber-toothed cats. The larger animals would come to drink at what looked like an ordinary watering hole, only to become trapped in the asphalt tar. The crazy thing is, the tar's never more than a foot deep, but once they were in it, they were trapped. Then the wolves would come, thinking they had easy pickings to prey on. But then they would become trapped too. Some traps, I'm afraid, are as dangerous for predators as for prey." She sighs. "So much history hidden down there. That's all I wanted—for my history to stay hidden somewhere deep and dark."

"It was always a risk," says the man. "To allow your face to become so well known, so famous."

"Was it?" She still stares down, absently watching the slow, cold boiling of asphalt pitch and methane. "I was so young when I left. I've changed. It wouldn't have been a problem if it hadn't been for Briggs. They won't let it go now. They'll keep after me for what happened back home." She sighs, almost wistfully. "But there's nothing can be done about that now. I must disappear."

"Where will you go?" he asks.

She doesn't reply straightaway but continues to stare into the tar pit.

"Did you know that La Brea is Spanish for 'tar' or 'pitch'?" she asks him eventually. "Everything sounds nicer in Spanish or French, don't you agree? I still dream in French, you know. It's still the language of my soul."

The faint breeze has changed direction, and now brings with it the metallic clanging from the forest of oil derricks, which fades as the breeze changes direction again.

"Shouldn't you be gone by now?" he asks her. "Out of town. Before this all gets out of hand."

"I will. I just have to tie up some loose ends. But I have somewhere safe to go. You know it: out where the stone theater is. I'll be fine. Once everything here is tied up."

"Is there anything I can do?" he asks. "You know I would do anything for you. I always have."

"I know," she says. "I have just one last thing; then you're free."

"Name it."

Anastasie sighs once more. "Secrets should stay buried. Those bodies they found down there—the mammoths and the dire wolves and the saber-toothed cats—they had lain hidden here for thousands of years. Their secrets were safe all that time. And they say there are thousands more down there."

"What's your point?" he asks.

"Just this . . ."

Anastasie's movements are so swift, the object she removes from her pocket is so indistinct in the twilight, that he doesn't have time to make sense of it. The loud report he hears he thinks must have come from the drilling rigs.

The first bullet hits him in the chest. The second and third in the face and forehead.

He sinks, almost gracefully, to his knees, then keels over.

Anastasie sighs. She had hoped he would have fallen straight into the tar pit. Putting her gun back in her coat pocket, she puts the pointed toe of her shoe to his shoulder and flips him over. The body rolls down the gully's edge. As it continues to roll across the lake's tarry edge, it becomes a pitch-and-dust-coated shadow. For a moment it rests on the surface, then sinks into the thick, viscous black tar. His face, blackened by the clinging asphalt, stares upward. One tar-gloved hand seems to point to the night sky.

Anastasie turns and heads back to where her automobile waits. When she gets back, she'll arrange to have the dead man's vehicle removed from the scene.

The only other thought that occurs to her is how long it will take for the body to be discovered, or whether the slow, cold boiling of tar will bubble and lap around him, slowly covering him up.

If he lies undiscovered long enough, she wonders, what will archaeologists of a new millennium make of these strange remains?

41

As her eyes dart around the café, Sadie Ehrlich chews a thumbnail edge. She looks shadow-eyed tired, yet at the same time radiates a hectic nervous energy that seems to run through her body like electricity. Mary Rourke has been around enough Hollywood blocks enough times to recognize that there is something narcotic, probably cocaine, stoking the generator.

"You look hungry, Sadie. You hungry? You should eat something." Rourke beckons to the guy behind the counter and orders a plate of stew and a cola. She asks Betty if she wants something, but Betty shakes her head.

They wait until the stew arrives.

"Okay, Sadie," says Rourke. "What is it you have to tell me? Do you know what happened to the other girls?"

Ehrlich looks uncertainly at Rourke, then to Betty, then to the door, then back to Rourke.

"It's all right, Sadie," says Betty. "Tell Miss Rourke what you told me."

"Yeah, I know what happened to the girls. At least, I think I know some of it. They got into something bad, real bad."

"What? Bad how?"

"They—*we*—got involved with these people. Did work for them. Then they went missing, and Lucille turned up dead. I got out before the same thing happened to me. But they're looking for me. I know they are." A tremolo of fear shivers through her voice.

"It's all right, Sadie," says Rourke, and rests a hand on her forearm. "We can get you somewhere safe. I know a cop—"

Sadie pulls back from her. "No, no cops. There were cops there. Cops involved with it all."

"Where? Involved with what?"

"The Resurrection Club."

Rourke frowns. "What's the Resurrection Club? Does it have anything to do with Hiram Levitt?"

"Who?"

"Never mind. Look, just go through it all. From the beginning . . ."

Sadie pushes some stew around her plate, her expression mournful. "There was four of us to start with. Me, Lucille, Betty, and Susie. We all arrived in Hollywood about the same time, all looking for our spot in the movies, and we all stayed at the Studio Club to start with. We were all on the nut, all four of us, all looking for a way to make a buck. Susie was just a kid, and we all looked out for her; Lucille was like Betty." Sadie looks across at her friend and smiles. "She always tried to stay on the straight and narrow. I feel real bad that I got her kicked out of the Studio Club—it was my idea to sneak the boys in, and Lucille kept trying to talk me out of it, that and smuggling the booze in. No, Lucille was a good girl. She had no folks and had been brought up in some kinda orphanage in the Midwest, and I guess they served up a lot of religion."

"So she had no other relatives living?"

Sadie shakes her head; then something occurs to her. "Oh, wait— I think there was one relative, an uncle or something, back in the Midwest. But that was all."

"So the four of you were at the Studio Club. What about the fifth girl that went missing?"

"Don't know nothing about her. And of the four of us, only Lucille and Susie ended up working at the Resurrection Club. Betty here told us we oughta be careful who we worked for. She didn't want no part of none of it. We shoulda listened." She looks over at Dupris, tears welling in her eyes.

"Tell me about the Resurrection Club. What was it?"

"It was, I don't know, like some kind of secret society. To start with, I thought it was just a gimmick for a speakeasy—you know, there are so many of these crazy societies and clubs in L.A.—all just excuses for boozing and other things. But it wasn't that, it was something much worse. But it didn't start with the club. It started with the yacht."

"What yacht?"

"The *Temptress,* it was called. A yacht moored in a small bay an hour or so down the coast. Near Laguna Beach. They set up a big top next to the yacht and threw some kinda big party there, and they was looking for girls to serve drinks and such. It was all studio people, so we thought we'd maybe get a break. So me, Lucille, and Susie worked it. We was real itchy about it, though, it being so isolated and all."

"Whose yacht was it?"

"Robert Huston's, I guess. His or Veronica Stratton's."

"You sure?"

"It was Lucille who got us the job. Huston had been talking about getting her a screen test and told her that there was a way she could make money and meet the right people. Lucille had been wary at first, but she said that she'd met Veronica Stratton too, and she had made it clear that it was all on the up-and-up. I mean, you wouldn't expect a woman to be a white-slave trader, would you?"

"I guess not. So this party was full of Hollywood people?"

"Yeah. But mainly to do with the movie that they was about to make. You know, the horror movie everyone's talking about."

"*The Devil's Playground*?" Rourke fights to keep her expression empty.

"Yeah. The one they say is cursed."

Rourke thinks for a moment. Every press function, every party, every event related to *The Devil's Playground* had passed across her desk first. And there had never been a party in Laguna Beach, far less on a yacht.

"I need you to think carefully, Sadie. Who was at that party? As many names as you can remember."

"I didn't recognize everyone," she says apologetically.

"Just tell me who you did recognize."

"There was Robert Huston and Veronica Stratton, of course. And Norma Carlton, who was going to be his leading lady in the movie."

"Norma Carlton was there?"

"Sure. She was there, so was the studio bosses."

"Harry Carbine?"

"Yeah, him. And Clifford J. Taylor. Taylor gave me the heebies. He was real free with his hands, you know? And he got more cop-a-feely with the booze."

"Who else?"

"There was the director, you know, the Kraut—"

"Paul Brand?"

"Yeah. He was none too interested in us girls. Mainly because none of us was as pretty as the boy he came with. And there was a Negro. Not serving or nothing—like he was a movie actor too. Real good-looking too. There were two non-Hollywood types. One was a fat older guy who looked like a professional boozehound, I don't know who or what he was. And another older guy, a real fish-outta-water type—looked like a banker or something like that. There was another feller there, and I got the idea he was a real butter-and-egg man—you know, an out-of-towner with a bankroll. He kept talking to people about this hotel he had by a lake somewheres, like he was trying to get them to invest in it. Thing is, it was like Veronica Stratton was backing him up. That's when she first mentioned these 'special parties.' She said that they had them out at this lake, where the hotel was. They kept talking about something called the 'stone theater.'"

"Special parties?"

"Yeah. That's what I think happened to the girls. But I'll get to that. The only other faces I recognized were the usual party-hounds. Marion Davies was there with that newspaper guy who bankrolls her. Charlie Chaplin was there for a while, and he took a real interest in Susie. Susie was the youngest of us, and looked even younger. There was some Russian broad who I guess was famous enough but I didn't recognize her. The rest was mainly men. There wasn't that many there, I guess. Maybe twenty in all."

"And did anything bad happen?"

"No. Not really. I just got a bad feeling about the whole thing. They was serving booze in plain sight, but we was told that wasn't any kind of problem, 'cause it's only illegal to buy it or sell it, and they had a certificate to prove what we was serving was from pre-Prohib stocks they had. It was all horsefeathers, of course—like I said, there were cops there too, at least a couple of plainclothes bulls—and I think they was there to make sure there wasn't any trouble with local coppers. Not that I thought any'd turn up—like I say, this place was so far outta town."

"But you got a bad feeling about it all?"

"Yeah. Not real bad. More like an instinct. Didn't like the way we was being looked at—me and the other girls, I mean—like we was, I dunno, like we was being sized up or something."

"And the other girls—did they get the same feeling?"

"No. Well, yeah—but they just thought it was the usual bug-eye. Men look at women like they're meat in Hollywood. All over, I guess, but they don't try to hide it in Hollywood. That's all Lucille and Susie thought it was. Lucille told me everything was copacetic and I shouldn't worry—and she was the one of us who was most careful. Me, I got this funny feeling. Like I say, an instinct."

Rourke nods, for a moment thinking through all Sadie has said. "None of this sounds like a secret society. More like a normal Hollywood party."

"I guess it was. But they had this heavy there. A great big guy, and tough-looking with it. It was clear he wasn't a guest, more like he was in charge of security or something. He had a couple of men with him, and he kept talking to the cops."

"Did you hear him speak? Did he have a really deep voice?"

"Yeah, that's him." Sadie's eyes narrow in suspicion. "You know him?"

"I think I might know who he is. Go on. . . ."

"Well, this big guy was the one who paid us at the end of the night. He said they had other work for us if we wanted it. He said he worked for someone who ran a club—a real ritzy place, and did we want to try out for it. He gave us the same phonus balonus about it being a great way to meet producers and directors. He said our uniforms and everything would be provided free, and we'd be paid even more than we was being paid for that night."

"So you took the job?"

"No. Not me. The other girls did. I just wanted out of it."

"So where was this club? I take it this was the Resurrection Club?"

"Yeah, it was. And I don't know where it was. That's where it all gets really weird. The girls—I mean Lucille and Susie—I could tell they were shook up about it but they didn't want to talk about it. Turned out later that they *couldn't* talk about it. It was only later that they seemed to relax a little about it and seemed happy with the money they was making. It turned out they was paid good—and I mean crazy good— for not much work. I guess they was paid so much to keep their mouths shut. It was only later, after Susie went missing, that Lucille started to talk about it. She wanted out, but she was afraid. She told me these people wasn't just bad, they was powerful. Real powerful."

"So this Resurrection Club, was it in a speakeasy?"

"No, not a speakeasy, it was more than that. It was a club—a real secret kinda setup—like a membership-only type of place. It was somewhere underground. Under the city. Lucille, Susie, and the other girls would turn up for their shift by waiting outside a disused Red Car tunnel. The real heavy type I talked about, he would turn up with a truck and make them get in with hoods on their heads until—"

"Wait—hoods on their heads?"

"Yeah. They were super-secretive about this club. No one was to know where it was, and the girls were led there blind. They was all told not to tell anyone else about their work. No friends or nothing. That was the first bad sign—that they was told all kinds of bad things would happen to them if they blabbed."

"And that didn't worry Lucille or Susie?"

"It did to start with, Lucille more than Susie, but I guess they got used to it—and the fact that they was making so much money helped. The other thing was that it was the same deal with the guests—they got there the same way. No one knew where this club was. So Lucille got used to it, I mean, she knew it was illegal and all that, but she just thought they was making sure the Treasury didn't raid them. The other thing was that Susie was all right with it. She kept telling Lucille not to worry so much. But Lucille never liked the setup."

"What type of setup?"

"She said it was weird. Scary. She said it was all voodoo-themed. There were both men and women in this club. Lucille said a lot of them was rich—at least from the way they was dressed. She got the idea that most of them were from Hollywood studios—she heard snippets of conversations as she served booze and snow. Everyone wore these weird masks, so it was difficult to recognize them, but Lucille thought some of them was famous movie stars. The club was divided into two parts. There was the main bar lounge, where she, Susie, and the other girls would walk around half undressed, carrying silver trays with glasses of champagne, boxes of reefers, and these little silver snuff-boxes filled with cocaine. Like I said, snow."

"What was it like, this lounge?"

"She said it was huge. Lucille said it looked like a factory hall or something, but under the city. She said there was giant pipes running along one side of it. It gave her the heebies—she said it had all been painted this dark-red color, like blood. All the furniture and stuff was real expensive. She said that it sounded like the truck drove through tunnels to get in and out. Then they had to go down these steps. Lucille thought they was far underground. She said she could sometimes hear the rattle of streetcars way up above them. There are miles of tunnels down there, you know, under the city."

"I know. But not much of it is big enough to drive a truck through. How come you know all this, Sadie?" asks Rourke. "I thought you said all the girls were sworn to secrecy."

"Susie never said nothing about it. It was Lucille that told me. She said Susie was asked to do a special party for them—not in the club, but somewheres else."

"In L.A.?"

"I don't know. Lucille wasn't sure neither, but thought it had something to do with this stone theater that they talked about. All she knew was that Susie changed when she came back. Wouldn't say a word about where she'd been or what happened. Susie was always funny, always a real pistol. But after that special party, she went quiet. Didn't even tell Lucille what happened. Then, one day, she was gone. It was after that that Lucille told me everything."

"Did Lucille recognize anyone?" asks Rourke. "I mean, I know they wore masks, but did she think she could make out who anyone was?"

"She didn't say. She was pretty scared. Real scared after Susie went missing. But she said the whole thing was headed up not by a man, but a woman. She never saw her, she was always in this other room. But Lucille said it was like everybody was scared of her. Real scared."

"Wait—what do you mean, 'other room'?"

"Lucille said there was another room to this underground place. It had a big iron door. Lucille and the other girls weren't allowed to go in, and only a few of the guests were allowed in. But she thought it was for something special. She thought they must have had some kinda orgy or something in there, because there was all these weird noises, she said."

"She had no idea what went on in there?"

"She said she heard some people say it was where resurrection happened, whatever that means. It was all to do with voodoo, she said. The club's walls was all painted with symbols and stuff. There was a huge painting above the iron door into the second room. Lucille said she thought it was specially important to them, because some of the women wore a charm with the same thing on it."

"What was the symbol?"

"She said it was a snake. A snake that was in the shape of a circle, like it was eating its own tail."

42

Mary Rourke sits in the kitchen of her Larchmont Village bungalow. It is bright, the air rich with the aroma of freshly brewed coffee. Sitting with her at the kitchen table are the two men she needs to help her. She had expected friction, but Jake Kendrick and George Blevins had shared a few staccato exchanges about the war, who had served where with whom and had done what, and they seemed to bond, silently and gloomily, as if members of some dark freemasonry. She would, she realized, never understand men—not because of their complexity, but because of their simplicity.

Rourke runs through everything Sadie has told her about the Resurrection Club. As she goes through what Lucille experienced, she sees something dark gather in Blevins's otherwise wound-immobile face.

"I've been asking around about this Dahlman and Darke traveling magic-lantern show," explains Rourke. "A lot of people in the movie industry started off in the magic-lantern business. I haven't been able to find anyone who worked in that particular show directly, but old Bob Milhouse, who works sets at the studio, used to be a roustabout in a similar setup. He said that he'd heard about Dahlman and Darke—it was one of the most highly regarded shows in that circle. He told me that the show folded—most of them did when nickelodeons, then picture houses came along, but Dahlman and Darke gave up even earlier. According to Milhouse, the show had been hugely successful, and it had been Boy Lindqvist who had turned around its fortunes. He was known in the business for creating great spectacles."

"Then why did it go bust?" asks Kendrick. "If it was so successful."

"There were *incidents*." Rourke italicizes the word with her tone. "In one town a girl was found half naked, wandering the streets in a state of confusion. She couldn't account for what had happened to her, and anything she did say didn't make any sense. The one thing she kept repeating was that she had seen the devil."

"What happened to her?" asks Blevins.

"Milhouse doesn't know any more than that, but he thinks she was put in an asylum or a sanitorium. He said there were other girls who went missing in different towns; again, he's sketchy on detail, but he does know that people started to connect the disappearances to the arrival in town of the Dahlman and Darke show. Eventually, a mob in one of the places attacked the show and burned the tents, the wagons, the whole thing down. The carnies had to make a run for the hills. What happened to them after that, no one really knows."

"This Lindqvist guy, was your guy able to give any kind of description?" asks Blevins. "It would be good to know what to look for."

"No. I asked him what Lindqvist looked like, but he never met him, just heard about his lantern shows and the rumors about him. Reading between the lines, that's who Milhouse thinks was the chief suspect in the girls' disappearances."

"What about this woman and her daughter?"

"Hippolyta and Anastasie Cormier? Milhouse didn't recognize the names, but did say there was supposed to be a fortune-teller attached to the show. Other than that, he didn't really know much more than he told me. He wasn't too sure that what he did know was that reliable— he said traveling people, carnies, were a superstitious bunch and were prone to exaggerating stories. Whatever the truth, something happened to cause the Dahlman and Darke show to disappear off the face of the earth."

"It seems to be a habit," says Kendrick. "Disappearing off the face of the earth. I took a drive by Madame Erzulie's. Place is empty now. No forwarding address. Apparently, the house had been rented, not owned. No sign of this guy Jansen you mentioned. Do you think he could be Boy Lindqvist?"

"I doubt it," says Rourke. "Too young."

"So what is the connection between this traveling show and the Resurrection Club?" asks Blevins.

"I don't know. But my guess is, Veronica Stratton is the link. Let's just assume for a moment that the 'resurrection' in the Resurrection Club is that all the members have had past lives they've put behind them, either through Hiram Levitt rewriting their histories or some other way. Maybe they're bound together by the fact that Levitt was blackmailing them."

"So that's why he was murdered?"

"Could be." Rourke frowns. "But I feel there's more to it—more to the club, I mean—than that. Though I am pretty sure that Levitt was murdered because he had the goods on someone and was milking them over it."

"That's a pretty long list of suspects," says Kendrick.

"Yeah—but my guess is that 'someone' was Veronica Stratton, maybe Robert Huston too. If Stratton is or was Anastasie Cormier, and Levitt had the goods to connect her to what happened in Leseuil, he had the power to put a Louisiana noose around her neck."

"So what do we do now?" asks Blevins.

"You're in the best position to keep an eye on Stratton and Huston. Try to keep note of when they go out, for how long, times, et cetera. And, of course, keep tabs on who comes and goes to Mount Laurel. I intend to make a visit myself and see if I can stir things up."

"Okay," Blevins replies. "The only thing is that I haven't seen Huston for a couple of days. But that ain't that unusual. There's been a lot of activity up at the main house, though. Like you said about the voodoo woman's house—stuff being packed in crates, trucks coming and going."

"Maybe I've stirred things up too much already," says Rourke.

"You really think Veronica Stratton is the queen bee in all this?" asks Kendrick. "You do know, speaking as a cop, that there's nothing I can officially pin on Stratton, Huston, or even this Resurrection Club? There's no connection I can see to Norma Carlton's death, and even if there was, that's a murder that never happened if we want to keep you and the studio out of it. Again, all we got is speculation that she or someone working for her killed Hiram Levitt."

"What about Lucille?" asks Blevins.

"Same thing. We got suspicions, but we ain't got much else."

"So that's it?" asks Rourke.

"Not quite. There are the Louisiana murders. The ones Sheriff Briggs—or ex-Sheriff Briggs—came all the way up here to solve. Those are a matter of record, and Anastasie and Hippolyta Cormier are wanted in Louisiana for them. I wired Terrebonne Parish Sheriff's Office, and they confirmed there are still warrants outstanding. Extraditing her out of the state will take more than we've got. At the moment, it all hangs on one thing."

"What?" asks Rourke.

"If you truly believe that Veronica Stratton is Anastasie Cormier."

As she stares at Kendrick, Rourke's face is fixed and hard, her gaze resolute. "Veronica Stratton *is* Anastasie Cormier, I'm convinced of it. And Madame Erzulie is her mother, Hippolyta Cormier. I think she's been hiding in plain sight all these years. There are no photographs of her when she was younger, and there are precious few people left alive who could recognize her—and I'm guessing she looks a whole lot different than she did back then."

There is silence between them for a while, each contemplating what's been discussed. Rourke refills coffee cups.

"It's funny, the things that come back to you," says Blevins as he gazes into the black well of his coffee cup. "Back in the war, in France, I had this master sergeant—he was from Kansas, as a matter of fact. Anyway, he was a career soldier, a couple of decades older than the rest of us, tough as nails, and had been through all kinds of crap. Somehow, he had managed to come out of it all with his hide intact, so us doughboys listened to every word he said. Not just because of his rank. Anyway, he always told us that it was at night you were most likely to get yours. He swore that you don't think straight like you do in the day. The night eats at you, he'd say, it's at night you make mistakes." Blevins is temporarily lost in a moment ten years and five thousand miles ago. "Anyway, our unit saw a lot of night patrols, gathering intelligence on German deployments and gun positions. Before every sortie we'd listen to this old leather-faced Jayhawker warn us about the night." Blevins gives a bitter laugh. "The irony of it all is that when his time came it came out of a clear blue midday sky, courtesy of Uncle Sam, delivered by a misaimed friendly shell landing a mile short of its intended target.

I saw it happen. Had a grandstand view, as a matter of fact." Blevins's hand moves unconsciously to his scar.

"What are you getting at?" asks Rourke.

"Just that we're beginning to get a picture of what's going on. I just hope we're not looking in the wrong direction."

43

When Mary Rourke pulls up at the gates to Mount Laurel, one of the security men watches disinterestedly from the gatehouse while the other saunters over to the Packard.

"Can I help you, lady?" a uniformed George Blevins asks, as if he and Rourke had never met before.

"I'm here to see Miss Stratton. My name's Rourke."

"Is she expecting you?"

"I telephoned earlier; yes, she is."

"Okay." As he did on her last visit, he points past the gates along the drive to the paved square parking lot. "Park up there, on the left. No automobiles other than the owners' are allowed past that point." Then his voice lowered. "I'll keep an eye on the wagon. By the way, no sign of Robert Huston. Ain't seen him for two days. Stratton's still getting stuff packed. Same deal as Madame Erzulie's. I reckon she's going to blow town, like we thought." He pauses. "Mary—be careful."

"Thanks," she says, loud enough for the other security man to hear.

She parks in the same spot as the last time and walks up to the main house. The door is answered by Parsons this time, and the butler's steady demeanor is slipping.

"Hello, Parsons, ol' bean," says Rourke breezily, and steps past him without waiting to be asked in. "Miss Stratton is expecting me."

This time, Parsons leads Rourke wordlessly to a slightly less grand reception room. The décor is different from that of the rest of the house, and Rourke senses that this is a more personal space for the movie star. Veronica Stratton sits by the window at an antique French escritoire, going through paperwork. The sunlight from the window makes a halo of her rich blonde hair.

She stands up and smiles when she sees Rourke. If the movie star is rattled by recent events, or has any idea she is under suspicion, then she's giving the best performance of her career.

"Ah, Miss Rourke—may I call you Mary? How lovely to see you, Mary," she says as she crosses to her and takes Mary's hand in both of hers. "I do believe we're going to be seeing much more of each other from now on."

"We are?"

"Oh, haven't you heard? Harry Carbine has finally managed to come to an agreement with First National. If we agree on terms, I'm to be loaned out to your studio for this new movie he wants to go into production next year. A talkie. So you'll be looking after me." She takes another step forward, still holding Rourke's hand. "Won't that be peachy?"

"The talkie that Norma Carlton was supposed to do?" asks Rourke, surprised. She removes her hand from the movie star's grasp, but takes the opportunity proximity offers to check Stratton's face for any hint of a birthmark. She can see none, though that might speak only to the efficiency of Stratton's concealer.

"I guess it is." Stratton smiles and reveals perfect teeth. "Norma won't be doing any talkies, that's for sure, unless she can project her voice from the grave. That really would be putting the 'medium' into the new medium. . . ."

"The last time we met," says Rourke, "you gave me the impression that you hated Norma Carlton. Respected, yes, but hated."

"Did I?" she replies airily.

"Yes. Specifically, you called her a bitch."

"How succinct of me. What of it?"

"Just that you seem to have spent a lot of time with her, from what I hear."

"From what you hear?" Stratton overdoes the mischief in her expression. "You do seem to be taking quite the interest in me."

"But it's true that you visited her at her home—actually, quite frequently—before she died?"

"You know, Mary, you are beginning to sound . . ." she makes a show of searching for the most apt description ". . . like a dime-novel detective. Have you some mystery you're trying to solve?"

"You haven't denied you visited her regularly."

"All right, then, yes, I did visit her from time to time. I said I didn't like her, and that much is true. We were rivals, and we fought for parts, but Norma Carlton was an exceptional woman. I was secure in my position at the top of my profession, and I respected Carlton for challenging that position. We met. We talked. We had things in common." Stratton sighs with affected wistfulness. "But now here I am, about to take on a role that was tailor-made for her."

"In fact, you could say you wouldn't have got the role if she had lived," says Rourke.

"Of course you could say that. The role was conceived for Carlton. If she had lived, she would have played it, not me. But you know yourself how often a lead role imagined for one actor or actress becomes famous through someone else's interpretation. And, as I'm sure you appreciate, I am not exactly struggling to find roles—and certainly not desperate enough to have competitors bumped off, if that's what you're implying." She pauses, raises a finger as if an idea has just come to her, and says, "Oh, but you can't be implying that, can you? Because Norma committed suicide. Or died of a heart condition. Which was it? Sorry, I'm usually good at remembering a script."

"If you have this big role coming up, why are you leaving town?"

"Leaving town? I'm not leaving town. Oh, you mean the packing cases. I'm packing a few things for a trip, that's all. Something to put all this nastiness behind us."

"Us?"

"Me and Robert, of course. I thought we could have a second honeymoon. Sailing around the islands. I'm quite the accomplished sailor, you know."

"Yes, your yacht is the *Temptress*, I believe."

Stratton looks surprised. "My, you are well informed."

"I've read your press bio."

"Ah yes—but this is something that is less *embellished* than the usual. I really do enjoy sailing. Even Robert has his sea legs now, and I do believe he enjoys it too. Do you sail, Mary?"

"'Fraid not. I'm a both-feet-on-solid-ground type."

"Really?" says Stratton. Her smile is a predatory baring of teeth, her eyes catlike again. "You should give it a try. It's good to try something different. A girl should be open to new experiences. You never know, you might develop a taste for the soft wave over the firm earth."

"I doubt it," says Rourke. "May I ask you something?"

"I don't see why you should start seeking permission now. You've done nothing but ask since you arrived." She holds her hands in an open gesture. "But please do. . . ."

"Where are you from? Originally, I mean?"

Stratton frowns. "You said yourself that you've read my press bio."

"Exactly. Where are you really from?"

"What it says on my bio happens to be true, Mary. I'm from Boston originally. My parents were both immigrants from England. Maybe that's why I had a soft spot for Robert's accent."

"I see. So you have no connection with Louisiana?"

"Louisiana?" Stratton frowns.

"Specifically, a place called Leseuil?"

"Whatever makes you ask that?"

"Do you?"

"No. I've never even been there."

"I see. Did you know Hiram Levitt?"

"The Resurrectionist? Yes, I've met him at different things—you know, parties, press galas, that kind of thing. Strange little man. Oh— I see. . . ." Stratton's expression is of realization. "You want to know if I'm some swamp flower from down ol' New Orleans way that Levitt cultivated into a rare California orchid?" She laughs. "No, I'm afraid you're barking up the wrong tree."

"Did you hear what happened to Levitt?"

"I heard he'd been murdered, if that's what you mean. Robbers breaking into his apartment, is what I read."

"I have a theory about that."

"Oh?"

"I don't think it was a random burglary. Not at the Talmadge. I believe whoever gained access to his apartment did so specifically to murder him."

"Why would anyone want to do that?" asks Stratton.

"Because Levitt had the dirt on some of the biggest—the very biggest—names in Hollywood. And I have a sneaking suspicion that he was using that dirt as a pension policy."

"Blackmail?"

"How do you know Madame Erzulie?"

"Who? I don't. Oh, wait—that's the spiritualist woman. I think Norma Carlton mentioned her."

"More voodoo-priestess type than spiritualist, from what I can gather. You've never had any contact with her?"

"No," Stratton intones as if the question was stupid. "I haven't a superstitious bone in my body. And, frankly, I was surprised Norma did. Why do you ask?"

"It's just something that came up." Rourke pauses. "Have you any family here in Hollywood? A mother tucked away somewhere, maybe?"

"You *have* read my bio? Of course I don't. Both my parents have passed."

"Just curious, is all," says Rourke. "As you've suggested yourself, what Hollywood studio biographies say about their stars isn't anything to go on. I knew Lillian and Dorothy Gish before they became virgins."

"Why do you ask specifically about my mother?" asks Stratton.

Rourke shrugs. "It's just, everything I'm dealing with seems to revolve around mothers and daughters."

"I see." Stratton drops the sultry act. The eyes no longer smolder but glint with ice. For the first time, Rourke notices that their particular brightness comes from their being emerald. The same color, almost, as her own. "I guess that has a lot to do with your own experience," says Stratton.

"My experience?"

"When someone starts to sniff about in my affairs, I sniff about in theirs. And I'm lucky enough to have access to professional sniffers for that kind of thing. I know about your husband. And your daughter. I believe Jack Rourke had a promising future as a movie lead. Pity he succumbed to patriotism. It's a disease that so often proves fatal. He's buried in France, isn't he?"

Rourke makes no reply. She focuses on keeping from her expression any hint that the movie star is rattling her.

"I am genuinely sorry about your daughter," says Stratton, and, strangely, Rourke believes her. "That was a tragedy. Spanish flu, wasn't it?"

"So your mother is dead," says Rourke flatly. Again, she keeps any emotion from her voice or expression. She has never spoken to anyone about her daughter; she certainly isn't going to with Stratton. But the same old thought stabs through her: I'm a fixer, I fix things; I couldn't fix that.

"My mother died ten years ago." Stratton's tone is flat, her eyes cold.

"Have you ever heard of something called the Resurrection Club?"

"The what?" Irritation now. "No, I haven't. Listen, Miss Rourke, I need to get on with my day. This has all become rather tiresome."

"Oh, I'm Miss Rourke again? I thought we were on first-name terms, Veronica."

Stratton presses the button to summon the butler. "That's when I thought we'd be working together. I rather think that if I do this movie with Carbine, I shall ask that you have nothing to do with it."

"That's if you do it," says Rourke as she stands up. "A lot of things can happen between now and then. Plus," she adds airily, "there's always Carole Ventris."

"Who the hell is Carole Ventris?"

"She was the stand-in for Norma Carlton. Everybody says she's just like a younger Norma. I have to say, she took me aback when I saw her. I believe she's being groomed for great things. Maybe even this talkie. And like I say, there's a lot that can happen between now and then. So there's the whole chicken-and-counting thing—"

She's interrupted by the arrival of the butler.

"Well, hello, Parsons," Rourke says. "Could you lead me out of this marble maze?"

As she once more emerges into the bright day, Rourke continues to wear the smile she dressed her face with in Stratton's day room. Only when she is sure she is out of sight of the main house does she let it slip, and succumb to the fluttering in her chest.

She has just, she realized, prodded a dangerous animal to angry wakefulness.

She stops at her automobile, climbs in, sits for a few seconds, then walks over to the gatehouse. Blevins and the older security man sit idly behind its window.

"I'm having trouble starting my car," says Rourke. "I wondered if one of you would do the whole knight-in-shining routine."

"It's okay, Jimmy," says Blevins wearily. "I got it."

Blevins walks with Rourke back to the Packard.

"How'd it go?" he asks quietly. He nods to the automobile. "Pop the hood and I'll make a show of it."

"I don't know," says Rourke. "She kind of lost her cool."

"Well, that's good, ain't it? You got to her."

"I guess so. It's just that I would have thought she would make a real effort to keep her act together. Maybe it's just that she feels the net closing in."

"No word about Huston?"

"Just that they're about to take a boat trip together."

"A boat trip?"

"I know. It could be a one-way ticket to Mexico or South America." She frowns. "But as for the net closing in, it's not much of a net. She knows we can't do anything about Norma's death without incriminating ourselves. The only thing that Jake Kendrick can bring the police into safely is Hiram Levitt's death, and we have no connection to Stratton or Huston with that. We can't even link them conclusively to your niece's murder or the disappearance of the other girls."

Blevins leans in, as if examining something in the engine more closely. "So you went out of your way just to spook her?"

"I guess. The best way to find tracks you haven't found is to get someone to try to cover them."

"So what now?"

"They seem to trust you. I guess your overzealous treatment of that photographer was designed to achieve just that. Ask Stratton if she or Huston need you to do any more bodyguard work. Tell them you need the extra hours."

"And if they don't bite?"

"Then they don't bite. Don't push it to the extent they start suspecting you. In the meantime, let me know if and when Huston makes an appearance. And keep note of when Stratton leaves the house and where she goes, if you can. Any other comings and goings too. In the meanwhile, Jake is getting as much information as he can from Louisiana. Problem is, he's getting heat from his brass about why he's spending time on it. I don't think it's because they're concerned about taxpayer dollars."

"What are you going to do?"

"I'm going to see if I can dig up anything more about Hiram Levitt. Like I said before, if Levitt was blackmailing even a quarter of his clients, then we've got more suspects than we can deal with."

"I know," says Blevins. "It also means that whoever killed him might have absolutely nothing to do with who killed Lucille—and both might have nothing to do with whoever killed Norma Carlton."

"That's the size of it," says Rourke, sighing. "But I'm convinced they're all tied together, and tied up with this Resurrection Club."

Blevins straightens up, as if he's found the problem with the engine. "You best head off," he says, "before Jimmy decides to come over and poke his nose in. By the way, no one has been near the car since you were up at the house. Unlike the last time, I was watching out."

"Okay, thanks," says Rourke. "But I'm still going to check the brakes before I hit that incline. . . ."

44

It is after midnight and Mary Rourke is in bed when she gets the call. She is not, however, asleep: her head has been filled with a fluttering confusion of thoughts like moths trapped in a lamp shade. Clifford J. Taylor makes no apology for calling at this hour, but there is something very different in his voice—none of his usual arrogance, and little self-assurance in his tone.

"You have to come to the studio, Mary," he says. "Now. I'll be waiting for you when you arrive."

"Now?" She looks at the bedside clock. Her confusion turns swiftly to suspicion. "Why? What is it that can't wait until the morning?"

"There's been a fire. A bad one. The whole vault has gone up. We've lost everything. Mary, there's more. . . ."

And he tells her.

There is a huddle of fire tenders around the large warehouse-type building that contains Carbine International's archive of film. The building is still brightly aflame, lighting up the sky the same way the Ouxbois set had when it had been set alight. But no fire hose is engaged on the burning vault. Instead, water is directed at the neighboring buildings, not yet aflame. The fire chief stands and watches impotently as the structure burns.

The instant she steps out of the car, she can feel the heat on her face, bright and sharp and intense. Clifford Taylor is standing next to the fire chief, and she walks over to them. Taylor's face is hard-etched by shock and the light of the blaze.

"Thanks for coming," he says. Then, in explanation, "There's nothing they can do. We just have to let it burn."

Rourke nods. She knows, as everybody in the business knows, that when cellulose-nitrate film burns, nothing can put it out. It can't be doused, it can't be smothered: the nitrate is so oxygen-rich that it will even burn underwater.

"Where's Harry?" she asks.

"In his office." In the light of the burning building, Taylor's face looks drawn and empty, like that of a boxer whose last ounce of fight has drained from him. He leads her across to the main building. They stop and turn at the deafening crash and roar as the film vault's roof collapses and the fire punches a bright, balled fist into the sky in triumph.

There is no one else in the main office complex, and Taylor leads Rourke through the marbled reception, along the hall with the studio's stars arranged along its walls, and into Harry Carbine's office.

Carbine is seated behind his desk. Behind him, the door of the wall safe yawns open.

"Oh, Harry," she says as she stands in front of his desk. Harry Carbine doesn't answer. He can't. His head is thrown back and looks upward at the ceiling. A small wound under his jaw wells blood, and crimson-and-gray matter has splashed onto the wall and open safe behind him.

Rourke steps around the desk and sees that Carbine's arms hang limply at his sides. His revolver lies on the floor, where it has fallen from the studio boss's hand.

"All the prints of *The Devil's Playground* have gone up in the fire," explains Taylor. "But there was one kept here in Harry's safe for exactly such eventualities as this. Someone's obviously taken it. Harry sunk everything he had into that film, sunk himself and the studio into massive debt to make it. We're in hock up to our armpits, and we're underinsured. I guess, when Harry saw that the only print of the movie that wasn't in the vault had been stolen, he knew he was ruined. That the studio was ruined. I guess he couldn't take the shame."

"So who took the final print?"

"I have no idea. I'm guessing whoever set the fire—it's just too much of a coincidence. We're in a mess, Mary. I knew Harry relied on you, so I'm relying on you now."

"What can I do? Cover up Harry's suicide?" Rourke's tone is scoffing. She walks over to the safe and, with her gloved hand, pushes it shut, examines it, then opens it again.

"No, of course not. What I mean is that I am going to have to steer the studio through this—*if* I can steer it through this. I mean, if I can find a way to avoid bankruptcy. The press are like wolves when they smell blood. You know as well as I do that there's nothing Hollywood enjoys more than seeing one of its own going under."

"Have you called the cops yet?"

"I was waiting for you first. I tried to get Sam Geller too, but there was no reply."

"So how did this all play out?"

"I got the call from Studio Security—I'm their first point of contact for anything to do with the fabric of the studio, but they'd already called the firehouse. I called Harry, and he met me out at the vault. It was already too late. Harry told me to wait while he checked on the print in his safe. When he didn't come back, I went across and found him there, like that. Then I telephoned you."

"So you think someone used the fire as a distraction, and to destroy all the stored prints of the movie, while they stole what they knew would be the last surviving print?"

"I don't know," says Taylor. "But that's what it looks like to—" He stops dead when he sees what Rourke has removed from her coat pocket.

"Why don't you take a seat over there. . . ." Rourke nods to where two couches flank a low coffee table. Taylor doesn't move, but stares at the gun, with an expression of frightened confusion on his face. "Move," urges Rourke.

Taylor does as he is told and sits. He seems to have recovered something of himself. "What the hell do you think you're doing?"

"I'm just filling in some gaps," says Rourke.

"What gaps?"

"Like how come, when I closed the wall safe's door, it had blood on it, like the rest of the wall. It's clear Harry's blood hit it when it was closed, not open. Like how there's a three-sheet poster for the movie out in reception that has a demon spreading its wings over the city— and it was you who came up with that idea. An idea you got from a magic-lantern show when you were younger."

"What the *hell* has that got to do with anything? Yes, I saw that when

I was a kid and it impressed me, so what? And, anyway, Paul Brand closed the movie with that image, so it's not all mine."

"Yeah," says Rourke. "I asked Brand about that. He said he added that touch after you had described your memory from the magic-lantern show. I'm guessing it was the Dahlman and Darke show."

"The what?" He shakes his head in angry disbelief. "Why are we even talking about this?" He is shouting now. "Harry is dead! If you're saying the safe door was closed when he shot himself, then, yes, I can see why that's odd. But what the hell does who came up with the idea for a movie poster have to do with anything?"

"Oh, that's an easy one. I got something wrong, you see. I thought Robert Huston was someone he wasn't. And it turns out you're the person I thought he was."

"I've had enough of this. . . ." Taylor starts to rise from his seat but is checked by Rourke's taking more precise aim and shaking her head. He eases back onto the sofa. "I'm confused, Mary—who the hell am I supposed to be, exactly?"

Rourke smiles malevolently. "You're not some New England blue-blood, are you? All the riding around sets on your Thoroughbred, the lockjaw accent, the jodhpurs and riding boots—it's all a big perfor-mance, isn't it? You see, a mistake I made was to think that Hiram Levitt only reincarnated actors and actresses. He obviously did the odd number on a producer. Yep, I know who you are, all right." She smiles coldly. "You're Boy Lindqvist. . . ."

"Who?" Taylor affects an expression of bewilderment.

"Boy Lindqvist," repeats Rourke. "Creative genius behind the Dahl-man and Darke magic-lantern show. And chief suspect in a series of disappearances of young women."

"I have no idea what the hell you're talking about, but I'll tell you this, you're going to regret this. You're going to regret this big-time." Taylor's expression shifts to one of indignant outrage. Oh, you're good, thinks Rourke.

"You know exactly what I'm talking about, Boy, so cut the act," she says. "You forget I've had to cover up for you here, for the studio, and it made me sick to the stomach. Now, you just sit tight there like a good little boy. And keep your hands where I can see them." Rourke, who has remained standing, moves across to Harry Carbine's desk. Without looking at the dead studio chief, she takes the telephone earpiece from its cradle and with the same hand dials the operator before asking to be connected to a Glendale number.

"Hi, Jake, it's Mary. Sorry to trouble you so late, but I need you to come to the studio. You better bring some detective chums. Harry Carbine's dead." She listens for a moment. "That's my guess, but it's been made to look like suicide. Lot of that around, it would seem. By the way, you'll have no trouble finding your way here—the studio film vault is lit up like the Fourth of July. And, Jake, hustle some, would you? I'm pointing that toy you gave me straight at Boy Lindqvist."

After she hangs up, Taylor eyes her malevolently, some of his composure restored.

"I don't know who you think I am," he says with measured malice. "I don't know what you think I've done. But I'm going to ruin you because of this. I promise you that when I'm done you'll be through in Hollywood. You've just made one really huge mistake."

"Maybe," she says dully. "It wouldn't be the first time. Where's the film? You have someone waiting to take it away? Golem Geller, by any chance?"

"Geller?" Taylor's confused expression is so convincing that Rourke herself is taken aback. "What's Sam Geller got to do with this?"

"He's a member of your little secret society, isn't he? The Resurrection Club. Party nights with girls snared by Veronica Stratton and Robert Huston—girls who end up dropping off the face of the earth. You like scaring women, don't you, Boy? And God knows there's a constant supply of them here. But there was a lot of other stuff going on at the Resurrection Club. Veronica Stratton's—or should I say Anastasie Cormier's—little voodoo ceremonies."

And there it was, in his eyes. Her last comment had really hit home. The mention of Cormier's name. Yet there's something unexpected in his reaction. Something that doesn't quite fit the script she has sketched out in her head.

"You think you have it all wrapped up," he says. "You think you have all the answers. Trust me, you don't know what you're talking about."

"Don't I? Well, let's see what the cops make of this little mise-en-scène." She nods to Harry Carbine's body.

"Christ, Mary, that's got nothing to do with me. Whatever else is going on, you've got me confused with someone else. I don't care what you think I'm involved in, or who the hell you think I am, I didn't kill Harry. I don't know anything about whether the safe was open or closed when he died, but either way it's pretty obvious he killed himself. There are things you don't know. Things about the movie and the studio. We're ruined without this movie, and Harry got financing from some very dangerous people. Whatever you see here, you're not looking right. And I'm not who you seem to think I am. I can show you proof, in my office."

"We're staying right here, nice and quiet, till the cops arrive."

There is a moment of quiet between them.

From outside, there is a great crashing sound. It startles them both, and Rourke turns her head. Before she works out it must be the film vault's walls collapsing in, Taylor grabs the heavy marble ashtray from the coffee table and hurls it at her head. She reacts quickly and the ashtray misses her temple. In a reflex action, her finger squeezes the trigger, and the gun goes off impotently into empty space. Taylor is up on his feet in an instant and slams into her. She lands on her back with Taylor's weight on top of her. The impact drives the air from her lungs. He grabs the wrist of the hand that holds the gun and twists viciously. The gun falls from her grasp and lands out of reach of them both on the thick office carpet. Taylor grabs Rourke by the throat with both hands.

"You bitch," he hisses. "You fucking bitch. Who do you think you are?"

The grip on her throat tightens, and she can't draw breath into her air-starved lungs. The room begins to turn gray as the blood to her brain is choked off. As she begins to lose consciousness, she sees the vicious triumph in her attacker's eyes.

Not this way, Mary, she tells herself. You're not going out this way.

Taylor screams and releases his grip on her throat as she stabs the varnished nails of each thumb into his eyes. He grabs her wrists and tries to wrench her free. She digs deeper into his eyes before he pulls her hands away. He stands up, bent over and blinking, weeping tears and blood. Rourke gets to her hands and knees, sucking big gulps of air into her lungs. Her hand falls on the onyx ashtray. She gets to her feet, her arms swinging loosely, the ashtray hanging in her grasp like a bell on a rope. Taylor turns to her, squinting through watering, bleeding eyes, his face contorted with rage. He lunges at her with an inhuman scream.

Rourke swings the ashtray at his head, catching him on the temple, its edge splitting his scalp. Taylor staggers for a second, then topples sideways, crashing onto the floor.

Rourke, still sucking air into tortured lungs, staggers over to where her gun lies and picks it up, training it with a shaking arm on Taylor. She lets her arm drop when she sees he presents no threat, lying unconscious, his breathing hissy and labored.

At that moment, Jake Kendrick bursts into the office with three uniformed cops.

Rourke, leaning against Carbine's desk, smiles weakly.

"Jake Kendrick to the rescue," she croaks with a shaky half-laugh.

Kendrick looks at her, at Carbine, and at Taylor unconscious and oozing blood onto the expensive Persian carpet.

"Yeah?" he says. "But who am I rescuing from who?"

45

Another fire, another departure point illuminated in the night, thinks Anastasie Cormier as she watches the glow flicker orange and white in the distance. She tries, this time, to feel regret, remorse, but the only pain that bites into her is that of loss: that she has achieved so much, has come so far, and she now has to turn her back on it all. But if she stays, she knows her history will catch up with her. And they're not averse to hanging women in Louisiana.

This time, however, she is wealthy. Her fortune grows each day without any effort on her part. She has accounts under different names where she keeps money accessible—a sum that most people would consider wealth in itself, but the vast bulk of her fortune is planted in that most fertile of financial soil: Wall Street. And, as everyone knows in 1927 America, Wall Street is where fortunes are guaranteed to grow.

Anastasie stands next to the automobile she has pulled over to the roadside, watching the fire, distant but bright in the night. She sees the lights on another automobile as it approaches. She checks her watch. One a.m. He is on time, as he always is.

The car pulls up behind hers and the lights are killed. A massive man unfolds from the car like the unfurling of a huge shadow.

"I know this was difficult for you," she says.

"He was my friend." Sam Geller says in a deep, rumbling baritone. "I worked with him from the beginning."

"He was my friend too," replies Anastasie. "But it had to be done."

"I'll never forget the look on his face," he says. He is a dark voice and a dark shadow in the night. "He was so confused. He didn't understand how I could betray him."

"You're free now," says Anastasie. "You're free of him and free of me.

And you're free of the threat of prison. You have more than enough money to live your life out in comfort."

"You're going?"

"It's all arranged," she says. "I'll be gone tomorrow. You fixed everything with the yacht?"

"It's all ready. Just like you said."

"Fine." Anastasie pauses, watching as a fireball, small but bright in the distance, surges into the sky. "Do you have it?" she asks.

Wordlessly, Geller walks back to his automobile. He takes a large carryall from the trunk, returns to Anastasie's automobile, and places the carryall in the passenger seat.

"I guess I will never see you again," Geller says, but there is no sadness in his tone.

"No, best that way," she says. "Thanks for everything. Good luck."

"You've destroyed me," said Geller dully. "You've destroyed all of us. You had so much; why didn't you accept that?"

"Because it was given to me by men. And what men give they take away without a thought. The only currency that matters in this town, in this world, is power."

"What happened there," says Geller, the dark tones darker with shame, "out there at the stone theater. What happened to those girls . . ."

"I seem to remember you took part in it all. Enthusiastic part. I know others call you the Golem. For me you'll always be Père Malfait—the bad you have done has been for your own sake, not mine. Don't blame me for exploiting your weakness; blame yourself for being weak."

Geller says nothing, instead turns silently and heads back to his parked vehicle.

After he has driven off, Anastasie climbs into her automobile, opens the carryall, and checks its contents, using the flame of her lighter as illumination. The disk-shaped metal canisters gleam in its light and she can read the labels:

THE DEVIL'S PLAYGROUND. A CARBINE INTERNATIONAL PRODUCTION.

46

From the row of ceiling lights, the too-bright bulbs beneath the white enamel shades scowl starkly down, flooding the room with a stark, nauseous, yellow-white light. They sit in a bleak whitewashed room at the Hollywood Division, in a station house on North Cahuenga Boulevard that the LAPD shares with the City Fire Department. Rourke sees that Kendrick's face looks old, tired, and long-shadowed, and she guesses she must look pretty much the same. Her head is pounding; her throat, despite the glasses of ice water, rasps with every swallow.

"You really did a number on him," says Kendrick with a mingling of censure and admiration. "Remind me never to get on your wrong side. And I'll never call you toots again."

"Will he be okay?"

"The doctors say he'll live. But he's still out for the count. In the meantime, I'm running a full background check on him. I've also asked Kansas if they have any kind of description of Lindqvist. What about you? Shouldn't you have a doctor check you over?"

"I tried to get Doc Wilson, but he's not at the clinic. I'll leave it—I'm fine. What now?"

"I've wired Kansas to inform them that we have in custody a suspect we believe to be Boy Lindqvist. They maybe don't have enough on him to warrant extradition. And unless we can come up with the goods, we've nothing to hold him on."

"What about the blood on the safe door? It means his story doesn't fit."

"I get what you mean, Mary, but I'm being overruled here. Carbine's death is being ruled a suicide. In fact, I had to talk my captain out of taking a closer look at you for attempted homicide on Taylor."

"Lindqvist," Rourke corrects him.

"That remains to be seen."

"Listen, Jake, I'm pretty sure Stratton and Huston are going to make a break for it. We may not have much on them, but if they get wind that we've got Lindqvist, on top of us trying to connect Stratton to Anastasie Cormier and the Louisiana murders Briggs was investigating, I'm guessing they'll make a run for it. Start off somewhere new."

"How could she?" asks Kendrick. "Veronica Stratton has one of the most recognizable faces in the world."

Rourke shrugs. "Anastasie Cormier has managed it at least once before. She'll manage it again, somehow. I'm sure she already has somewhere safe lined up. I'm going down to where the *Temptress* is moored. I'll get Blevins to come with me. I suggest you join us there as soon as you're freed up here."

"I think you should wait for me."

"Blevins can handle himself. Anyway, we're just going to watch. If Stratton and Huston turn up, then we'll call you and you can get the local cops down there."

"And what are we going to say is our reason for stopping them?"

"I don't know," says Rourke frustratedly. "That you're waiting for a confirmation from another state that Stratton is wanted for murder under another name. The main thing is that we don't allow her to slip off the face of the earth again."

"Take it easy, Mary," says Kendrick. "We still don't know what we're dealing with."

"I have a pretty good idea. . . ."

The interior of the automobile is gilded with warm light as the sun rises from behind the mountains, reaching golden fingers into the dark-slumbering Pacific Ocean. As arranged, Blevins had picked her up from the precinct. It feels strange to sit in the passenger seat of the pale-gray sedan she had so often checked her rearview mirror for. The other thing that strikes her is, sitting looking at Blevins's right, unscarred, profile, she could see that he had been a handsome, if hard-looking man. His profile is strong, his hair a lighter blond than Kendrick's. The girls would have been after you, she thinks, before your face was messed up.

It takes them an hour to get to Laguna Beach, then another twenty minutes backtracking to find the rough track that leads to the cove. They park up above the sunrise-painted cliff and make their way to its edge. Below, a pale crescent of pristine sand gently cups an azure disk of water. The pale finger of a wooden jetty points out to the mouth of the cove and the Pacific beyond. The yacht sits tied to the jetty.

"A bootlegger's paradise," says Blevins. "Nothing for miles."

"That's why they chose here, I guess. It must be the only safe shelter. Do you see them?"

"Nope," says Blevins. "If they turn up, you sit tight. I'll drive back down the coast to the town and call the cops. They won't have time to set out before they get here."

"I hope not."

"Don't worry," says Blevins. "If push comes to shove, the cops will send a launch after them. They can't outrun that."

"I guess," says Rourke doubtfully.

"Like I say, don't worry, Mary. They won't get away."

"Maybe not. But unless the Louisiana sheriff's office comes up with something concrete, she'll get away anyway."

They find a rocky outcrop farther along the cliff, perched on its edge. It allows them an oblique view down to the yacht. As the morning sun takes command of the sky, it beats down on them.

"We're very exposed here," says Rourke.

"They'll never see us."

"I want to bring this to an end. To reach some kind of conclusion. To find out what happened to these girls, to your niece."

Blevins nods grimly. "So do I. This is where it all ends."

Jake Kendrick looks at the information on the desk before him. Mary was wrong. Or part wrong. He has no doubt that Clifford J. Taylor, still lying unconscious in an expensive private hospital room, has something to do with the Resurrection Club, maybe even, given what he's found out, with the missing girls. But one thing is certain: Clifford Taylor is not Boy Lindqvist. There has been no reinvention, none of Hiram Levitt's magic. Clifford Taylor's past is a matter of record: there are photographs from back east, college yearbooks, society columns, official documentation.

The arrogant, entitled blueblood image isn't an act, it's who Taylor is.

There had, however, been a scandal when Taylor was a freshman at Yale. There had been a party, things had gotten out of hand, and a young debutante had accused him of rape. It was the most serious such accusation against him, but by no means the only one. Taylor had fancied himself as a lounge lizard and one for the ladies, but when they didn't share his high opinion of himself, he quickly turned into a wrong gee. But that was it.

He wasn't Boy Lindqvist. And already his lawyers were turning up the heat. Ah, Mary, thinks Kendrick, when you're wrong, you're really wrong.

He thinks it all through. He doesn't have a single substantive piece of evidence against Veronica Stratton. And with Taylor out of the frame, if Huston really is Lindqvist, they have no way of proving it. The net is closing in on their quarry, but it's a net full of holes.

It's time to cut losses and get Rourke and Blevins out of it before things get even more messed up.

He grabs his hat and jacket and checks his watch. It's eight-thirty, meaning it's ten-thirty in Louisiana and Kansas. It's worth checking, he decides, and on his way out to the precinct lot, he calls in to the front desk, where wires are brought in from the wire office.

"Anything from Louisiana, Pat?" he asks the duty uniform.

"You keep askin'," says the sergeant, "and I keep tellin'—I'll let you know as soon as something comes in. Nothing from Louisiana, but there's a wire just in this minute from Kansas. You sure like having pen pals." The sergeant thumbs through the telegrams in the in-tray and hands one to Kendrick. "Like I say, just got it . . ."

"Thanks, Pat." Kendrick takes the telegram and reads it.

AS PER YOUR REQUEST(STOP)BOY LINDQVIST SUSPECT IN
KIDNAPPING RAPE MURDER(STOP)INSUFFICIENT EVIDENCE TO
INITIATE EXTRADITION(STOP)DESCRIPTION BLOND MEDIUM
HEIGHT EASILY RECOGNIZABLE BY SEVERE SCAR ON LEFT SIDE
OF FACE(STOP)PLEASE ADVISE IF LOCATED(STOP)

47

1910
Kansas

The last one had been one too many. And he had been sloppy. She had gotten away before he could finish her, silence her for good, like he had the others. But how he has savored her fear. How he had savored all their fear. It had been easy for him: he was handsome and he was strong. They fell to his charm so easily; then, when they realized that what lay beneath was so terribly ugly, it was too late, and all that was left to them was their fear. And how he had drunk that fear.

He had been so alone with his burden, so terribly alone. But then they had come. Hippolyta and Anastasie. They brought with them the kind of beauty and grace and bright darkness he worshipped. When he first saw Anastasie, he had thought how she might yield to him, how she might offer up her fear for him to drink. But he quickly realized there was no fear in her, and in its place was something bright and hard and cold and sharp.

And it was he who came to fear her.

She found out about what he did. About what happened to the girls in each new town, each stop along the way. He had feared that she would destroy him, and he knew she was capable of destroying him, for his crimes against her sisterkind. Instead, she helped him. She helped him choose, then brought them to him. The gender they shared made them trust Anastasie. She brought him what he needed, and in return she demanded only one thing: his complete, lifelong, and unquestioning loyalty. And that he follow her command and no other.

He gladly, joyously, agreed.

But he had come full-circle, and Boy found himself returned to the edge of his hometown. And he had seen her: Nancy Stillson, the girl he had desired so many years before. She was still young, still fresh, still in bloom. She had not recognized him, not just because he was taller, more handsome, his hair brightened and his skin darkened by carnival seasons in the sun—but because she had never noticed him, registered his existence, when he had been neighbor and schoolmate.

Then he had unleashed himself upon her. Her fear had been so deliciously, perfectly bright. It had, to start with, filled him with pride that he had acted alone, but he feared Anastasie's wrath. This girl must never be found, must never tell anyone about what he had done to her, about how he had drunk her fear.

Nancy had screamed. Boy's choice of location had been flawed, and her screams had been heard. He had heard voices raised in shouts as others came toward them, and so had Nancy, and she had screamed more. Boy had run desperate, headlong, careless in concealment, back to the encampment. He had barely had time to explain it all to Anastasie when the mob fell upon the show. There were screams and cries. Old man Dahlman had appealed for calm but had been knocked down, beaten, trampled. The tents, the big top, the stalls—they had set fire to it all. Everything had burned brightly in the night.

"Another flame to light our departure," Anastasie had said to her mother. They had fled. Boy had led them out into the vast black prairie, but their progress had been slow because of Hippolyta's infirmity.

"You must lead them away from us," Anastasie had commanded, and as always he obeyed. He had run close enough to the camp to be seen in the torchlight and the flames from the burning tents. He had run, and the mob had followed.

They had caught up with him. Yells and oaths and fists rained on him; angry hands seized him. He was terrified, but he thought of Anastasie escaping into the night and it gave him courage. They would kill him, but she would live. They held him until the girl and her father arrived. Nancy Stillson's father wasn't a large man, but he was wiry, compact, as if woven from steel cable. Something had flashed and glittered in the farmer's tight-balled fist: a crescent of white steel turned golden in the torchlight. It was a hand scythe. Stillson raised the scythe above his head and brought it down with all his strength.

Boy Lindqvist felt no pain to start with, just the jarring impact as the sickle's blade sliced into the bones of his face, parting skin, sinew and muscle as if they weren't there.

Hands released him, and he fell into the prairie grass. Then, like the dawning of a black sun on the prairie, the pain found him and he screamed. There was another arcing flash, and he felt the tip of the scythe pierce his chest.

As the world slipped away from him, he imagined he saw the demon from the magic-lantern show, his eyes ember-red and his great wings spread wide and filling the sky. It must just be the fire and smoke from the camp, thought Boy, as death came to claim him.

He could not make sense of it to start with. There was a great green vaulted ceiling high above him, and he thought he was in a cathedral for a moment. Then he realized it was a forest. He was in great pain, he knew that, but something had detached him from the pain, something flowed through his veins that placed him at one remove from what was happening to his body. There was something clinging to the left side of his face, covering that eye. His nostrils were filled with smells of the earth, of fungi, of soil, of damp wood, of worms, of death and life.

He saw her. Her face. Her beautiful, terrifying face.

"It's all right," she said in that strange accent of hers. "You have been resurrected, you have been reborn, and it is all going to be all right," said Anastasie Cormier, and Boy knew it would be.

48

1927
Hollywood

Jake Kendrick assembles four men in two cars. Before they set out, he telephones the Orange County Sheriff's Department and tells the duty officer what is happening and gives a description of Blevins/Lindqvist. He also gives the name of the cove where Rourke was headed.

"I'll get someone out there right away," says the deputy. Kendrick tells him that he's on his way and will be there in an hour.

"Watch out for Lindqvist," he says. "He's full of tricks."

The heat from the sun, the desert of wakefulness that lies unbroken between her and her last sleeping, the arid, raspy grating in her throat, all combine to dull Mary Rourke's responses. She and Blevins have been sitting there for an hour or more, and Rourke's limbs ache; her pulse throbs in her temples.

"Are you okay?" asks Blevins.

"I'm fine," she lies weakly. "I'm just— Wait, look!" Suddenly animated, she points down to the cove. A small motor tender rounds the promontory and heads toward the yacht. Rourke can see there are two men in the tender, plus a woman whose blonde hair was all but covered by a scarf. "It's Stratton."

Blevins takes the binoculars from her and looks. "You're right. You stay here, I'll fetch help. Don't move, and don't let them see you." He heads back to the automobile.

Rourke trains the binoculars on the yacht. The party of three is boarding. She'll do as Blevins suggested and sit tight. But only for so long. She reaches into her clutch bag, but her fingers fail to find what they seek. She puts the binoculars down and scrabbles in her bag. It's gone. The pistol Jake Kendrick gave her is missing. Maybe it has dropped into the footwell of the car. She has to try to catch Blevins before he leaves so she can retrieve the gun.

But when she looks over to where Blevins parked the sedan, she can see it is still sitting there, unmoving. He isn't heading up the track to the main road. He hasn't even started the engine. Instead, George Blevins steps back out of the automobile and starts heading back toward her. And he has something in his hand.

Under that bright, hot sun, a cold, dark realization coalesces in Mary Rourke's chest.

She stands up, searching the ground around her for a rock, a stick, anything to defend herself. There is nothing.

Blevins is close now, the hunting knife gleams in his hand. His smile is malicious, twisted by more than the deformity of his face. It is, she realizes, an expression of malevolent anticipation. He's telling himself he's going to enjoy what comes next.

For an instant, the yacht and its occupants are forgotten. This cliff-top universe is filled only with the two of them.

It is then that the sound of a car, coming along the track at speed, distracts them both.

The two LAPD automobiles bump along the rough track to where the cliff edges the bay. There is a knot of three Orange County Fords already sitting there. A group of five men stand watching them approach: none wears a uniform. The tallest of them, a big middle-aged man in a business suit and a hat so wide-brimmed it wouldn't look out of place on the range, walks over to meet the approaching city cops. He rests an elbow on the roof of Kendrick's car and leans into the window. Kendrick sees a brass eagle–topped badge pinned to his breast pocket.

"You Kendrick? I'm Sam Jernigan, Orange County sheriff."

"Thanks for your assist on this, Sheriff. You got Mary Rourke?"

"Start off, we ain't assisting. You're on my bean patch now. And no, no sign of anybody here."

"What?"

"Like I said, I got a boy down here within minutes of your call. There weren't nobody here."

Kendrick opens the door and steps out, forcing Jernigan to take a step back. "But this is where we were supposed to meet," protests Kendrick. "This is the name of the cove I was given."

"Who gave it to you?" asks Jernigan.

Kendrick opens his mouth to speak, then remembers George Blevins handing him a note with where the yacht was supposed to be anchored. "Shit, Lindqvist . . . He gave me the wrong location." He shakes the thought from his head and looks earnestly at Jernigan. "Sheriff, I really need your help here. This is the wrong cove—we've been deliberately misled. I need every cove and bay where a yacht could be anchored checked out."

"That's a lot of coastline, friend."

"Believe me, Sheriff, a woman's life depends on it."

Blevins is turned to watch the car approach, and Rourke frantically runs through her options. Without a weapon, and with Blevins armed with a knife, she has none. Maybe the approaching car is the local sheriff, she thinks.

She knows it isn't when Blevins turns from watching it to face her again, the twisted, malicious grin returning to his face.

Rourke looks down at the cove and sees that the yacht has loosed its mooring and now is heading out to the mouth of the cove and the ocean beyond, the motor tender towed behind it. It's too late, she thinks. It's all too late.

She turns back to Blevins, who still eyes her with grinning, malevolent intent. Looking over his shoulder, she sees the new arrival pull up next to Blevins's gray sedan. The door opens and a man climbs out. He is tall, very tall, and heavily built.

Whatever hope Mary Rourke was clinging to evaporates as she watches Golem Geller make his way, slowly and deliberately, toward them.

They abandon the LAPD vehicles and split up between the Orange County automobiles. Kendrick goes with Jernigan, who has assigned each car its own stretch of coastline. Kendrick has taken an instant and deep dislike of the local sheriff, but pushes his antipathy and frustration down. Jernigan has the local knowledge. And he's the only game in town.

"I hope you know this is a whole needle-haystack thing," says Jernigan. "What's it all about?"

Kendrick tells him, cutting out as much unnecessary detail as possible.

"So you think these people are making a run outta territorial waters?"

"That would be my guess."

Jernigan thinks for a moment, then brakes hard. He three-points the automobile with grinding of gears and a cloud of dust. "You know somethin'? I think I might know just the spot."

"Are they gone?" asks Geller as he reaches them. He looks at Rourke without comment, his eyes empty.

"They're gone. Out at sea by now," says Blevins. He turns to Rourke. "Just got to deal with her."

"We could just leave her," says Geller. Blevins turns to him, the smile dropping from his face.

"Are you crazy? You know what she's like; we'd be looking over our shoulders for the rest of our lives. And so would Anastasie. We promised her, remember?"

"Yes," says Geller. "We did. We promised her a lot of things."

"Anyway," says Blevins, turning back to Rourke, the leering grin back on his twisted face, "I want to have some fun first. I'm going to enjoy this."

"You think?" Rourke fights to keep the fear from her voice. "Trust me, handsome, I'll make sure both sides of your face are a perfect match first. I'm not so easy to scare, Boy. I've got it right this time, haven't I? You're Boy Lindqvist."

"Knowing that won't do you any good."

"So what about the real Blevins? Jake Kendrick got details on him."

"He's in some nuthouse. Shell shock or the likes. I got access to his records."

"So it *was* you who fixed my brakes."

"Yeah. Not good enough. But I'm gonna put that right now. You've ruined everything. For me, for Anastasie, for everyone. You don't know what you've been messing with. And Anastasie has told me to make sure you suffer before you die. And I aim to please."

"What about you, Sam?" she asks Geller. "Why did you get involved in all of this?"

"I don't know," he says glumly. "I guess just like a fly don't know how it ends up in a spider's web. I ain't proud of what I done, Mary. I need you to believe me."

"Why? What does that matter now?"

"Yeah . . ." Lindqvist frowns. "Why are you coming over all repentant? You got what you wanted out of all of this, like all of us did."

"Did I?"

"Looked to me like you did, out there at the stone theater. Anyway, we gotta get this done. Like I say, I'm going to have some fun with her. You wanna watch?"

"No," says Geller. "I've seen too much."

Lindqvist turns again to Rourke, raises the knife, and steps toward her. She responds by backing away until she is at the cliff's edge. "You're not going to have any fun with me, you rat-ugly piece of shit. I'll go over the edge first."

"Either way," says Lindqvist, "the job gets done."

Rourke jumps at the sound of it. Lindqvist too looks surprised. He lets the knife fall from his grasp and pulls at the front of his shirt, already blooming red from the bullet's exit wound. He turns and looks at Geller, as does Rourke. A heavy-caliber revolver smokes in his hand. Lindqvist opens his mouth to say something, but Geller fires again, and he falls, silently, to the ground.

Rourke stares at Geller. She doesn't know what's to come next, and half expects him to shoot her too.

"I'm sorry, Mary," he says, and she can see the pain in his eyes. "You don't know her. You don't know how she can make you crazy. Make you do things. I'm so ashamed. I'm so sorry."

"Talk to the cops, Sam," says Rourke, and she takes a step toward him. He checks her with a movement of the gun barrel.

"And finish it all at the end of a rope? No, Mary, I ain't going out like that." He takes a deep breath. "Promise me you won't look for her no more. You won't look for Anastasie. There's nothing to come of that but pain. Sorry it had to end this way. Bye, toots."

Geller places the barrel beneath his jaw and pulls the trigger. There is a plume of blood and matter; then, like a felled tree, Golem Geller topples onto the ground.

She sits watching the sea for nearly an hour, her thoughts vague and unfixed. It all started, somehow, with a movie. She's still sitting there, flanked by the bodies of two dead men, when Kendrick and the Orange County sheriff arrive.

PART FOUR

49

One Year Later
1928

Hollywood

The world has changed in the year since it all happened. After the sun sets on the eve of Yom Kippur, 1927, a small Jewish singer wearing blackface opens his mouth on a New York movie-theater screen and rocks all of Hollywood, all of the world, to its core.

Al Jolson tells the world, "You ain't heard nothin' yet," and in that instant the movies become the talkies.

And with the change, the scope and the art and the ambition of movies has been shrunk, literally: the bulk and comparative immobility of synchronized-sound film cameras and the need for actors to be within feet of a microphone has reduced the scale of shots, diminished the epic visions of directors. Because of this, some producers and directors defiantly forge ahead with silent movies, but a hungry-eared public, used to hearing stars on the radio and now on-screen, shun visual spectacle in favor of spoken word.

Many recently released silent movies are recalled and, along with those nearing completion, have sound sections grafted into them. Hollywood, always quick to find a catchphrase, begins to call the practice "goat-glanding" movies: a reference to the dubious vigor-restoring surgical practices of John Romulus Brinkley.

The dark shadow of the microphone is cast over the silver screen. Those whose faces have been their fortune now find their voices are their ruin. Famous cowboy stars are revealed to have impenetrable foreign accents; sophisticated leading ladies' voices ring unmusically with Boston brogues or Bowery twangs; romantic male leads reveal effeminate or reedy tones.

Many of Hollywood's greatest stars disappear overnight.

Despite the frantic focus on the new medium, *The Devil's Playground* and the tragedies surrounding it have not been forgotten. The loss of the film, the death of its glamorous star, and the suicide of its producer have become the stuff of Hollywood legend—as has the disappearance at sea of its male lead, Robert Huston, along with his wife, the legendary actress Veronica Stratton. Everyone has their own theory, their own take on it.

Mary Rourke offers no thoughts on the subject. She has kept her opinions largely to herself since she and Jake Kendrick took their story about a secret society—the Resurrection Club—to the top of LAPD's detective bureau. The skepticism and scorn with which their initial claims were met have become more muted, less outspoken. Someone, somewhere, has told the bureau to give the appearance of looking into it. The eleven miles of known underground tunnels have been searched, they claim. No sign of any such club has been found.

It is a dull June day when Jake Kendrick and Mary Rourke take matters into their own hands. The Los Angeles Police Department, Kendrick knows, makes use of the tunnels themselves to allow safe transfer of prisoners from headquarters to the city courthouse. It is a starting point. Rourke and Kendrick spend two whole days, and half of the next, navigating the dark passageways and wide tunnels underneath the city. Occasionally, they rise to near street level again, and daylight, voices, and footsteps reach down from busy sidewalks above them. At other times they make ringing iron-runged descents into the black pools of stairwells. A couple of times they have to kill their flashlights and press against cold stone when they hear the nearby sounds of bootleggers moving carts of illicit alcohol.

"Probably Mayor Cryer's people," whispers Kendrick in the dark. "Shifting booze to and from City Hall. Gotta love them Republicans."

At one point, they stumble upon an underground speakeasy, and only Kendrick's badge, gun, and calming authoritative manner saves them from unpleasantness.

It is midafternoon on the third day that an access corridor between two Red Car tunnels suddenly opens out into a huge hall. Scanning the space with his flashlight, Kendrick finds a double-pole lever power switch on the wall. He flips the switch, and rows of pendulum and wall lights flicker into brightness. The whole place is brightly, bleakly illuminated, and Rourke catches her breath.

"This is it," says Kendrick. "Isn't it?"

Rourke nods. She recognized it instantly from the secondhand description Sadie Ehrlich had given her. It is wide and high-vaulted. Huge pipes and conduits run snakelike along one side, and the plastered brick walls and riveted steel panels are all painted blood-red. Kendrick suggests that it has been some kind of machine hall, perhaps for ventilating the now unused Pacific Electric Red Car tunnels, but that it has long since had its machinery stripped out.

Rourke says nothing and gazes around the space. She imagines it dressed for voodoo rituals and drinks—and drug-fueled excesses. Bad things have happened here, she thinks. You don't need to know its history to sense it. Something bad lingers in the air.

They find the iron door. Turning the wheel lock releases bolts, and it creakingly offers entry into a second chamber. This room is huge too, but the walls are rendered dark green while the pipework and power conduits have been painted the same dark-crimson color as the outer chamber. It gives the room a nauseously organic feel. A single pendant light hangs from the center of the ceiling, casting a bright, circular pool of light on the stone-flagged floor.

"Do you think this is the stone theater?" asks Kendrick.

Rourke shakes her head. "This was the resurrection chamber. The stone theater was somewhere else. Somewhere far from here. I guess we'll never know where."

There is nothing else in either room to suggest that these spaces are in current use or have been anytime recently. No paintings of serpents, no voodoo symbols, no furniture, no illicit bars. But Rourke senses something lingering in the stale air, like the scent of a woman who has passed through the room, or the echoes of just-stilled voices. A streetcar rattles past somewhere far above them, again just as Lucille had described to Sadie, who had in turn described to Rourke—as if to reassure them they really are in the right place.

"I was beginning to wonder if it was all real," Kendrick says, looking around the inner chamber.

"Real or not," says Rourke, "they've cleaned the place out. Like everything else, all we have is a story to tell and nothing to back it up."

The sky has brightened, and the sun dazzles them when they emerge at street level once more at the Hall of Records entrance. They stand for a moment, as if the Los Angeles landscape has suddenly become an alien geography and they are each unsure which direction to take.

"Well, that's that," Kendrick says.

"Would appear so," Rourke replies.

"Do you think they've been scared off?"

"Only to some other location. Or maybe, with Anastasie Cormier gone, they've lost their raison d'être."

"Come again?"

"Never mind. It's French."

"I guess we'll never find out what happened to those girls."

"I guess."

Kendrick removes his hat, runs fingers through his thick dark-blond hair, and looks squintingly up at the vast, castlelike Hall of Records and the clearing sky beyond.

"Well, I best be going," he says as he replaces his hat. "See you around, Mary."

"See you around, Jake." She watches him walk down Spring Street, with that strange mix of athleticism and the ghost of a limp.

"Jake . . . wait!" she calls out, and when he turns, "I've got an idea . . ."

Three significant things happen over the following three months.

First of all, Mary Rourke, free after Carbine International Pictures goes bust, sets up office on Sunset Boulevard. Taking a leaf out of the late Hiram Levitt's book, she offers services to all Hollywood's studios based on unshakable confidentiality. Her shingle states she's a publicity consultant, but Mary Rourke remains what she's always been. A fixer.

Jake Kendrick is viewed with mistrust by his police colleagues—seen as someone with an inconvenient surplus of curiosity combined with unhealthily honest tendencies. His pursuit of the truth behind the Resurrection Club has meant the wrong toes were trodden upon, too often, and his LAPD career outlook has become decidedly myopic. It therefore doesn't take much persuading from Mary Rourke for him to quit the department, apply for a PI license, and become her partner in the new venture.

They are kept busy. Rourke's track record and Kendrick's police experience and contacts prove an attractive combination for studios keen to keep their stars' names out of the papers and their stars' carcasses out of jail. Rourke hires Sylvie, her former assistant at Carbine, to help deal with the volume of work.

It's all going well. Despite the fact that something continually itches at the back of Rourke's brain, they never discuss *The Devil's Playground,* Veronica Stratton's disappearance, or Hiram Levitt's murder, which remains unsolved.

Until the two other events. Resurrections, of a sort.

Like everyone else, Rourke finds out about the first discovery in the newspapers. A geologist working for one of the oil companies made a grim discovery out at La Brea Tar Pits: the body of a man, partly submerged in the dense, black asphalt pitch, had been discovered during a survey. He had been dead for several months, but has been identified by his wallet, still on the body, and the identification has been confirmed by dental records.

Frank Quinlan at the *Examiner* sums it all up in his headline: PHYSICIAN TO HOLLYWOOD'S RICH AND FAMOUS FOUND SHOT TO DEATH IN TAR PIT. Beneath the headline is a photograph of a heavyset man in a tuxedo at some social gathering. The article explains, "Doctor John Henry Albertus Wilson, head of the Appleton Clinic, where Hollywood's great and good sought treatment, victim of unknown gunman . . ."

The news stuns Rourke. Doc Wilson hadn't just taken off, as he had hinted he might. His disappearance seemed odd at the time, but he had briefed his deputy, Davidson, to take over. In any case, the vault fire at Carbine International, the death of its chief, and the subsequent collapse of the company had diverted everyone's attention. The Appleton Clinic itself had fallen victim to its parent company's going belly-up, and the clinic had been bought out by an insurance company. Wilson's unavailability had been inconvenient and puzzling for a while, then had been forgotten.

But now Doc Wilson is back in everyone's mind. The itch in the back of Rourke's brain is suddenly, irresistibly intensified. Unbidden, the memory comes to her of Boy Lindqvist sitting in her kitchen and pretending to be George Blevins. She remembers his tale about a Jay-hawker sergeant who had been looking out in the wrong direction, at the wrong time. It had been nothing but a fiction to explain his disfiguring facial scar. But he had had a point. Mary Rourke is convinced she has been looking in the wrong direction.

Doc Wilson was murdered.

Doc Wilson was murdered, Norma Carlton was murdered, Hiram Levitt was murdered. It is a bleak equation that has an answer, she knows it with every fiber. It is an arithmetic sequence that has a product—and that product is not the one her previous calculations have given her.

A week later, she and Kendrick talk it through in the office.

"I met up with Dan McMenemy, the detective investigating Wilson's homicide," explains Kendrick. "If you can call it investigating: that suggests activity, and there ain't much of that. I took him to Cole's." Cole's was a bar that had turned coffeehouse for Prohibition and sat half below street level, next to the Pacific Electric Red Car depot. If you had a face they knew and trusted, your coffee mug would be filled with under-the-counter bourbon.

"What has he got?" asks Rourke.

"Not much to nothing. Other than that Doc Wilson was carrying close to a thousand bucks on him when he died, added to which he had bank accounts that don't add up. I guess he was paid well at the Appleton Clinic, but he had over a quarter of a million between banks. Looks like Doc Wilson was on someone else's payroll too."

"It sure does." Rourke thinks for a moment. Everything is different. Focus is shifted. "So what's the cops' take on it?"

"Well, you know they're not big thinkers—they've got Doc Wilson running a pill mill and selling thebaine and other narcotics on the side. To be fair, there seem to be some discrepancies in his drug books, but nothing so significant that he'd pull in that kind of dough."

"And that's it?"

"That's all they got. Or that's all McMenemy was willing to share. And they ain't looking none too hard for anything else. Why? What are you thinking?"

"Just that Doc Wilson may have had something to do with Norma Carlton's death," says Rourke. "When he showed me her body in the morgue, I saw the bruising around her neck. Maybe that wasn't the main cause of death, because he made sure the lights went out before I had a good enough look at her body."

"Why would Wilson murder Norma Carlton?"

"I'm not saying he did. I'm saying he wasn't as innocent a participant in the big cover-up as he made out. Anyone who knew how I operated could be guaranteed the only medic I'd call would be Wilson. Maybe I'm becoming paranoid, but I'm beginning to think an elaborate Hollywood production was put on for an audience of one. Me." An idea strikes her. "Do you know Pops Nolan?"

"Pops, sure . . ." Kendrick frowns. "Everybody knows Pops. Thirty-year man in the department. I ain't seen him in a while, but, yeah, I know him. Why?"

"Renata, Norma Carlton's maid, said that she was surprised how quick the cops got to the house after she called, like they had just been around the corner. It was Pops Nolan and . . ." She shakes her head in irritation. "I can't remember the young cop's name. I paid them both off, but maybe they'd already had a paycheck."

"Pops Nolan?" Kendrick shakes his head doubtfully. "I can't see that. But I'll look into it. But none of this helps us with the question of who killed Norma Carlton, and why."

"I've got nothing to connect her death to Veronica Stratton, other than they knew each other better than everyone thought." Rourke shakes her head. "I don't know—maybe she found out about the Resurrection Club and heard girls were going missing. Carlton was there at the yacht party. Norma Carlton was someone people would listen to, and maybe they decided to shut her up before they did."

"That's an awfully long stretch, Mary."

"I guess."

With other, paying matters to deal with, they drop the subject, agreeing that they will never know the truth. And all the while, Sam Geller's dying request that she forget about it all and get on with her life echoes in the background.

"It was Harry Carbine who got me mixed up in this whole mess, and Harry's dead. I think I have to accept the hero's journey is at an end."

But it continues to nag at Rourke, tugging at the thread ends of her thoughts, trying to find the one that will unravel.

—

The third discovery comes a month later. And with it comes renewed interest among the press and public in the *Devil's Playground* curse.

The Coast Guard is on constant lookout up and down the Pacific Coast. Their quarry is illicit booze-laden vessels seeking out hidden coves like Crescent Cove or isolated spots on Laguna Beach to land their goods. The Coast Guard, and everyone else, call it the Rum Patrol. It's a huge task, and the Navy has transferred twenty four-stack destroyers to the Coast Guard for the job.

It was one of the Coast Guard destroyers that found her.

The *Temptress* was derelict and adrift, her mast sheared, shrouded in her own rotting sails. The hull was unbreached, but barnacle-crusted, and the yacht showed signs of seven months' sun scorching and storm lashing, yet still floated.

The boarding party had been spooked by the experience, as most seafarers are when they find a derelict. The belowdecks were stuffy, and entering them had been like breaking open and stepping into a tomb. But a tomb without any bodies. Food sat rotted on the galley table, lifejackets hung unused in lockers, but there was no sign of Veronica Stratton or of Robert Huston. The yacht's small tender was missing, but no evidence was found of any calamity on the yacht that would have compelled them to abandon it and take to the open sea in a small rowboat.

The press go crazy with the story: MISSING MOVIE STARS' BOAT FOUND. HOLLYWOOD'S MARIE CELESTE. BLONDE SCREEN GODDESS DISAPPEARED. Grainy photographs show the exterior and interior of the yacht. There is something unnervingly corpselike about it.

Mary Rourke is shaken by the discovery. But, as she points out to Kendrick, it neither proves nor disproves that Stratton still lives.

"Odds are they're both dead," says Kendrick. "It is a strange one, though. By the way, there's something else. I've been asking around about Pops Nolan."

"And?"

"He took early retirement. Him and his wife have taken this house down the coast. Nothing fancy, but it seems quite a stretch, given his pension. There's a new automobile as well."

"So you think I'm right about him?"

"Could be; the jury's out. You want me to pay him a visit?"

"No, not yet. There's something about all of this that still isn't sitting right with me. I don't know what it is."

The office telephone rings, and Sylvie answers it. "It's for you, Miss Rourke."

"Who is it?"

"It's Miss Drescher."

"Margot Drescher?"

"She says it's important."

50

It started life as the L.A. County Poor Farm, and still has parts devoted to offering food, shelter, and field labor to the indigent of Los Angeles. Immediately after the war, it served as a major hospital for treating victims of the Spanish flu. As she approaches it, it looks to Mary Rourke like a fully self-contained small town. Situated in a landscape of orange and olive groves between Downey and Hollydale, the State Insane Asylum is a community sitting in verdant, fence-bound isolation.

When she arrives at the main administration building, Rourke is directed to Eucalyptus Avenue, where, she is told, she will find the "psychopathic wards."

Instead of the towering walls and watchtowers she was expecting, she is surprised to see that Downey Asylum comprises a complex of pleasant-looking single-story buildings, each like an extended bungalow, arranged along a tree-lined street and backed by flower gardens.

When she finds the appropriate building, Rourke is subject to the horn-rimmed scrutiny of a thin-lipped chief nurse. But when Rourke tells her who she's there to visit, the thin lips break unexpectedly into a smile.

"Oh, you're here to see Theodore? He's very dashing—quite the charmer, you know."

"I can imagine," says Rourke.

"Are you a relative?"

"No, I'm a former colleague, from his studio days."

"Oh, really?" says the nurse. "That must be exciting."

"It has its moments."

"Are you an actress?" asks the nurse hopefully. "Will I have seen you in anything?"

"No. I work behind the scenes."

"Oh." The nurse fails to hide her disappointment. "Well, anyway—I'll take you along to see Theodore." She leads Rourke along a corridor and into a large open area. There is a huge square recess in the high ceiling, which in turn gives way to a tented glass roof. The result is that the space is flooded with bright light.

There are tables spaced at intervals across the floor. At each table sit patients involved in various activities, from playing chess and cards to engaging in all kinds of arts or crafts. Rourke notices that no one rocks back and forth, no one contorts or rants or raves. Madness seems unobtrusive and convivial here. If it were not for the fact that everybody wears the same outfit—white shirt and pants for men, white blouse and below-the-knee skirt for women—Rourke could imagine she is in a Hollywood studio cafeteria.

Sitting by himself at a table near the far side of the hall sits a man of around fifty, reading a book. He has a handsome face—not movie-star handsome, Rourke notes, too much character for that—but there is something vaguely aristocratic about him. His gray-flecked dark hair is retreating at the temples and has formed a stark widow's peak. His eyes are bright blue under arching black eyebrows. There is something mischievous about him. Not mad, mischievous. The aquiline nose and the strong, almost pointed chin give him the look of some clubbable devil, and Rourke reluctantly understands what Norma Carlton saw in him. He wears the same white shirt-and-pants outfit as every other patient, but somehow does so with more panache, and Rourke wonders if his loony suit is personally tailored for him.

"Theodore," says the nurse, "there's a young lady here to see you."

"Ah, Nurse Willard . . ." He puts the book down, and the handsome face breaks into a broad, boyish smile. "No female companionship could ever be quite as delightful as yours."

Nurse Willard giggles almost girlishly, a sound as comely as a blocked sink draining. "I'll leave you to it."

He waves as she leaves, then turns to Rourke. The smile fades without disappearing, but the eyes become harder, more suspicious.

"Please, sit," he says. She does.

"Hello, Mr. Woolfe. My name is Mary Rourke, I wonder if I could ask you—"

Woolfe silences her with a fingertip held to his lips. He leans forward, resting his elbows on the table. His shoulders hunched, he casts his gaze to both sides, as if checking they are not overheard.

"Keep it down," he urges in hushed conspiratorial tones, "or the Earthlings will hear you. Have you been sent by the Venusian ambassador?"

"I beg your pardon?"

"It's all right," he whispers. "I know what the Martians are planning, and I have a message to send to Venus. His Excellency the Ambassador is expecting it. Have you come to collect it?"

"I . . ." Rourke is lost for words.

Woolfe suddenly sits upright, throws his head back, and laughs uproariously. "I'm sorry, Miss Rourke, I couldn't resist that. The sane are so uncomfortable around the mad, and I so seldom have the opportunity to have fun with someone from the outside." He indicates their surroundings with a wave of the hand. "Welcome to the booby hatch. Quite the place, isn't it?"

"It doesn't look too bad. Lots of light and air."

"Yeah." He looks up at the huge, tented skylight abstractedly. "That's the thing—these people think that light and air are the cures for madness. They believe psychiatric medicine should be all about banishing darkness, lighting up dark corners, and eliminating shadows, all that fine guff." He gives a small laugh. "The truth is, they've got it all wrong. Insanity isn't darkness—it's light. Bright, hard, sharp-edged light. I never saw more clearly than when I lost my marbles. It's the sane who live in the dark, who are made of shadows. Everyone here is a little ray of sunshine. Mad sunshine, but sunshine." He examines Rourke carefully, and an expression of recognition crosses his face. "Wait a minute, I remember you. You screen-tested for me once. A long, long time ago." He nods enthusiastically, as if the action stimulates his recall. "Yes—yes, that's it—you auditioned but didn't get the part. Aren't you the girl who broke Stroheim's nose?" He frowns thoughtfully as he struggles to retrieve the memory. "Or was it Louis Mayer? No, no— Darryl Zanuck?"

"I work in publicity, Mr. Woolfe. I'm not an actress."

"Publicity?" The dark eyebrows arch in surprise. "What on earth can I do to help someone from publicity? Or, when you say you work in publicity, do you mean publicity like Eddie Mannix and Howard Strickling work in publicity?"

"That's what I mean."

"Ah, right—you're a fixer?"

"For want of a better word."

"Not wanting to be impolite, but there are no better words for what you do, and many that are worse. What can I do for you?"

"I've been trying to sort some things out. I got a call from Margot Drescher, the agent. . . ."

"Oh yes." Woolfe smiles. "I know Margot. She's all right. How is she?"

"Fine," says Rourke. "Margot has asked I meet with her tomorrow, but she suggested I talk with you first. She said you would help me understand things a little better."

"Oh," says Woolfe breezily. "What things?"

"It's about your ex-wife."

His expression darkens. "Norma? What about her?"

"You know what happened to her?"

"They told me she's dead. A year back, or more. I was informed very solicitously, very cautiously. I don't know what they thought the news would do to me, but then they pumped so much Somnifen into me that the lights turned out and didn't come fully back on for a week." He nods in the direction of the other patients. "They're great believers in sleep cures here, which is why everybody is only half awake."

"Were you upset that Miss Carlton has died? Or were you pleased?"

He leans back in his chair and eyes Rourke appraisingly for a moment before answering. "I was neither."

"You threatened to kill her yourself, at one time. That's why you're in this place. You came at her with a gun. Now that she's dead, haven't you gotten what you wanted?"

"Why I'm in this place isn't as straightforward as you might think. When all that *hoo-hah* happened—when I went crazy—I was desperate. What you and everyone else can't seem to understand is that it wasn't that I wanted Norma to die, it was that I wanted to live. I wanted to be free. Anyway, the reason I'm neither upset nor pleased is because I'm not convinced."

"Not convinced of what? That she killed herself?"

"No, not that. I *know* Norma didn't kill herself. That's all baloney and bull, if you'll pardon the expression. What I'm not convinced about is that she's dead at all."

"Believe me, Norma Carlton is dead, Mr. Woolfe, I can confirm that. I saw her dead body with my own eyes."

"Well, I didn't with mine, and that's what it would take to convince me that she's dead."

"I can assure you—"

"What is it you want from me, Miss Rourke?"

"I'm just trying to make sense of what's happened."

Woolfe regards her for a moment. She senses an intensity in his eyes—something fierce and penetrating—and for the first time since she sat opposite him she feels his madness, intense but fleeting, blaze through the space between them. Like the sun flashing off a window opened and closed, it is there and it is gone. He smiles knowingly. "It's Norma, isn't it? She's gotten to you. She's gotten under your skin."

"As I say, Norma's dead," says Rourke.

"If Norma really is dead, then someone has had the courage to kill her. That's why you're here—to see if there was any way I could have had a hand in her death. But I sense you've started to understand the truth about Norma. Trust me, it's better not knowing."

"No, you're wrong, Mr. Woolfe. The truth is exactly what I'm after. What is it that I'm missing?"

He regards her for a while, his eyes bright, intelligent, piercing. "Have you traveled much, Miss Rourke? Have you been outside the U.S., seen other countries, other peoples?"

"I've traveled some," she says.

"When you're abroad, when you're in a different country, you encounter customs you're unfamiliar with, perspectives on things that are different from yours. People behave, to your eyes, oddly. They speak a language you don't understand."

"I don't get—"

"This . . ." He waves his hand airily to indicate their surroundings. "This is a foreign country. The nation of the mad. I'm a long-term resident, but not a native. I've toured this fine land's principal attractions: Norwalk State, Patton State, and now here. I reside as a rich expatriate and have the resources to live that little bit better, in that little bit more comfort, than the locals. And although I speak their language, I still do so with the grammar of the sane."

"I'm sure you have a point," says Rourke, "but I'm sorry, I don't get it."

"Just as if I had run away to Europe or Mexico or South America, I am here to hide. I've never contested my diagnosis or confinement. In fact, I welcomed it, encouraged it. You'll probably have heard that a little incident I was involved with has stopped my planned release. It wasn't a psychotic episode; it was the sanest thing I have ever done. It made sure I stay in here—or even somewhere more secure. You see, Miss Rourke, this is my asylum in every sense of the word. I came here to feel safe."

"Safe from what?"

"From Norma Carlton. As long as I am in here, she can't reach me. I'm safe from her."

"You'll excuse me if I point out that that in itself sounds paranoid," says Rourke.

"Does it? Maybe I should be more honest with the Medical Review Board. Maybe they'd keep me in for telling the truth."

"So you're telling me Norma Carlton was dangerous?"

"Norma Carlton was the most beautiful woman I have ever known. The most desirable. But I got to see what lay beneath that beauty, and it was ugly. So terribly, terribly ugly. There was a darkness to Norma that was unfathomable." Woolfe's face is filled with something like awe. "It is almost impossible to describe how black her soul was. She could make me, make any man, do unspeakable things. Sometimes it was to serve her purposes, at other times simply to see how far I would go to please her. Eventually, when I had lost all but the last shreds of who I was, I realized it was she who was mad. Completely insane. And, from what I could gather, her mother had been insane too. Be warned, Miss Rourke, if you are following Norma's trail, then you're going to come across footprints filled with blood."

Rourke tries to hide the thrill of discovery that runs through her. She clearly fails.

"Oh my God," says Woolfe, smiling. "You really have been hunting the devil, haven't you. And now you've found her, is that it?"

"Her mother?" Rourke recovers herself.

"Norma kept me away from her, but I know she had her close."

"Where was Norma from? What was her real name?"

"That I don't know for sure. She never admitted that Hiram Levitt did a number on her, but I'm pretty sure he did. The little creep was always hanging around her. Everybody was always hanging around

her. Everyone thought they knew who, *what,* they were dealing with."
Woolfe leans back in his chair. "Truth is, nobody knew Norma Carlton. Their impressions of her were just what she chose to reveal to them. I need you to believe me—Norma was the most intelligent, cunning person I've met. She was also the most evil creature I have ever come across. She destroyed so many men. So many women, for that matter. They say I tried to shoot her because I was insane with jealousy because of her infidelities. It wasn't that. I determined to try to kill Norma because I wanted to save myself, save my soul. Norma Carlton is the devil, Miss Rourke. That's what I saw, and my only mistake was to believe I could kill her. But you can't kill the devil."

Rourke's mind races. "What about Veronica Stratton?" she asks after a moment.

"What about her?"

"What was she to Norma?"

"Another moth that fluttered around the flame, that's all. They had this fiction going, this supposed rivalry, but Stratton's star had risen as far as it could, and Norma was about to outshine her."

"And that didn't trouble Stratton?"

"Like everyone else, Veronica Stratton was completely, insanely in love with Norma. She would do anything for her. Lay down her life. Perhaps that's what she did. I read about the yacht being found."

"And Robert Huston?"

Woolfe laughs scornfully. "Huston? He was the pet they shared. He simply did as he was told."

"What about the Resurrection Club?"

"What's that?"

"You haven't heard of it?"

Woolfe shrugs and shakes his head.

They are interrupted by the nurse returning into the hall, pushing a large white trolley. She goes from patient to patient, handing out small paper cups containing pills.

"Ah," says Woolfe. "Cocktail hour already. Allow me to escort you to the door before I'm too somnolent to find the way."

"I'm sorry . . ." says Rourke as she rises.

"Oh, please, don't be. There's peace in stupor."

"I'm just seeing my guest to the door, Nurse Willard," he says as they pass the trolley. "Keep my martini chilled—I'll be right back."

Willard smiles with uncomely girlishness. "Be quick, now, Theodore. I hope you've had a nice visit."

He escorts Rourke to the exit. She notes that an orderly has to unlock the inner door and is surprised when he allows Woolfe to see her to the main door. "They're very relaxed here," explains Woolfe. "Or, more correctly, they keep us relaxed."

A scent of oranges is carried on the breeze, and it reminds Rourke of that first evening at Norma Carlton's house.

"You've been very helpful," says Rourke. "Thank you."

"Oh, I really do hope I haven't," says Woolfe, his expression serious. "I sense I've given you an answer that it would have been better that you never found. Promise me something, Miss Rourke. . . ."

"What?"

"Go live your life. Forget about Norma Carlton. Whatever truth you feel you have to uncover, leave it buried. In fact, heap more dirt on it and walk away. Whether she's alive or dead, you don't want to find where following Norma's footsteps will lead you."

Rourke makes her way back to where her automobile is parked outside the main administration building, trying not to think how Theo Woolfe's caution about Norma Carlton echoes perfectly what Golem Geller, before he blew out his brains, said about Anastasie Cormier.

51

The following morning, Mary Rourke sits in the living room of her Larchmont Village bungalow. She looks at her watch, then looks at it again a few moments later, with the itchy unease of a reluctant patient in a dentist's waiting room.

Jake Kendrick won't be coming with her. He won't even be following at a discreet distance. Margot Drescher has been very clear on that.

"Come alone," she had said. "Make sure no one follows you. A man's life depends on it."

She thinks back to what Harry Carbine had said to her about "the hero's journey" and how it had all seemed guff at the time. It all seems guff now. It's a journey that she wishes he had never handed her a ticket for. She thinks of Carbine. Poor Harry.

She checks her clutch bag for the pocket pistol Kendrick gave her. It's a habit she's gotten into since she dipped her hand into her bag on an isolated clifftop and came out empty. Slipping the gun back into the bag, she checks her watch once more. Time to go, she thinks, or near as damn it. She rises and puts on her hat and coat, picks up her keys from the dresser. Leaving the house, she pauses as she passes the cabinet. She looks at the photograph, and once more the face of a girl who looks so like her looks back out at her. As so many times before, Mary Rourke folds up her grief and slips it away somewhere inside.

The temperature outside has dropped a couple of degrees, but the air clings to Rourke like damp cloth. A dull ache infuses itself into the bone of her forehead and the bridge of her nose. Before she steps into her automobile, she looks up at a sky turned to a sheet of pale silk, the color of milk. Considering her mission, and Margot Drescher's dark cautions to secrecy, and the fact that Rourke has felt the need to hide a pistol in her clutch bag, she feels she could do without the omens of coming storms.

The downtown parking lot is easy to find: it's one of those places making a buck out of a temporary opportunity. It sits between two business blocks on a site cleared of one building and awaiting the construction of its replacement. In the meantime, it offers secure all-day parking. She pulls up at the booth, pays for the day, and is told by the elderly ticket guy that there's some space left at the back of the lot.

She finds a space and waits in the Packard, as she's been told to. A few minutes later, she is startled by the rap of urgent knuckles on her side window. Margot Drescher waves a bony, ring-laden hand in an impatient beckoning that Rourke should get out and come with her. She does, and follows Drescher across the lot. Rourke can sense the small woman's usual electric energy, but this time it's anxious, darker. They stop at an Erskine sedan, which Rourke knows is not Drescher's usual automobile. A rental, she guesses.

"Nobody knows you're here?" asks Drescher. Her face is paler, more drawn, than usual.

"Nobody. Like you told me. You're really going to introduce me to Nathan Milcom?"

"That's what I said."

"Where is he?"

"Not here. I'll take you to him."

"Is all this secrecy necessary, Margot?" asks Rourke.

"Christ, Mary," says Drescher. "This whole thing's littered with bodies. You should know that more than anyone else. Get in; we've got quite a drive."

Drescher climbs in behind the wheel of the Erskine. She looks even smaller and frailer as she hunches forward, the thin fingers wrapping around the steering wheel.

"You heard about Veronica Stratton?" asks Rourke.

"I heard."

"So what do you think?" asks Rourke. "Is she dead, or is it a staged disappearance?"

"She's dead," says Drescher flatly. "She was probably dead before that boat set sail. She maybe was never on it. And my guess is, Robert Huston had been killed long before. You see, Mary, you've been chasing the wrong ghosts. You've written the wrong villain into your script. Did you see Theo Woolfe yesterday?"

"I did. He claimed Norma was evil—that she was insane. And that her mother had been insane too."

"Then you're beginning to get the picture."

"Where are we going?" asks Rourke.

"You'll find out."

Drescher drives silently and grim-faced out of town and into the Hollywood Hills. They pass through Glendale, heading toward Pasadena.

"Is it far?" asks Rourke.

"Less than an hour now," says Drescher.

"You know about the Resurrection Club, Margot?"

"Yeah, I know about it," she says without turning to Rourke.

"How did you get to know about it?"

"From the person we're going to meet."

"Nathan Milcom?"

"He told me about it. He was invited to join—he said he went along with it just to get close to the real power in Hollywood. Something that wouldn't be easy for him otherwise—you'll understand that soon. But then he made the connection between these missing girls and whatever went on with the so-called inner circle. He wanted out before he got pulled in deeper. Whatever went on at the inner circle's little desert get-togethers, he knew that if he got involved, he could never get uninvolved."

"Wait a minute," says Rourke. "How could they invite Nathan Milcom to join? That's the whole big thing, isn't it? The big gimmick—that no one has ever met the writer of *The Devil's Playground*, except you."

"He wasn't invited as Nathan Milcom."

Rourke turns on the Erskine's bench seat to face Drescher's profile. "'Milcom' is a pseudonym? He's well known under another name?"

Drescher turns to her. "You'll find that and everything else out soon." She turns back to the road, her body again hunched forward, her eyes only just above the level of the steering wheel. "Then I'm done with this whole thing. This whole business. I'm getting out of town," she says blankly. "Going back east."

"But your business," says Rourke, "the agency. It's taken you years ..."

Drescher gives a bitter laugh. "When I started out, there was only me. Hollywood studios were free to rip off naïve actors who couldn't find their contractual asses with both hands. Now there are twelve talent agencies in Hollywood, and more coming along almost every month. There are a lot of younger and hungrier fish out there. David Selznick's brother, for one—young Myron is getting quite the reputation as an agent and is always looking to expand. Trust me, I won't have any trouble getting more than one to bite when I dangle the bait of me getting out of the business."

Rourke frowns. "Why, though, Margot? Is it because of all this stuff that's going on?"

"You mean everybody ending up dead or missing? Harry Carbine blowing his brains out—or someone blowing them out for him? Doc Wilson taking a mud bath out at La Brea? Robert Huston and Veronica Stratton taking a swim to Japan from their yacht? Yeah, all that's been preying on my mind, you could say. But it's mainly about Norma."

"What about Norma?"

"I thought I knew her. Or at least I thought I knew her as well as she would allow anyone to get to know her. I was her agent, for Christ's sake. But it turns out I was in the dark about Norma as much as anyone else. Hollywood can be a real lonely place when you realize no one is who you think they are and the connections you thought were real are just as fake as the stuff on the screen. Anyway, the way this has all been going, I'd like to keep this old hide of mine intact."

They fall silent for a while. Drescher pulls into a gas station just outside Pasadena. While the pump attendant fills the tank, Rourke notices that Drescher continuously surveys the road behind them, clearly checking for any sign that they've been followed. They move on.

For some time now, the San Gabriel Mountains have edged the horizon to their left. As they approach Azusa, the mountains' presence becomes looming. Drescher takes the route north from Azusa, and the road shakes off the vestments of civilization. Rourke is aware they are now climbing steeply into the mountains and are surrounded by forest, ravine, and the shoulders of the mountains. The air feels cleaner and colder, but Rourke notes that the sky's milky gray sheet of silk has become rumpled and shadowed with clouds.

"I thought we were going to meet Nathan Milcom, not Grizzly Adams," says Rourke dryly as they turn up a narrower mountain road. The older woman doesn't answer.

Drescher turns off the road, onto a track. They jolt along for half a mile before they come to its end and she turns in to a scrub-fringed bay where the car is partially hidden from the track.

"Christ, Margot," says Rourke as they step out of the Erskine. "Where the hell are we?"

"Listen Mary, you should know by now how dangerous these people are. It doesn't matter how screwy the mumbo-jumbo they believe is— these are very powerful people with the right kind and the wrong kind of connections. Trust me, you ought to thank me I should be so cautious. It's up this track." Drescher leads the way up the scrub-fringed trail. Rourke can't help but smile at the image of the small, bent, expensively dressed talent agent as she marches purposefully and unsteadily up the mountain track. Rourke can hear the sound of water ever more distinctly. Suddenly, the chaparral opens out to reveal a wide, broad, open space.

"My God," she says. "What is this place?" She looks around the clearing. The ground beneath their feet is now paved, if crumbling, with sagebrush bursting through cracks. There are the relics of more than a dozen buildings, some stone ruins like worn-down teeth, others half-collapsed wooden skeletons. Several low stone structures like wellheads or firepits are dotted around the space.

"This place?" Drescher turns and sweepingly opens her arms. "This, Mary, is the perfect analogy for Hollywood. This is a place where great dreams blossomed, then died. Welcome to Eldoradoville."

"Eldoradoville?"

"It's an old gold-rush town. At its height it had hardware and grocery stores, blacksmiths, butchers, a hotel, half a dozen saloons, buildings for stores and equipment, and prospectors' shacks. It was going to be the big thing back then. Look around you—this is the future of Hollywood. They thought this would stand forever, or at least until they had mined the last nugget or panned the last grain of gold dust from the river."

"What happened?"

"Nothing less than biblical," says Drescher. "The Great Flood of 1862 washed it all away. Overnight, almost."

"Why here, Margot?"

"I was here years ago. Louis Mayer wanted to film a gold-rush western here. Decided to go for the authentic feel instead of filming on a backlot. He wanted Norma to play the heroine, but it was a bad part and I advised her to turn it down. Mayer had me and Norma limousined up here for a champagne picnic—trying to persuade us that it would be good for Norma, going through the script, sharing his vision, the whole nine yards."

"I take it, it didn't work? I don't remember Norma Carlton being in a movie like that."

"It was before she was exclusive to Carbine. And, no, it never was made, with or without Norma." Drescher's expression gives way to a fleeting, malicious grin. "Mayer had to cut the picnic short. He went into the bushes to take a leak, walked straight into poison oak."

"So why are we here now?"

"Because it's remote and it's safe."

There is the sound of an approaching car engine, then of tires on dirt as it coasts to a halt.

"That him?" asks Rourke.

"Should be." Drescher's face is animated, fearful. "Maybe we should duck out of sight, till we're sure."

She leads the way, wobbling across the uneven ground to one of the skeletal wooden sheds. Rourke follows, fearful that Drescher will break a bird-thin ankle. They duck inside the shed. The rust fossils of mining equipment are scattered across a floor rotted through in places. There is an unpleasant animal odor in the air. Peering out through the gappy boarding of the shed, they both fix their attention on where the path opens out into the clearing.

Rourke reaches into her clutch bag and pulls out the pocket pistol. Drescher turns her wide-eyed gaze from the clearing to the pistol to Rourke's face.

"Who are you? Big Boy Williams or Will Rogers? We're meeting a photoplay writer, not holding off a tribe of Comanches."

"Then why were you so nervous on the way up here, Margot? The way you—"

Rourke is interrupted by the sound of footfall on the dirt track. They both peer through the gaps in the planking. A tall figure emerges from the trail and steps warily into the open.

"You are kidding me . . ." Rourke says under her breath.

"No joke," says Drescher. "Put the gun away, Mary."

"I'll hang on to it just for now, if you don't mind," says Rourke. "You've dealt me a wild card, Margot. But I guess you knew that, and that's why you didn't tell me till we got up here. I think I'll hang on to my comforter until I'm surer of the lay of the land."

Drescher shrugs. "If it makes you feel happier. Things are complicated, that's for sure. But don't go waving it around. Come on."

The man who has just arrived turns abruptly when he hears them coming out of hiding. Relief washes across his handsome face, then is replaced by a frown when he sees the small pistol in Rourke's hand.

"What can I tell you," says Drescher to the man. "She's the suspicious type. I can't say as I blame her, given everything."

Rourke stands and stares at the man for a moment, her mind racing through everything his presence here means.

"So you are Nathan Milcom?" Rourke asks the tall, handsome Black man. "You wrote *The Devil's Playground*?"

"Yes. I am Nathan Milcom," replies Lewis Everett.

52

"Why are we meeting out here?" asks Rourke. "Why are we an hour and a half out of town, in the middle of nowhere?"

Drescher snorts a laugh. "I'm a Jew and he's a Negro. Where do you think we should meet? The country club? Anyway, everyone thinks Lewis Everett has disappeared. It's good to leave it like that. At least for the moment. And there are people looking for him."

"Are they?" asks Rourke. "The cops aren't. Norma Carlton's death is done and dusted. There'll be no investigation now. No one is looking for a murderer."

Everett nods at the gun in her hand. "No one?"

"Someone played me for a patsy, and I'm none too keen on that. Norma was strangled, then her death dressed up as a suicide long enough for me to be conned into tidying it all up. I'm beginning to think that Doc Wilson was involved and it cost him his life. Whoever's behind it all, it's someone who knows how the system works. How studio foot soldiers like me work these messes."

"I see. And I know the studio system, is that it? You're thinking I killed Norma?"

"I don't know what I'm thinking. All this is a little ... *discombobulating*, if you catch my meaning. But I'm guessing you have your reasons for wanting to have this little catch-up in the mountains. I'd like to hear them, but I'll hang on to this until I do. Just in case you have any ideas about me becoming the latest victim of the *Devil's Playground* curse. It's a good place up here to lose someone permanently."

"You really think I'd be part of something like that?" asks Drescher.

"I didn't think Golem Geller would be, but he was. But, no, Margot.

I don't. And I don't think Mr. Everett here is a killer. But let's play it safe for now. Let me hear what you've got to say."

"We're exposed here," says Everett. "Can we go down into the gully by the river? There's a camping ground there that's sheltered."

Rourke nods for Drescher and Everett to lead. They find the spot and sit on log cuttings improvised as camp seats. The San Gabriel River slides by beside them, surprisingly quiet.

"First of all," says Rourke. "You're telling me that you really are Nathan Milcom? You really wrote *The Devil's Playground*?"

"What's wrong?" says Everett. "Not what you were expecting? Wrong shade?"

"You're a recognized photoplay writer and movie director. Why go to all this cloak-and-dagger stuff over this particular script?"

"Are you really that naïve?" It's Margot Drescher who answers. "Because he's a Negro. Do you really think that Louis Mayer or Cecil DeMille or Harry Carbine would openly buy a script from a Negro? Especially a script about European moral corruption? It was my idea that we made up a pseudonym and never had a face-to-face between studio and writer. Anyway, it all added to the mystique of the script."

"What about the book the script was based on? Does that exist?"

"There is no novel," explains Everett. "Or all there is of it is the bits of it I wrote to draw the studios in. Pierre Lanton, the name I chose for the book's supposed author, was a Black Haitian soldier who fought in the Haitian Revolution, not a white European priest, I borrowed the name part as tribute, part as part of the joke."

"Joke?"

"The whole thing's a satire," explains Drescher. "A satire so subtle and clever that Harry Carbine, Cliff Taylor, and Paul Brand were all too dumb to see through it."

"Then I'm dumb too—I've read the script and I'm not in on the gag."

"Really?" says Everett. "The city of Ouxbois, famed for its painters, sculptors, and makers of great images? A city that becomes distant from the reality of the poverty-and-plague-ridden world that surrounds them? A self-absorbed populace that becomes ever more hedonistic and lascivious, eventually turning to orgiastic worship of Belphegor, the Lord of Sloth and Unearned Riches; Beelzebub, the Lord of Gluttony; and Asmodeus, the Lord of Lust? Doesn't it all ring a bell? I made up the name Ouxbois. It's a contraction of the French *houx bois. . . ."*

"Holly wood . . ." Rourke gives a small, bitter laugh.

"And the forces of the Inquisition," says Everett, "are the forces of the Hays Office. But I also liked adding the touch of them rampaging through the streets in robes, masks, and conical hats. An *hommage,* you could say, to dear old D.W. and his racist epic."

"All a joke? This whole thing is all a joke?" Rourke feels a surge of anger. "People burned to death performing your little satire on Hollywood."

"Well, if it makes you feel better, the joke's on me. I doubt I'm going to live much longer. The Resurrection Club funded the whole movie. Bailed Harry Carbine out of the hole the studio was in. I guess they won't have much of a sense of humor about the whole thing."

"If the Resurrection Club still exists. They've lost their queen bee, one way or another."

"You mean Anastasie Cormier?" asks Everett.

"Also known as Veronica Stratton, yes, that's who I mean."

Both Drescher and Everett laugh. "Didn't you learn anything from Theo Woolfe?" asks Drescher. "Haven't you worked out that Veronica Stratton wasn't Anastasie Cormier?"

"If she wasn't, then who?" asks Rourke, but she already knows the answer.

"Norma Carlton. Norma is Anastasie."

"*Is*—you mean 'was'?"

"I think you should know how the Resurrection Club worked," said Everett. "It was the usual Prohibition frat-house-type secret society that was a front for booze, narcotics, and sex. It was by invitation only. And to be invited, you had to have been someone reinvented by Hiram Levitt. He was in on everything, but he got greedy. Anyway, you have to understand the kind of person Norma was."

"I'm sure Theo Woolfe filled you in on what a monster Norma was," says Drescher.

Rourke nods.

"Norma was obsessed with control, with dominating those around her for her own aims," continues Everett. "She had to control every-thing, everybody. She was using Levitt to blackmail just about every big name in Hollywood. Not always money—sometimes they had to do things for her. Anyway, I got an invitation. I don't know why, but I did. And there were other Negroes, and Hispanics. Race didn't seem to be an issue, but I guess that was because there was this voodoo background to it. But the main belief was supposed to be reincarnation. That death wasn't the end of anything but the beginning. That, every time you died, you were born again stronger. And that was what happened to the inner circle. There was an initiation ceremony—this rebirthing. You were stripped of your clothes and dressed in a robe. It was all hogwash, you know the kind of thing. But there was this other, second room. Only a chosen few were allowed into this room. It had a huge iron door. Behind it was the Resurrection Chamber."

"What happened in there?"

"I was only invited into the Resurrection Chamber a couple of times—and only when I was clearly being considered for full membership of the inner circle. What I saw in there was enough to convince me I needed to get out. When I was asked to become a full member, I refused. And I quickly found out that you didn't refuse Norma. She had loved the script for *The Devil's Playground*—and the fact that it was a satire on Hollywood. Without her, it would never have been made. Harry Carbine was about to go under. He was desperate for a big hit but didn't have the funds or the credit to make one. So Norma got the members of the inner circle to fund it."

"Wait . . ." Rourke frowns. "Are you saying that Harry Carbine was part of this voodoo club?"

Everett shakes his head. "He was at a few parties where there were club members, but he didn't know what was going on—never attended any of the ceremonies or other gatherings. All he knew was that Norma had saved his bacon with the finance she had put together. As far as he was aware, Clarence Van Brenner at Consolidated Californian Bank was the main source of cash, but he clearly suspected there were dangerous people lurking in the background. The only conditions Norma made were that Carbine put everything into *The Devil's Playground* and use some of the investment to part-fund my movie, *Silas Torn*."

Rourke processes the information. It all fits now. All Carbine had known was that Norma had saved his studio. That was the hero's journey he had set Rourke on—to find out if Norma had paid for it with her life.

"And the Resurrection Club—they just coughed up the cash because Norma told them to?" she asks.

"They would do anything she told them. Not just because they were in her thrall, but because the inner-circle members—and some other powerful or influential people that they needed onboard—took part in these ceremonies. Weird sex stuff, with girls that Boy Lindqvist supplied."

"This happened in the place in the tunnels under the city?"

"No, these were special. The rumor I heard is that they took place somewhere out in the desert. They talked about a 'stone theater,' whatever that was. I think bad stuff went on. Whatever happened, my guess is it was photographed or filmed or whatever. All I know for sure is that whoever went there was completely under Norma's control."

Rourke thinks about what Everett has told her. "So who murdered Norma Carlton? And why?"

"That's why I wanted to see you," says Everett. "You see, to become a member of the inner circle, you had to go through resurrection."

"You mean this symbolic rebirth you talked about?"

"No. That was just for the general members. To become a true member of the Resurrection Club, to join its inner circle, you had to undergo true resurrection."

"What does that mean?"

"It means what it says. You had to die and be brought back to life. In that room, the inner chamber, people would die. Then they came back. Reborn. It was a voodoo ritual that Norma—or Anastasie—had done before, many times. She made the acolyte drink a special potion—*coup de poudre*—she called it. And then they died—everyone else there was to bear witness by feeling for a pulse. But there was a member who was a doctor, and he would give the corpse an injection of something and they'd come back to life."

"A doctor?" Rourke feels an electric thrill. It all falls into place for her. She thinks back to the night in the Appleton morgue: Doc Wilson switching off the light above Norma Carlton's corpse before Rourke could examine it closely.

"And you believed this?"

"I saw it for myself. These people died on the altar. They had no pulse, weren't breathing. Then they came back. I started to believe it all: that Anastasie really was some kind of voodoo priestess. And I think she believed it all herself. She claimed that she herself had been reincarnated many times—an infinite number of times. She said that her mother had given birth to her without the seed of a man. And her mother before her, her mother before her, and so on and so on. Parthenogenesis, one generation after another."

"So she was delusional?"

"She was insane. I made sure I disappeared before it was my turn."

"So what now?" asks Rourke.

"Now I'm going to disappear again. I've got enough money to live my life out someplace where a Black man won't be noticed, so long as his wealth isn't too obvious."

Again Rourke thinks it all through. She sees again Norma Carlton lying on her bed, her skin cool to the touch, no pulse beneath Rourke's fingertips. Later, Carlton's body lying on the morgue table, bruising around the neck, her skin blotched and waxy. Lon Chaney explaining how Norma had made him tell her all about his makeup techniques.

They sit in silence, the three of them. Rourke watches the ribbon of the San Gabriel River slide by like a snake glistening in the sun. It is a good five minutes before Rourke breaks the silence.

"Norma Carlton is alive," she says to herself more than the others. "It was Norma Carlton all along."

"Yes," says Margot Drescher. "And there isn't a damned thing any of us can do about it now."

Rourke turns to her, the emerald of her eyes flashing in the sun.

"I'm going to do something about it. I don't know how, I don't know when—but one day I will," she says. "One day."

EPILOGUE

53

1967
Sudden Lake

There is a flickering silence in the hotel's subterranean movie theater as the terminal title card on the screen announces to the audience of two that they have, indeed, reached the end. The card disappears. There is a moment of blackness until the projector rattlingly releases the last few inches of film from its sprocketed grasp, and a beam of its raw light slices emphatically through the theater's darkness.

"Now you have your answer, Dr. Conway," she says. "*All* the answers you sought. Your quest has reached its conclusion. So what do you think? Is *The Devil's Playground* the greatest horror movie ever made?"

He makes no reply, but continues to gaze at the screen, as if struck dumb by what he has witnessed, hypnotized by the intensity of the experience; still awestruck and confused as to how Paul Brand had achieved what he had achieved. The shapes, the forms, the writhing demons and devils hidden but not hidden in the shadows. He feels he has not been watching a moving picture but a moving painting, painted in silver, gray, and obsidian. He questions his own sanity as he remembers forms taking on three dimensions, the screen taking depth, dark hands and bright faces reaching and looming out at him. Was it real, he thinks desperately, or was it in my mind?

But through it all is the awareness that something is wrong. Something is terribly wrong.

"Now you know all the secrets hidden in *The Devil's Playground*," says the old woman. "All of my secrets. But I have to tell you, it's not as privileged a position as you might think." She stands up, and the ancient theater seat flaps back clatteringly into position. Conway remains sitting, silent, but in the flickering light from the projector she sees a tear glisten on his cheek.

"I was less than honest with you when I said you would be the first in forty years to see *The Devil's Playground*." She leans down, reaches over to him and jabs two fingers into his neck, just at the angle of his jaw. She holds them there. He can feel their pressure, but only just, the sensation distant and weak, like the sound of a voice from another room. "There have been others before you—not many, but there have been others—and there will be others after you. You see, Dr. Conway, I know who sent you."

She feels a pulse—weak, faltering, fading, but a pulse—then removes her fingers from his neck.

"I'm so glad that you were able to linger long enough to watch the whole movie."

She leaves him alone in the theater for a moment. Incapable of turning his head to see where she has gone, what she is doing, he feels his heart beating. His fear is so total it should be beating faster, pounding in his ears. But it doesn't: his pulse marks time softly, fainter with each beat.

Every instinct is to escape, to flee the prison of the dark screening room, of the darker hotel. He thinks of escape into the light, into the hard, hot brightness of the desert. Now he sees it—now he understands what they meant when they talked of the special beauty of the desert. The beauty of freedom.

He must escape. While she is out of the theater, he must make his break. He focuses all his concentration on moving something—a finger, a toe, anything—but a wildfire of claustrophobic panic surges through him as he acknowledges he is completely bound within the straitjacket of his own body. The architecture of this prison, he realizes, isn't the desert-rock walls of the theater, or the wood and stone of the dark, ugly hotel, but his own bone and flesh.

And yet the movie haunts him through his terror. The demons, the darkness. Paul Conway, who has always confused and conflated the real and the celluloid worlds, finds himself wondering if it was a movie, after all, or simply a premonition: a glimpse into the hell that awaits him.

She returns, but he still cannot turn to see that she has brought in the wheelchair he saw outside the theater. With surprising strength, she places her forearms under his armpits and hoists him out of the seat and onto the wheelchair.

"It's time to go, Dr. Conway. I enjoyed your visit. And I always welcome any opportunity to watch *The Devil's Playground* again. But all good things . . ."

She steps around the wheelchair, disappearing behind him. He waits for a feeling of forward motion, for her to push the wheelchair.

"By the way, if you're wondering, it was the lemonade. Made with fresh lemons and spiked with a neurotoxin cocktail. I grow all kinds of things in the greenhouse: jimsonweed, datura, silverleaf nightshade, chondrodendron . . . Where I grew up, the way I grew up, how my mother taught me, I learned all kinds of skills like that. Traditional ways, you'd call them, I guess. Anyway, I put a few drops into your lemonade. It completely paralyzes your body, but you can still see and hear—still fear. In fact, it heightens your senses, exaggerates them, makes your imagination ten times more powerful. I don't know what you saw when watching the film—how much was what was on-screen and how much was hallucination—but I was careful in my dosage. I didn't want to detract from your enjoyment of the movie."

Behind the poisoned and paralyzed film historian, and outside his field of vision, she picks up the half-inch-thick snake-leather cord she had left in the aisle behind them.

"It's the same potion I used back then, you know," she says conversationally. "The one I used—or, more correctly, Doc Wilson used—to fake my death. It'll wear off soon." She leans forward and whispers in his ear conspiratorially. "I know who sent you. You're not the first she's sent, you know. She's sent others before you." Straightening up, she loops the cord around the unresisting film historian's neck. She twists and tightens the corded leather at the nape of his neck. She jams a short stick into the knot and turns it, as if using a corkscrew, making the leather cord into a garrote.

Conway feels the cord tightening, hears a wet, wheezing sound that he realizes is his breathing. Then it stops as the passage of air to his lungs and blood to his brain is stilled. It takes him a minute to die; but a minute filled with unspeakable horrors. More terrifying than his own suffocation, he sees the screen in front of him come back to life. Yet no projector paints with light the images he sees. These come from darkness. He sees the monstrous figure of the sorcerer Archambeau twist and contort and change once more into Beelzebub. The demon Prince of Hell stretches his arm out free from the confinement of the screen, his bony finger indicating Conway. The last thing the film historian sees is the bull-headed, talon-clawed demon, his insect eyes fire-red, as he surges free of the flimsy prison of lenticulated silver fabric to seize and claim him.

The last thought Dr. Paul Conway ever thinks is that his scream is totally silent.

The old woman again presses her fingers to his neck to check for a pulse. Satisfied Conway is dead, she leaves him while she collects the film reels from the small projection cabin and replaces them in the old metal canisters, which she in turn stacks in the leather carrier.

The sun is now low in the sky as she carries the film outside and across to the gleaming, polished-steel Airstream trailer. Inside, powered by the line fed into the trailer from the hotel, the air conditioner maintains the steady cool temperature that has protected the film print for all these years. She replaces the reels in their allocated place on the shelves that line one wall. She looks around the trailer at the dozens of posters and lobby display cards pasted to the other wall, filling every inch of its surface.

And from half of them, her younger self gazes back at her. Norma Carlton, in smooth-skinned youthful perfection. As she looks at her unflawed image, her fingers involuntarily reach up to her face and touch where the birthmark, no longer concealed by makeup, further darkens the already dark-tanned, aging skin.

The beautiful woman in the rest of the cards and posters could also, fleetingly, be mistaken for the young Norma Carlton. But that's not who she is. The other posters span the new age of Hollywood, the age of sound and color, from the Thirties to the Sixties, and show a movie star, a real movie star, make the transition from fresh-faced ingenue to mature leading lady. There are flashbulb smiles from photographs of her holding Academy Awards. Stills from a dozen movies where she plays opposite Grant, Tracy, Stewart, Bogart, Cooper . . . It is the chronicling of a glorious, decades-long career, and of an enduring beauty. All the posters and cards are top-billing emblazoned with her name.

Carole Ventris.

The old woman who was Norma Carlton, and before that was Anastasie Cormier, stands for a silent moment in the air-conditioned cool of the Airstream. She smiles as she looks at the images of the young actress whom she had championed to be her stand-in for *The Devil's Playground*—and who, after Norma's feigned suicide and Veronica Stratton's disappearance, had outshone them both. Had gone on to outshine Crawford and Davis, Lamarr and Leigh, Monroe and Taylor.

A true Hollywood star.

Anastasie had known, way back then, that night of bright flame that illuminated her and her mother's departure from Leseuil. She had known then that the next incarnation, the next iteration in that endless cycle of mother and daughter, was already growing in her belly.

That was why they had to die. Old man Trosclair burned not only because he had tried to kill Hippolyta and Anastasie out there in the beautiful dark of the backswamp, but because he would never have accepted that the child was a magical renewal of an eternal cycle, and not the result of his son's siring.

Boy Lindqvist and the Dahlman and Darke Phantasmagoria had given them sanctuary. Hiram Levitt and Hollywood had given them rebirth.

Anastasie had become Norma Carlton, Hippolyta had become Madame Erzulie and been housed in comfort. The child had been cared for by both in secret, until she had been sent to a blueblood boarding school back east. Norma Carlton had become a star.

It had been perfect.

She had used her power over men to gain the control she needed, bound them to her with dark acts, leading them to fulfill their darkest desires.

But then an old man had come to Hollywood from another world, seeking resolution at the end of his days to a question that festered deep inside him. A retired sheriff from the old days, the old places. Hiram Levitt, the small, dark keeper of secrets, had already been squeezing Norma for more money. Levitt had realized the arrival of Sheriff Briggs provided a lever with which to pry free more cash.

Lindqvist had dealt with Briggs, Geller with Levitt. But she had known it was only a matter of time before echoes from a Louisiana swamp would bring scandal, or the renewed attention would lead a policeman or a forgotten-about relative to her door with questions of missing girls. A brilliant career would end in ignominy. And they hanged women in Louisiana.

Just as Hippolyta had handed the baton to Anastasie, it had become her time to pass it on to the next regeneration. The cycle renewed. Norma Carlton's star was extinguished so another could shine in its place—shine brighter, unclouded by scandal.

Carole Ventris. Her replacement. Her stand-in. Her daughter.

She sighs, turns from the images, and locks the Airstream behind her as she leaves. She has work to do.

54

One Year Earlier
1966

Santa Barbara

The drive up the coast has been pleasant. The low-hanging June Gloom clouds that had huddled close to the sea when he had set out have now worn thin to slow-fluttering tatters against the blue shield of sky.

His destination sits quietly waiting for him where Montecito and Santa Barbara meet. Paul Conway reaches the top of a long driveway that is edged with manicured shrubs, and parks in front of a house of dark glass and blond stone. The architecture is modernist. And expensive.

A woman in her fifties, wearing an apron, answers the door.

"I'm Dr. Conway," he explains. "I have an appointment with Mrs. Morgan."

The woman smiles. "Yes, sir, she's expecting you. She's out on the veranda and asked if you would mind joining her there."

"Not at all."

The maid—Conway assumes the woman is some kind of domestic—takes him through the house, along the hall that cuts through to the back. The size of the house, the quality of its construction, and the taste of the furniture and art that dress it all tell him that the occupier is very wealthy. The dubiety he felt when he received the phone call—and the strange offer contained in it—starts to evaporate. It had only been when he realized whose widow Mrs. Morgan was—and who she herself had been, back in the day—that he committed to driving up from L.A.

He knows he's dealing with Old Hollywood royalty. Yet the house and its interior don't have that overdone, opulent Golden Age grandness in which people from back then seem to cocoon themselves. He notes pieces of art as he glances from the hall into large, open-plan spaces; he thinks he spots a Giacometti sculpture and a Warhol canvas.

At the rear of the house, the panoramic sliding glass doors are already open, and the servant leads Conway out onto a wide veranda of white stone. The veranda's elevated position offers a view out over Butterfly Beach, the Santa Barbara Channel, and the ocean beyond. Despite it being early afternoon, the heat is calmed by a breeze that carries a cool, salt scent up from the ocean. Bright sun diamonds sparkle on the aquamarine of a pool set to one side.

A nice spot, thinks Conway.

"Mrs. Morgan . . . Dr. Conway," the servant makes the introduction. A woman whose age he can't pin down, but who he knows must be somewhere around her late seventies, is sitting at the patio table, in the shade of a parasol. She stands up with the ease and grace of a much younger woman. She wears a broad-brimmed sunhat and sunglasses; a loose sand-colored kaftan hangs airily around her form.

"Thanks for coming," Mrs. Morgan says, and takes his hand. Again, her voice is that of a younger woman. The tenor is friendly but authoritative—a tone that seems to come naturally to her.

"My pleasure. You have a beautiful home."

"Thank you," she says. "Please, sit. May I offer you some lunch, Dr. Conway? I'm just about to have some myself."

"No, thank you, ma'am. I stopped off in Ventura and picked something up there."

They both sit at the patio table.

"Something to drink? Some tea?"

"I'm fine, thank you. I'm rather keen to get down to business, if you don't mind. I was somewhat taken aback by your offer."

She nods, turns to the servant, and says: "Thank you, Gertrude."

The maid retires into the house.

"It is a genuine offer," she says when they are alone.

"That is a lot of money. An awful lot of money."

"I married well." She pauses, then corrects herself: "I *remarried* well.

Or at least I did on the third attempt. Money is something I have no shortage of. You are aware that my husband died six months ago. I now have the financial resources to fund this project."

"I know who you are, of course, Mrs. Morgan," says Conway. "I mean, I know all your late husband's movies, naturally. But I know about you, yourself—that you were important behind the scenes, back in the day. A very important woman. Powerful, even."

She waves a hand dismissively. "I know you'll already know this, given you're an expert on the era, but there were a lot of us. Women, I mean; there were more women working in Hollywood in the Twenties—as writers, producers, directors, technicians, even studio chiefs—than there are today. Have you heard of Tressie Souders?"

"I have, as a matter of fact, she directed *A Woman's Error.*"

"Yes, she did. She was a woman, and she was Black. And she made movies. Wrote them, directed them, produced them. Her race and her gender didn't stop her in the Twenties. People like her and Oscar Micheaux did for Negro filmmaking what the Harlem Renaissance did for Black literature. And now? It's all been snuffed out. Do you know what Tressie Souders has been doing since then? Working as a domestic. A servant in a white household." She sighs. "It all changed. It all came crashing down. And you know what did it? The microphone. Movies became talkies, and all those unique voices were silenced."

"Mrs. Morgan, I don't see . . ."

"Anyway, there is talk now of 'New Hollywood,' of a new creative direction," she continues, ignoring his impatience. "Maybe things will change again. But you're not much interested in New Hollywood, are you, Dr. Conway?"

"I'm a film historian. It is your age that interests me. The Golden Age. The silents."

"And that is why I got in touch with you. I read in the *Times* about you locating a print of *Queen Pharaoh.* And people in the know tell me you're tracking down the 1910 version of *Frankenstein.* They say that, if anyone can find the print, you will."

"That's what you're offering me all this money for? To find Dawley's *Frankenstein* for you?"

"No, Dr. Conway. I'm hunting even bigger game. There's only one movie I'm interested in, the movie I want to get my hands on. And it's the greatest horror movie ever made."

Conway thinks for a moment, then frowns. "*The Devil's Playground*?"

"Yes. You know about it?"

"Of course I know about it. Everyone with any interest in movie history knows about it—and everyone knows about all the deaths and disappearances and crazy stuff associated with it. It's a lost master-piece, but they say it's a cursed production. Just like theater actors call *Macbeth* 'the Scottish play' because it's supposed to be cursed, movie actors have all kinds of superstitions about *The Devil's Playground*. Even today. But no one has seen it. Or no one still living. And there are no suggestions anywhere of it having survived. I'd love to take your money, Mrs. Morgan, but the truth is, I wouldn't know where to start looking. Mainly because there isn't anything to find."

"What if I told you you're wrong? What if I told you there *is* a print surviving?"

Conway looks at her and he can see she is serious. This is no mad old lady, and he feels a thrill at the idea that there *is* a copy of *The Devil's Playground* out there—and maybe, just maybe, he could be the one to find it.

"Why?" he asks. "I mean, why do you want to find it? Why is it so important to you?"

She doesn't answer him for a moment but looks out over the grassed lawn and the beach and sea beyond. In her profile he can see some-thing of the woman she had been, back then. They say she'd been a real looker. Back then.

"Let's just say I have some unfinished business that I want to finish. I will pay you a quarter of the sum we discussed if you agree to look for *The Devil's Playground*—the rest when you deliver it to me. And, Dr. Conway, I'm as much, maybe more, interested in who has kept it hidden as I am in the film itself."

"That's all good and well," says Conway, "but, like I said, I wouldn't know where to start looking."

"I think I can help you with that," she says. She lays a sealed envelope on the table. "In there is a check for one-quarter of the commission I mentioned on the phone, and a note of the total sum I am prepared to offer the possessor of the print for its purchase."

Conway reaches for the envelope, but she places a hand on it.

"There's one more thing in there," she says. "A piece of information, a name. It is the name of the person who I believe has the last remaining print of *The Devil's Playground*. You see, I believe I know *who*, but I don't know *where*. That's the name in here." She taps the envelope with the crimson-varnished tip of a tanned finger. "But before you read that name, I must have your undertaking to complete this assignment—and to keep all its particulars, including the name—*especially* the name—I've given you strictly confidential. Well, Dr. Conway, do you accept?"

He looks at her for a moment. She still wears the sunglasses, and her eyes are hidden behind the black lenses. There is nothing to be read in her expression other than a fixed determination.

"I accept," he says, and she lifts her hand from the envelope. Conway slides a thumbnail beneath the flap, opens the envelope and examines its contents. Last among them is a folded sheet of expensive vellum writing paper. He unfolds it and sees a name written on it, nothing else. Two things strike him instantaneously: confusion, and a tingling electric thrill running up his spine.

"This . . ." He shakes his head, his expression one of wonder. "This is impossible. It doesn't make any sense. This is who you say has the movie?"

She nods her head. "I have a story to tell you, Dr. Conway. A story where nothing is ever what it seems . . ."

They sit for another two hours in the shade of the parasol, cooled by the breeze from the ocean. She tells him a tale of a great movie, of a curse hanging over it, of a great movie actress, of a real-life drama even greater than the one that played out on screen. Of a time and a place where deception came naturally. She tells him a tale of Hollywood.

After he leaves Mrs. Morgan to her pleasant view out over the beach and the water, Conway sits in his car for a while, his mind racing through all she has told him. All those secrets. The name—*that* name—she gave him as if it were a simple matter of fact. The tingle in the nape of his neck and scalp whenever he thinks of the significance of it all.

He looks at it again. *Norma Carlton.*

Whatever mission she thinks she's sent him on, despite whatever guarantees of confidentiality he has given her, he knows there is a book in this. This could make his name, move him into a different league.

He'll do as she asked, all right: he'll keep everything he finds out to himself until he delivers the film to her. But then . . . Then there'll be the book. All these years writing Hollywood history, he'll now become world-famous for *rewriting* it.

He becomes aware that the servant is watching him from the doorway, and he starts the car.

All those secrets. He shakes his head in wonder. God knows how many more secrets she has to tell, he thinks as he steers his Rambler down the driveway. She must have been quite a woman, back then, he thinks. Everyone in Hollywood had known her—her and that ex-cop partner of hers. Every studio chief, every hotel concierge, every Hollywood desk sergeant, every reporter, had known her number by heart.

Back then, before she married a rich director. Before she became Mrs. Morgan.

When her name had been Mary Rourke and she'd been Hollywood's top fixer.

55

1967
Sudden Lake

No sky is more beautiful, more majestic, Norma Carlton thinks to herself, than that of the desert at sundown. Yet she remembers loving a different landscape, as different from the desert as it is possible to be, when she was younger: a landscape of closed, green-vaulted skies, of dark waters and dense, humid air. When she was younger; when she had been Anastasie Cormier. But that landscape and that name are remote and faded now.

Tonight, a vast furl of cloud, high and distant, slides like a crimson velvet curtain drawn across the turquoise-blue screen of the sunset sky. She stands on the stoop of the hotel, looking out at the sky's drama. She has waited for the day's astringent, unforgiving heat to dissipate from the moistureless air, knowing that she and Golly will have a long walk back to the hotel.

With the film historian's lifeless body propped up in the passenger seat, his head lolling loosely with every bump, and her dog lying in the back, Norma Carlton drives Conway's Rambler across unpaved desert, out to the edge of Sudden Lake. She passes one, then another of the abandoned lodges, untouched and undisturbed for forty years, painting their sunset-stretched shadows on the bleached canvas of the salt flats. At the far edge of the pan, a rocky bluff presents its weathered face to the setting sun, and she seeks out the crease in it—impossible to find unless you know where to look, and even then only once you are upon it.

In turn, the crease reveals itself to be a cleft in the bluff, high-walled and shadowed night-dark, but too narrow to be called a canyon, the sides too vertical for it to be called a gulch. It is only just wide enough for a car to pass. She switches on the Rambler's headlights and eases it between the rocky walls, aware that if she becomes stuck, or the car breaks down, she won't be able to open the doors wide enough to escape.

Eventually, the narrow ravine opens out into a tear-shaped gully, a vast projection of rock overhanging it like a canopy, the dark eye socket of a cave set deep and low in the back wall of the gully. It seems a space outside time, shadowed and silent, the air motionless. The gully is a natural amphitheater, the rock overhang its velarium. That was why it had been used, all those years ago. That's why those dark dramas, in which her role had been central, had played out here. The Stone Theater.

An audience waits for her.

There are four of them—five now, with the new arrival. Four automobiles, each from a different decade. They sit grit-crusted and dust-coated, but otherwise perfectly preserved and rustless. Each a car-grave for a pilgrim who came in search of a lost majesty.

She eases the Rambler into a space between a 1950s Oldsmobile 88 sedan and a 1930s Ford station wagon. Through the dusty side window, she sees a woman in the passenger seat of the Oldsmobile, sitting exactly as she had been left fifteen years before. The air of the gully is so hot, so dry and still, so ancient and undisturbed, that the body of the dead woman, like the others, has mummified. Her skin is bronzed parchment, her flesh shriveled. Her eyelids have shrunk back from the gray-brown globes of her eyes, and such decomposition that has occurred has loosened her lower jaw, which now flaps wide. It looks for all the world as if she is staring and screaming at whatever it is her dead eyes see on the stone screen of the gully.

Without taking the keys from the ignition, she leaves the Rambler there, leaves Conway with the others whose secret missions had brought them to seek, and find, the true nature of the *Devil's Playground* curse.

She calls her dog and wearily heads back out of the hidden gully. As she does so, she tries to imagine the urgent torrent that had once coursed and tumbled through it, out through the narrow ravine and into the bone basin of a lake that had waited millennia for waters to fill it. And now waits again.

All things, she thinks, form a cycle.

Emerging from the shadowed cleft, and before she starts the long walk back to the distant hotel, she once more looks up at the shadow-play drama of dying red-gold light and growing velvet shade playing out on the vast screen of the desert sky.

It is magnificent, it is epic, it is timeless.

It is silent.

THE END

ACKNOWLEDGMENTS

The Devil's Playground was a dream to write, mainly because immersing myself in Golden Era Hollywood, a period and setting that fascinates me, was such unalloyed joy. I am therefore hugely grateful to all of those who supported and encouraged me in the writing of this novel: my wife, Wendy, whose belief in the project remained absolute throughout; Jason Kaufman, my editor at Doubleday, for his unwavering enthusiasm for the novel and invaluable insight during its crafting; and my agent Esmond Harmsworth, whose counsel and belief in my writing have encouraged me to push creative boundaries.

I'd also like to thank Lily Dondoshansky and Ana Espinoza at Doubleday for their hard work, and Michael Windsor for his superb cover design.

ABOUT THE AUTHOR

CRAIG RUSSELL is an award-winning Scottish author whose books have been translated into twenty-five languages. His previous works include *The Devil Aspect,* the Fabel series of thrillers, and the Lennox series of noir mysteries. He is the only two-time winner of the McIlvanney Prize (2015 and 2021) as well as the winner of the 2008 Crime Writers' Association Dagger in the Library prize. He lives in Perthshire, Scotland, with his wife.